P

A Weddin ... Como

"A reminder of the golden days of youth and a testament to the lasting power of forever friendship, *A Wedding in Lake Como* is Jennifer Probst at her finest. Readers will be swept away by this powerful story of loss and redemption that proves it's never too late to carve a new path, chase a new dream—or fall in love all over again. A breathtaking Italian setting is the icing on the cake. Don't miss this enchanting novel!"

—Kristy Woodson Harvey,
New York Times bestselling author of *A Happier Life*

"Glorious. A perfect story told with so much heart. Plus the food and the clothes. And Italy! You'll be delighted."

—Susan Mallery,
#1 *New York Times* bestselling author of *The Summer Book Club*

"Part coming-of-age and part found family, *A Wedding in Lake Como* beautifully illustrates the impenetrable bond and enduring power of invincible friendships. Readers will travel alongside the characters as they embark on an emotional journey full of heartfelt developments, including the healing power of an apology and a second chance with the one that got away. This is a true gem of a novel."

—Tracey Garvis Graves,
New York Times bestselling author of *The Trail of Lost Hearts*

"If there's one thing Probst is going to do, it's convince readers that Italy is where they'll find themselves. . . . *A Wedding in Lake Como* is a novel about the dynamics of female friendship amid a backdrop of self-discovery that fans will enjoy."

—*Booklist*

Praise for

The Secret Love Letters of Olivia Moretti

"The ultimate escape into Italian sunshine and a romantic mystery."

—*New York Times* bestselling author Tessa Bailey

"Jennifer Probst digs deep and true in this richly textured novel. You'll fall in love with these very human sisters, captivating setting, and perfect ending."

—Susan Elizabeth Phillips,
New York Times bestselling author of *Simply the Best*

"Travel to beautiful Positano through the eyes of three estranged sisters and the mother they only thought they knew in Jennifer Probst's breathtaking page-turner."

—Jane L. Rosen, author of *Eliza Starts a Rumor*

"Hidden love and a rediscovered sisterhood await readers in Probst's latest. . . . Probst once again proves her talent at writing female relationships that will resonate with readers of contemporary women's fiction."

—*Booklist*

Praise for
Our Italian Summer

"The novel is carried by the rich interactions between the women, as well as the lush Italian landscape, city descriptions, and culinary pleasures. Probst consistently charms." —*Publishers Weekly*

"*Under the Tuscan Sun* meets *Divine Secrets of the Ya-Ya Sisterhood* as Probst (*Searching for Someday*, 2013) explores the dynamics of womanhood between three generations against a picturesque Italian backdrop. . . . Filled with family drama amidst a lush setting, plus a touch of romance, *Our Italian Summer* will provide a delicious escape for readers." —*Booklist*

"In *Our Italian Summer*, Jennifer Probst captures the essence of Italy and celebrates the bond between mothers and daughters. With food worthy of an Italian grandmother's kitchen and descriptions to make the Travel Channel jealous, you'll want to join the Ferrari women on their unforgettable journey."

—Amy E. Reichert, author of *Once Upon a December*

"*Our Italian Summer* beautifully navigates the complicated relationships between families in a heartfelt manner in this multigenerational novel set against the splendid backdrop of Italy in all of her glory. Jennifer Probst whisks readers away on an unforgettable journey. The perfect novel to satisfy your wanderlust!"

—*New York Times* bestselling author Chanel Cleeton

Praise for the novels of Jennifer Probst

"Achingly romantic, touching, realistic, and just plain beautiful."

—*New York Times* bestselling author Katy Evans

"Tender and heartwarming."

—#1 national bestselling author Marina Adair

"Beautiful . . . and so well written! Highly recommend!"

—*New York Times* bestselling author Emma Chase

"Jennifer Probst pens a charming, romantic tale destined to steal your heart."

—*New York Times* bestselling author Lori Wilde

"Probst tugs at the heartstrings." —*Publishers Weekly*

"I never wanted this story to end! Jennifer Probst has a knack for writing characters I truly care about—I want these people as *my* friends!"

—*New York Times* bestselling author Alice Clayton

"For a . . . fun-filled, warmhearted read, look no further than Jennifer Probst!" —*New York Times* bestselling author Jill Shalvis

"Jennifer Probst never fails to delight."

—*New York Times* bestselling author Lauren Layne

Titles by Jennifer Probst

The Meet Me in Italy Series

Our Italian Summer

The Secret Love Letters of Olivia Moretti

A Wedding in Lake Como

To Sicily with Love

The Sunshine Sisters Series

Love on Beach Avenue

Temptation on Ocean Drive

Forever in Cape May

Christmas in Cape May

Stay Series

The Start of Something Good

A Brand New Ending

All Roads Lead to You

Something Just Like This

Begin Again

Billionaire Builders Series

Everywhere and Every Way

Any Time, Any Place

Somehow, Some Way

All or Nothing at All

Searching For . . . Series

Searching for Someday

Searching for Perfect

Searching for Beautiful

Searching for Always

Searching for You

Searching for Mine

Searching for Disaster

Marriage to a Billionaire Series

The Marriage Bargain

The Marriage Trap

The Marriage Mistake

The Book of Spells

The Marriage Merger

The Marriage Arrangement

Nonfiction

Write Naked

Write True

Writers Inspiring Writers: What I Wish I'd Known

TO SICILY WITH LOVE

JENNIFER PROBST

BERKLEY
New York

BERKLEY
An imprint of Penguin Random House LLC
penguinrandomhouse.com

Book design by Katy Riegel

Library of Congress Cataloging-in-Publication Data

Names: Probst, Jennifer, author.
Title: To Sicily with love / Jennifer Probst.
Description: First Edition. | New York: Berkley, 2025. |
Series: Meet me in italy; vol 4
Identifiers: LCCN 2024015791 (print) | LCCN 2024015792 (ebook) |
ISBN 9780593546062 (trade paperback) | ISBN 9780593546079 (ebook)
Subjects: LCSH: Sicily (Italy)—Fiction. | LCGFT: Romance fiction. | Novels.
Classification: LCC PS3616.R624 T6 2025 (print) |
LCC PS3616.R624 (ebook) | DDC 813.6—dc23/eng/20240408
LC record available at https://lccn.loc.gov/2024015791
LC ebook record available at https://lccn.loc.gov/2024015792

First Edition: February 2025

Printed in the United States of America
1st Printing

At its core,

this story is about family. Family of blood and DNA;

family chosen in friendship; family

bound not only by joy and love,

but pain and forgiveness.

This book is dedicated

to my own family, those here and

those who have passed.

Thank you for being part of my life.

Without you, I could not have written this book.

Sicilians build things like they will live forever
and eat like they will die tomorrow.

—Plato

TO SICILY WITH LOVE

PART ONE

ONE

I PULLED UP to the curb and stared at the familiar Cape Cod house. Bright white. Black shutters. A light dusting of snow covered the usual thriving flower and vegetable garden. Two wicker rocking chairs on the front porch held grinning snowmen cushions. Leftover lights from Christmas still wrapped around the railing, the only bright spot in the dreary winter evening. Holding back a sigh, I shoved the endless buzz of thoughts and tasks and ideas igniting my brain to the side and got out of the car.

It was time to see Mom.

I squared my shoulders and tried not to dread my visit with each step. I was horrible. I loved my mother. But these consistent check-ins were beginning to grate on my nerves, especially when each second was precious. As I told my clients regularly, dreams don't work unless you do. And damned if I didn't have a ton of both to conquer.

I walked inside and found her in the kitchen. "Hi, Mom."

"Aurora! How are you, sweetheart?" Guilt hit again as she

lit up and hugged me like it was the first time we'd seen each other in ages, instead of only two days. Have mothers always acted like puppies, with a warped sense of time?

Maybe I'd have children one day and find out.

"Good. Really busy. You said you needed help with something?"

She made a sound of annoyance and began waving her hands in the air. "It's the TV again! I tried to save money by switching to the app instead of the cable box, but it doesn't work. I called the company and they said no one could come out because I was doing it wrong." A frown creased her brow. "I'm not an idiot. I know it's broken."

Frustration simmered, but I fought it back. This wasn't an emergency I should be running over to fix, but no matter how many times I explained my schedule, Mom said she understood and wouldn't bother me. Then did. "Let me look at it. The bedroom?"

"Yes. Thank you. I don't know how your dad dealt with all this tech. Are you hungry? I made a quiche and salad. Why don't you stay?"

"Can't. I'm meeting Jason for dinner."

Her silence was answer enough, but I refused to let her piss me off on my date night. It took me less than five minutes to work the two remotes and click on the app causing the trouble. "Mom, come here. You were hitting the wrong button."

"No. That's impossible."

I half closed my eyes. God, she was stubborn. Probably the most stubborn person on the planet. Dad used to laugh and say she'd tire out a mule, but there was no better quality when it came to sheer grit and staying power. "Look, I'll show you."

Her gasp would have made me laugh if I hadn't been so stressed. "I can't believe it. Thank you. Have some water. I bought the vitamin stuff you like."

I was about to tell her no, but the look on her face made me pause. The flicker of longing in her dark eyes, as if she craved company. Crap. Why did she have to feel so lonely? Why couldn't she find some pursuits to fill her time instead of depending on me? It had been five years since Dad passed. She was in her mid-fifties, not her seventies. Was it wrong that I expected more independence from her? I forced a smile. "Sure, Mom."

She practically ran to the kitchen and presented me with the bottle proudly. I took a sip, studying her in the fading light that beamed from the window.

My mother was still beautiful, retaining a timeless elegance. Her rich dark hair was her best asset, with only threads of gray she kept under control with dye. Big brown eyes dominated her face, with lush lashes that any woman would envy. A classic Roman nose, full lips, and heavy slanted brows gave off an earthiness that matched her curvy figure. I'd encouraged her to begin dating, knowing she'd easily attract men with her looks, but Mom refused. She said Dad was the love of her life and she wasn't interested in finding another.

I'd have been happy to see her score a dinner date.

Though we looked alike, we'd always been different. I had the same thick dark hair, though I'd cut mine years ago, to my mother's distress. Now the strands were smooth and curled under my chin in a stylish cut. People always commented that we were like twins. I always wished I'd inherited my father's light blond hair, hazel eyes, and trim build. Instead, I got stuck with too many curves, a too-large nose, and an excess of body hair.

But behavior-wise? Yeah, I was completely my very English dad. I looked at the world in crisp blacks and whites and had laser-sharp focus on tasks that furthered my goals. Rest was my nemesis, along with messy emotion. I'd managed to turn my practicality into a career but lacked the patience my mother held when it came to listening to rants or endless whining. I didn't believe in "poor me." I believed in fixing it.

My mom exuded a warm, nurturing persona that sucked in everyone who craved a listening ear, a hug, or a favor. She loved cooking, naps, gardening, and long conversations that had no real point.

We were opposites who couldn't seem to understand each other. It had made for some epic fights when I was a teen, during which Mom had surprised me with her legendary Italian temper. Dad always said when she reached her limit and snapped, no one wanted to be near the explosion.

Too bad I was an only child. It really sucked not to have any siblings. Mom had multiple miscarriages after me, so they'd eventually decided to stop trying. Both my parents were also only children. I'd grown up without any type of extended family. I literally had no grandparents, cousins, or aunts or uncles, which was a bummer around the holidays, but at least I got full attention and all the presents.

Unfortunately, presents no longer mattered, and I was the sole target of my mother's scrutiny.

Lucky me.

"What are you up to this week?" she asked.

I shook my head at the thought of my schedule. "It's nonstop. I'm booked with client appointments, and I want to get a handle on the new season of the podcast. Plus, I fell behind on the book, so I need to get some writing done." I chattered on about the other responsibilities on my plate, hoping she'd get a sense of how busy I truly was.

She nodded, but a tiny frown caused her brow to crease. "When was the last time you saw Hannah or April?"

"I don't know—six months, maybe? I had to cancel our last meet-up. But they're doing well."

The frown deepened. "Honey, I don't understand why you lost touch. They were your best friends all through college. It's like you've suddenly dropped them."

And here we go.

I tried not to get irritated. "Mom, we're all busy. They have young kids now and I'm building a business. Things change."

"Some things should be prioritized," she said gently. "Like good friends. Work can't take the place of relationships."

"Meaningful work can," I shot back. "Plus, I have Jason. We're getting serious and that's my priority right now."

I could tell she wanted to say something but held back. The irritation grew into anger, especially when I spotted the gleam of disapproval in her eyes. Not only for Jason but for my choices as well. For the work I put my heart and soul into that she didn't understand.

For my entire life.

Why couldn't my mother be happy with her own life instead of trying to manage mine? She always wanted something from me. A call, a text, a visit. Poking at my choices, consistently telling me I needed to slow down.

I'd finally invited Jason to Sunday dinner, hopeful Mom

would see all the wonderful things I did. Instead, there was an underlying tension that hung heavily over the dining room table.

I hated the way she'd immediately judged his muscles and good looks. She never said a word of criticism, but I knew. It was obvious in her gaze as he politely refused most of the food that contained carbs and spoke about ambition and doing better than our parents. His passion steered the conversation as Jason explained his future plans of running a fitness empire. When she revealed the *torta setteveli* seven-layer cake she'd spent hours baking, he refused, joking that sugar was the hidden demon causing weight gain and diabetes, giving me a wink as if we were on the same team.

I'd squirmed with embarrassment and resentment in my seat, hating that I still sought her approval like I was a needy child. There was no reason for her to question Jason or my choices in relationships. Afterward, we'd had a fight and I'd walked out. We hadn't mentioned it since, but the words flung back and forth still hung in the air between us, like a cloud of pollution, dark and heavy and poisonous. Now we were circling back to this conversation.

"I see you making choices with your head, not your heart. I only want you to lean in to all the wonderful surprises out there. Not close yourself off because it doesn't make sense or meet a certain goal. Do you understand?"

Yes. I did. That was the terrible part. The disconnect between us was growing and I was getting tired of her criticism. Of her judging my life based on ideals I could never accept or understand.

Slowly, I put down my water bottle and gave her a tight smile. "Sure, Mom. I gotta go. I'll check in next week."

I gave her a quick hug and headed for the door.

"Wait—I'll see you Sunday, right?"

I stiffened. "Probably not. I have a lot of work, Mom."

Her hands flew up in the air. "All day Sunday? Honey, it's our only chance to spend some quality time together. Just come and eat. You're too skinny—you need a good meal without constantly scrolling through that phone. All that social media isn't healthy."

"I'll let you know, okay?"

"Fine. Text me. I love you."

I muttered it back and hurried out, sending a quick text to Jason that I was running late. As I sped away, I let out a breath. Finally, I'd get back to my real life.

On cue, my phone belted out Carrie Underwood's song "The Champion," which always pumped me up, and I quickly put my earbuds in to answer. I held strict appointments with all my clients but was always available for emergencies. Being on call for the people who depended on me was important and had helped expand my life-coaching business quickly. Referrals and reviews were key.

"Hi, Millicent. How are you?"

A deep, depressive sigh. "I need help, Aurora. I wrote down all the goals I'd like to achieve, but when I got up today I felt overwhelmed. So I made breakfast and watched Netflix and had a chat with my sister—who never makes me feel good—and now I'm on my couch."

I winced. The couch is the place where success goes to die.

Since she was a new client, I knew I'd need to give Millicent a little more hand-holding to retrain her mind. I launched into my step-by-step routine to bring the woman out of her immediate funk, forcing her to move her body.

By the time I reached the restaurant, I had her pumped up and in the right mindset. I got out of the car, hitched my purse higher on my arm, and spoke into the empty air with all the passion I could muster.

"Millicent, you've forgotten the most important step in changing your life. What did we speak about yesterday? Repeat it to me."

My hands gestured wildly in the air, a genetic trait from Mom's Italian heritage I couldn't seem to break. My client's hesitation told me she was desperately trying to remember the motto I drilled into every person's brain, including my own.

A short silence hummed over the line. "Action?"

"That's right! Nothing changes unless you do."

I pushed open the door to the restaurant, nodding to the hostess as I threaded my way to our usual corner table. Jason raised his hand to signal me over, then dropped it when he realized I was in work mode. I shot him an apologetic look, but he smiled and went back to perusing the menu. He was used to my packed schedule and never resented it when work seeped into our time. Another reason he was the perfect boyfriend.

"Now, give me the sound of victory!"

I winced at the loud hooting but was satisfied with the enthusiasm. "Get to work, Millicent. Make your dreams come true!"

"Thanks, Aurora—I am unstoppable!"

I gave my own hoot, said goodbye, and removed my earbuds.

Jason shot me an amused look. "Owl power?"

"Very funny. Sorry I'm late—I had to stop at Mom's."

"You're worth waiting for." He reached over and took my hands. "I think we should go with the mahi-mahi. Abe said it's fresh from the market and the pineapple salsa is homemade."

"Done. I'm too tired to make decisions." I smiled and studied him from across the table. Jason's thick blond hair was kept short but with just enough surfer wave to give him a boyish look. As a fitness trainer and nutrition guru, he kept himself in peak health. At a towering six three, he possessed eight-pack abs, bulging biceps, and thighs the size of tree trunks. Blue eyes held both intelligence and an intensity that had attracted me immediately.

Not sexual intensity, though we met each other's needs nicely. Jason ate, breathed, and slept work. But not just work to be busy. He was obsessed with meeting and smashing through goals, with achieving perfection with not only his body but his mind and emotions as well.

Jason was the male me. And the moment we'd met, I knew he was meant to be my partner. People told us all the time we were couple goals, and whenever I posted anything of us together, my social feed interaction doubled and I got a ton of new subscribers and followers.

Our waiter, Abe, came over, his gentle face wreathed in a smile. Jason and I had been coming regularly to Riverview restaurant for six months and he knew exactly what we liked. "So nice to see you again. Have we made our choices for the night?" His clean-shaven head gleamed and his dark eyes shrewdly glanced at the table, noting the candle was lit, the linens were pressed, and our water glasses were full.

"Thank you, Abe. We'll both have the mahi-mahi. Grilled, no butter," Jason said.

"Very good. Asparagus instead of the potato?"

"Definitely."

"House salad? With olive oil, lemon juice, and a dash of sea salt?"

Jason glanced at me, hesitant, and I took the reins. "Let's switch it out for arugula with some fennel tonight."

"Perfect. Shall I bring the Saratoga sparkling water now or with dinner?"

"Now, please," Jason said, thanking him. I relaxed in the chair. The first time Jason and I had dinner together, I was struck by his commitment to health, and he'd helped fine-tune my body to a lean, green fighting machine. My energy doubled, which meant I could double my workload. We were a power couple, each pushing the other consistently to be and do better. Only on our weekly dinner date at Riverview did we allow ourselves to take a few precious hours to relax. The rest of our time was dedicated to achievement and enough sleep to recharge.

"How is your mom?"

I hesitated. "Frustrating," I admitted. "She called me twice this week to fix something in the house, then guilted me into staying for a longer visit. I don't mind if there's a real problem, but she doesn't respect my work schedule. Plus, she still gets upset if I don't come over for Sunday dinner."

Jason regarded me thoughtfully. "Babe, I know you love your mom, but it's time for some tough love. How long has your dad been gone now?"

"Five years."

"You can't keep feeling responsible for her happiness. Maybe these Sunday dinners are harmful. She learns to keep being dependent on your company, and you get upset. I hate that she can't see how your work changes people. She minimizes the importance."

I sighed. "Yeah, she just doesn't get it. I'll cancel this Sunday and give us both a necessary break."

"That's my girl." His smile warmed me. "What do you have going on this weekend?"

I sipped my cocktail slowly and savored my Friday night indulgence. "I begin my new season on the podcast, so I'm doing some research on my guests. I've got some powerhouses who agreed to come on the show, which will definitely help preorders of the book."

He nodded. The lights shimmered and highlighted the golden strands of his hair. Those sky blue eyes fastened on my face with a sense of urgency. "Did you finish writing it yet?"

I tried not to wince. "I'm close. I just need to work out these last few chapters." Actually, there were more than a few left, but I'd blocked out serious writing time to finally get to the end. Jason didn't need to know how much I had left, so it wasn't really a lie. I shifted in my chair as heat prickled on my skin in a warning.

Dammit, I shouldn't have stretched the truth.

When I was young and got nervous, I broke out in an allergy: hives would suddenly appear and itch like crazy. Any type of lying always initiated the breakout. After testing, the doctors had agreed it was stress and recommended a psychologist.

My parents dismissed the suggestion, citing that I was perfect and I'd outgrow the rash. I suffered through school, freaking out over dates or public speeches, not knowing when it'd crop up and humiliate me. But I'd spent the last decade transforming the shy, nervous girl I was into a powerhouse and despised when weakness slunk back in. I took a deep breath, filling my lungs from the diaphragm; imagined a bright white light washing over my skin with healing; then slowly released.

The prickling eased.

I focused back on Jason. "You need to make that your first priority," he said. "How are your clients doing?"

I gave a half laugh. "They're making progress. I'm proud of them being dedicated to change. I know firsthand how hard it can be."

Jason looked at me with a spark of pride that made me squirm in my seat with satisfaction. There was something about his approval that made me feel invincible. "But you didn't even need life coaching. You were strong enough to do it all on your own."

I remembered after my dad died how it was as if I'd reached a crossroads. One path held ongoing agony, depression, and grief. The alternate path was filled with action and a chance to transform. Mom had spiraled, and I'd recognized one of us had to be strong. So I fought through my messy, weak emotions. I relied on sheer grit and an actionable plan to get to the other side and re-create myself.

"Well, I read books and attended some life conferences. No one ever does it alone," I said mildly. I thought of the list of mentors I'd listened to, how I dug deep inside myself for the change I encouraged in others. My breakthrough was a realization that I was here to guide people like me who were struggling to find their true selves. I took classes and was certified as a life coach, then began to create my own philosophies and share them on social media. It took a while, but eventually my followers grew and I began doing a podcast. The past two years, I finally became profitable. My podcast was highly rated on Spotify, my life-coaching business was flourishing, and I'd signed a publishing contract for my first self-help book. I was living my dream and thriving under pressure.

Nothing worthwhile was easy, but I loved how Jason believed in me. He only made me want even more for myself, for him. For us.

Jason's face softened. "I love that you're humble in your success. I remember after I opened my first gym, everyone told me I could finally relax. That I'd done it. But it was just the beginning for me. Unfortunately, most of those people dropped away. I needed to surround myself with people like us. People who don't get lazy or give in to an emotional mindset of negativity."

The busboy stopped at our table and dropped a basket of bread between us.

I stiffened, afraid to even breathe as a little puff of steam rose from the linens, carrying the scent of freshly baked dough to my nostrils. Like a recovering smoker, I tried to suck in the delicious smell before it disappeared forever. Sometimes, I had no shame.

Jason picked up the basket and handed it quickly back. "No bread, thank you," he said firmly. "Carbs will kill you."

"Oh, sorry," the guy mumbled, racing away.

I cleared my throat and took another sip of my cocktail. That was a close call.

Jason kept talking like the incident had never occurred.

"I'm running the half-marathon next Saturday. Did you decide to join me? I already registered you."

Running wasn't my favorite thing in the world. I'd worked like crazy trying to tame my generous curves, which I'd inherited from Mom, and found the perfect combination of food/sugar avoidance, weights, and kickboxing. Something about running bored me to tears. I think it was all that empty time with nothing to do but think. But Jason thought running was the bread and butter of exercise, so I tried to compromise.

"I can't, babe. I've got clients, writing, and podcast research. I'll need to pass this time."

"Understood. My gym is sponsoring the event, so I probably won't be around that whole day."

Tamping down a sigh, I pushed thoughts of my family out of my mind. The fish was delivered and we feasted on dinner. We traded work stories and upcoming calendar events and discussed the newest nonfiction books we were reading. I finished my cocktail, sucking down the precious last drops, and smiled.

Jason tilted his head. "What is it?"

Satisfaction sung in my veins. "I'm happy. With me. With us. With everything."

He smiled back. "Me, too."

I stared into his blue eyes. He'd mentioned long-term commitment a few times, but we still hadn't exchanged the big *I love you*s yet. I never pressured him. I wasn't the type. I'd turn thirty-five this year but was in no rush for children. Nowadays, I had plenty of time and options for a family. It was as if my life were on the edge of a breakout, from my love life to my career, and all I needed to do was keep pushing and manifesting and working my ass off. I'd finally have it all.

"Want to go back to my place or yours?" Jason asked.

"Let's do yours tonight." I hadn't cleaned for a while and he hated a messy home.

"Great, let's get the bill." He lifted a finger and Abe appeared with the leather portfolio, sliding it in the middle. Most of the time, we split the check, but this time Jason took it, shaking his head when I reached for my purse. "My treat."

"Thank you."

We went back to his place and I spent the night. I woke up with a sated body, a fire in my belly, and a brain buzzing to get the day started.

Until I got the phone call.

Years ago, when I received the news that my father had died in a car crash, I believed it was the most defining moment of my life. I believed if I rose to the challenge and conquered that tragedy, the rest of my future would play out the way I hoped.

Now I knew different.

I guess God had bigger plans for me.

Because my mother had been found by my neighbor, collapsed on the kitchen floor.

She'd had a cardiac arrest.

And she was gone.

TWO

SIX MONTHS LATER

I STUDIED MYSELF in the mirror, carefully applying my favorite red lipstick and smoothing down some flyaway strands of hair. The woman who stared back at me looked different. She was thinner and sharper, with a pointy edge to her chin and defined cheekbones. Dark eyes were rimmed with liner. A touch of gold glitter shadow swiped over her lids emphasized full black lashes. She was clad in a fashionable mustard wrap dress that showed off her leaner figure, and I was surprised at how calm and in control she was. As if she had everything figured out.

I peered harder into my reflection, my gaze clashing with my twin's. It was then I saw the duplicity.

The woman's eyes were beautiful, but they were dead. No emotion gleamed there, just a surface flatness no one would ever notice as long as she didn't let them look too hard.

I drew in a breath, held a moment, and slowly released. The familiar prickling danced beneath the surface of my skin, but that was the least of my problems. I had to be my best at this event. I'd postponed twice already, and though everyone seemed understanding because of the circumstances, I'd run out of time. If I didn't show, I'd risk my stable of followers and fans, which I needed desperately to keep, and the new ones I needed desperately to sign.

I can do this.

Pulling my shaky fingers into fists, I left the bathroom in a cloud of Dior and grabbed my beaded vintage purse. Jason had a late meeting with investors for his new gym, so we'd decided to go separately. I wished he was at my side to walk in and greet everyone, but he'd sacrificed enough. I couldn't expect him to continue putting off his workload to babysit me. It was time I showed him I was truly back to my powerhouse ways and the woman he'd fallen in love with.

I am strong.

I am capable.

I am all.

My mantra was firm and powerful even as my gut clenched with fear. It was new—this anxiety that washed over me when I was confronted with people. At first, I gave myself grace to pick up the pieces, canceled a few appearances, and delayed the new podcast season. After all, my entire world had blown up with a phone call. The daily motivational videos I posted slowed to once a week. My editor gave me an extension on the book and pushed out the release date. At the respectable three-month mark, I decided I'd grieved enough and dove back into work, confident it'd been enough time.

I guess it hadn't been. I suffered from hive breakouts, panic around crowds, and a brain fog that made it impossible to focus.

Jason was patient. But as time passed and things didn't get better, I began to wonder why I couldn't go back to my old self. It was the exact time frame I'd needed years ago when I lost Dad. Three months of hard grief, then slow, achievable steps to break out of my emotional paralysis. By six months, I should be putting in regular days. I didn't expect to be back to my full self until after a year, but why wasn't I even able to complete simple tasks?

I couldn't afford to keep myself out of the spotlight any longer. Tonight, I needed to prove that I could run my business, charm clients, and grow my fan base.

Everything depended on it.

Lifting my chin with determination, I repeated the mantra to myself as I climbed into my sleek white convertible and drove to the restaurant. Harvest on Hudson boasted warm elegance, impeccable food, and a gorgeous setting on the Hudson River. The late spring night was warm and the patio was open; twinkling lights, a full bar, and appetizers made their rounds under a sky filled with stars.

I walked to the main dining area, nodding with approval at the elegant decor. With sparkling crystal, bright white tablecloths, gorgeous floral vases, and accents of rich wood, it dripped with the aura of accomplishment and success. The bar was an icon of dark mahogany and gleaming granite, allowing plenty of seating and space for networking.

My planner, Penelope, had nailed it. The new season of my podcast may have been delayed, but now I was back and intended to dazzle. I'd decided to throw a celebration party with an impressive guest list to thank my current audience and expand to new members. Press had been invited, along with several huge social media influencers and previous podcast guests. Signs and a giant banner advertised my glowing face next to the famous hook line: **STEP INTO YOUR SUCCESS!** I did a walk-through, tidied up last-minute details with Penelope, and got ready to begin greeting guests.

I had created a reputation of getting people to be real with themselves and their limitations, but if I was counseling myself, I'd say it was time to push through. I couldn't bury myself in a cave when the world needed me. Life didn't shut down because I was struggling with a difficult loss. Showing up as my best self was exactly what my audience needed to see—growth and determination after being hit hard with tragedy. I was a living, breathing symbol of all I counseled, and I refused to fail.

"Aurora!" I swung around to greet Sheena, one of my most successful clients. She looked impeccable as usual, dressed in an emerald green beaded dress, her honey blond hair done in an elaborate twist to show off her delicate features. "How are you doing? Better, I hope?"

Her face reflected a sympathy and swirling curiosity that immediately jerked my hackles up. Losing my mom had given my followers a bit of gossip, becoming a hot topic as a swarm of condolences choked my daily feeds. People reached out with their apologies, love, and prayers. And of course, positive thoughts. Many were friends. Many were strangers. It was a beautiful thing to see the world show up to support me after my loss, but I also experienced something horrible and dark growing inside me, like mold slithering and threatening a clean surface.

Resentment.

Because I was in the public spotlight, people nosily inquired about the details of my loss. The consistent prodding to share my experience, my heartbreak, and the gory details of how it felt to be an orphan created a deep well of rage that shocked me. Memories of my father's car crash began surfacing, and I didn't want to deal with others poking into the losses I'd endured, greedily devouring my grief like I was a reality television star.

But I recognized that part of the grief cycle was anger, so I tried to accept my dark emotions with grace. I was confident the feeling would dissipate.

I smiled and pushed all the mess down with a hard shove. "So much better! Thanks for asking. I'm excited to get back to work. I hear congratulations are in order for renewing the series?"

Sheena had come to me as a struggling actress desperate to make it. She was beautiful and talented but lacked confidence. After a year of deep work, she landed a role in a television pilot that was eventually turned into a series. Sheena's role as the beautiful bitchy neighbor grew in popularity, and now she was a household name. She offered a blurb for my website and was a guest on my podcast, praising my services. It had been the beginning of my own breakout, and my podcast began to climb the charts. She was a symbol to me of the people I could help with my philosophies and action plans.

Her glossy pink lips opened to emit a delighted laugh. "Yes, we're in season three—can you believe it? My agent is sending me movie scripts now. As you've always told me, when your time comes for success, you need to be ready and have done the work. I'm going full throttle while my name is hot."

"That's wonderful. You know I'm here whenever you need me."

"Same, Aurora. My heart truly broke for your loss. I'm glad to see you thriving again."

I swallowed past the tightness in my throat and chatted a bit more before easing to the next group of guests. The waiter glided by and I snatched a glass of champagne, clutching it gratefully. Alcohol was allowed this evening. God knows, I needed a little liquid courage tonight.

The next hour was a blur of faces, condolences, and superficial niceties. I did my best to bring my usual enthusiastic and bold personality, but my skin began to itch under my beautiful dress, and sweat dripped between my breasts, even though the air was chilled. I had to make my speech soon to pump everyone up. Usually, the pull of the crowd and the possibility of changing people's mindsets flooded me with gratitude and adrenaline.

But not now. Now I only felt my heart beating faster and louder. My voice rose in conversation as I tried to struggle past the roaring noise in my ears. I was just about to duck into the ladies' room to calm down, but my gaze suddenly fastened on Jason, easing through the crowd to reach me.

Relief dropped my shoulders. He was dressed in an immaculate blue suit, with a starched pink shirt. He wore Italian loafers and no socks. Blond hair curled over his brow. Sky blue eyes kept me in focus as he stopped at my side, bending down to kiss my temple. "Sorry I'm late," he whispered. "How's it going?"

"Great. I'm so happy you're here." My words contradicted my body as I leaned into him for support. He allowed it for a few precious seconds, then eased back. Jason had told me multiple times he'd fallen in love with me for my fierce independence, self-reliance, and inner strength. My need factor had been high these past months, and I knew he was hoping I'd rally and prove I could push through anything for success. Even grief.

Even by myself.

"Good. I didn't want to miss your speech. This is a good turnout," he said, glancing at the crowded room. I looked around and tried to see what he did, but the colorful, glamorous gowns and sleek suits and sparkling crystal glasses seemed distorted, as if I viewed the scene through a dirty lens.

"How was the opening?" I asked.

"Exactly what I hoped—we were at capacity." Satisfaction settled over his face. "I manifested my vision and now I have three gyms. Plus, I just got a sponsorship for Quake protein drinks. They're interested in partnering with the gym for marketing purposes. Isn't that incredible?"

"Incredible," I repeated.

Jason's schedule was already maxed. Once I stopped working twenty-four seven, I noticed how little time we actually spent together outside work. But of course, I was happy for him. He was getting everything he dreamed of. It just felt odd that I wasn't racing by his side, hand in hand. I'd tripped and slowed, watching him pull ahead.

I needed to pick up my pace or he'd cross the finish line without me.

The idea caused fear to poke its ugly head out from the dark cellar. I kicked its head and shut the door. It remained closed.

For now.

"You worked hard and you deserve this success," I said firmly.

"Thanks, babe. Now it's your turn. I know things have been hard, but this is your moment. Go claim it."

Why did his tone irritate instead of inspire me? I ignored the question and smiled, grabbing another glass of champagne. His frown told me he disapproved, but this time, I didn't care. I just needed one more to get through, then I'd drink water the rest of the night.

We networked like the power couple we were, and I finally nodded to Penelope, who immediately dimmed the lights and began the opening music for my podcast. Applause thundered as I took the stage. I was reminded once again that I'd spent years scrambling for this day, this exact scenario. People now looked to me for advice and support and counsel. I was the focus of a lavish, exclusive cocktail party to celebrate a podcast I'd built and made successful. I'd changed lives for many in this room. I'd proven my significance.

I gave a dazzling smile and hooted into the microphone with my trademark call to action.

"I'm so happy to be here, surrounded by the doers, the creators, the believers!"

More applause. My gaze took in the blur of faces, all turned toward me, waiting to be dazzled, expecting me to give them what they showed up for. I waited for the rush to fill me up and flood my veins, allowing me to be that change for them—to help them believe in themselves like I did.

But I felt . . . nothing.

Just a slow unraveling of anxiety building to a low, thrumming panic. I kept my arms held high in the air, big smile pasted to my face, and relied on the power of my voice to keep going.

"We've done all this together. There is no me without you—and this party tonight is so much more than an opportunity to dress up and drink bubbly champagne and network. This is about stepping into our real selves. The powerful, beautiful people we are inside, ready to be unleashed. Ready to be our best. Ready to . . ."

I waited and hoped they'd take the bait.

"Step into success!" the audience roared back.

My stomach loosened. Breath came easier into my lungs. *I got this.*

"That's right! Tonight, I've brought you together to take a new step into the future with me. I've got a new action implementation plan to make things easier for you to break through blocks. More stories to inspire and help you remember your power. More guests on the podcast to tell their truth and help us create real change for our lives and our future, full of all our dreams, such as financial freedom, love, contribution, and passion! Who wants it *all*?"

The music crashed through the speakers and the lights flashed and everyone clapped wildly. My gaze scanned the crowd, snagging on Jason, who looked up at me with pride and satisfaction. That elusive adrenaline hit finally crashed through, and I was back, ready to lead.

Until Jason looked down, frowned at his phone, then quickly lifted it to his ear. In the middle of the pumped-up crowd, in the middle of my rousing speech, he pivoted on his leather heel and walked out of the restaurant.

It was a simple thing. A minor inconvenience that would have normally made me a bit irritated. Maybe I would have said something to him later on, he would have apologized, and the entire incident would have been erased.

But right now, the emptiness inside me gaped open like a bleeding wound, like Jason had ripped off the bandage and exposed my vulnerability to the world. Within seconds, I saw flashes of our past relationship and how he liked things to be tit for tat. I saw our connection not as true emotion but as a convenient arrangement, a bargain to push the other toward greatness and achievement.

What I didn't see in those awful, flickering moments?

Jason showing up for the ugly stuff. The hard things. The mess that lurked behind greatness but was always present and waiting to jump out.

The devastating truth was too much to process so quickly, but then the second crisis occurred right on its tail.

My mother's voice rose inside me and the memory bashed into me with a touch of violence, yanking me into the past.

"I'm worried about you, Aurora. You're becoming a person I don't recognize anymore."

We were sitting on the front porch. My mom was curled up in the rocker, a glass of red wine cupped in her long, tapered fingers. Her hair fell in messy waves over her shoulders, stray grays intermingled with coal black strands. She wore loose oatmeal-colored pants and a matching well-worn cardigan sweater. The sun was setting, turning the sky to warm pinks and blues, bleeding into one another like a child's crushed crayons. We'd just finished dinner, and I'd spent most of the time excitedly telling her about my exploding business. Mom had just nodded, thoughtfully staring at me with those stirring dark eyes, stripping past the barrier right to my soul. My frustration with her inability to celebrate my success grew, so I'd asked her to talk out on the porch.

"Mom, why don't you understand work makes me happy? Do you see the amount of people who need me? I'm changing lives!"

Her sigh floated on the warm spring breeze. "You misunderstand me, Aurora. Seeing you happy makes my heart full. But you're chasing happiness in the wrong direction. There's a difference between wanting to help people and wanting to be loved and needed. I think you're confusing the two."

I felt like screaming at her stubbornness. I'd never believed Mom would want to hold me back in my career—she'd never been one to push the "stay at home, get married, and have children" role. But now I wondered if she wasn't disappointed that I'd passed thirty and wasn't close to settling down. My voice sharpened. "I'm sorry you believe I'm pathetic enough to chase after adoration with strangers, Mom. I mean, really? Do you realize I'm making a difference in the world? I've built real connections! How does that translate to neediness?"

Her lips pursed and I knew she was just as frustrated as I was. "I'm simply asking you to look deeper. Do you realize you never see your old friends anymore? You used to visit Hannah and April in Chicago regularly, but you haven't gone in over a year. I can barely get you to commit to a Sunday afternoon dinner, and if you do come, you're always in a rush. And the last time you went to church was Christmas."

"I'm busy building something for myself. Is that so wrong?"

"No. Work is important. Goals and passions are important. But so are family, friends, and faith. I'm afraid for you, darling."

I blinked and regarded her in shock. "Afraid of what? That I'll be rich and well-known and deliriously happy?"

Sadness and some type of grief shone in her gaze. I jerked back, confused at the obvious pain and secrets swirling in those depths, but then it was gone and she was just my mom again.

Her voice caught and drifted in the playful breeze. "I'm afraid when you reach that lofty peak, you'll look into the crowd and see no one you truly recognize. That you will be alone."

I'd gotten offended, refusing to listen. I'd chalked the whole lecture up to her being upset that I'd changed. Just because I had no time to have a four-course dinner full of carbs or go to church to hear the priest ramble on didn't mean I'd be alone. I said as much, and she backed down, but the words couldn't be unspoken or unheard.

I blinked wildly, trying to clear my vision. My gaze sought out familiar faces to prove my mother was wrong. I recognized all my clients, new and old. Influencers whom I'd gotten to know on a first-name basis. Actors, artists, writers, and self-help gurus who dotted the landscape with their own fans. My staff. Acquaintances whom I occasionally grabbed coffee with to share ideas.

But no one I loved.

No real friends who knew me from before. No family. No Jason.

Dear God, had my mother been right?

Grief crushed me and I became helpless beneath the weight. Within moments, I'd completely lost my focus. The heart that had been full for my audience filled with sadness and an aching loneliness I'd never experienced before. I felt untethered in the world and in this room, where I'd carefully curated a group of supporters to help share in my joy of success.

Instead, I felt horribly isolated and overwhelmed.

I want my mom and dad back.

The noise level dimmed.

I want to go home and be safe.

A low hoot of encouragement rose to my ears. The lump in my throat grew bigger, choking me, and my skin began to itch.

"I—I can't thank you enough for being here. I'm so grateful."

I bit the inside of my cheek hard as silly tears threatened. I would not let this happen. I was bigger than my emotions. I'd spent the past years proving myself over and over so others could do it, too. I could not fail at my own launch party, with cameras flashing and videos whirring and important influencers hanging on my next words.

"This is going to be an epic year for all of us."

My booming, kick-ass tone fell flat. Murmurs arose. In horror, I watched hives begin to break out on my bare arms, popping up like Rice Krispies cereal in an angry, blistering red.

I had to get off the stage before it was too late.

Frantically, I looked around for someone to save me but found no one.

"Let's take a step toward owning our future." My voice wobbled, hitched, broke.

A hush fell over the restaurant, and hungry, curious gazes poked and prodded every inch.

"Let's—"

From a distance, I heard the music begin to play. Penelope tried to gain me those precious seconds to flee the stage before the disaster came, but it was too late.

I burst into tears and began to sob in front of my guests.

Then I ran away.

THREE

"I JUST DON'T understand."

Jason paced back and forth in my apartment. I was too exhausted to try to get him to sit, so I just watched, sipping my tea. Jacket shed, shirtsleeves rolled up, face set with concentration, he seemed to be working himself up to a big lecture. I studied his rock-hard muscles and the lithe prowl he'd perfected to show off how good healthy can not only feel but look.

He'd always seemed to fit in my apartment, which I'd furnished with careful thought to feng shui and Marie Kondo. If I didn't love something, I got rid of it. I rented a charming old Victorian in the eclectic town of Cold Spring, situated by the Hudson River. The place was filled with character—from the gorgeous wooden plank floors that creaked to the solid plastered walls painted in bold colors: purple, yellow, and robin's-egg blue. The rooms were filled with pieces of antique furniture: a curio cabinet with various-size drawers, coffee tables with scrolled floral art etched on the top, ornate framed mirrors with beveled glass, handmade braided throw rugs. I'd found a deal on a canary yellow sectional with velvet tufted cushions and invested in fluffy modern pillows and blankets to cuddle up with. Jason called it a fun house since I hadn't stuck with the modern, simplistic flair he preferred, but what he saw as chaos I viewed as story.

Large bay windows looked out to a wild garden with benches. I wasn't a gardener or good with plants like Mom, but when I could squeeze out half an hour, I loved to sit outside under the trees and watch bees hop from bloom to bloom while I wrote my lists and plans in my leather-bound journal.

Cold Spring was filled with New York City transplants and well-off creative types and entrepreneurs. Main Street boasted numerous cafés and shops filled with antiques, art, and custom design fashion. Menus catered to vegans, and dogs were just as important customers as people. The local train station allowed an ease for commuters that rocketed rent and mortgage prices, so I was lucky to have grabbed the opportunity as my career and finances leveled up.

Jason lived a few towns over, in Beacon, so it was a quick drive, but his place looked like a converted warehouse, with high ceilings and plenty of space for his training equipment. He'd mentioned if we decided to move in together, we'd go to his place, but the thought of leaving my safe haven concerned me. I was excited about furthering our commitment, but I knew we weren't ready yet, so it was easy to wave off and continue things as they were.

But the last few months I'd been a bit more demanding of Jason, and we were both beginning to see the frays in the solid fabric of our relationship. Tonight had not helped.

I didn't know how to respond to his comment. My freak-out was already blowing up online. Most comments were sympathetic, but others were almost gleeful in their scorn. My career was being picked apart and analyzed because the fickle public adored a good freak-out. All of the press made me squirm with humiliation. I was supposed to be the one to lift others—I'd made it the crux of my career with life coaching, writing, and the podcast. Having the world suddenly question my stability, trading opinions about whether I was "pushing too hard, too fast" or "needing a self-care retreat," made me burn with shame.

"What was going on in your head? I've never seen you have a public breakdown before. The sobs. The hives. Running out in the middle of a party you hosted. Do you need Benadryl for your allergies?"

My skin still itched, but once I'd gotten out of the restaurant and headed home, the giant bumps began to fade. I didn't like the look of distaste on Jason's face. I knew they were ugly, but he was being completely unsympathetic to my embarrassment. He'd been silent on the drive over, lost in his thoughts.

"I'm good now."

Jason turned to study me. I felt like a new species of insect he desperately wanted to figure out. "Aurora, we need to speak frankly."

A chill raced down my spine. I hugged my knees to my chest and tried not to shiver. Why did I just need him to crawl next to me and give me a hug? For tonight, couldn't I cry on his chest while he soothed me? "What is it?"

"I feel like I've been patient and supportive. You've gone through a difficult time. Losing your mom would throw anyone off, so I gave you these months and tried to focus all my attention on your needs. Have I done that for you?"

I blinked. Did he really want me to answer? "Yeah."

He nodded firmly. "Yes. But you've had enough time to steep in grief. I completely understand and support you! But it's been six months, and you're not doing any better."

I tried to swallow but my throat wouldn't work. "I'm trying," I managed to squeak out.

"I know, babe. But your mom is gone," he said gently. "She's not coming back. Would she like seeing you screw up your future because you want to wallow in sadness?"

I jerked back. "No."

"No," he repeated. "It's time to rise up, Aurora. You've done it before, after your dad died. You took that event and turned it into a successful career helping others. Now it's time to do it again. Shed your story and create a new one—one full of power and action. Tonight was your opportunity and you gave in to your weaker self. And I can't keep picking up the pieces, baby. I just can't. I've already sacrificed months of progress on the gym opening to take care of you, but we need to move on. Do you agree?"

A low, boiling anger simmered in response to his words. Jason had never dealt with death or illness or catastrophe. His parents were still around and happily married. He had two siblings who were just as successful, and whenever someone tried to share their hard-luck story with him, he had no patience for it. I'd always found such strength of purpose admirable. But lately?

Not so much. Lately, I wondered if Jason couldn't relate because he'd never faced true adversity.

I tried to squash the uncomfortable thought. Jason was the only one I had left and I couldn't lose him. I managed to choke out one word. "Yes."

"Yes!" he repeated. Why did I want to slap him for treating me like a wayward child? "I've been thinking about what's best for you and I have a plan. You need to push past your block. Focus solely on action-oriented tasks—I'll be happy to work with you and compose a chart. Didn't you tell me that works for most of your clients?"

It had. I'd made a name for myself creating and trademarking my special task planner that helped focus on breaking up large action blocks into smaller tasks and linking it to the true motivation of the goal. For instance, losing weight or feeling more confident in your body seemed like an insurmountable task, but if it was broken into simple steps, such as *drink one gallon of water*, success was easier. I had them imagine their cells hydrated and happy, healing traveling into their bodies via white light, and what activities they could do with more stamina. Then I built the blocks until each segment led to the final goal.

But watching Jason throw my own tool at me made me really, really mad.

I buried my head down toward my tea and managed a nod.

"Good. We'll build your plan together to help get you out of this mess. In the meantime, I think there's only one way to guarantee you relearn to stand on your own and gain back your power."

I dragged in a shaky breath. My spidey senses tingled with dread. "What?"

"We need to break up."

I peered up at him, my insides raw and broken, and wondered if I'd misheard him. "Did you say you wanted to break up?"

"Of course not! I said we *need* to break up—it's completely different. Hear me out, Aurora, and I'm sure you'll agree. I've done a lot of thinking about it this past week but was hoping tonight you'd be better and I wouldn't have to go to Plan B."

"Plan B?" I echoed faintly, wondering if I had dropped into an alternate reality.

"Sure. Plan A was to coddle you and hope you get better on your own. Obviously, you need more help, so I created Plan B. I did some research and I think you're struggling with feeling lost and abandoned. Perfectly understandable when it comes to losing parents, of course."

Oh, this was going to be bad. My hands began to shake, so I carefully put the teacup on the table and tucked them under the blanket. This time, I couldn't manage a word, but he didn't seem to care, continuing blithely as he began to pace again.

"The problem is, you've turned to me in order to feel safe. At first, I was perfectly happy to play that role. I loved being your rock and didn't mind putting my own needs aside. You're special. I've been wanting to tell you this for a while." He paused his steps and turned to face me. "Aurora, I love you."

A gurgle of astonishment bubbled from my lips. WTF? I'd been waiting for his big announcement, hoping we'd be vulnerable to each other and confess our emotions. I imagined candlelit dinners and moonlight or maybe even whispers in the dark, tangled in sheets, after lovemaking.

But . . . didn't he say he was breaking up with me?

He must've registered my shocked expression and figured I was over-the-moon happy. "That's right. I love you. But we moved into an unhealthy relationship, and that's dangerous for both of us. The longer I satisfy your needs, the longer you'll be hindered and choose to isolate yourself. The world needs you, babe. I need you. So it's best if we take a break from each other while you figure this out."

I continued to stare at him mutely, having no clue what he wanted me to do. Thank him? Bow my head and admit I was a screwed-up mess? Promise I'd do better to save our relationship? Tell him I loved him back?

He tilted his head and placed his hands on his hips. The shirt stretched across his broad muscles and squeezed his tight biceps. His brows lowered, gaze worriedly scanning me. I suddenly felt like a project to him rather than the woman he claimed to love.

"I don't want this," he said gently. "This hurts me as much as you, but I'm hoping you understand. If I step away, you'll be forced to take action. I know you can do it. You can fix this mess and be stronger than ever. Think of the role model you'll be! Going through grief, struggling with the fallout, and stepping to the other side. It'll be a perfect segue to your book and podcast. You'll be bigger than ever, babe. But for now, you need to be stripped of all your crutches."

He stepped forward and knelt before me. His hands stroked back my hair like I was fragile, and though I despised myself, I only wanted to grip his palm and bring it to my cheek and beg him not to do this. Not now. Not when I needed him the most.

I had no one else. I'd pushed them all away in my hunt for . . . more.

"We'll make our way back to each other," Jason vowed. "And then we'll be ready for the future—our future."

He kissed me with a gentle touch like I was the finest, most delicate, most adored china, his lips skating over mine.

"I love you, Aurora. Now, go fix your life and come back to me."

Then he left.

FOUR

THE NEXT DAY, I got a call from my editor.

"How are you, Aurora?" Claire asked. Her voice oozed with sympathy and warmth, which I knew was trouble. It meant she'd seen the blowup on social media and assumed I was falling apart. A self-help, motivational figure whose mental health was suddenly being questioned would not sell a lot of books. Or maybe it would for the drama, but the book wasn't about that. I'd broken the trust the moment I sobbed at my own party.

"I'm much better, thank you," I said, trying to sound forceful and confident. "I'm sure you've heard about the incident this past weekend. I'd planned to call you myself and let you know there's nothing to worry about. Last week, a few triggers appeared, but I've worked through them and I'm ready to finish this book."

Claire hummed over the line, her tell for when she was about to delicately suggest something I might not like. "I'm thrilled to hear that. Truly, I've been so worried about you, and slightly guilty that I've pushed my own agenda when you're still struggling. But I actually have news I think you'll agree is quite wonderful. We've decided to push out the due date to give you the time you need."

"Oh? How long will that delay publication?" I closed my eyes, dreading the answer.

A pause. "Two years. That will give you another year to work on the book, and then a year to get it ready for release. And if you need more time? Well, that's fine!"

No, no, no . . .

"Claire, I can't thank you enough for trying to work with me, but I'm so much better. In fact, I began writing this morning and I'm flying through the pages. I'm sure I can deliver the manuscript within the month."

Sure, I was lying, but if I had to write, *All work and no play makes Aurora a dull girl*, I would. I'd do anything to keep this contract. Pushing it out ruined all my carefully built plans. I couldn't guarantee I'd be at the top in two years, or as relevant. The book was slotted for the spring, to coincide with the podcast and events Penelope had been securing to overlap with my publisher's book tour.

Now? I would be pushed aside to make way for other leaders, the ones nipping at my heels and hungry for the spotlight. Hungry to steal my spot.

Claire laughed, startling me. "You are simply amazing. I appreciate your work ethic, but it's already been decided. This way, we'll be able to have the best book possible for our team to sell. Your job is to take the time you need and heal."

"I'm healed," I said desperately. "Are you sure I can't convince you to keep our pub date, Claire? Honestly, I know I can deliver a great book."

"This is good news, Aurora! You keep the advance, and I'll send over an amendment letter with the new deadline date. It will be worth waiting for. I know your audience will love it."

The air whooshed out of my lungs. There was no convincing her, so I'd better pretend to like the decision. "Thanks so much for your thoughtfulness," I said, trying not to choke. "I truly appreciate it."

"You are so welcome. Let me know if you have any questions, but we'll be in touch."

I thanked her again and hung up.

My short-lived ambition to tackle my email and shoot a motivational video withered away. I looked at my laptop and camera lying out on the desk, abandoned. I needed to return several voice mails, go food shopping, and work out. But I was still clad in my robe, pj's, and socks on a sunny Tuesday afternoon.

The yawning emptiness was waiting to devour me. I struggled for a bit, then gave in. It was so much easier than trying to be fabulous and have all the answers. Like a trail of dominoes, each part of my life had begun to topple, leaving me with nothing.

Jason was gone. I was angry for a while, but then the fear and loneliness wiped it out, leaving me in a panic state. The apartment was eerily still. I'd picked up the phone to call my mother, then remembered she was gone and I'd never talk to her again. Never hear her warm laugh or feel her hand in mine or gaze into her beautiful dark eyes. Losing Mom had triggered my grief over Dad, so now it was as if I were right back where I'd been after the car crash. I'd never golf with him again or listen to his crisp British voice as he called people he disliked wankers like in *Ted Lasso.* There was no one in my life to share their memories with. I felt as if I were floating in a vast ocean, clutching a raft and wondering if anyone could really see me in order to rescue me.

You rescue yourself, the inner voice whispered. *Get up and own your life. Show the world how winners live.*

It was a motto I'd built my entire career around, but now I was simply a fraud. I had no idea how to help myself. I'd believed it was willpower, positive mindset, and determined action. But as I wandered around my silent oasis, touching books on my shelf, picking up family pictures and cradling them against my chest, I realized I'd never known what I was doing. I'd shouldered the first loss and believed I was bulletproof and knew all the secrets.

Now I was going to pay the price for my hubris.

Blinking back tears, I'd returned to my permanent perch on my couch when my gaze caught on a sleek white box. I slid it from the bookshelf and stared at the DNA test Jason had gotten me for Christmas. I'd been talking about how I wished I'd had siblings and cousins, and he mentioned many people had discovered lost relatives by doing the tests.

Curious, I opened the box and read the instructions. It was simple enough. I provided a saliva sample, sent it to the ancestry company, and they returned the results. I'd confirm my cultural heritage and be able to track down any family members via a family tree site. Taking the box, I typed the site onto my computer and quickly read the summary.

I already doubted that anyone was out there for me. Dad

had said he came from a long line of only children—both his parents and grandparents. But maybe there was a hint of royalty in there from England? It would be fun to find out.

Mom had always been brusque about her past and childhood. She just said her parents had passed away when she was young and she was also an only child. After she graduated from high school, she left her guardians—whom she wasn't close with—and worked a variety of jobs until Dad came along. Dad met her at a pizza place and they immediately fell in love, got married, and started building a family. Whenever I asked about her past, Mom just told me her life began the moment she saw Dad, at nineteen years old.

My fingers automatically reached around my neck to stroke the silver medal my mother had always worn. Dad used to joke he could buy her precious diamonds or pearls, but she'd never give up her St. Lucy medal. The simple circular piece of jewelry held a delicacy of craftsmanship. I used to get frustrated that she wouldn't take it off even for a holiday, when she had flashier jewelry, but she'd just shake her head and tell me St. Lucy would always keep her in the light, and it had once belonged to her mother.

Now the medal pressing against my skin brought me comfort, connecting me to her and her past.

What if there was someone out there related to us in some weird way? The possibility of finding any type of long-lost aunt or uncle soothed my raw heart. I wanted someone to share my parents with, someone who would care and understand how special they were.

It didn't take long for me to complete the sample, get it in the mail, and register for an account. A shiver of excitement raced down my spine. For a few wonderful seconds, I felt strong enough to open up my inbox and tackle some work. Maybe I needed something like this to hope for in order to get out of my rut. Any type of action begets more action and allows the universe to open up the flow of energy, pulling us forward.

I'd written that line in my first chapter. Now that the pressure was off with my deadline, I bet my muse would peek her head out and give me some words. My fingers tapped the keys, and I threw my shoulders back. I'd work, get dressed, and go for a walk. Connecting with nature was an excellent way to re-ground and move past blocks.

I clicked on an email from my producer, Eliza, for *Step into Your Success*, hoping for the finalized schedule of guests. We'd been shifting through candidates to find the perfect fit for the new season, finally able to recruit some bigger names. After delaying the initial episode, I hoped my audience would find the show was worth the wait.

Until I began to read.

Eliza had forwarded me the emails. All were polite and apologetic. All cited work schedule complications and offered to try again in the fall. All wished me well. One referred me to a grief therapist. Another said that she admired my bravery to show vulnerability in public. The final one mentioned self-care and pointed me to another podcast that focused on the theme.

Slowly, I began scrolling through more emails. Eliza had supplied a list of alternates to approach, citing a bunch of in-office emergencies. Penelope was frantic to pull all the current advertising to reflect the cancellations. Events needed rescheduling. New client intake forms required reading. Each task that didn't get done snowballed into more and put me further behind.

The swirl of helplessness took hold, turning into a tsunami. I snatched my fingers back from the keyboard and groaned, trying to fight the gut-wrenching black cloud swallowing me up.

Everything was falling apart and I didn't know how to put it back together.

Even worse?

I wondered if I'd stopped caring. I'd become the exact type of person I counseled, but my action plan wasn't working. Hopelessness curled inside like a familiar friend and pushed me back to the sofa, back to the blankets, back to the nothingness where I could find rest.

Tomorrow. I'd be better tomorrow. I'd write my book and answer emails. I'd call back Penelope and we'd fix things. I'd print out the intake forms, make my notes, and reach out. I'd do it all.

Tomorrow.

"TELL ME WHAT brings you today, Aurora."

One week later, I'd finally sought help. Fighting my sense of failure, I reached out to a therapist. I couldn't stand back and watch my entire life shatter because I was embarrassed to admit my fail-safe action plans weren't working on me. Dr. Sariah Peterson came highly recommended from reviews, was covered by my insurance, and had a cancellation, so she could fit me in. I liked her immediately and was positive she'd get me going again. A tall Black woman with her hair pulled back in a sleek chignon, cheekbones that could cut glass, and a rich voice that made me want to close my eyes and listen. I felt confident in her ability to help me. I spent the first session telling her about my parents, my crumbling career, and the separation from Jason. I finished with explaining how important it was that I get back to work.

Amber eyes reflected concern as she stared back at me, matched with a tiny frown creasing her brow. "I appreciate your wanting to get back to your life and become productive again," she said gently, "but that's simply not going to happen, Aurora."

I blinked, trying not to panic. "What do you mean? If you think meds will work, I'm willing. I just need to get over this hump. That's the reason I'm here."

A sigh escaped her lips. "I don't think you're appreciating the challenges you've been faced with. Grief is unique to everyone, and there's no timetable on when it finally integrates into our lives. You lost your mom without warning. You lost your dad only five years ago. The man you trusted walked away, wanting to fix you. Your public show of emotion ended up being a punishment and caused you further trust issues. There's a lot to unpack here."

Hearing her list, I began to realize that maybe I was dealing with more than I originally thought. I was so used to not allowing a self-pitying story to control my life, I'd pushed away the reality of my circumstances. "What do you think I should do? I can't keep lying on the couch and hoping for motivation. I can't be afraid to meet with people in case I cry or break out in hives. It's ridiculous."

"I think the first step is trying to be kinder to yourself. Sometimes, the greatest teachers are the worst students. All of these solutions that helped others aren't working for you because you're too close—there's no neutral observer to see what you're capable of and what you're not."

I blew out a frustrated breath. I'd come here for solutions, but the session was over and I'd gotten nothing. "No pills?"

"Not yet. I'll need a few more sessions before I can diagnose you with clinical depression. For now, let's see each other next week, and your job is to do one thing a day that makes you feel productive."

"I need to do thirty to get out of this hole."

"For this week, it's just one. One daily task of your choosing. If you feel like crying, cry and don't judge it. Instead of fighting or criticizing the emotions that come up, welcome them in. Emotion is energy, which promotes healing."

"I know that."

A slight smile curved her lips as she scribbled in her notes. "I know you know. With your head, not your heart. We need to break through some of your emotional barriers to get to the other side."

"I know that, too," I muttered. I wanted to explain that I had no emotional barriers, and other than my parents' dying and leaving me alone, nothing else was wrong. I was still angry at Jason, but in some weird way, I agreed with his plan. We'd never set up our relationship to be needy. It was wrong for me to suddenly expect him to be fine with changing the rules. Once we got past this hurdle, I'd need to make some changes between us so we didn't have this issue again.

I allowed Dr. Sariah to dismiss me and made an appointment for next week.

I headed home and walked into my lonely apartment. I

made myself a protein shake and forced myself to drink it, even though I was having the strangest dreams about pasta. Mom had mourned my decision to stop eating pasta and bread, but I'd never wavered or had regrets. Until now.

I fiddled on my phone and opened up IG. I'd been sneaking peeks at Jason's social media feeds, half hoping he'd tag me in one of his posts, or at least hint that he was having a hard time. Instead, it was a festival of muscled pics, motivational quotes, and shots of him in the gym. His followers had increased after the third gym opening. I scrolled past a video of him gazing into the camera with those striking blue eyes, naked chest glistening with sweat.

"Commit to a better self and I'll get you there," he said in that rumbly voice.

Irritation hit. God, was he trying to sell sex to gain traction? Because he was definitely succeeding—there were a million hearts and comments about all the ways his followers wanted him to commit.

He still texted me every day, but it was always a GIF or quote centered on motivation and belief in self. At first, it was comforting to still be in communication, but as time passed and he never bothered to personally check on me or try to talk, I got pissed.

Muttering under my breath, I tried to push Jason out of my head and focus on my own career. I had a few FaceTime appointments with clients today, and I was determined to show up as my old self. Maybe I just needed one appointment with a therapist to feel better. I quickly typed out an action list. No tears today. No couch. I was dressed with makeup on and ready to work.

I opened my inbox and spent a few moments skimming until I saw the results of my DNA test. Biting my lip, I hovered between waiting to read the results later as a reward and diving in right now. Curiosity won. I'd just take a quick look and study it more later.

I started with the DNA report, which confirmed a mix of English, Italian / Southern Italian, and a small percentage of Greek.

I was surprised there wasn't a bigger mix of nationalities scattered in, which must have meant both my parents were close to one hundred percent English and Italian.

Dad's side confirmed there were no close DNA matches, which meant no English relatives, but a few names were listed as possible ancestors going way back. As I scrolled down, Mom's maiden name jumped from the screen.

Serafina Lucia Romano.

I lifted my hand and touched my finger to her name. I wished I could have asked her more about her childhood, even though it made her sad. I would have loved to hear some stories about my grandparents. She'd only told me they were Italian and both passed when she was a teenager. I'd tried to probe a bit more, but Mom shut down behind a wall and I always let it go.

But back then I had figured I had my whole life to talk and laugh and argue with Mom. If only I'd known our time would get cut short, I would have done so many things differently. I counseled living with no regrets, but now every time I went to sleep, I was haunted by all the unspoken words and missed moments with her. Especially my regrets over our last visit. I wished I could have stayed to eat after fixing her TV instead of rushing out. I tortured myself by wondering if I could have saved her by staying late that night and making her happy. The doctors said it was arrhythmia, and there was nothing I could have done, but maybe CPR? Calling 911? Instead, I'd left and gone to dinner with my boyfriend. My rational brain knew this wasn't a productive thought train to chase, but I couldn't seem to help it.

Tears stung my eyes. Instead of heeding Dr. Sariah's advice, I choked them back, determined to salvage the day. I was about to close the email, but my gaze caught on the top of a heading.

DNA MATCH

Holding my breath, I read a long list of names underneath.

GRANDPARENTS:
Bellomo Romano, Rosa
Romano, Giovanni

AUNTS:
Caruso Romano, Philomena

UNCLES:
Romano, Agosto

COUSINS (FIRST):
Caruso, Catena Isabella
Caruso, Teodoro Alberto
Romano, Emilio
Romano, Luigi
Romano, Teresa

My heart began to beat crazily in my chest. Were these my grandparents who'd passed? But if my parents were only children, why were there aunts, uncles, and cousins listed?

I read through a few times, then slumped with disappointment. These couldn't be exact matches. I knew the site gathered thousands of names from registrants and they could be several generations removed. The first cousins must be a mistake. I knew Italians usually had large families, and that was another reason Mom didn't like to talk about her childhood. She'd been lonely, she'd said several times. I'd always felt guilty she didn't have any siblings, but I guess sole children ran in our genes.

Maybe I'd do some research later on the site, but right now, I wanted to complete at least one task while I was still feeling motivated.

I drew in a deep breath and began writing emails.

A few days later, for the second time, my entire world blew up.

FIVE

Dear Aurora,

Are you my cousin?

I just received a message with your information on the ancestry site, and it looks like we are related! This makes me so happy and I have many questions. My name is Catena and I live in Sciacca, Sicily, but my family is from Lucca. We have many aunts and uncles and cousins here. I would love to talk. This is my number on WhatsApp—please message me!

Catena

I read the email with growing excitement. Somehow, there must've been a child Mom didn't know about. I knew Romano was a popular name in Italy, but maybe there truly was a connection between us. I imagined being able to talk to someone who was a blood relative, someone who would know something about Mom and her past. It was a thread to tug on.

I immediately responded with my phone number and asked if she was free to speak that night. She responded and we set up a time.

The hours dragged. I managed to counsel a few clients, but the podcast schedule had been hard to fix. After losing such big-name guests, we put the word out to some influencers, but only a few responded—with scheduling conflicts. Anxiety had begun to stir and grow as I realized I might have lost a lot of my progress because of my decreased social media posts and daily videos. People said they understood and were patient, but the world was moving at light speed, and if you didn't continue putting out content, you were forgotten.

I reminded myself of my worth and that moving at a slower pace wouldn't destroy me. Unfortunately, the achiever part roared its disapproval and tried to mentally berate my body for being so weak . . . so lazy . . . so average.

Finally, it was time, and I called the number.

"Aurora! It is so nice to talk with you!"

I caught my breath at the sound of her accent, rich and lilting, like music. "I feel the same way. I can't believe this is happening. When I did the DNA report, I didn't expect anyone to really show up."

Her laugh was warm and infectious. "I'm the opposite. We have such an extended family, I'm excited when there's a new connection popping up. But there hasn't been one in a while, and never from America! Where do you live?"

"New York. A few hours north of Manhattan. Have you ever been?"

"No, but I dream of going someday."

My mind whirled with questions, greedy for all her stories

and information. "Catena, how are you related to my mom? She never mentioned you or any family connections in Sicily, and she was an only child."

Catena paused, then made a low humming noise. "I do not know. But it shows that you are my first cousin, which means Serafina was my aunt. I need to ask my family. I have not had time to tell them about you yet. My parents do not like me being on the app. They say not to mess with God's plans by poking our noses in others' business. Maybe a half sibling no one knew about? Imagine a secret baby somewhere!"

A scandal surrounding my mother? Fascination over this new mystery gave me a shot of adrenaline. "Tell me all about you and your family."

Her voice was light and gossipy. "I am twenty-four and have a brother, Teodoro, who's two years older. Mamma's name is Philomena, and Papà is Alessandro, but his name is Caruso, not Romano. I have many cousins. I did a family tree you can look at! It will give you all the names."

I frowned, trying to piece things together. "How many siblings does your mom have?"

"Only one, my uncle Agosto."

"So that means my mom should be related to Philomena and Agosto, right?"

"*Sì.* But I am not sure how. My grandparents only have my mom and uncle."

I nibbled on my lip.

"Maybe we can talk to your mom and mine? I'm sure we can find out and solve the mystery!"

Pain and sadness washed over me and I held my breath to ward off the emotions. No matter how smart it sounded to move energy and just feel, I hated being helpless and tossed around like a raft in the rough ocean waves. I'd take numbness over this gripping grief. "Unfortunately, we can't. My parents have both passed. Dad died years ago in a car crash, and I just lost my mom recently."

I heard a gasp over the line. I was used to people's sympathetic reaction to such news, but something about this girl across the world, this person who might have a touch of my family's blood flowing in her veins, made me feel better. Someone to share my mourning. "Aurora, I had no idea. What a terrible thing to go through. And you have no siblings?"

"No. That's what brought me to do the test. I was curious because both Mom and Dad were only children. I wanted to see if there was anyone out there who maybe knew them."

"My heart breaks for you. To lose both your *mamma* and *papà* so close? I could not live—I would have a complete breakdown! Oh, I must talk to Mamma about this, and maybe my grandparents. We will find the connection. I just know we are family—I feel it!"

I did, too. Which made no sense, and my rational brain said I was only looking desperately for any type of relation so I wouldn't feel alone, but I didn't care. My gut sang its confirmation that Catena was meant to have contacted me. I didn't know what would happen, but I was ready to walk this new path.

"Can you tell me more about Lucca and your family?" I asked.

And she did. She painted a picture of a small Sicilian town where her entire family lived close, where farming and fishing were king. Catena and her brother owned a pub in Sciacca, which was close to Lucca. Most of her cousins attended school or worked in her aunt and uncle's pizzeria. They also owned an olive oil business. I listened greedily to her description and wondered about my mother's connection to any of it.

"And you? Please tell me all about New York!"

"I live in a small town called Cold Spring. It's by the river and mountains, and the train can take you into Manhattan. New York is fast-paced and competitive and bloodthirsty, but I love it. My job is being a life coach, so I have a bunch of clients I counsel to live better, and I do a podcast called *Step into Your Success*. I'm also writing a book."

Another gasp. "You are famous! My cousin is famous!"

I laughed. "No, I'm really not. But I'm hoping to keep building my reputation and trying to help more people."

"I cannot believe you are a writer and do all of these things. I have never heard of a life coach. Do you tell people what to do?"

"No. I just guide them to be their true selves and feel confident. I try to get them to take action on the things they want."

"I need one of those!"

I laughed again, enjoying her easy warmth. It already felt like she was a friend. "Consider all my advice free. Family discount," I teased.

We chatted a bit more, trading stories. Catena asked me to give her details about my mom, and I savored being able to share with someone who cared. Finally, we were ready to say goodbye. "I will talk to my family about you and call you this week," she promised.

"Thanks, Catena." My throat clogged with raw emotion. "This meant a lot."

When we ended the call, there was a flicker of hope burning bright inside, the possibility of more out in the world. Something bigger than me to take away this awful hungry pain that was my constant companion.

For the first time in a while, I was excited for tomorrow.

AFTER A PRODUCTIVE day, I felt like I was back to my old self.

Eliza pulled off a miracle and retained the up-and-coming actress turned motivational speaker Marley Greene to be our first guest on the podcast. Because of her schedule, we had a tight turnaround, so I went into the studio to steep myself in research and compose a Q and A. Since the party had gone badly, we'd decided to do something to grab attention: we were doing the podcast and simultaneous YouTube live.

I usually wasn't afraid of live recordings. I did well on a mic and in front of a camera and had learned skills to create an intimate dialogue with my guests. Lately, though, my behavior had been unpredictable, so I doubled down on doing everything exactly right. With only a few days to announce the change of guest and promote the opening season, my team and I went into overdrive.

This time, I couldn't afford to fail.

I left the couch and sadness behind and knew this was a turning point. Maybe the hard grieving was finally done. Maybe going to a therapist had allowed me an outlet, and speaking with Catena had given me hope. I even thought of reaching out to Jason but figured the best move was to prove myself by killing on my podcast premiere to show how wrong he'd been for leaving me. I wanted to return on an upswing and have a serious talk. If we were going to be together long-term, we needed to straighten some things out between us. Combining a declaration of love with a departure was screwed up, even if he believed he was doing the right thing.

On cue, my phone buzzed and I glanced down.

"You must do the thing you think you can not do."

—Eleanor Roosevelt

My fingers clenched into fists at the mockery of such a quote. Really? Jason was sending me Eleanor? I mean, the first lady was incredible, but it was the type of quote I cut my teeth on years ago. He didn't even have to dig for that one! That quote came up at the top of every Google search under quotes to motivate.

Was this the man I wanted as my partner?

I hadn't even been able to say *I love you* back because he left me. Did I love him? I thought I did, but all my emotions were mixed up like ingredients in a blender. I couldn't separate any of them.

The question was too deep right now, so I pushed it aside and kept on working. By the end of the day, I felt satisfied with the progress I'd made. Dr. Sariah would be pleased—I'd done much more than one task and I hadn't cried all day. I was definitely better.

Even my staff made comments on my focus, welcoming me back. Confidence rushed back in full force. Why quit now when I still had more to do? I called a few clients to check in so they knew I'd returned ready to counsel, and soon my calendar was packed again.

I nibbled on my lower lip as I saw my appointment with Dr. Sariah for tomorrow. I was so much better, I probably could push it off to next week. Then I'd have free time to catch up on all the work I'd missed.

I quickly called her office and rescheduled.

I made some more calls, shot off more emails, and soon I was buried at my desk in peak form.

I'm back, baby.

When I got home, it was late, but energy bubbled in my veins. I sipped lemon water and scrolled through my feeds, dropping random comments on various posts to show I was ready to engage again. A text flashed up on my screen.

Aurora, can you talk? I found out about your mother.

I trembled and shot Catena a message to call me right away.

When the phone rang, I tried not to show my greediness for information. "Hi, Catena. I'm so excited to hear about my mom. Is she a relation to your family? Does anyone know her?"

An eerie silence settled over the line. I wished I could see her face on the screen to help navigate the sudden dread washing through me. As if I knew her next words would change everything and I'd never be the same person again.

Catena's voice wobbled over the phone, increasing my fear. "Yes. I asked my *mamma* about yours last night. She was very shocked and wanted to know how I knew that name. I told her about the site and talking to you. Oh, Aurora. I didn't know. They never told us."

My heart galloped like a herd of Thoroughbreds. "Told you what?"

I heard a gulp as if she were fighting tears. "I think it's best if you talk to my mother now. She wants to tell you the story."

"Wait—why can't *you*?" I practically shrieked, but there was a low crash and then another woman began speaking. Her Italian accent was thicker than Catena's, and a new heaviness forced me to pace back and forth, helpless to do anything but wait for her explanation.

"Aurora." My name sounded like a prayer from her lips. A torrent of Italian came over the line, and then Catena's voice yelling, "English, Mamma!" and then she switched back.

"I am your aunt Philomena. I did not . . . I did not know about your mother's death. If we had . . ." A deep breath. "I hoped one day she would come back, or write, or call, give us some sign that we could mend things, but after she left, there was nothing."

My head spun and nausea pitched in my gut. "I don't understand what you're talking about," I said, shaking. "This makes no sense. My mother was an only child. My grandparents died when she was a teenager. I have no family."

"Oh, *mia nipote*, you do have a family. Serafina was my sister. She grew up in Sicily with me and my brother, your uncle Agosto. You have many cousins, aunts, and uncles in Lucca Sicula."

Lucca? Aunts and uncles and cousins? How was this possible?

Why had my mother lied and cut me off from my relatives?

Struck mute, I struggled to make sense of this information

bomb. "Why?" The word broke from my lips in a half whisper. "Why wouldn't she tell me?"

More Italian. Yelling and knocking in the background. "Serafina left when she was nineteen. It was a terrible scandal, an awful thing. Your grandfather told her if she left us to marry, she would never be able to return. The next morning, she was gone—she'd disappeared without a goodbye. We were all broken, Aurora. It was a terrible, terrible time."

I dropped to the couch, suddenly dizzy. "My dad? She left Sicily to marry my dad?"

"The Englishman?"

Oh God, yes. "His name was Peter York. He was a wonderful dad and I loved him."

A long breath. "*Sì.* Sera always loved big. I am not surprised she chose to follow. Her heart would not have been whole without him."

"What about my grandparents? When did they die?"

This time, the silence seemed to fill with surprise. "Your grandparents are still here."

I sucked in a breath. "They're alive?"

"*Sì.* Sera never told you anything about us?"

"No, I knew nothing." Bitterness and anger and a wallowing sadness overtook me as my mind furiously tried to sift through this information. "No one kept in contact with my mom? No one knew she died?"

"We did not know. *Mio Dio*, I did not know I lost my sister." Deep sobs rose to my ears, but the familiar numbness edged through to protect me. It was too much to understand right now. Mom had lied about her entire life. She had a war with her family and I was the casualty. Dad had known, too.

They'd both betrayed me. "Is there anyone else? A brother or sister?"

"No. It's just me." Ice prickled my skin. "It's always been just me."

More sobs and a litany of Italian and then Catena came on the line. "Aurora, we are all in shock. No one told us we had an aunt or a cousin in America. But you are one of us! We must meet each other and talk. Come to Sicily, Aurora."

I blinked. "I can't," I said automatically. "I'm sorry, I need—I need to go. I need to think about all of this."

"Yes, of course. You will have questions. Call me back, and I will make sure you get your answers. We both deserve them, no? We deserve the truth."

The truth. My entire family background was a lie. The shadows in my mother's eyes when she talked about the death of my grandparents. The flicker of pain in her brown eyes when she stared out the window and didn't realize I was watching her. As if she were gazing into another time and place.

It hadn't been my imagination. She'd left another life behind, one with her siblings and parents and a home across the ocean. I hadn't gotten to choose. If she'd sat me down and told me the story, would I have sought out my relatives sooner? Would they have all been able to forgive for the greater good?

I'd never know because it was too late.

I stumbled over my goodbye to Catena and hung up.

I'd stood alone at my mother's funeral and watched her being lowered into the ground. Other than Jason and my college friends, whom I'd lost touch with, no one was there to share in my stories about her, in the laughter and tears of the past. I alone held her memory, and I wasn't big enough to carry her legacy. Until right now, I hadn't realized that our parents are the only ones to love us unconditionally, passionately, generously. They are the first ones to turn to in celebration or heartbreak. Without them, I'd built no other foundation, and being alone had made the knowledge so much harder to bear.

But I did have family. I shared blood with people who'd known my mother as a girl. Who'd raised her and seen her fall in love with my father. Who'd challenged her and forced her to choose between family and love.

There was no defense against the secrets she'd kept from me, and that made my heart hurt so much worse. If only the lawyer had read a will after she passed, a personal letter explaining the details of her family and allowing me to choose. But this wasn't some novel or Netflix series where everything worked out in the end.

Mom was gone and it was up to me to put the broken pieces together.

Lethargy crept in to save me from my aching head. My limbs gave out, and all the productive energy from the day whooshed away. I crawled into bed and pulled the covers over me. Tears stung my eyes, but I felt too awful to cry. The image of my mother's face drifted behind my closed lids, and mercifully, sleep came to take me away from all of it.

SIX

A WEEK PASSED.

I'd been haunted by the phone call and received another message from Catena.

Aurora,

I'm worried about you. I'm sorry for the call with my mother and all we learned about your mom. I cannot believe I will never meet her or your dad. I cannot believe they kept this secret from all of us. I spoke with my grandparents and the rest of my family, and we all beg you to come to Sicily. You are welcome here, and we must right all of these wrongs. Please come visit us, cugina. I want to hug you and show you beautiful Sciacca and Lucca. You can stay as long or as short as you'd like—there's a place for you here. Please, think about it.

Love,

Catena

Of course, I couldn't abandon everything here to travel to Sicily. I didn't know any of them, even if they were related to me. And my own grandparents had refused to accept my dad, so why would they suddenly accept me? The questions tore me apart until I felt like I was going out of my mind.

All the momentum I'd achieved disappeared. I met with two new clients, and even I knew the consults were terrible. Who'd want to sign with a life coach whose voice sounded dead when reading motivational passages from her unfinished book?

By the time my podcast premiere arrived, I was a bunch of raw nerves. I tried hard to get myself together, using clothes as my armor—hello, Gucci business suit—and makeup to hide my puffy red eyes. I looked in the mirror and saw a woman dressed for success, but once again, there seemed to be no soul in her dark eyes. I pasted on a big smile and hoped it could make a difference. How many times had I told a client if you put a smile on your face, you trick your body into believing you are happy?

Now I knew I was full of crap.

Marley was a lovely guest. She exuded a calm, thoughtful energy as I interviewed her, and though she was becoming a big name in the entertainment industry, she didn't seem to be obsessed with her fame. I peppered her with questions about balancing the outside world's needs with our inner ones, and her ambitious shooting schedule while raising a family.

It was all going so well. I'd managed to seem enthusiastic and focused. I needed to prove to my sponsors they'd been right in trusting my podcast to bring in big numbers, especially after losing a bunch after my little breakdown. This kickoff episode was key to proving my worth. I caught a thumbs-up from Eliza and knew we were in the homestretch.

I leaned forward as if desperate to hear Marley's secrets. "I'm sure our viewers would love to learn what you always return to when things are falling apart. When you haven't slept all night and the dog runs away, and the children are screaming, and you're running late for the studio—what do you focus on? What are your techniques to keep pushing forward?"

She gave a low laugh and crossed her legs. The tasteful black skirt and matching jacket showed a woman of classic restraint, but the poppy red blouse underneath hinted at so much more. "I'm human like everyone else, and some days are just disastrous. My main goal to salvage the chaos is not to allow myself to be cruel or berate."

"You try not to take your mood out on others?"

"No, I don't take it out on myself," she clarified. "I believe in positive self-talk and kindness. If I call myself fat, or stupid, or lazy, all of that negative energy circles into the universe and comes back like a boomerang."

I nodded, loving her answer. "I agree. I like to ask myself if I'd say the same things to a friend. If the answer is a strong no, I realize I've fallen into the harmful pattern."

"Exactly. And when you feel like you still can't pull yourself out of the mental ditch, concentrate on one element that makes all the difference. It's been my saving grace and brings an inner power that turns me into my own superhero."

"Oh, who wouldn't want to be their very own Wonder Woman? Tell us."

Her face lit up and I was struck by the warmth in her voice and the way her gaze glittered with positivity. "My family. They are my true north. My parents, my husband, and my children. The days may be filled with things out of our control, but the people who love us are the foundation for everything."

I watched the woman across from me utter those words with complete confidence. Like she was bestowing a secret on the universe, and we should be grateful. And suddenly, a biting, awful resentment overtook me.

It hadn't happened to Marley yet. She hadn't dealt with the bitter loss of having someone she loved ripped away without explanation or preparation. Of facing secrets from the people closest to her and having to deal with the fallout. It was so easy to sprinkle out advice when she'd never been tested. She truly believed what she said, forgetting all the lost souls in the world who'd suffered personal losses and had no family to lean on.

My mind furiously begged me to back up. The rational part of my brain explained that I wanted to lash out because I was still in pain, and this poor woman didn't deserve my wrath.

But my damaged heart connected with the dark side and let it rip.

"How convenient." The words dropped like stone between us.

She blinked. Tilted her head. "Excuse me?"

I pressed my lips in a tight line. "I said it seems very convenient to use your family as a motivator. May I ask if you've ever lost anyone close to you?"

She hesitated, looking around as if waiting for a cue card. A tentative smile curved her lips. "Well, no. I've been very lucky. But I think I know what you're trying to say, Aurora. Many people don't have spouses or children, or even their parents. But family doesn't have to be blood. It can be the people we love and cherish and who we choose. Nothing else matters. Don't you agree?"

Oh, she seemed smug. I was smug once. I didn't think tragedy could sneak in and steal all the things I cherished, leaving me with nothing. Leaving me alone.

"No, I don't agree," I said calmly. "I think many of our viewers aren't all that lucky. Some of them deal with loneliness and grief. Some of them have experienced incredible loss and don't know how to get up in the morning, and they don't have anyone to help them. What would you say to those people, Marley?"

Eliza made a frantic cutting motion.

I ignored her.

Marley wasn't giving up easily. "I think you're talking about mental health. Depression is a serious illness and different from what I was referencing. If you're having trouble getting out of bed or can't complete simple activities, it's time to see a therapist."

"Of course." Eliza gave me the signal to announce the help line and I smoothly transitioned. "I'd like to tell our viewers we just flashed a phone number at the bottom of the screen for the national help hotline. Please contact them if you want to talk to someone or were triggered by this conversation."

"Mental health is the number one priority," Marley said a bit loudly, like she was making her point.

I began to back off. I'd already screwed up and I desperately needed to save the end of this podcast. "Yes, it is."

"And if you're struggling out there, go find a family member or friend to hug. Sometimes, we just need a reminder we are loved. No one is truly alone."

I jerked back like I'd been slapped. The image of my empty apartment flashed in my mind. Of my father being pulled out of the crumpled car without my being able to say goodbye. Of Jason leaving me in my weak state because it was for my own good. Of standing next to my mother's grave in the shattering silence, making me question what I'd been working so hard toward.

My breath felt strangled in my lungs, and a surge of emotion shot through my legs, wriggled in my stomach, climbed up my vertebrae, and sank deep into my chest. A terrible pressure forced the heavy wave to rise in my throat. I fought madly for control, but I was helpless underneath the vicious onslaught.

The tears gripped me, slowly at first, then pushing sobs out in great gulps.

Marley gasped, obviously horrified at such a dramatic display of emotion, and quickly came over to hug me.

I jerked back, not wanting anyone to touch me, and crashed out of my chair.

Then fell on my ass.

The camera whirred on, casting the entire incident live to our viewers.

Finally, everything went black.

THE NEXT DAY, I went to see Jason.

He'd heard about the debacle and texted me to check how I was doing. I took it as a sign that maybe he was regretting his decision to walk away in my time of need, so I asked if I could come over.

I walked into his place, taking in the familiar scatter of training equipment, inspirational art, and life-size image of da Vinci's human body sketch hung on the far wall. I'd thought it was strange at first but got used to it. Jason always told me he wanted to be reminded of the human body at all times, because he'd dedicated his life to healing in a different way than a doctor does.

The furniture was leather and cold to the touch. The kitchen was small but well equipped to create any shake or recipe he desired. Decorated in stark black and white, it was an austere home that was male-centric, but I'd always managed to make a place for myself. I'd bought him a cheery yellow blanket, luxury hotel feather pillows, and a red ceramic bowl to put his fruit in. We'd been moving slowly and carefully toward getting into each other's private space but assumed our goal of living together would eventually occur.

As we hugged and I caught the faint scent of musk and sweat, I wanted to stay longer in his arms. I craved a bit of softness with him, but Jason rarely encouraged too much vulnerability. He was a good lover, but public affection wasn't his thing, and I'd gotten used to it. I'd assumed we were growing toward sharing some deeper emotions, but even now, he quickly pulled away to walk into the kitchen and grabbed a can of my favorite lemon Spindrift. I tried to fight the disappointment at the short embrace.

"I've missed you," he said.

My heart eased a bit. Maybe this break had been good for us. Missing each other was a sign of a healthy relationship. "I missed you, too."

"You look so thin." A tiny frown creased his brow. "But, babe, I can tell you're not doing your weights—there's no muscle definition. You don't want to ruin such great weight loss by not toning."

I tried not to feel insulted at the comment. Jason said he'd loved my body when we first began dating, but then praised each pound I shed, which was a complete contradiction. I shook off the prickle of alarm because there were more important things I needed from him now. "Jason, some major things have been happening and I really need to talk."

"Of course. Come sit."

We settled close on the sofa and I told him everything. The words spilled out in a convoluted rush, but he didn't interrupt. His blue eyes widened with shock and he took my hand, squeezing in comfort, nodding as he listened. When I was done, relief softened my shoulders. I hadn't even seen my therapist yet—canceling my appointment had caused me to miss two weeks now—so Jason was the first one to know about my sudden new family. I really needed his perspective—I'd always trusted his opinion.

Jason rubbed his head in obvious disbelief. "I can't believe it. Your mom never gave you a clue you have all these relatives? Why would she lie about this? It makes no sense."

"I know. I keep trying to figure out why. They said she ran away and they banned her, but I feel like I'm missing so much more."

His fingers interlaced with mine and I savored the support. "There must be a bigger story, but I'm not sure how you can forgive her. She literally abandoned her entire family in Sicily without a word."

The wound from the news throbbed at his words. I shifted with discomfort, not liking his bashing my mother, even though I was enraged with her. Still, he was right. "I guess so. I feel like I'm in a nightmare and I can't wake up. I spent my life wishing for more family, but I didn't expect this. They want me to come to Sicily."

"What? That makes no sense. They don't even know you."

I ignored my sudden flare of annoyance. "Yes, but they knew my mother. I'm part of the family and they want to meet me."

"If there's any truth to the story, your mom ran away because they wouldn't accept your dad. I'm sure you don't want to be trapped over there with a bunch of people who cut them both off and didn't want to even know you. Talk about awkward."

I pulled my hand away to take a sip of my drink. Somehow, he wasn't making me feel better about anything. "They seemed shocked at her death. Maybe they regret their actions and want to meet me."

He looked doubtful but patted my leg. "I'm sure they understood when you declined. Aurora, I'm sorry you're going through all this. Watching the podcast was . . . painful."

I swallowed back humiliation. Why had I hoped for him to understand? It was like the more I craved connection and understanding, the more I felt isolated. "Yeah, I kind of lost it. Hearing Marley talk about leaning on family triggered me."

"It was just her opinion," he said carefully. "I'm sure she didn't mean it to come out the way you took it."

"I know." My heart ached to try to explain in a way he'd relate to. "Losing my mom changed me, Jason. I'm struggling with this constant fear and loneliness I've never experienced before. Like I was plucked from this safe place and put into a wild forest, and now I have to survive on my own."

He nodded, regarding me thoughtfully. I felt like a bug under a microscope rather than a woman he claimed to love. "You didn't have this problem after your dad, though, right?"

I swallowed. "No. But the things I did before aren't working now."

"Did you go to a therapist?"

"Yes. She's good, but after the first session, I felt so much better that I pushed out my second appointment. Then this podcast happened and I'm back where I started." Despair swirled inside me. "I lost one of my big sponsors, Jason. They said they wanted to wait until the new season stabilized before they invest. My next guest delayed the taping because watching me with Marley probably scared the crap out of him and he's thinking I'll freak out on air. I feel like everything is closing in around me, and I don't know what to do."

"Oh, baby, come here." He gave me a warm hug and I sighed with relief. "You already know what you need to do."

I held on tight, not caring if I seemed needy. "I do?"

Too soon, he pulled back, studying my face intently. "Yes. You need to accept responsibility and do the hard stuff, even if you don't want to. You can do hard things, Aurora."

Coldness seeped into my bones. I shifted away from him. "Glennon Doyle said that in her book *Untamed*."

He ignored me and kept talking. "No one can pull you out of this mess but yourself. I think that podcast was you hitting rock bottom. Tomorrow, you should call up your sponsors and tell them you're going to use your breakdown as fodder for teaching. You're going to take something painful and hard and transform it. I know you can do it. You have an incredible power and drive to help others. Don't let this bump in the road divert you from your mission."

Had he just called the loss of my mom a bump in the road?

My perspective shifted as he continued speaking. I sensed a

new distance between us. I observed the sheen of excitement in his sky blue eyes, the way his voice deepened and accelerated, as if he needed the momentum to carry him forward. How odd I'd never noticed it was almost like a performance, rather than his open heart speaking to mine.

Was this the way I was with my clients? Had I placed myself on a pedestal, pretending I shared their pain and cared for their progress, yet only focused on the goal? Had I looked at their success as my win? I preached about steps throughout the journey. I advised on movement of body to shift energy, listening to mentors and reading from leaders who'd been through difficult times. I was great with sharing quotes and speeches and trying to lift people up.

But was I truly invested in the person, or more interested in boasting that I could fix someone who was broken?

Like I was broken now.

Like Jason was trying to fix me.

I interrupted his impassioned speech. "Are we together, Jason? Or taking a break for my greater good?"

He hesitated, studying my face with a touch of doubt. "Of course we're together! I'm invested in this relationship. I took a step back because I felt you needed some space. I'd never want to hurt you."

Truth rang out in his voice. I nodded but avoided his gaze. Why did the whole thing still feel icky? "Okay."

He kept talking, sprinkling opinions in the air like fairy dust. "Maybe knowing you have family will allow you to rally. You don't have to go to Sicily to have a connection. You should think about a family get-together over Zoom. Even though it was a shock, this could be good for you. Sharing grief and making sense out of your mom's choices could be what you need to push past these blocks."

Jason liked to help. I hadn't noticed how much before because I'd never been his focus. I stood up. "Thanks. I have a lot to think about."

He tried to lean in to give me a kiss, but I smoothly turned and reached for my purse, and he didn't push the issue. "What are you going to do with the rest of the podcast?"

I shrugged. "Not sure."

He pressed his lips together. He seemed to be battling between the desire to give me another lecture and accepting my answer. "Why don't we have dinner this week? I don't think I realized how bad things were. I was devastated watching you cry on live stream."

I tilted my head up in challenge. "Were you? Or did you judge me for wrecking the entire interview?"

Jason frowned and squeezed my shoulder. "Babe, it was heartbreaking. I'm not sure why you seem mad at me, but I truly am trying to be supportive. Why don't you text if you want to see me this week? We'll leave it up to you."

Dammit, why did I still get the sense I was being patronized? Maybe I was sorting through a mess of emotions and our relationship was bound to take a hit. I kept thinking about Mom's silent disapproval of Jason's actions that night at dinner. I'd defended him, but her judgment had leaked into my own mind, making me question things I never had before. It had been easy to ignore when things were good between Jason and me, but with these sudden cracks, I was beginning to wonder.

I said goodbye and thought about Jason's easy rejection of my going to Sicily. He made good points. We could meet and talk over Zoom. And if my grandparents had disowned their own daughter over a simple disapproval of her choices, they sucked. Why would I want to even know them? And why would they want to meet me after years of not caring? Unless Mom's death had made them regret their actions.

Questions exploded in my head. I'd gone to Jason to calm my mind and share, but I returned more confused than ever. My tentative rise in confidence and work productivity had slid down, and I'd avoided calling back my clients or going on social media. My public humiliation was making its way through various feeds, and though most had been supportive and sympathetic, there was an underlying judgment I couldn't get out of my head. The slightly patronizing sympathy of people who had no idea what hell was. Or if they did, they'd quickly forgotten, comparing me to their own experiences and finding me lacking. Especially when my entire platform was built on helping others move forward with positivity and action. I represented the worst example of my teachings.

I got back to my apartment and looked around. Other than my comfy sofa and blanket, where I pretty much stayed, the rest of the place seemed like a ghost town. I'd lost too much weight, choosing to forgo nutrition for sleep, and lacking motivation to cook. My meals came from Instacart at Whole Foods and were keeping me alive. There was no evidence of pets or a boyfriend, no personal belongings or mess scattered about. Just a trendy, perfectly nice space to house any occupant. All those personal touches I'd carefully picked out were nice but had no intimacy.

Dear God. The place had no soul.

All the things I'd boasted about, believing I was a success

story, faded away. I walked to the dresser and picked up my parents' photo. They were holding me between them, their faces laughing, squeezing me tight with the ocean roaring behind us. I remembered that day, remembered running across the sand under the hot sun and licking melty sweet ice-pops and searching for seashells that pricked my feet. I remembered the feel of the scratchy towel Dad wrapped around me and the way my mother's olive skin shone and gleamed with suntan lotion, the wet strands of her hair falling over her shoulders in tousled dark waves.

A longing hit hard and I sank to my knees and cried, wondering what I was going to do next.

SEVEN

"You canceled your last appointment," Dr. Sariah said in a mild tone. "Would you like to share why?"

I bit my lip. "I thought I was better and didn't need you."

A slight smile curved her lips. "Understood. It's been done before, but I'm glad to see you back. Unfortunately, if it happens again, I won't be able to get you back in. I have a waiting list."

I winced. "I'm really sorry. I'll be more careful."

She inclined her head, accepting my apology. "Would you like to tell me what's been happening?"

Her question made me snort. "Besides my life getting even worse? Let's just say I have a story you're never going to believe."

Gentle curiosity lit her gaze. "I'm listening."

And she was. For the second time, I poured my heart out, telling her about what had been happening, from my lost family up to my podcast breakdown. When I was done, I slumped over. "I bet we're out of time now. That was a long story."

"We have time. Aurora, how do you feel about having family you didn't know of?"

I thought hard and tried to be honest. "Mixed-up. I'm so happy to know I'm not alone, but I'm mad they dissed my mom. If I hadn't done that test, I would've never known. Then I'm angry at Mom and Dad for keeping such an important secret."

"Good. And what about the podcast? How did you feel about showing your feelings in a public setting?"

My body shook at the memory. "Horrible. Vulnerable. Ashamed and humiliated. Pissed off at Marley for pushing my buttons and pissed off at myself for my weakness. I lost a big sponsor and my next scheduled guest canceled. My producer can't even look at me because she's afraid I'm going to freak out. The premiere did well on Spotify, but it was more to watch me have a breakdown than for my content. I'm falling apart and I need help."

Dr. Sariah kept her gaze on mine, not afraid to look at me like everyone else was. "Grief is a multilayered, thorny thing, Aurora. It's not something we fix overnight, and it's sneaky. Sometimes, we feel strong enough and think it's in the past, then a simple occurrence throws us back into the pain. What you're going through is normal. In fact, you've been very forthcoming with your feelings. You're not trying to pretend you're okay."

I winced. "Well, I did last week."

"Yet you came back here. I'd like to talk about what happened when you saw Jason. How do you feel things are with him since he took a step back?"

"There's a lot of questions here about how I feel," I tried to joke. "I came here looking for action items."

Her face reflected gentle patience. "Most patients are. But emotions take action hostage sometimes, and it's important we do some digging to unearth them. Make sense?"

I wrinkled my nose. Wallowing in feelings didn't seem very productive. I'd always allowed my clients to tell me how they felt, and then I built them a step-by-step action plan to follow. I subscribed to the theory that it didn't matter how you felt as long as you were taking the steps, but I guess Dr. Sariah had a different theory.

Maybe I should just wrap this up and find a new doctor. Someone who'd fix my problems rather than have me talk about them. But I liked her and really wanted this to work. I also didn't have time to find another one covered by my insurance, go through another consult, and start over again. I took a deep breath. "It didn't go the way I hoped," I admitted.

"What did you hope for?"

My face turned red at my weakness. "I wanted him to hold me and say he understood. Which he did, for a little bit, but then he gave this motivational speech and I got upset."

"Did you not feel like he was accepting your pain?"

I jerked back at the question. Suddenly defensive, I tried to backtrack. "Maybe. But Jason knows that wouldn't be helpful. Our relationship works so well because we push each other to be better. He wants me to write my book and do my podcast and stop having silly breakdowns at inappropriate times." I gave a half laugh. "I'd probably say the same if he was in my position. We're both used to tough love, I guess. We believe wallowing in useless emotion isn't helpful."

Dr. Sariah tapped her pen. "You said 'we.' Do you believe that, too? That emotions are a block to progress?"

I squirmed a bit in my chair. Did I? No, I never tried to reject my clients' feelings if they were sad or depressed or feeling hopeless. I worked with them to believe in themselves again and transform their bodies and minds. Jason did the same work in a fitness format.

"I think there's a balance that needs to be maintained," I said slowly. "Emotion is energy. Flow and acceptance are important, but there's a point where you can't let emotion rule. You need to be strong enough to work past it so it doesn't ruin your life. You need to push it aside and take action to change your life."

A memory hit.

The group of girls who used to bully me in high school. They'd follow me down the halls, slam me against the lockers, insult my body and my hair and my face. I'd fallen into a terrible position by attracting the interest of a boy in school whom the leader liked. She declared war by making me feel small on a daily basis, slowly torturing me until I'd withdrawn into myself. Mom and Dad tried to find out why I'd changed, but I kept my secret tight. I kept my grades up and I endured.

Until the new girl came in and took my place.

She was overweight and socially awkward and I was relieved to finally have attention shifted off me. I stuffed down the guilt when I caught her suffering through the same stuff I had, and kept my head ducked down and hurried past.

Until that day.

Walking back from school. Hearing a loud cry. Peeking into the deserted side street where we'd cut through the fence to get home and finding the girl on the ground, crying. God, I wanted to run away. Wanted to keep myself safe. But the voice inside who said to stop being steeped in fear and shame began to rise, filling my head.

This time, I raced toward them, not away.

With a banshee cry that would have made Mel Gibson from *Braveheart* proud, I launched myself at the three bullies, kicking and punching and pushing with all my backed-up emotion. They fought back for a bit, but they'd always relied on mental torture, with their long nails and pretty styled hair and designer clothes they were so proud of. They weren't street kids and had no idea how to handle me.

They ran away, calling me batshit crazy.

I helped the girl up, looking at her tearstained cheeks and snotty nose and the gratitude in her eyes, which made me feel like Captain Marvel after saving the planet.

It was that exact moment I was pushed into my calling. Helping others through action. Talking nicely to those girls wouldn't work, and neither did running away or ignoring them. Crying never helped. Praying hadn't, either.

But kicking their asses did. And I intended, from that day on, to keep walking the action path rather than allow myself to be a victim to my emotions ever again.

Odd: I'd used that same motivation after Dad died to build a career out of rising from misery and creating a life I could love again. The inner voice told me it was time to take all that emotion and surge forward with a plan.

"Aurora? What are you thinking about?"

I shook off the memory, feeling chilled. How odd that I'd remembered that. I'd shoved that time of my life aside, not liking to think about those high school years of losing myself over other people's bad behavior. "Nothing."

"Hmm. I don't think it was nothing. Maybe one day you'll share with me."

I gave her a guilty look, but she didn't press me. "What does this have to do with moving forward? I need to know what to do. Do you think I should do a Zoom meeting with all of them? Should I try to keep doing the podcast and ignore the critics? Work on the book and see if my editor will publish it earlier so I can prove I'm better?"

Dr. Sariah tilted her head. "Sit with every one of those questions for a moment, and then speak from your gut. Do you want to do any of that?"

I tried not to get annoyed at her psych games and did what I was told.

The voice, which had been pretty quiet since I'd beat up those girls and lost my dad, suddenly rose and roared.

No.

Startled, I looked around like there was someone else in the room who'd screamed in my ear. "Um, no."

She nodded. "Now ask me another question."

It was hard not to roll my eyes. "Should I have dinner with Jason this week and get back together? Forget my icks and just move on?"

Dr. Sariah kept silent.

I let out an impatient breath. "Fine. I'll ask my inner self."

The voice grumbled and shook with such powerful intensity, I jumped.

No.

This was getting majorly weird. "Well, guess that was also a no."

"I think there's one last question you want to ask yourself, Aurora."

I blinked. "What? I'd like to ask when I'm going to get back to normal, and move on from this inactive nonsense I'm struggling with, or when my career is going to get back on track, but I'm feeling like that's not the question you want me to ask."

Another small smile. Dr. Sariah almost seemed amused, like she was having fun with this ridiculous dialogue.

"Do you want to go to Sicily?" she asked.

I chuckled at that one. Sure, leave everything in my life behind me in tatters to chase a family I didn't know, in a place I'd never been, halfway across the world, with no plans in place. Sounded like a living nightmare and the easiest answer I'd ever utter.

I played along. "Do I want to go to Sicily?"

I snorted when there was silence. But then Dr. Sariah gave me the look and I tried not to huff. Speaking to my inner self for the last time, I repeated my question. *Do I want to go to Sicily?*

The voice bellowed from every dark corner in my body, rattling my brain and searing my insides with a pulsing intensity. I didn't stand as much as jump up like I was starring in a horror movie and the chain saw killer had found me in the closet and reached over to grab me.

Yes.

Dr. Sariah didn't move or even look concerned. There was a knowing gleam in her eyes as she took in my reaction, and then she scribbled something on her pad as I stared back with my jaw unhinged.

"Yes," I squeaked out, trembling.

"Yes." She ripped off a piece of paper. "I want you to schedule a Zoom appointment with me every week—I'll make sure I make room, even with the time difference."

I blinked. She smiled.

"Our time's up. Have a good trip."

I walked out of her office in a trance.

That week, I packed my bags and flew to Sicily.

PART TWO

Sicily

EIGHT

What have I done?

I asked myself that question over and over during the long plane ride and received no answer. Sure, the voice had gone silent after pushing me to do this impulsive, ridiculous thing. Nerves jumped in my belly as I got closer to my destination in Sciacca. I'd been traveling now for an entire day, taking a plane to Rome, then to Palermo, and hiring a driver to make the trek to Sciacca, where Catena lived.

I'd decided to carve out ten days for the trip. After I returned from Dr. Sariah's office, I made a detailed list of what I wanted to accomplish while I was in Sicily, including seeking answers to questions about my mother's past, hitting the sightseeing highlights, and meeting everyone in the family. I hadn't had any type of vacation in the past five years, preferring to focus on work, and I thought the time away could be the refresh I desperately needed. I could still work with my clients but take a step back from the daily chaos and reset. It was a perfect compromise.

When I called, Catena flipped out with excitement, chattering so fast I could barely listen. She'd insisted I stay in her apartment, but I pushed back, explaining I needed my own space. I'd arranged a Vrbo near the marina so I'd have relaxation and privacy and be close enough to walk to cafés and shops. My grandparents, aunts, and uncles lived in Lucca Sicula, a tiny town in the Agrigento region of Sicily. Since there weren't many guest homes or hotels there, and I wanted to be closest to my cousin, I'd decided to stay the bulk of the time in Sciacca rather than Lucca. Still, my driver said it was only a half hour drive to Lucca from where I would be staying. I could go back and forth and also poke around some of the other small towns I'd researched.

Of course, I'd immediately looked up how far Taormina was, since the only place I knew in Sicily was from *The White Lotus* show, but it was about three hours away from where I was staying.

The drive from the airport to my rental gave a new definition to the word *horror*. I'd experienced Manhattan driving, had been in cabs beeping and cutting lanes and speeding through yellow lights like it was a contest, but driving in Sicily was a whole other level. Instead of slowing down when a pedestrian was crossing the street, my driver sped up, muttering an array of Italian I assumed was curse words, as if disappointed he hadn't made contact. Lights and stop signs didn't seem to make any difference. I almost screamed when in a busy intersection, he decided to roar past the red sign that clearly warned him to stop, barely missing an epic crash. He must've sensed my distress, because he shot me a big grin, waving his hands in the air and off the steering wheel as he probably explained I shouldn't worry. I was too scared to pull out Google Translate to find out.

I began to second-guess my plan to rent a car here. I'd be safer paying drivers or relying on public transportation. I'd have to see how things went.

Finally, we arrived at the apartment. I dragged my exhausted, dusty body out of the car, refusing help with my luggage as he pointed up the steep flight of stairs, angling that he'd drag it up for me. I only wanted to catch my breath and be alone for a little bit. My driver happily left with a decent tip and roared away to try to kill some other pedestrians.

The host had been in touch and arranged some food and water to be ready. I stared up at the faded yellow building with white shutters, squinting in the hot sun at the third-floor wrought-iron balcony, then down at my bulging suitcase.

It was a good thing Jason had trained me, because I was about to get a workout.

I dragged my stuff up three flights of stairs, used the code, and pushed my way through the doors.

Then caught my breath.

Oh, it was charming.

Bright floral ceramic tiles welcomed me into the space, where a square table was set with a robin's-egg blue tablecloth. Window shutters were painted the same blue. The small sitting area had a lemon-colored couch and chair, with a TV and carved wooden coffee table. A curved staircase led up to the second-floor bedroom. As I walked through, I peeked into a bathroom of gorgeous sea blue tiles, with a bidet and nice-size shower. The kitchen had modern appliances and a butcher-block-style island.

The decor made me smile. Cheerful accent colors filled the rooms, in yellows, turquoise, reds, and whites, from the throw pillows to the ceramic bowls and the paintings on the wall. I grabbed a bottle of water and explored. My bedroom was airy and light, with a veranda that held two lounge chairs and a table. I pushed the doors open and stepped outside, stunned at what I saw before me.

Paradise.

The water was right below, in a gorgeous deep blue that made me gasp. Fishing boats of all sizes rocked gently in the marina or glided smoothly out underneath a cloudless stretch of sky. People strolled the narrow streets below, and a vast array of houses in pale pink, mustard yellow, and umber squeezed together in jagged rows, spread out before me like a scenic gift.

I feasted on the panoramic view while the breeze playfully tugged at my hair, cooling the sweat from my skin. Seagulls screeched and dipped in coordinated dances. I drank my water and allowed myself a few moments to rest and just be. The trip here had been fueled by anxiety and doubt. I was used to a million thoughts rumbling through my brain, but at this very moment, there was only silence.

Finally, I went back to the kitchen and grabbed a few things for a quick snack. The peach I bit into was juicy and fresh, and the yogurt I'd requested was creamy and smooth. I palmed a few almonds for some protein, guzzled the rest of my water, and brought my suitcase to the bedroom. After setting up my toiletries and hanging up some of my dresses, I took out my phone and texted Catena.

I'm here! Love the apartment. It's beautiful and
overlooks the marina.

She responded quickly. I'm so excited! Why don't you rest and I'll pick you up at six pm? I can take you to the pub to meet my brother.

My stomach clenched. Now that I was here, I realized I had to actually meet these people face-to-face. Since I'd decided to take the trip, I'd been running on adrenaline and impulse. Now I'd be trapped with strangers who were actually related to me, and I had no idea what would happen next.

I swallowed back the tightness in my throat and texted: Can't wait.

There was no turning back now. I'd need to deal with the unknown.

I put my phone on the dresser, tugged back the covers, and crawled into bed. Immediately, my body gave in to the exhaustion. I'd think about all of it later. Right now, I just needed some rest.

With the veranda doors open and the faint sound of activity from the marina, the soft breeze blowing in, I closed my eyes and fell asleep.

I FOUGHT THE urge to wipe my sweaty palms down my sundress and shifted from foot to foot. I'd picked a simple black dress that floated above my knees and paired it with flat strappy sandals. My hair was pinned up and gold hoops adorned my ears. My purse was coveted Chanel, also in black. I wanted to look nice to meet my cousin, but not overdone. I had no idea what to expect, so keeping it in classic black, New York–style chic, was my best bet.

A knock sounded on the door. I drew in a deep breath, opened it, and faced my relative.

The woman standing on the threshold had long, straight dark hair with angled bangs. Large brown eyes with heavy brows peeked beneath the fringe. Full lips curved in a big smile, painted in dark red. Sharp cheekbones and nose dominated her angled face. She was average height, a bit curvy, and dressed in a fashionable silky V-neck blouse tied at the waist and white shorts that showed off her long, tanned legs. Red sandals with a chunky heel completed her fashionable look. I stared, searching for features similar to my mom, my heart pounding loud in my ears.

"Aurora?"

I nodded fiercely. "Catena?" I asked hesitantly, though we both knew who the other was.

"Sì."

We stared at each other for a few moments, and then she let out a shriek, jumping into my arms.

I almost stumbled back from her enthusiasm, then returned her hug. The delicious scent of her floral perfume drifted to my nostrils. She was laughing and chattering at the same time, and I was struck by the sudden rush of warmth surrounding me, from her voice to her embrace to her open joy at meeting me.

"I can't believe you are here, *cugina*!" She pulled back, her face glowing with happiness. "It is almost like a dream come true. I cannot wait to show you around my home and for you to meet my family. No—your family!"

I laughed. I sensed then that Catena was genuine, and even

if everything else imploded on this adventure, I'd made a lasting blood connection. "I'm a little overwhelmed," I admitted. "I've never traveled to Europe before."

She waved a hand in the air, flashing red-painted nails to match her lipstick. "We will take good care of you." Her gaze flickered around my rental. "This is beautiful, but I know Mamma will want you to stay with her in Lucca. We will meet her on Friday, along with Babba and Nonna. Are you going to rent a car?"

I hesitated, thrown off by her remark. I hoped no one would pressure me to give up my space. I needed privacy. "I can't drive a stick and I'm a little nervous."

"In Sciacca, it is better to walk—most roads allow no cars. Theo or I can drive you around to sightsee or to Lucca. Are you hungry? We can eat and have drinks with my brother. I know it was a long trip."

"That sounds good."

"Let's go!" I followed her to a tiny white car that looked like a strong breeze could crush it and climbed in the passenger seat. Catena chattered on, saving me from making conversation, while we shot away from the marina, veered around pedestrians, and maneuvered through endless narrow side streets. Scooters whizzed past us, practically brushing the mirrors. I bumped along, trying not to grasp desperately at the door handle, and reminded myself she was an expert. She would probably not kill anyone.

"I cannot believe you are famous in the US and a real author. No one has met a writer before. I am following you on TikTok and I love your videos. I am inspired after I listen to you! How did you get this job?"

My eyes widened as we barreled through a red light and bumped over a pothole-ridden street. There was no way two cars could fit. Catena glanced at me, not even worried about the road in front of her. It would be rude to remind her she should look straight ahead, right? "Um, thank you. *Grazie.* But I'm still writing my first book, so I don't feel like a real author yet. I love helping people accomplish their goals, so I started with videos and trained as a life coach."

"How do you learn to be a life coach?" she asked curiously.

"There's a special program where you train and study various coaching techniques. Learn about brain science and motivation and personalities. I read a lot, but first, I practiced on myself. Then I opened up my own business. It took many years for me to grow, so it wasn't fast or easy. I began a podcast and a publisher messaged me about doing a book because I had a large audience."

Catena nodded. "*Sì*, you work very hard. I see this. I like to do new things for the bar to get new tourists. Maybe you can help!"

"I'd love to help, though I don't know much about the restaurant industry here."

"That is why you would be a good person to talk to. Think outside the box, no?"

The idea of giving something to my new cousin gave me a sense of satisfaction. If I made myself useful while I was here, I'd feel better. I was taking up their time and resources, especially if they were driving my ass around. "Absolutely. And you get the family discount. Free."

We both laughed and then we peeled out onto a side street, where she squeezed between two other miniature cars with barely an inch of space to spare. Holy crap, they should require helmets to drive here.

I got out and took a look around. Bar Sciacca had a colorful ceramic sign on the archway of a door leading into a brick building. Chairs and tables were scattered out on the sidewalk with an array of people drinking and eating. The lyrical hum of Italian chatter filled the air along with delicious scents, from grilled meat to cinnamon and coffee. Bunches of flowers were placed on each of the tables, their vivid blooms adding a cheerful atmosphere. I followed Catena through the door, entering a cooler dimly lit interior that I loved immediately. The place was a cross between an old-fashioned pub, with dark wood furnishings and a giant bar, and a trendy wine bar, with the far facing wall carved into an extensive wine rack filled with bottles. The other wall had a beautiful mural painted on the brick, with colorful wine bottles lining tables with a view of the sea and fishing boats. Mosaics were stamped in different designs edging the ceiling. Music played in the background—was that Frank Sinatra?—and two male bartenders poured drinks, shouting back and forth with the customers in an easy, friendly manner. The vibe was laid-back and comfortable, and I immediately relaxed.

This was no competitive New York bar with women dressed to impress and cutthroat competition to snag a man's gaze. It didn't even have that artistic, broody vibe I occasionally got from Cold Spring, where health and creativity were God. I liked that the crowd didn't seem to be mainly male-centric, and there was a nice mix of old and young.

"This is the family business," Catena said. Pride etched her voice, but she was staring at me as if waiting for my approval. "It was my aunt and uncle's, but my cousin went to Roma and didn't want to run the bar. Theo and I decided to buy it, so it's now ours. We did a few updates to make it more fun and decided to focus on *vino* rather than competing with Murphy's, which is the Irish pub."

"I love it so much," I said honestly, reaching out to touch her arm. "I wish I had a bar like this back where I live. It's a place where everybody knows your name."

Catena frowned. "Many tourists come here and do not know one another's names."

"Sorry, that was just a phrase from an old TV show. I meant to say I feel welcome here."

She beamed at my words. "I am so happy! Come, let's meet Theo. He's been excited to see you."

Catena grabbed my hand and led me over to the bar, speaking rapidly in Italian to a group of young guys who shouted her name in greeting. She shouted something back, making them laugh, and they moved to allow us space. "Theo! She's here!"

A guy with sandy blond hair and chocolate brown eyes met my gaze. He was dressed in jeans and a casual black T-shirt. His jaw was clean-shaven, and when he smiled at me, I was struck by how he looked like a male version of Catena. He leaned over the bar and stuck both hands out, palms up. "Aurora, I'm so happy you came. I'm your cousin Teodoro. Everyone calls me Theo."

He had a slightly serious tone and seemed a bit more formal than his sister. I placed my hands in his and smiled back. "I can't believe I'm here. It's nice to meet you. This bar is amazing."

A glint of pride like Catena's sparked in his eyes. "*Grazie.* What can I get you to drink? I have a plate coming out for you to eat."

"Red wine? Any kind—you can pick."

Catena pushed me onto a stool. "The good stuff, Theo! Aurora is going to help us with the bar and give us tips to get more people in. She is very famous in America. She coaches life to people!"

Theo poured a glass of ruby red liquid and slid it over. "I did not know this was a job until I saw your videos. Coaching is big in New York?"

"It's becoming popular. I think people are more screwed up today."

They laughed. I sipped my wine, and the rich taste of earth and blackberry coated my tongue. So. Good. I'd forgotten how much I loved the nuances of a good wine, since Jason frowned upon drinking due to calories and sugar content. "Delicious."

"We get this from a family vineyard in the area. Maybe we can take you there? How long are you staying?" Theo asked.

"Ten days."

Theo and Catena shared a sad look. "We were hoping you could stay a little longer. Our cousin Magdalena is getting married, and we really want you to be a part of it."

It was a sweet invitation, but I didn't belong at such an intimate family function. "Oh, that's so nice, but I have a ton of work back home. I am looking forward to seeing as many people as possible and doing some touring. From the little I've seen, Sciacca is very beautiful."

"We will make sure you see as much as possible," Catena said. "We'll get Quint to cover the bar."

Theo waved and motioned the other man over. I stared curiously as he slung a dish towel over his shoulder and strode over. He moved with a lean, pantherlike grace, holding my attention. He was about six foot and, like Theo, dressed in a T-shirt and jeans. He stopped in front of me, tilting his head as his gaze crashed into mine.

Theo patted him on the back and spoke. "Quint, this is my cousin from New York, Aurora. We found out we were related through one of those genetic tests, and she came to visit."

A strange breathlessness came over me as I stared into beautiful umber eyes with flecks of green, the odd color urging me to look deeper and linger. His coal black hair was cut on the shorter side, showcasing a face of rough planes and angles. A short beard framed his lips and hugged his jaw, giving him a bit of a sexy lumberjack look. I imagined him in flannels with an ax, then wondered if I was going nuts.

I didn't read romance novels, dammit. Had nothing against them, but they just weren't my jam. I'd never described men in my head with such sexy terms, so I was briefly thrown off.

"Aurora, it's nice to meet you. I'm Quint."

He put out his hand to shake. His voice was heavily accented but rich and deep. I blinked and put my fingers in his, enjoying the firm grip. I refused to blush or stutter just because this man was drop-dead gorgeous. "Nice to meet you."

Catena chattered on as we seemed to be caught up in each other's gaze. "We may need you to cover the place so we can take her sightseeing."

"Of course." His lips curved in a smile. I noticed his upper lip was thinly defined, and the lower was plump. "Though there's not as much excitement around here compared to Palermo."

"Oh, I have a ton of work to do anyway, so I'm not going to bother anyone to play tour guide."

"Are you not on vacation?" Quint asked, a touch of playfulness in his tone.

"Aurora is a famous life coach and author," Catena bragged. "Her work is important."

I tried not to blush at my cousin's misinformation, especially under Quint's interest. God, if only she knew the extent of my failure. But how could I explain that my mom's death had brought on a personal breakdown? They might be related, but they'd never met my mom or known how bad things had gotten with me. Much easier for them to think I led a charmed, successful life. "It's really not a big deal," I managed. "And I'm still writing the book. I don't have anything published."

"It is still a worthy accomplishment," Quint said in perfect English. "I'm glad you are here."

I lost the battle, feeling my cheeks turn red. Thank goodness I was saved with the arrival of my food. Quint placed it on the bar with a flourish. "We gave you a small taste of everything," Theo said. "*Buon appetito.*"

I stared down at the generous amount of food spread out on the platter. There was a fried ball of something covered in sauce, a variety of sliced meats, a delicate fish in oil and lemon, pasta with eggplant, and a basket of crusty bread. My goodness, was this a regular meal here? I knew Italians ate a lot, but Mom had respected early on that I preferred to eat light portions and limited carbs. I'd just arrived, though, and I didn't want to make a fuss, so I just smiled and thanked them.

"The fish is caught fresh every morning," Catena said. "Sciacca is known for fishing, and it's how most people here make their living. I can take you to the market one morning if you'd like."

I loved the idea of farm to table, and there was nothing like eating sustainable food with no preservatives. "Yes, that would be wonderful." I forked up a piece and nearly groaned. It was perfect—light and flaky with just the right amount of seasoning. Jason's voice was like a mantra in my head, lecturing about the evil of carbs. I'd just avoid the bread, pick the eggplant from the pasta, and eat the meat. "How long have you both owned the bar?"

"Three years now," Theo answered. "Mom and Pop were hoping we'd run the pizzeria in Lucca, but we preferred a bar. It worked out, though—our other cousins took over there, so now we all have a business we love."

I couldn't imagine having endless cousins and family-run shops to take over. Dad had worked in a bank with crusty financiers and strict schedules. Mom had stayed home with me until I went to college, then transitioned to a part-time job at the local boutique in town. I'd always burned to make my own way, in a nontraditional business, but now I imagined the security of knowing there was a place built from the ground up that was your inheritance. It was a beautiful idea that made my heart suddenly ache and wish I had my mom here.

I ignored the feeling and focused on my plate. The cured meat had the perfect bite of salt, so I nibbled on the end. "Have you always been a bartender, too?" I asked Quint. The flash of amusement made me pause, wondering if I'd sounded judgy. I had no idea how the job market was in Sicily and didn't want him to think I looked down on the career. "Which is great! Bartending is a difficult skill to learn."

His lower lip quirked, as if he found my rush of words adorable. I found myself staring at him. How did he make every expression seem sexy? "Theo and Catena allowed me to buy a stake in their business," he said easily. "I've worked in restaurants my whole life, so I'm comfortable here."

Theo thumped him on the back. "He's a master at multitasking on a Saturday night and a great chef. Also keeps the women coming back."

Quint shook his head, but I caught a flash of red on his cheekbones. Ah, he was a player. That would make sense with his ridiculous good looks and running a bar. I refused to wonder about the flicker of disappointment unfurling within me, reminding myself that Jason and I were still together. We just needed to mend some of the loose threads of our relationship and we'd get right back on track.

We chatted comfortably for a while as Quint broke off to serve customers. Each time someone interrupted us, Theo and Catena would enthusiastically introduce me as their newfound cousin, and I'd be enveloped in a welcoming embrace or invited to dinner. It was so different from New York and the cool, independent, distant vibe the place thrummed with. Here, everyone seemed to know one another.

I'd finished my plate and tried not to eye the bread or pasta. I knew the comfort of carbs and the slippery slope Jason had warned me about. I'd tested out the fried ball thing with two bites and almost wept. Crunchy, creamy, with arborio rice and sauce and cheese, it was a dish I'd probably dream about tonight. But definitely not healthy, and it wasn't like I was exercising or doing weights lately. Someone called over Catena and Theo, and I covered the uneaten portions with the napkin.

On cue, Quint leaned over the bar, catching me in the act. "Don't like the bread? We bake it fresh."

I blinked, caught off guard. Something about those glowing eyes staring into mine without apology made my stomach drop in a funny way. "Um, it looks delicious, but I'm full."

He peeked under the napkin and I tried not to blush. "No pasta? Gluten allergy?"

"No. Just a volatile relationship with carbs."

He frowned. "Volatile?"

"Like toxic? Bad for you?"

His face brightened. "Yes. Ah, makes you sick."

I wanted to agree but refused to lie. "No, it makes me fat." I made a face and patted my hips.

His gaze swept over my body and he frowned in confusion. "But you are beautiful."

I jerked back slightly. Men didn't think of me as beautiful, and I was okay with that. Jason called me interesting, strong, and dynamic. My ex-boyfriends had termed me pretty, and I'd never had a problem with it. But the simple statement uttered by Quint rocked me a bit more than I expected. Probably said it to all women. Italians were different from Americans and knew how to compliment.

"Thank you, but not with an extra twenty pounds," I joked.

I expected him to wave a hand in the air and laugh, but those dark brows slammed together in a deeper frown. "No. You are beautiful any way as long as your body is happy. Eating should be from the soul, not the mind."

Stunned, I stared at this stranger who'd uttered a haunting truth I'd never given any consideration to. My relationship to my body had been a common one—fraught with doubt, hate, envy, and eventually, acceptance. But sheer love? Viewing food as a joy rather than in the context of weight or health or judgment? It was an alien concept.

A strange awareness hummed between us as his last comment hung in the air, surrounded by noise and laughter and rowdiness, yet a silence filled my insides. It was a calmness I rarely experienced outside my attempts to meditate or brief moments of focused clarity.

Catena and Theo drifted back and jolted me out of my revelation. "Quint, can you check on the kitchen? They're getting backed up," Theo said.

Quint nodded at Theo, glancing once more at me, then taking my plate and disappearing through the doors. I let out my breath and shook off the encounter. The last thing I needed was a flirty bartender distracting me, even if he seemed genuine.

I finished my wine, declining a second glass from Theo. "Do you have plans for tomorrow?" he asked. "Anything particular you want to see?"

"I'm going to work in the morning, and then I figured I'd explore around town. See the main sights here—the piazza and churches and museum. Chiesa dei Cappa—"

"Cappuccini," Theo finished. "Catena can take you around tomorrow to sightsee and you can join us for dinner. Some of our other cousins would like to come, if that's okay?"

I ignored my initial reaction to say no and hide in my room. It was not the reason I came to Sicily. "Sounds great."

"Are you nervous about meeting everyone?" Catena asked. Her gaze held a serious reflection. "I keep thinking about what happened. We tried to talk to my mom about it, but she got really upset and refused to discuss it. Uncle Agosto got very drunk when he heard and ran out. Everyone was in shock, asking questions that were never answered. I think we all deserve to know the truth of what happened."

My throat tightened. "I searched everywhere to see if Mom wrote a letter or hid photos—any indication she left an entire family behind. But I didn't find a thing."

Theo shook his head. "Makes no sense. Cannot imagine Babba or Nonna cutting their daughter off and keeping it a secret."

"Or our mom not telling us she had a sister," Catena added.

I thought of the pain my mom had gone through, losing her family, forced to pretend she was an only child. My cousins spoke of their tight-knit family here, but was it all a facade? No matter what my daughter did wrong, I'd never send her away. I needed to know the whole story so I could make my own decision and bring some peace to my mom, wherever she was now. "Are you sure they really want to see me?" I shifted in my seat with discomfort. "Maybe they want nothing to do with her child if they sent her away."

"No, Aurora, they all begged for you to come," Catena said, her voice forceful and loud. "They did not know about you or your mother's death. They wailed and cried and Nonna went to her room, refusing to come out for two days."

Theo gave a sigh. "It was very bad. Having you here is important, and we are happy you made your way to us. We are family."

The word jolted me, and suddenly I was overwhelmed and exhausted. The emotions from the trip, meeting my cousins, and prepping to introduce myself to the rest of the family made me want to crawl under the covers and shut down. I needed some time to get myself together.

"Catena, would it be okay if I went home instead of seeing your place? I'm getting a headache—probably from the plane ride." I smiled in apology and hoped she wouldn't get mad.

"Of course! We will have plenty of time together. Let's go."

Theo came around to hug me goodbye, and I was enveloped in a flurry of *arrivederci*s and *buona notte*s as if leaving old friends. Finally, Catena got me home, promising to see me tomorrow and urging me to get some sleep.

I let myself inside my temporary home. It didn't take me long to get ready for bed, but I was drawn back to the balcony, gazing out into the night of a place I'd never been, ready to uncover the secrets of my mother's past.

The stars sparkled from a blue-black sky like jewels spread over the spill of houses dotted on the cliffs. Boats rocked gently in the water below. The air smelled of brine and damp heat and fish, yet it was also the scent of newness and adventure. Loneliness washed over me, even though I was now close to family. I reached for my phone and texted Jason on impulse.

Arrived in Sicily and met my cousins. It's beautiful here. I miss you.

I waited for his response, but it never came. After all, I was six hours ahead and he was probably in his staff meeting. I didn't blame him, of course. He was sensible to avoid all distractions even if he knew I'd landed in Sicily today and hadn't checked on my arrival.

My mind flashed to Quint, and I wondered if he'd pick up in the middle of a meeting to answer his girlfriend, sensing her need to connect.

I attached my phone to the charger, slid into bed, and waited for my exhausted mind to catch up with my body.

I needed to be ready for tomorrow.

NINE

I TRIED TO work for several hours the next morning, but my brain wouldn't cooperate. I tried to write a chapter on channeling emotion into productivity. After I read it back, I realized the words sounded flat and lifeless. How could I lecture readers on something I was still failing at?

I decided to freewrite while I was here. I'd heard capturing random thoughts on the page helped flush out the junk in the mind. Spending twenty minutes, I filled up three pages of notebook paper with ridiculous fragments that made no sense. At least I felt accomplished. I was intent on finishing the book by the end of the summer and dazzling my editor with my proficiency. I needed to stay relevant in the industry, and the book was key. Already, I noticed my followers dropping, especially since the podcast disaster and delaying the next few episodes. My coaching appointments had also diminished, so I'd reached out to my clients and rescheduled our meetings to when I returned. I'd have better focus and not half-ass our sessions.

I managed to do a few videos and post motivational quotes, but nothing felt authentic. Maybe I'd use my trip to Sicily to spark some new interest by journaling my travels. I bet Catena would love to be part of my posts. I didn't have to say anything personal, just that I was enjoying a getaway and wanted to share my experiences.

The idea lifted my spirits, and I began a bit of research on the area to see which hot spots would be the best to film. I'd told Catena I'd meet her in the Piazza Scandaliato this afternoon, which would give me some time to poke around on my own.

Jason called as I was getting ready to leave. I considered not answering since I was a bit miffed he'd waited so long to contact me.

But that would be immature and our relationship was already strained. I clicked on FaceTime to accept.

"Hi, babe. How was the trip?"

I took in his relaxed pose and easy smile. He'd obviously just worked out. He had that glow from endorphins and a light sheen of sweat glistening on his forehead. Meaty biceps strained against his T-shirt as he crossed his arms over his chest. I focused on his handsome face and wondered why I wasn't as happy to see him as I'd expected.

I choked back the guilt from my disturbing thought and forced a smile. "Good. Long. I ended up taking a nap and going to bed early last night. So far, Sciacca is beautiful. My rental is on the marina. Wanna see?"

"Sure."

I tilted the phone and walked around so he could see the space and the view from my balcony.

Jason whistled. "Wow, pretty fancy. Looks like it'll be a great place to write and work. You'll be inspired."

I tried not to wince. I hadn't told Jason about the book's being delayed. I swore I would when I got home. "Hope so."

"Have you met your cousins yet?"

"Yeah, Catena picked me up and took me to their bar. She owns it with her brother, Theo, and a friend, Quint. They were so nice." I filled him in on the details of our meet-up, enjoying sharing my story with someone. The pang hit me once again that I'd normally tell my mom or dad, but now no one knew me like that anymore. I was suddenly grateful that Jason was in my life and vowed to be more patient with him. After all, he hadn't changed. I was the one who'd begun to challenge our dynamics.

"I'm so glad it's working out. I was worried about you. When are you seeing your grandparents?"

"Tomorrow. I guess it's a big family dinner where everyone is invited, so it may be overwhelming." I nibbled on my lower lip. "Catena is taking me sightseeing this afternoon and I'll meet more of my cousins."

"Damn, how many cousins do you have?"

I laughed. "Apparently, a ton. They even mentioned inviting me to a wedding, but I'd need to extend my stay."

"You'll have your answers by next week," Jason said firmly. "Then you can come home and things will be better."

He made it sound so black and white, like I could return to my normal life without a hitch. But I already sensed a change within me. How could I be the same person ever again when I'd lost my parents? Was it possible that time would stitch and heal the wound, and I'd forget this whole crisis of identity ever happened? Would discovering my relatives fill the empty hole inside me?

I didn't respond. There were too many questions that Jason seemed confident I could answer in ten days. He took my silence as an invitation to launch into work mode, detailing the flood of new clients at his third gym. He spoke about all the wonderful things in his life, and though I was happy for him—I really was—there was an odd type of disconnect, like I was conversing with an old friend rather than my current lover.

"Hey, want me to tag you in one of my posts? I noticed you lost some followers. Also, I referred you to one of my clients. He lost thirty pounds, but now he wants to transform some other things in his life, and I thought you'd be perfect. I'll text you his name and number. Can you get a hold of him quickly, though? Follow-through is a big thing to him and he's an important contact. Gets me tons of business."

Uh-oh. The irritation was back. Had Jason always treated me like a work assistant and this was the first time I'd noticed? Half of me wanted to tell him I couldn't take on more clients, but I also didn't feel like getting into a go-around about dropping my responsibilities when my entire name was built on action. Because he was right. We'd both told each other numerous times we didn't understand people who just couldn't seem to get things done.

Now I was one of them.

I smiled through gritted teeth. "Sure. Send it over."

"Great, he's going to adore you. I better head out. I know the time difference is messed up, so no worries if you're unable to get a hold of me."

Seemed like he wasn't worried about texting me back. I was getting ready to click off when he said my name. "Yeah?"

"I love you, babe. Get this sorted out and come home to me."

The genuine warmth in his voice almost negated my doubts about our conversation, but I wondered if I was just starved for affection. I opened my mouth to say the words back but, once again, found I couldn't.

"I will. Bye."

I ended the call before he noticed. Hopefully, this trip would solve some issues and I would stop getting pissed off by everything Jason did. Maybe it was a rite of passage with relationships reaching a certain amount of time. My past boyfriends averaged only a few months, and I'd never experienced a big, passionate love. Honestly, I didn't think they existed. I thought there were many layers and levels of affection, and love was quieter and more dependable. Trustworthy. I'd known how much my parents loved each other, but it was as if I hadn't been a part of their relationship. They'd always been private with their affection, and the occasional times Mom would lose her temper, my father's English demeanor always remained calm. They seemed like a perfect balance for each other.

I'd believed I was the same with Jason. When I imagined waking up to someone years from now, it made sense that we shared the same goals and values and wanted the same future. I saw us running an empire together and being happy.

Lately, though, I wasn't sure. I hoped Sicily would help me figure stuff out.

I grabbed a bottle of water and my Coach cross-body purse and headed out. I studied Google Maps and knew which way

I was heading. I had a solid sense of direction, so I was comfortable venturing out alone before it was time to meet Catena.

Today, I wore casual white shorts, Skechers sneakers, and a hot pink T-shirt that said **I AM THE STORM**.

I began my walk by the marina, taking the sloping pathways downward, my skin already heating under the fierce sun. I remembered being mesmerized the first time I visited New York City and witnessed the splendor of towering buildings thrusting toward the sky in fierce competition. The chaotic vibrancy of crushing crowds, neon billboards, street vendors and food trucks lining every inch of space gave me a sense of aliveness. Here, I was struck by the serene, gorgeous landscape as endless homes squeezed together in perfect, messy symmetry spilled over the cliffs, a wall of color and angled roofs framing the glassy blue water of the sea.

Surrounded by faded, dusty buildings in earth tones, with arched windows and wrought-iron balconies bursting with colorful blooms, I felt like I was stepping back in time, to a simpler way of life. There was a sprawling emptiness in the street that edged out to stone pillars lining the marina waters. Stately trees swayed in the breeze and played witness to the rolling clouds and turquoise skies, to the stone and stucco and brick of the ancient structures' surroundings.

Fishing boats bobbed in the waves, cutting back and forth as a few fishermen greeted one another in loud Italian. I made a note to go with Catena when she bought seafood at the market so I could take part in such a classic tradition.

I snapped pictures, each more stunning than the previous, doing a few selfies to caption later. Climbing a set of steep stairs, I began to make my way upward, peeking into several shops that displayed brightly colored pottery painted with blood oranges, lemons, and the fishing village scenery. Most of them were closed, which was odd at the height of the day. The scent of espresso hit me as I passed a café, nodding at a lone couple sipping the hot brew at an outside table under a red umbrella, munching on a pastry filled with cream.

The slap of my sneakers on the cobblestones and the fluttering of the Italian flags in the hot breeze were the only sounds as I meandered deeper into the center of the city. Sweat began to drip between my breasts. I sipped my water and made a mental note to bring a fan or sun hat next time. I had no idea it could be this hot here.

With each step, I relaxed into the sights and sounds around me. The roar of the occasional scooter seemed far away, and it looked like the road I was on was too narrow for cars. I calculated that I was circling around the Piazza Scandaliato, so I headed in the general direction of the former Church of Santa Margherita, which was on my list of sights. I'd save the museum for later.

The square was empty, so I took my time taking some pictures and studying the outside of the distressed mustard building. It was simple and understated, with three wooden doors and a few carved-out archways displaying statues of saints. There was one stained-glass window in the center, topped with a plain cross at the top. Some fancy scrolled architecture winged the sides of the structure.

When I entered, there were only three people inside. My breath caught as I stepped farther into the shadowy, cool interior.

The pews had been removed, and I took in the empty space

with black-and-white checkered tiled floors in comparison to the gorgeous white and rose gold marbled details. Rich gold edged the marble and appeared throughout the walls and the beautifully sculpted holy figures and vivid frescoes. It was heavily decorated in the Baroque style with an ornateness I appreciated, contradictory to the church's teachings on simplicity.

Quietly, I approached the nave, where the wooden statue of Santa Margherita welcomed visitors. I stared at the altar, imagining parishioners praying on the benches, listening to the priest as he said Mass in this glorious historic monument. An old pipe organ was displayed on the balcony, and I could close my eyes and imagine the soaring notes of orchestral music filling the air.

Mom had dragged me to religious classes until my confirmation, raising me as a strict Catholic even as my dad rolled his eyes and pronounced his Protestant ways much easier to satisfy. I hated going to Sunday church and engaged in epic battles when I tried to refuse. I'd stopped going these past few years, though it devastated her, but she'd staunchly attended weekly Mass on her own, a staple in her faith that I had never seemed to inherit or grasp.

I'd tried praying after I lost Dad, but I felt as if I were uttering words to an unknown entity and empty space. I tried again after Mom passed but abandoned the practice shortly after and hoped she would forgive me from the other side.

But here, in the quiet and beauty of the peaceful church, I felt something shift. An energy bubbled up within me, not the kind I channeled into concrete action, but a peacefulness in knowing all was okay. My parents' faces floated in my memory and I squeezed my eyes tight, holding on to the image. I waited for the breakdown that had been happening over the past few months, but this time, I only felt a spark of gratitude for this fleeting moment. Standing in a beautiful place with holy figures guarding me, my parents' memory hugged tight to my heart.

All is well, my love.

The voice whispered in my brain and I could swear I caught the scent of my mother's perfume, a light floral that always reminded me of sunshine and daffodils.

My eyes flew open and I looked around, but there was nothing here.

Weird.

I hugged myself, trying to shake off the clichéd feeling of someone walking over my grave, and finished my tour. I blinked in the bright light, sliding my sunglasses back on, and began walking. It was almost time to meet Catena.

I headed to the piazza and she ran to greet me immediately, dressed in an orange sundress that floated above her knees in a gauzy fabric. "*Ciao, mia cugina!*" She enveloped me in an enthusiastic hug, which I returned. I could get used to such nurturing. It was as if my needy soul craved comfort, and my cousins thought nothing of physical affection. My mom had been like that, but Jason was more distant, so I'd trained myself to hold back.

"How was your day? Tell me what you did. Do you like Sciacca?" Catena asked in a rush, linking her arm with mine as she led me across the piazza.

I glowed under her attention. "Yes. I explored the marina and some of the town and saw the former Church of Santa Margherita. It was so beautiful."

"I am glad. There are many churches here to discover. My uncle owns an olive oil farm in Lucca, so we will take you there. And the local vineyard, and you must see Castello Incantato, which is our enchanted castle. Oh, and we must go to the beach. But I am afraid Mamma may snatch you from me—she cannot wait to meet you tomorrow."

I imagined meeting my mother's sister and swallowed back my nervousness. Would she look like Mom? Talk like her with big gestures and a passionate voice? Would she smell like her floral perfume and give big, tight hugs that lasted forever? "I can't wait, either. I brought some pictures with me to show them."

Catena gave an excited squeal. "I want to see and hear everything. But first, let me give you a tour of all the things I love about Sciacca. Then we will meet Emilio and Teresa at Eros Bar for a cocktail. Yes?"

"Yes. But why are we going to a competitor's place?" I asked curiously.

She laughed and waved her hand in the air. "Oh, we are all friends here. We go to each other's places for drinks and food. We compete for the tourists, but it is not in a mean way."

I nodded. With such a small, close-knit community, probably every business overlapped with another. I matched my pace to hers while she pointed out landmarks in the piazza, leading me upward to show me the most spectacular views. "We're heading toward the historical center, to one of our four main gates that leads into our city," she explained. "This is the Porta San Salvatore. The architecture is from the Renaissance period and there are many details to see."

I stared at the giant gate with two columns and a graceful

arch. It was as if a benevolent old king welcomed me into sanctuary, and a shiver shot down my spine. I'd never stepped on ground with such history before, a place with ancient stories to tell that were wrapped in silence, witnessed by the town's architecture.

Catena pointed out the elephant carvings on either side of the arch, and the three coats of arms that screamed of dignity and honor and protection. I snapped a few pictures. "Take a selfie with me?" I asked.

"Of course!"

We stood in front of the gates, looking small against the massive stone entryway. "Perfect. I'll post later and I'd love to tag your bar, too. Get the word out about Sciacca for you."

Her face lit up. "*Grazie!* I will tag you and then all of my friends will become your followers. Maybe you can do life coaching in Sicilia."

I laughed. We spent the next hour in tour mode as she walked me through the historic city center, sharing stories about the town along with some town gossip. "Oh, here is my favorite *pasticceria*—let's grab a gelato. My treat." I walked beside her into the small bakery, where a big selection of pastries, baked goods, and ice cream spread out before us. The scents of sugar and bread filled the air, and I wanted to take giant gulps of it and get a contact high.

Catena chatted in Italian with the old man behind the counter while my eyes bugged out at the pastries. I loved a good bakery, but this was on another level. I didn't know what they were named, but many resembled cannoli dipped in icing and pistachios, mini pastry puffs with powdered sugar and cream oozing out, and cookies of all shapes and flavors. Some people imagined dying in a bookstore or a florist shop or on a beach at sunset.

I'd happily die in this very bakery.

"What flavor?" my cousin asked. I glanced over the colorful array in the display, my usual excuse that I wasn't hungry dying on my lips. "Mango, please. Small."

I figured it'd be like sorbet and the lightest in calories. After all, I couldn't come to Italy and not taste the food and treats. It would be criminal. I just needed to be careful of what I picked and pace myself.

Catena ordered pistachio. My first taste was like the first ray of sunshine after a long winter. The tangy, juicy fruit flavor hit my tongue while the rich cream immediately melted in the perfect combination, eliciting a low moan from my lips. My cousin laughed and bumped my shoulder. "Good, right? You must eat gelato every day here. You are on vacation."

"I think I agree with this rule."

She dragged me into a few shops displaying gorgeous artwork and ceramics. I lingered over the handmade bowls painted with bright lemons and blood oranges, admiring the detail on different pieces. "All the shops were closed a few hours ago," I mentioned, fingering a crisp linen towel with flowers spilling over a balcony. "Are they only open in the evenings?"

"They close for lunchtime," Catena said. "Besides the high heat, it is when we eat our lunch, which is our big meal. Feast is from noon to around five p.m. Then they reopen till late in the evening."

I stopped and stared at her. "Wait—you eat for five hours every day?"

"No! Only for about three. We nap for the other two. Come, it is time to meet our cousins."

She ignored my open jaw at the Italian schedule, and I followed her out. When did anyone work? How could you run a business by closing all day? I trotted after her. "You close the pub during the day?"

"No, we stay open most days unless we have something we'd rather do, and then we close. I don't mind serving lunch and cocktails. Many cafés stay open, but it all depends on the mood. It would not be a problem to close if we'd like."

The idea of a mood dominating work fascinated me. "But what if your job is on a farm or vineyard or you're a fisherman? Are they different from shops and eateries?"

"*Sì.* Fishermen work their hours around the fish. Farmers work their schedule around the crops. And the grapes tell us when to pick and when to harvest. Here, we listen to other things besides time. It is different with you?"

I laughed. "Um, yeah, it's different. We like to work, well, all day."

"What about food? Sleep? Family time? Church?"

I finished my gelato and threw out the cup. "We do that, too, but work is primary. We can't not show up because we're having a bad day or want to go to the park to play."

Catena paused and looked at me with serious dark eyes. "How sad," she murmured. "It is like a prison?"

A laugh gurgled from me. "No! We like it that way. I love my work, and it's my identity. It's my passion."

"So working all day and night makes you happy?"

"Yes, exactly."

She wrinkled her nose and resumed walking. "I love my

pub, but it is only a portion of what I love. But I am not famous like you, so I do not know much."

My cousin uttered the word—*famous*—with no ill intention or jealousy, just a simple fact. I almost groaned aloud at how it sounded to my ears. I wasn't explaining things correctly. I loved other things, too. Like my mom and dad. My dog Rufus, who'd died. My college friends whom I grew up with. And Jason. I loved Jason. I thought.

My feet stumbled over each other as I realized in that awful flashing moment that all those things were now gone, leaving me with . . . work. I had no time to analyze the troubling thought because we arrived at Eros, the name displayed on the small sign above the doorway. There was a decent crowd gathered at tables inside. A guy stood up and waved us over. Catena grabbed my hand and pulled me toward him.

"Emilio! *Come stai?* I have found her—our cousin Aurora." She chattered rapidly in Italian and his gaze met mine, a slow smile curving his thin lips. He looked different from Theo, much shorter, with blondish hair and blue-gray eyes. His long face and round cheeks gave him an almost cherubic look, but his grin was full of mischief, like he was the jokester of the family.

"Aurora, I am so glad you are here. We have all been waiting to meet you. Welcome, *mia cugina*." He gave me a quick, hard hug.

The woman beside Emilio elbowed him off me in a teasing manner. "Stop hogging her," she admonished, jumping in front and pulling me in for her own hug with a squeal. "You are like a miracle! I could not believe when Catena told us you showed up on the site and that we had family out there. And an aunt I never knew. Oh, the gossip around here over this—it is bigger than when Luisa broke her engagement to marry the contractor who fixed her house!"

I couldn't help but laugh at Theresa's bright, gossipy chatter. She reminded me a lot of Catena and was quite beautiful, with reddish hair and light eyes like her brother's. She wore jean shorts with a designer belt and a white silky T-shirt tucked in. Her body was all gorgeous curves I admired on her. Her curly hair was pinned up on top of her head and giant gold hoops adorned her ears. "It's nice to meet both of you."

Catena motioned for me to sit. "What are you drinking?" she asked.

I looked at my new cousins. "Aperol spritz," Teresa said with confidence. "Get two more. We must catch up and need time."

Catena nodded and disappeared inside. I stared at my cousins and suddenly felt tongue-tied. Where did I even start with my questions? I felt overwhelmed and I hadn't even walked into the big family dinner. I tried to tap into my podcast training and asked questions. It was the fastest way to connect. "Okay, can you remind me who your parents are? I know Catena told me, but I'm still a bit jumbled."

Emilio chuckled. "You cannot remember dozens of cousins, aunts, and uncles you just met? We are disappointed in you."

Teresa rolled her eyes but looked at her brother with affection. "Ignore him; he thinks he is the family comedian. Our dad is Agosto, who is Philomena's brother. Philomena is your mom's sister."

"Okay, got that."

"Our mom's name is Grazia. Me, Emilio, and Luigi are all

siblings, so we are your first cousins. Luigi is working, so he couldn't be here. Then Catena and Theo are on Philomena's side—also first cousins."

I nodded, getting a clearer picture of the family tree.

Emilio jumped in with what I was already thinking of as his trademark grin. "It's the extended cousins that will mess you up. Babba and Nonna have a ton of siblings—five each—so when we have a gathering, there can be a dozen aunts and uncles and their kids, who will be your second cousins."

I couldn't imagine having that many people trying to eat together. Or have a conversation. It would be like hosting a banquet. "Are all of them coming this weekend?" I asked tentatively.

"Many of them," Teresa said. "But no one will expect you to remember names or relations at this point. Please do not worry. We only want you to enjoy yourself and honor you as family." Her eyes filled with sadness. "We are so sorry about your mother, Aurora. I cannot imagine how hard this is."

Her sweet compassion made me blink back sudden tears. I still wasn't comfortable with this new emotional me, who cried at random and felt like her insides were broken fragmented glass. I forced a smile. "*Grazie.* It has been harder than I thought."

Catena came back with four spritzes, easily balancing all of them in her hands. "Let us toast!" she announced, holding her glass high in the air. "To our cousin!"

We clinked glasses, sipped, and fell into conversation. Within minutes, any awkwardness was erased and I relaxed, blooming under their affection. Teresa worked at the pizzeria in Lucca with her brother Luigi, and Emilio attended a university for business. They filled in the details of who did what within the family so I had a better idea of my mother's siblings. We ordered another round, and the fizzy bitter drink danced in my veins with celebration. I'd forgotten how enjoyable it was to sit outside with a cocktail, soaking in the sun and lively dialogue with people I cared about. When was the last time I'd allowed myself to take a break? My meetings with clients were centered on work, even if we shared a meal. And my friends? Well, after too many times of not returning their calls, or canceling our meet-ups, they'd gone quiet, disappearing into their own lives. I consoled myself by saying we'd grown apart and needed to move on, but now I realized I had just not taken the time and care to keep the relationships going.

"Do you have a boyfriend, Aurora?" Teresa asked.

I only hesitated a moment. "Yes. His name is Jason."

Catena leaned in eagerly. "How long are you together? Is it serious?"

"We've been together a year." I tried to tread carefully, wondering why it felt odd describing our relationship. "He owns a few gyms and is big into fitness. So far, we've been a good team."

Emilio shook his head. "So sad. I have many friends who will fight to take you out."

Teresa sighed. "Trust me, it is good you have an excuse to say no to my brother's friends. They are all children who only want to drink and party."

Emilio raised his brow. "And you do not?"

She punched his arm, then turned back to me. "Are you sure you do not want to stay with us? I do not like the idea of you being in a Vrbo."

"Catena already offered, but I'm happy with the place. It's right on the water, and that way I can get my work done."

"You must come to the pizzeria," Emilio said with a wink. "We make better food than Catena and Theo's pub."

"You don't even work there, Emilio," Teresa teased.

"I do on breaks. Plus, I only speak the truth."

Catena gasped. "Our menu is much more extensive! We do not just create pizza, and our *arancino* is famous."

"Tell that to Nonna. You stole her recipe."

Catena glared. "You cannot steal from family."

Emilio kept a straight face. "Good to know. I guess you only borrowed Teresa's precious designer Dolce and Gabbana shoes, then, for the past few years?"

I watched Teresa's face tighten. "Are you trying to start a fight, Emilio?" She launched into expressive Italian with hands flying, and then Catena jumped in.

"I will give them back! How about I bring them to dinner?"

Fascinated by the argument, Emilio seemed smug, like he enjoyed being in the center of trouble. Catena and Teresa shared a look, then glanced at him.

"I think I'll call Luigi and tell him you kissed Mary after he broke up with her," Teresa said with innocent wide eyes. "You weren't trying to steal his girlfriend, right? You were only borrowing her?"

Her brother stared back in shock and a hint of panic. "Don't be mean, T. Come on, let's just forget about it. Aurora is going to get the wrong idea about our family. Don't scare her."

The girls pealed with laughter, and I joined them. I'd never had anyone to fight with, but I liked the sense of humor they brought into their zings. Had my mom quarreled with Philomena and Agosto? Had they been close? And if so, how could she possibly have left them behind?

"Why did she leave?" I suddenly asked. "My mom. Do you know?"

Silence fell. They stared at me with compassion, and when Teresa answered, her voice rang with sincerity. "We pushed for the story but know none of the details. Dad cried. I've never seen that before, and when we kept asking why we didn't know about Aunt Serafina, he just said she ran away to get married when she was nineteen and never returned. He shut down after that. Like Catena, we think having you there will finally force them to tell us the whole story."

"What about your dad?" Emilio asked. "Does he know anything?"

Heaviness pressed on my chest. "Dad died five years ago in a car crash."

Teresa sucked in her breath. "So you lost both of them?" she whispered.

I managed a nod.

"We will get all of the details," Catena said firmly. "There must be an explanation for all of this."

I hoped so. God, I wanted everything to make sense again, and even if I couldn't get Mom back, I craved some peace about what had happened in her past. "Who will be at dinner?" I asked.

They all shared a glance. "Everyone," Emilio finally said. "They all want to meet you. But don't worry, *cugina*. I will protect you. If you feel scared from so many questions, I will get you out of there."

"So will we," Catena added. "And Theo. You do not have to worry."

The tight-knit support eased my tension. I was grateful for their understanding of my overwhelmed feeling going into the dinner.

"*Grazie*," I said, smiling at them. "I am so happy I met you."

Catena squeezed my hand. "Now, let's take this party back to the pub and eat!"

We finished our drinks and headed to Bar Sciacca. Theo and Quint were both there, serving patrons and making cocktails, but the moment I entered, I heard a slight cheer as people from last night greeted me. Astonished at the welcome, I said my hellos and spent the next few hours nibbling on amazing food, avoiding carbs, and talking to a ton of new people.

Before long, they were closing up, and I waited for Catena outside, where I could grab some fresh air. My head was spinning from so many interactions, and my feet ached from my long walk today. Probably water retention, too, I reminded myself, thinking of the cocktails and gelato. I'd have to be more careful, like I was back home. Though I knew I could stand to gain a few pounds.

"It is a lot, no?"

I turned and found Quint beside me. Immediately, I remembered his simple compliment, which still thrilled me and allowed me to push aside any lingering thoughts about my diet. I hadn't talked to him much tonight, since he was busy and I was inundated with family. I tilted my head and regarded him. "What is a lot?"

His lips quirked in a smile. I tried not to stare, but I was having a hard time not admiring the rough carving of his features, his dark beard, which clung sexily to frame his mouth and cover his jaw. I wondered if it was smooth or course to the touch. "Meeting so many strangers at once. Being in a new country. Getting used to suddenly having a family. I think it must not be easy."

His voice was naturally deep, with the lilting musical accent softening the edges. Something about it made me want to close my eyes and just listen to him speak. I smiled back. "Yes, I guess it is," I admitted. "I was an only child and had no other family. Emilio and Teresa had a little argument at lunch and I enjoyed listening to it."

His laugh pumped the air with life, rattling fully from his chest. Jason rarely laughed with his whole body. He preferred a small chuckle before rushing on to the next comment, as if he had no time to waste on silly humor. "Did no one warn you about our Sicilian ways?" His eyes gleamed with amusement, a beautiful mix of brown and green I couldn't look away from.

"Maybe you should tell me so I'm prepared?"

He took a step toward me and I caught the scent of musk, leather, and whiskey, rich and heady. "Ah, that is a good idea. There are three things you need to know before you enter the lion's den."

I winced. "I hope I'm not the sacrifice."

"Not if you follow my advice."

"I'm listening."

"Number one. Sicilians yell very loudly. This does not mean we are angry. It is just our way and we are passionate no matter what the subject is. *Capisci?*"

"Got it. No crying if my aunt screams in my face."

Another laugh. It was a bit addicting, having a playful conversation that did not hold any goals or action items. "Very good. *Secondo*. You must eat."

I blinked. "I can eat."

He shook his head sadly. "No, I mean you must eat a lot. It will worry the family if you don't. It will cause great distress."

I tucked the information away but figured I had that covered. I was extremely polite and always had a bite of everything offered—I just never finished it. Leaving food on the plate was key in managing diet. "Got it. And the third?"

He stroked his beard and my fingers tingled to duplicate the movement. His serious expression was just as sensual as his laughter. God, this man must have a different date every night. He said something, but I almost missed it, distracted by his hotness. I asked him to repeat it and tried to hold back my blush.

"There are many, many duplicate names in our community, so we term people by their nicknames or jobs."

"I don't understand."

"There are dozens of Tonys, so one will ask, Tony the baker? Or Tony the butcher? Or Tony the one who got engaged to cousin Sara and broke it off? It is the way we keep track of our people."

"Is there another Aurora?" I asked curiously.

He lifted his hands and shrugged. "Perhaps? I do not know your family's past, but if there is, you may find a story linked to your name. Many times, the name is followed by the mother's name."

"Do women change their name after marriage here?"

Quint nodded. "*Sì.* But the woman's family name stays with her and continues also, so she is known with two last names."

I couldn't help my sigh of pleasure. "I like that. We do the hyphenation thing, but I still feel like we're wiped out from our history the moment we marry. I'm not sure why no one challenges such a patriarchal notion in this modern time."

"Family history is important. It gives us identity." I watched as a sudden shadow flickered in his eyes; a hint of pain skittered across his face but then was gone. I figured it was the moonlight, because he was suddenly smiling again. "I am glad you will be discovering yours, Aurora."

My name sounded rich from his tongue and a shiver raced down my spine. Our gazes met and lingered, while an odd energy squeezed the air around us. I'd never experienced such a strange sensation with a man before and found myself falling mute, unable to break the tension with a lighthearted remark.

What was happening to me?

"I am ready, *cugina*!" Catena's voice rang out and I jumped. The moment shattered and Quint nodded to me, turning away. "Thanks for keeping her company, Quint."

"Of course." He began walking away, then paused. "Enjoy your time with your family, Aurora."

"I'll remember the rules."

His lingering laugh echoed in my ears as he disappeared.

Catena drove me back to my rental as we discussed the evening and how much fun we'd had. "I will pick you up at noon tomorrow, *sì*?"

"*Sì*." I gave her a hug goodbye and watched her peel away. Then I got ready for bed, trying not to be nervous about what was ahead. I picked up my phone and considered texting Jason, then put it back down. We'd catch up once I met my family. There would be a lot to tell him.

I closed my eyes and thought about Mom and what she'd think if she knew I was here in Sicily. Would she be happy? Or angry I was stirring up the past?

I'd never know. But somehow, it felt right to be here. Like I was meant to discover her story.

I hugged the feeling to my heart and slept soundly.

TEN

LUCCA SICULA HAD a different vibe than Sciacca.

We drove away from the water and boats into a landscape of dusty browns and greens. The fishing community gave way to farming, where vast fields grew olives and blood oranges and grapes for wine. The mountains shimmered in the distance. Catena told me Lucca Sicula had a population of about two thousand, and as we drove down a bumpy, poorly maintained road that twisted in sharp angles, I got the sense I was diving further into the past.

Finally, the car stopped. Catena faced me.

"We are here."

I shivered with a combination of worry and excitement. There was a line of tall homes in a long row close together, painted in Tuscan orange hues with wooden doors. Wrought-iron balconies with colorful flowers overlooked the cobblestone streets. There were no grass or yards, and I blinked in surprise. I'd expected rolling hills with an old-fashioned Tuscan farmhouse, but this reminded me of the grit and close quarters of old city neighborhoods.

Children gathered together, laughing and playing a few feet away, and Catena called something in Italian to them, throwing kisses while they waved back. I wiped my sweaty palms down my tailored black pants. I hadn't known what to wear, so I fell back on classic New York black—sleek, cool, and comfortable. The sleeveless white silk blouse was light against my skin. I'd panicked when I saw Catena's jeans, but she told me I looked perfect for the occasion, so I relaxed and trusted her.

We paused before the door and I took a ragged breath. Catena met my gaze and nodded with support, then rapped out a quick knock.

The door immediately opened.

She led me over the threshold, and I saw a line of family behind a woman who looked similar to Mom. Catena hugged her, speaking quickly in Italian, then switching back to English. "Mamma, this is cousin Aurora. Aurora, this is your aunt Philomena."

I stared in shock at my aunt's face, greedily devouring the familiar features I missed so much. Her dark hair was threaded with gray and cut shorter than my mom's but had the same thick texture. Olive skin set off wide chocolate brown eyes with full lashes. But it was the dominant nose, sloping jaw, and heavy winged brows that were reminiscent to me. She was the same, yet different. Her body was shorter, more stocky than curvy around the hips and belly. The simple blue dress had pockets and was both practical and tidy.

I blinked and hesitated, not sure what to do as dozens of

stares centered on me, the newcomer, and for one wild moment, I wanted to turn and run away.

"Aurora. My beautiful niece." Her voice broke, and then she was weeping, gathering me gently into her arms as if I were the most fragile thing she'd ever handled. She smelled of citrus and warm baked bread, and I fought my own tears as I hugged her back, reminding myself over and over that this was my aunt, who'd grown up with Mom.

The embrace broke the spell, and then I was surrounded, squeezed in by one relative after another who introduced themselves, hugging and touching me, talking loudly in Italian while I tried to respond as my head whipped back and forth. I spotted Theo in the throng; he waved, and then Teresa was flanking Catena as they pulled me forward.

"Give her room, Mamma!" Catena said with a laugh. "You will scare her away."

My aunt refused to let go of my hand as she introduced me to her husband, Alessandro, then accompanied me over to a man who looked exactly like Emilio. Light hair receded from his high forehead. Bluish eyes stared back at me. A trimmed gray mustache gave him a distinguished air. A blue collared polo was neatly open at the neck, paired with navy blue pants, creased smartly down the middle. He wrung his hands together as if he were just as nervous as I was. "I am your uncle Agosto," he said in a heavily accented voice. "I was Serafina's brother." Grief reflected on his slightly wrinkled face. "Welcome to the family, *mia nipote*. We are all mourning the loss of your mother."

I cleared away the lump in my throat. "*Grazie*. It's nice to meet you."

He reached out and took my hands, gripping them. My chest tightened and I was finding it hard to breathe. Okay, this was a lot. My mind spun with a million thoughts, yet everyone was still speaking around me. My skin began to itch, and I prayed I wouldn't begin breaking out in hives. God, I should have scheduled a session with Dr. Sariah before this big meeting. What was I thinking?

His gaze roved over me in wonder. "You look like your *mamma*. So beautiful."

I bit my lip hard and tried not to lose it. "*Grazie*," I said again, feeling tongue-tied and lost.

"This is my wife—your aunt Lucy." I smiled at the petite woman standing next to my uncle. She had delicate, birdlike features and kind brown eyes.

"We are so happy to finally have you here," my aunt said.

Emilio pushed his way over and patted my shoulder. "Would you like a glass of wine?" he whispered.

Overwhelmed by the number of people I was meeting, I shot him a grateful glance. "Yes."

"Be right back. Papà, Mamma, this is a lot for her, too."

Uncle Agosto snatched his hands back like he'd done something wrong. Aunt Lucy pressed her lips together. He said something in Italian, as if in apology, but I shook my head and spoke up. "No, it's okay. I'm happy to be here. Happy to meet my mother's family."

He relaxed and smiled back, and that's when I caught a hint of the mischief he'd normally exude, just like Emilio. I was grateful I'd met my four cousins earlier; just like they'd promised, they were helping me navigate this reunion.

A glass of wine was pressed into my hand and I sipped the

liquid courage. I had a quick overall impression of my grandparents' house of simplicity, cleanliness, and warmth. The scents of cooking and lemon polish drifted in the air. The roar of window air conditioners was a steady hum amid conversations. Lots of dark wood was set off with colorful accents, such as mosaic figurines, photographs, and floral tapestry pillows. A large couch and multiple chairs in earth tones made up the main living area, with a small television and heavily carved tables. Sheer lace curtains covered the windows. An arched doorway opened to the kitchen, where I spotted many women gathered around in aprons, shuffling things from the stove to the countertops as they chattered with one another. Bottles of wine competed with hunks of bread, oils, lemons, and bulbs of garlic. Dishes of olives and cheese with cured meats were displayed on the dining table, which seemed to have two large leaves with chairs squeezed in tight next to one another. It struck me as a home filled with family and cooking and busyness, but I couldn't picture my mother being a part of it. In my mind, she belonged only to me, alone in the kitchen as she cooked for the two of us. Humming and drinking red wine, music in the background, hair pinned up as she served us with a joy I'd never understood.

I shook my head to clear away the images. Uncle Agosto shared a glance with Aunt Philomena, then smiled at me. "Come. You must meet your *nonna* and *babba*."

The strange endearments seemed too intimate, but I held my tongue as I was led through a group of aunts and uncles hovering nearby. My heart pounded hard against my chest as we closed the distance and a clear path was made for us, as if I were about to meet the queen and king. The back of my neck prickled and I gave a quick scratch, hoping my face didn't look red or broken out.

And then we were finally face-to-face.

These were my grandparents.

The three of us stared at one another. My grandmother's eyes were swollen and red-rimmed behind her clear-framed glasses, as if she had been crying all night. A broken gasp fell from her lips as her gaze roved over me, and she launched into a litany of Italian that I didn't understand, except for one perfect, precious word.

Serafina.

She called out my mother's name like it was something sacred, her wrinkled hands clasped together like she was praying. Her curly gray hair was cut short, and her face was a beautiful map of soft creases that bespoke a life well lived. Dark eyes clung to mine under familiar arching brows. Like Philomena, she resembled my mother, as I'd imagined she would have looked if she'd grown old the way she was supposed to. A green apron covered with lemons cinched her waist.

Aunt Philomena gripped my arm in support and responded to my grandmother in Italian, then spoke to me. "Aurora, this is your *nonna*, Rosa. And your *babba*, Giovanni."

A shattering silence fell between us. Slowly, my grandmother stepped closer, cupping my cheeks and staring into my face with wonder. Her hands were warm and firm, and in that moment, I experienced a fleeting sensation of complete comfort and care, reminding me of when I was little and would climb into Mom's arms.

"I did not know about you," she said, voice shaky. "*Mia*

bella nipote. I dreamed of you. I missed my Sera every day, and now she is gone." Ravaged pain shone in her dark eyes. "You are here now. You will make all of this right."

I blinked furiously, trying not to weep as my past and present crashed together in an emotional wreck. Her arms came around me and I leaned gently into her embrace, allowing myself to tumble straight into my fantasy. I was a lost grandchild now found. Yes, the circumstances were horrible, and I had a zillion questions about why this had happened, but for now, I was here, and it was a moment I'd never forget.

"I miss her so much," I whispered. "I wish she could be here."

She whispered my name like a prayer. "Your name. Aurora. That is my middle name. Your *mamma* bestowed on me a gift."

Shock pummeled me. I was named after my grandmother but had never known about the connection, the special honor of carrying someone's legacy. "I didn't know."

My grandmother—Nonna—patted my back and murmured in Italian, soothing my ears. When she finally pulled away, she gave me a small smile. "Giovanni, come meet your *nipote.* Come."

She pulled him forward and I noticed his reluctance, his guarded stare as he took me in. My grandfather was short and stocky, with big hands and a rough exterior. A frown creased his wrinkled forehead. Thick black-framed glasses perched on his wide, flat nose. Silver hair was slicked back neatly. He was dressed nicely in a collared shirt and pants and sensible loafers. Hazel eyes appraised me with a firm distance, and he immediately struck me as removed from the emotional scene my grandmother and I had just shared.

A flare of doubt hit as I waited for an embrace or a touch,

but he only nodded, his voice deep and heavily accented. "*Buongiorno.* Good to meet you. Aurora."

He said my name tentatively, almost like he didn't believe I was related to him. A barrier separated him from me, and ridiculously, hurt pummeled me. Was he the reason my mother fled? Was he mean and cruel and I hadn't known? I studied him carefully, nodding back with politeness but refusing to speak. Instinct screamed that he was the missing link in this story, and I didn't trust him.

Odd—he didn't seem to trust me, either.

We regarded each other in silent judgment, then I was guided into the kitchen surrounded by my grandmother and aunts and cousins. My brain worked frantically to keep up with the endless list of names and relations, but it didn't seem to matter, because within minutes, I was perched beside the table with my glass of wine, surrounded by women chopping and cooking a massive meal. Plates and cups clinked and clattered. Laughter filled the air. I was barraged with questions about my mom and dad, about America, about my job and my childhood. I answered all of them, glowing with the attention and being able to share things about my parents. Men drifted in and out to refill drinks but mainly stayed in the living room or stood out on the balcony manning a small grill, from which the rich scent of cooked meat drifted in.

I met my other first cousin, Luigi, who was charming and obviously adored his wife and three daughters, who were outside playing. Uncle Agosto told bad jokes when he tried to interrupt and was shooed out of the kitchen by his own family. Magdalena was my second cousin whose wedding was coming up. Her dreamy, excited expression as she spoke about her fiancé gave me an odd longing. I thought of Jason and wondered how I sounded when I talked about him. Something told me I was more lukewarm. The idea nagged in my gut, but I pushed it aside to talk about her wedding.

"Aurora, please try to come. I would love to have my new *cugina* there," she begged. She reminded me of Snow White, with her pale skin, dark eyes, black hair, and red, red lips. Her grandfather was my grandfather's brother and owned the olive oil farm nearby. I congratulated myself on remembering the connection. I was lost on all the others. Most of the names blurred and ended with *a*'s for the women, and the men seemed dressed all alike, with collared shirts and neatly creased pants. Most sported white or gray hair with mustaches. Their deep voices were rough and loud. They reminded me a bit of stepping into a scene from *The Godfather*.

"I would love to, but I'm only here for ten days. I have a ton of work waiting for me back home. Plus, my boyfriend."

Immediately, I received everyone's full attention. Teresa bumped my shoulder, obviously thrilled I'd spilled the tea early and she was in the know. "His name is Jason," she said loudly. "He owns a gym and does fitness. Sounds like he's hot."

"How long have you been together?" Magda asked.

"A year. We have very similar interests."

"And he's hot," Teresa said again.

The girls laughed. Aunt Philomena shook her head as she sliced hunks of bread with rapid ease. "Can you speak to Catena, please? She has not brought anyone home to meet me and she is old. It is time to settle down."

I pressed my lips together to keep from laughing. Catena was a few years younger than me, so I must be a full-fledged spinster. The remark brought a heated response from my cousin, and Teresa jumped in to defend her. "Mamma, things are not the same anymore. We don't have to get married young. We want careers."

"She's working at a bar and partying all night," my aunt shot back. "It is nonsense. I want grandchildren."

"Nonna! Tell her she's being mean," Catena whined, laying her head against my grandmother's chest.

I watched as Nonna patted her in comfort and kissed the top of her head. "You are a good girl, but your *mamma* is impatient. We need more babies."

Teresa shuddered. "Not me. I like doing what I want."

One of my other aunts—Maria?—wagged her finger at my cousins. "*Basta con queste sciocchezze!* You are almost thirty. Look at Magda—she is twenty-five and married before you. Stop being picky."

"Do you want to marry Jason?" Magda asked, obviously trying to switch the attention off my cousins' lack of spouses.

My tongue got stuck to the roof of my mouth. I thought over our last face-to-face conversation, when he told me he loved me, then left. I thought about how excited I was about our future and what a perfect fit he was for my lifestyle. What was love, really? A choice. Once lust and adrenaline faded, the stuff left was the sticking parts. Respect. Common goals. Shared interests. Jason basically hit all the marks.

"I don't know," I said honestly, surprised in the moment at my response.

My grandmother turned from the stove, wiping her hands on a dish towel. "Did your mother meet him?" she asked softly.

I gritted my teeth as pain stabbed me. "Yes, she did." I

didn't want to tell them Mom disapproved but refused to tell me why. Or share that one of our final times together dissolved into a fight while I challenged her on the reason she didn't like Jason. Or my behavior and obsession with my career.

I guess I looked sad, because Aunt Philomena patted my hand, and Catena refilled my wineglass, and then we were heading to the table for dinner.

My cousins pushed me into a chair, flanking me, and my elbows were squeezed close to my sides from the other seats jammed in tight. I noticed a separate, smaller table for all the children set up in the living room. My grandmother and aunts began bringing in dishes, filled with what looked like an array of vegetables in a sauce. I immediately perked up, relieved I was able to eat everything offered.

"Caponata," Teresa whispered to me, thanking my aunt as she placed a full bowl in front of both of us. I watched as each person was individually served by the women, and how my grandmother barked orders at everyone, nodding and directing as if they were performing an intricate dance routine. My grandfather sat at the head of the table as if lording over his servants. It was a bit disturbing.

"I feel bad not helping," I said, beginning to push my chair back to get out of my seat.

"No!" Catena practically shouted from my other side. "You are our special guest; they will not let you do work today. And I don't want to, either, so let's just keep sitting."

I chuckled at my cousin, then caught Aunt Philomena's shake of the head. Yeah, she'd heard that comment, too, but seemed amused by her daughter's remark. A memory sparked of how my mother used to serve my dad, and the way I'd rolled my eyes, teasing her that women didn't have to be subservient to men any longer. I hadn't listened when she explained cooking for the people you loved was an honor. Regret throbbed like a wound. Now it was too late to apologize. Watching the prideful faces on my aunts and grandmother gave me a new impression.

The bread came out piping hot, with sesame seeds sprinkled on the crust. My fingers curled in to avoid taking a piece. Some came out with what looked like a piece of dried meat on top, which I didn't recognize. I decided to skip that, too.

Finally, after much fussing, everyone took their places and they said grace, bowing their heads as they prayed. When I looked up, I found my grandfather staring at me, but he quickly looked away as soon as I noticed.

Tension tightened in my stomach. I decided to avoid him as much as possible. Until I knew the circumstances regarding Mom's disappearance, I had no desire to converse.

The caponata was fried eggplant mixed with other vegetables, olives, and capers, creating a delicious salty flavor that danced on my taste buds. Most scooped it onto the bread and made a mini open sandwich of the treat, and I enjoyed each morsel. "Try the bottarga," Teresa suggested. "It's crostini with dried fish and lemon."

Luigi passed me one, and I took a bite of the top with just the edge of the bread. God, that was unexpectedly good. The acidity and some other unique spice were rich and bold. I took another sip of my wine and relaxed. I liked this dinner. It was going well.

Suddenly, all the women got up from the table and began clearing. I knew it couldn't be over, so I figured we'd have another dish, then dessert. My grandmother patted my shoulder as she walked past, and I heard the roars of laughter from the children's table. Luigi's wife seemed to be the other table's director, because she'd admonish, shake her head, serve, and chuckle along with their antics. My grandfather had given up on staring at me and was talking with the uncles, their voices gruff as they argued about something I couldn't understand. Their voices got louder and I winced, waiting for the explosion, but my cousins just talked louder, and I remembered what Quint had told me about Italians yelling, so I relaxed.

New dishes were served and I glanced around for the explanation.

This time, Magdalena spoke. "*Involtini di pesce spada.* It's swordfish."

I perked up. I was thriving during this dinner! With enthusiasm, I forked the rolled-up fish, which was seasoned with breadcrumbs and some nuts. The rich, buttery flavor was moan-worthy, and I wondered why Mom had never made us anything like this. The fish was flaky and fresh. A beautiful salad was placed on the table, along with a plate of shrimp that had the shells on. Dad called them prawns, and these were gigantic and a bold red color.

I drizzled some lemon and peeled off the shells, sinking my teeth into the firm flesh. Succulent, with the distant flavor of salt from the sea. I realized how different things were when they were freshly caught or passed through a minimal number of distributors. I'd tasted fruit from the farm markets in the Hudson Valley, and no supermarkets compared. Sicilian food, so far, was quite delicious.

I enjoyed the overlapping conversations around the table, greedily ingesting the way everyone related in such a loving way. I talked about New York and my job to my aunts and cousins and answered a ton of questions. When the women got up again, I smiled.

"Dessert now?"

Catena had termed this meal dinner, but it was only two p.m. and no one seemed in a rush to move.

My cousins laughed. "No, third course," Teresa said.

Third course?

"*Anelletti al forno*, my favorite!" Emilio said as the large casserole dish was set down. Immediately, Aunt Philomena began to cut and serve, while my grandmother brought in more bread.

My luck had run out.

I was about to eat carbs.

And I was already full.

Pinning on a smile, I accepted the bursting plate of cheese, meat, and pasta oozing over my dish. Someone put bread on my plate. I forked up a small bite and popped it in my mouth.

Oh. My. God.

I'd never eaten anything like it. The melty cheese accented the firm ring-shaped pasta, and pieces of ham and—pork? veal maybe?—gave it a layered richness that made a sound of pleasure escape my lips. I had no idea what else was in it, but besides being the most calories I'd ingested in a few bites, it was also the most memorable.

Jason would die here.

My grandmother gave out seconds, dipping in and out of speaking Italian. I heard the word "*BASTA!*" from one of my second cousins, and my grandmother glared a bit, then sat down. I wondered what bad thing my cousin had said. I made a mental note to look it up and never say it.

Magda launched into talk about her upcoming wedding while the table was cleared. More wine was poured. I stuck to sparkling water and slumped a bit in my chair. No way was I eating dessert.

Until I realized dinner wasn't over.

A platter with a beautiful roasted chicken came out to the oohs and aahs of everyone. Other dishes were set around, and I found my eyes widening in denial that any one person could eat this much and live.

I guess, in Sicily, they not only lived but flourished.

Catena pointed to the various plates. "Potato croquettes, chicken, escarole. *Buon appetito!*"

Carbs after carbs? Pasta with potatoes and bread?

As if he'd caught my thoughts, my grandfather swung his head around to rest his narrowed gaze on me. It flicked to my face, to my plate, and back. A frown creased his wrinkled brow.

My heart began to pound harder. I couldn't offend anyone, especially him. I'd just . . . eat it.

And I did. I wondered over the juicy texture and flavor of the chicken, so light and citrusy, with the scents of rosemary and herbs. The potatoes were encrusted in a fried dough and creamy in the hot center. The bitter taste of the escarole leaves was balanced with lemon and capers, rounding out the rest of the dishes. I finished my plate, my one small act of rebellion staring me in the face.

My bread remained untouched.

"Do you like everything?" my grandmother asked, eyes flashing with worry as she analyzed my mostly empty plate. "More?"

"No, thank you! I love every single thing I tasted. Mom

never—" I broke off, biting my lip, as if I'd said something wrong.

A short silence fell over the table. My cheeks burned.

"She did not cook like this?" my grandmother asked, voice laced with pain.

"No. She loved to make pasta with eggplant in various ways. She made her own bread, too. And her favorite cake to make was *torta setteveli*. Dad loved it."

My grandmother gasped. "I taught her to bake that dessert for special occasions."

Murmurs of sympathy rose to my ears. I bit my lip hard. Imagining Mom had baked that cake with her mother, learning every careful step, probably complaining or fighting in the kitchen with my grandmother made my heart squeeze tight. I remembered visiting and watching her in the kitchen, smells of dough and salt permeating the air, her apron tight around her waist as her graceful hands pulled sheets of pasta from the maker. I remembered touting my new diet, which consisted of vegetables and no carbs. I remembered her face falling as she tried to create special things just for me in an obvious need to bond with her only daughter.

Shame burned through me. I'd treated her as disposable, uneducated as to how to be truly healthy. I'd gossiped with Jason about how hard it was to eat at my mother's house and keep true to myself, while he agreed enthusiastically and doubled up on our shared workouts.

My grandmother pressed her hands together. "I taught her many dishes before she left, but she was always sneaking away from the kitchen. To run around with the boys and explore and get messy."

My eyes widened at this important information. "She was? She was . . . wild?"

Aunt Philomena laughed. "Ah, your *mamma* always knew how to sweet-talk me into doing her work. She loved to run and play. Remember, Papà, how she used to beg to go to work with you in the fields? She could get lost for hours daydreaming or reading or dancing. *Piena di vita.*" My aunt shook her hands. "She was full of life."

I couldn't relate that image to the mom I'd known, so practical and nurturing, as if her entire existence had been built on having a family and she'd been disappointed to have only one child. But there were other images in my memory, buried deep, that suddenly sprang loose.

Mom reading late at night, worn covers and towering spines of books stacked on the shelves and tables.

Mom staring out the window, lost in another world, not hearing me call her name over and over. The distance in her face, the sadness in her gaze as she blinked, clearing it away before refocusing on me.

Mom dancing with Dad in the kitchen late at night, caught up in their own world as I stared at them with a longing I couldn't understand, as if I craved to be part of a secret club only they knew about.

The sound of Mom weeping through a closed door as my father quietly spoke in a soothing voice. Overhearing his comment, "You need to stop torturing yourself and let it go, my love." I hadn't understood, so I'd shrugged off the incident. Now I wondered if it was the past rearing up, the past she'd kept a secret from everyone, including her only daughter.

"You have not had any bread."

I startled; my gaze flew to my grandfather. He pointed at my plate and the large chunk left uneaten. A strange tension floated in the air. "*Scusi?*" I said, tilting my head.

Disapproval gleamed in his hazel eyes. He pushed his glasses up his nose in an annoyed manner. "You do not like the bread?"

I caught my breath as everyone stared at me. My grandmother seemed worried, as if I'd deemed her food unworthy. "N-n-no, I love the bread. I'm just very full."

"Babba, leave her alone. She's not used to eating so much in the States. Carbs are bad," Catena said, defending me.

A thundercloud passed over my grandfather's face. "*Il pane è la vita!*" he boomed out.

Now my grandmother looked distressed. Aunt Philomena sighed. "Papà, don't scare her. Let her eat what she wants."

Suddenly, the chair scraped back and my grandfather got up from the table. With a loud humph, he disappeared, leaving me shocked and embarrassed, with my jaw hanging open. He was a very mean man. I immediately didn't like him trying to bully me or make me feel bad. Was this how he'd treated my mother? No wonder she left!

The tension on the women's faces disturbed me, though, so I did the only thing left to keep the peace.

I grabbed the bread, and I ate it.

I caught Emilio's grin, the girls' supportive nods, and Aunt Philomena's relief. My grandmother watched me polish off every crumb with such pride, I decided it was worth the calories and compromise to please her.

My grandfather came back. He took in my empty plate and didn't comment. I burned with resentment as he conversed with my uncles again, ignoring my attempt to make him happy. He didn't like me, and I had no idea why. I just needed to get to the truth about my mom, and hopefully I wouldn't see him again. I'd keep close with my cousins and my grandmother and Aunt Philomena. It was enough.

The final clearing occurred, to my relief. Espresso brewed. Tiny cups of lemon ices were brought out—dubbed *granita al limone*—which reminded me of sorbet. Pieces of bitter chocolate were laid out with almonds. A beautiful multilayered sponge cake was served—filled with creamy ricotta. The flavor was sweet with honey and citrus, and the dessert was decorated with dried candied fruits in various shapes. All the months of avoiding sugar crashed into this one perfect moment. The grainy bite of the chocolate, the tartness of the lemon ice, the sugary cream of the cake, the bitter burning sip of espresso—all the culinary tastes and textures culminated in pure delight.

I closed my eyes and let myself soar.

"What in God's name is this cake called?" I whispered to Catena.

She grinned. "Cassata. Nonna's recipe is the best around—better than the pastry shops."

Food was religion here. It was a lesson I'd never forget.

Eventually, we all got up from the table. I helped clear, overpowering the aunts who tried to wave me away, and a coordinated cleanup crew took over. For such a small kitchen, everyone seemed to have their job and knew their place within the cramped space. The men stayed at the table and talked. Some ventured out to smoke a cigar. Family members began to leave with their kids, saying goodbye to me with warm hugs and invitations for dinner, many saying they'd see me for church Sunday morning.

Finally, everyone had left except Aunt Philomena, Uncle Agosto, their spouses and children, and my grandparents.

I sank into the sofa, perched on the edge, my knees and hands pressed together to calm my nerves. My grandfather drifted in and took his place in the main leather chair, facing me. My aunt was on one side, my cousin on another. My grandmother was the last to settle in, next to my grandfather. Without a speech planned, or specific questions to ask, we stared at one another in uneasy silence, as if no one knew where to start.

I was surprised when the words popped out of my mouth.

"Tell me what happened with my mother. I want to know everything."

ELEVEN

Nonna looked at my grandfather as if asking for permission, but his gaze was shuttered and he didn't respond. It was Aunt Philomena who spoke first. "I want to say how hard it's been for all of us. To know your precious mother is gone, and we never got a chance to see her or meet you. It is a blessing that Catena reached out and found you."

I bit my lip and nodded, trying not to cry. God, this was a lot. But I burned for the answers I needed to make sense of things. "Me, too. I don't understand why Mom never mentioned any of you. All I know is what she told me. Mom said she lost her parents very young and that she was an only child. She met my father when he visited New York from England and she was working in a pizza shop. He came to order a slice, fell in love with her instantly, and they were married a few months later in a whirlwind romance. She got pregnant on the honeymoon and had me. They tried to have more children, but she couldn't get pregnant again, and eventually they stopped trying. That's all I know."

My grandmother gave a sharp cry of pain. Philomena rushed over to console her, but my gaze was riveted on my grandfather. He sat silent and still, his face carved from rock. I shivered with dread. I only hoped he told the truth. No matter how bad it was, I needed to know so I could move on and make my own peace with the past.

"Please tell me about my mother," I pleaded. "Please tell me what happened."

Catena inched over on the sofa and clasped my hand. "Mamma? Nonna? It is time we know everything. You owe Aurora the truth."

Finally, my grandmother raised her head high, took a breath, and met my gaze. Grief ravaged her face, but her voice was strong when she began to speak.

"Your mother was our oldest child. She was very special to us. She was a good girl, but like Philomena mentioned, she had a rebellious streak. As she grew up, Sera was always testing us. She was strong-willed and we had many battles."

I couldn't help interrupting, greedy for all the information. "What type of battles? What did she do that was wrong?"

My grandmother sighed. "Maybe you do not understand, coming from America? We have certain ways here—the old ways. It is very important for children to listen and respect their elders here. To obey the rules. Your *mamma* had a bright light inside her that attracted others. Many boys flocked to talk to and date her, but we are very strict."

"So she snuck out to meet boys?" I asked.

"*Sì*," Nonna said. "We forbade her to see anyone we had not met and approved of. She began fighting with us a lot. Not wanting to go to church. Disappearing from her chores or staying out at dinner. We were very worried, so we gave more rules to protect her."

Philomena cut in. "Your mom was loved by many, *cara*. She was three years older than me, and I would do anything she asked. She was the most popular at school and had many friends. She began talking about leaving home to travel. She said she wanted adventure."

Agosto shook his head with a sad smile. "I remember when Sera would take me out for the day. She would make up stories as we explored the vineyards, about far-off worlds where children were kings and queens and fought dragons. We would climb trees and sit in the fields for hours until sunset. She made every moment magic."

I caught my breath in wonderment, remembering my mother's stories when I was a child. How she seemed to make everything bigger and better when I was around her. My throat tightened. "Did she want to go to school?"

"She wanted to go to America," Philomena said. "I didn't understand why. I thought she had everything here. Many boys wanted to marry her."

"We gave Sera many choices," Nonna added. "The pizzeria could be hers. Or she could work and study in Sciacca, or with the olive oil company. I even told her she could study cooking and open a fancy *pasticceria*. We wanted her to be happy."

I imagined Mom as a free spirit, feeling trapped in her tiny town and aching to burst out. Wasn't that how I'd felt myself?

That there was so much more beyond my mom and dad's house, waiting for me? Had I gotten my wanderlust and ambition from her, yet never recognized it?

"When did she meet my dad?" I asked hesitantly.

Nonna pulled out a hanky and dabbed her eyes, then crumpled it in her hand. "He came into the pizzeria. Sera was working that day."

I sucked in my breath. It was the same story she'd told me, yet she'd changed the location.

Nonna continued. "Your father was visiting from England for a few days. He'd served in the war overseas and was staying in Lucca before he went back home. He felt the same way about Sera, and the next day, he showed up at the house. He asked if he could take her out."

"What did you say?"

I knew already, though. I sensed the story taking shape, a modern Romeo and Juliet without Romeo's family dynamics.

Aunt Philomena gave a sound of distress. "I knew something bad was going to happen," she whispered, pressing her hand to her trembling lips. "She was in love with him. Kept saying he was her *anima gemella*."

Catena and Teresa both gasped. "Twin soul," Catena said in an awed tone. "How romantic."

"To a young child, it is romance. To us, it is *tragedia*."

I stared at my grandmother, her words echoing uncomfortably in the air. Still, my grandfather had not spoken. He studied the floor, refusing to meet anyone's gaze.

Uncle Agosto scratched his head. "I don't remember much of that time. Just that Sera was so angry at everyone. I had never seen her like that before."

"We forbade her to see your father," Nonna continued. "Your grandfather explained he was only here for a short time, and it was not appropriate. He was afraid she would get in trouble with him. Sera refused and disobeyed. We were very upset and your grandfather went to tell him that he must leave Sera alone."

"I bet that did not go well," I muttered, squeezing my cousin's hand.

"No. It was very bad." My grandmother's fingers trembled around her handkerchief. "We did not know how to control her. We hoped at the end of the week, he would disappear and we would have our Sera back. We spoke about sending her away to study so she could get out of Lucca for a while. But it did not work that way. Your father asked her to go away with him because he did not want to leave her. She told us about it, and we fought. Your grandfather tried to lock her in her room."

No one spoke for a while. I knew the ending but needed to hear it spoken.

"She didn't stay, though," I said softly.

"No. We woke up in the morning and she had left."

Philomena shook her head. "My memory is very foggy about that night. She cried to me and said she needed to go with him. I begged her to listen to Papà. I said they could write to each other or talk and maybe make plans for later. I finally calmed her down and she seemed okay. I thought she would sleep and we would talk in the morning. We would fix it. But it was too late. She only left a note."

My chin shot up. "She left a note?" I repeated.

Nonna's face collapsed into mourning. "*Sì*. It said only this: 'I am sorry but I love him. Forgive me.'"

A sob caught in my chest, but it was strangled, refusing to

be released. My mind spun from the story, which sounded like it belonged in one of Shakespeare's plays. I thought over my memories of my parents, trying to see if I remembered snippets that would hint at regret about their decision.

But I only remembered the love. The respect. The devotion. Their love story had been real, even if it had many casualties.

"That is so sad," Teresa said, breaking the silence.

"Can I see the note?" I asked.

Nonna nodded, taking a crumpled yellowed piece of paper out of her pocket and handing it to Uncle Agosto. He brought it over and pressed it into my hand with reverence. The words were in Italian, but I traced my fingertip over the familiar loopy script, my eyes stinging with fierce tears.

"We never heard from her again," Aunt Philomena said sadly. "We didn't know your father's last name or where they settled. Years later, your uncle Agosto and I finally hired a private investigator."

My grandmother gasped along with my cousins. "You never told me!"

Pain creased the features of my aunt's face. "I know, Mamma. The investigator found out she was settled in America and had married. We didn't know about you, Aurora. We decided not to go any further because Serafina didn't want to be found." A sob broke from her lips. "I believed we'd all have more time. Time for her to reach out on her own."

Uncle Agosto shook his head. "We felt it was best not to share this information. There was already so much pain."

This new revelation hit me hard. If the PI had reached out and made contact, would everything have been different? Or would Mom still have kept her silence?

I pictured my mother running away from her family to marry my father. Did she believe she'd never be able to convince my grandparents to accept him? Did she regret her impulsive actions and think about reaching out later on? Or was she afraid to take the chance, assuming she'd be rejected by her blood and forever damaged?

The questions whirled in my mind, questions I'd never get answered.

The words broke from my soul and launched into the room. "Are you sorry you let her go? Do you—do you have regrets?"

My family regarded me with a deep sadness carved into their features. Tears ran down Nonna's cheeks. "*Sì*. Every day. Every moment."

My aunts and uncles murmured their agreement. "We should have tried harder," Aunt Philomena whispered. "She was my sister."

Suddenly, my grandfather's voice sliced like a sharp blade through flesh, making me bleed. "Your mother broke the rules of our household. She betrayed her family and made her choice. That is the truth."

A tense silence descended. Shock held me immobile as I stared at him, not understanding how he could defend his actions. "But she was your daughter," I whispered. "You loved her. How could you stop looking? How could you let her go?"

I searched his gaze behind those thick glasses, hoping to find a shred of apology or guilt. But there was nothing but a wintery storm in his eyes. His lips firmed together in a stubborn denial of his own part in such a tragedy. I knew then that he'd shed my mother's memory years ago, and even her death didn't bring him regret. My grandfather had been the one to decide there'd be no further communication. He'd driven my mother away forever.

I blamed him for everything.

"I don't understand you," I said shakily. "She was a wonderful mother and wife. People loved her. You're the one I feel sorry for, because you didn't get to have her in your life!"

My grandmother broke into sobs and reached out for my grandfather, but he was already standing up, his posture stiff and straight. Without a word, he disappeared upstairs, the echo of his footsteps sounding like doom to my ears.

Uncle Agosto got up. "I'll check on him."

We watched him follow, and my grandmother struggled to speak. "Aurora, my darling girl. It was a confusing time. We woke up and she was gone. We looked for her, but when your grandfather discovered she'd run away with your father, he was heartbroken. This type of thing doesn't happen in our home. We all made mistakes."

"He doesn't seem to think so," I said bitterly. "My father was a good man. A wonderful father."

"I have no doubt," Aunt Philomena said. "Sera would have never chosen him unless he was worthy, and she had a wonderful life. She had you. What a gift you must have been to her! How can any of us possibly regret her having you?"

I swiped at my wet cheeks and leaned into the comforting words. Suddenly, I was surrounded by my cousins, offering support and loving sentiments that soothed the rawness.

"You belong to us now," Nonna said. "You are family and we will never let you go."

The words reached deep into my heart, lifted the grief, and allowed it to finally shake through me.

And my family was here to witness it all, without judgment. So, for the first time since my mother's death, I let myself fall.

AFTER I LEFT my grandparents', Catena and Teresa drove me back to Sciacca and stayed a few hours to make sure I was all right. All that emotion had taken its toll, so I slept in pretty late. I ate some fruit, still stuffed from the amazing meal I'd experienced, and strolled to the local café to grab coffee. I sipped the brew outside and stared at the Mediterranean Sea. The turquoise water glittered under the sun's rays and the screech of seagulls and conversations in Italian drifted in the air.

I had a Zoom meeting with Dr. Sariah later and figured I'd do more sightseeing. We hadn't talked about any further itinerary. Whatever happened, I knew I now had a bond with my cousins, aunts, and grandmother. Maybe I'd come back out next year and make an annual summer trip. Or maybe Catena and Teresa could visit me in New York. I had six more days to spend, so I might as well see as much as I could and spend time with my cousins when their work schedules allowed.

My phone pinged. Jason was FaceTiming me, so I answered. "Hey. How are you?"

His smile was tight-lipped, which was odd. "Busy. Had to get to the gym early—we're having a big promo and I'm offering my clients a special bonus workout. What are you doing?"

I gave a luxurious sigh. "Sitting on a bench, looking at the Mediterranean, drinking coffee. It's beautiful here."

The phone bounced and the background blurred. He was on the move. "Got up late, huh? Sounds relaxing. I'm sure you needed it. Did you see your family?"

I wondered at the curtness in his tone but figured he was distracted. "Yes, yesterday. It was a lot, Jason. There were so many people there, I was overwhelmed. But they were nice and I really bonded with my cousins and my aunt and my grandmother. I didn't like my grandfather, though. Oh, and they served like eight courses in the afternoon. And I found out about my mom. It's heartbreaking."

I kept talking, wanting Jason to know the details about this new chapter in my life. I was halfway through my story when I paused, sensing not only distraction but an odd tension. "Jason, is everything okay? Do you need to call me back?"

He stopped moving and stared at the screen so I could see him up close. "I'm sorry, Aurora. I know this stuff is important—it's the reason you went to Sicily. But it's hard for me because I'm at this critical point with the gyms, and I feel like I'm not giving you the quality time you need to really help you right now. I'm frustrated."

My heart warmed a bit. He seemed genuinely interested in connecting, and I knew it was hard for him when he was so wrapped up in work. I wanted to be understanding for him, too. "I get it. I know you have a lot going on and I'm not mad."

He nodded. "Good. But I need to be honest about my feelings, too. A healthy relationship doesn't leave room for lies. Right?"

I hesitated. "Right."

"Okay. I need to know something. Why didn't you call my client back?"

"Who?"

He let out an impatient breath. "Jerry. My client. I specifically asked you to call him and you never did. I know you're in

Sicily and sleeping in and seeing all this great stuff, but I promised him you'd call within twenty-four hours. He depended on both of us, Aurora. He was really upset. I almost lost his trust, and he's been referring me to many of his friends. It could have been a disaster."

The name suddenly blitzed in my memory. I'd completely forgotten. Guilt slammed through me, along with another emotion I didn't want to investigate. It would only make my relationship with Jason more strained if I gave it a voice. "I'm so sorry. I meant to reach out, but with the time difference, and the big family get-together, I completely forgot. Can I text or call him now? Explain?"

"No, I took care of it. Told him you lost your phone in Italy. I didn't like lying, but I had no other choice."

"Okay. Well, again, I'm sorry."

"Yeah, I know." An awkward silence settled. "Do you want to finish your story? Why you didn't like your grandfather."

The intimacy I'd thought we had disappeared. I stared at his handsome face while he tried to mask his impatience and felt something crack from the inside. I had no right to feel betrayed, but I wondered again how I ranked in comparison to his work. Was it the distance getting in the way? Would things go back to normal when I returned? Or was this the new dynamic between us?

"Never mind, I'll tell you later. You have to focus on your event."

The shadows lightened from his eyes along with his frown. "You're right. I'm sorry, babe. Didn't mean to call you out. I'm just stressed and can't afford to lose Jerry right now. I probably shouldn't have asked you to step up."

His words ruffled my nerves. "Sure. Well, good luck."

"I'll call you back tonight and let you know how it went. Are you able to get any of your work done in between visits and sightseeing?"

"I'm working today."

"Good for you! The next few days will go by fast and I bet you'll be back to normal. You were right to take this trip, Aurora. Bye. Love you."

"Bye."

I clicked off. Didn't he notice I never said *I love you* back? Did it bother him or was he just trying to be patient?

The memory dragged me back, like a shell flung into a rough wave and pitched into the water.

My mother's voice rose in my head like a ghost who refused to be denied any longer.

We sat on the back deck, staring at the full moon. Stars blanketed the night sky. We sipped red wine and didn't speak. Dinner was over, Jason had just left, and we'd already had words. I knew she didn't like him, but she refused to say anything specific, which was driving me crazy.

"I wish you would just talk to me straight. Dad would have."

She jerked back and I felt a little sorry. I studied her profile, her olive skin, plump lips, heavy brows, and Roman nose. Sadness cloaked her like a worn blanket. Finally, she took a breath and turned to face me head-on. Her voice hit me like a force.

"Life is an adventure, my darling girl. It is not a long line of tasks to complete, or goals to accomplish. It's not about winning or losing, success or perfection."

Uncomfortable with her sudden probing and general assess-

ment of my life, I challenged her back. "I had no idea you knew the secret to life, Mom. Are you going to share it with me?"

She ignored my smart-ass remark and gripped my hand, squeezing too tight. "Yes. It's about love, and pain, and loss. It is laughter and tears and failure. You've kept yourself in a box, but one day, the lines will blur and you'll be faced with a choice." My mother's beautiful dark eyes stared into mine with a fervor that made fear trickle down my spine. I'd never seen her so serious, leaning forward so our faces were inches apart. "And I'm terrified you'll take the safe route and stay in your lane. You'll settle down with a nice man who checks all your boxes. If you do, you may not have regrets. You may sleep peacefully at night. But, Aurora, playing it safe will destroy you in the end."

My mouth fell open. "You want me to make mistakes and get my heart broken by some other man? Jason is a stand-up guy. He's all the things I'm looking for. You should be happy—you're not making sense!"

Frustration snapped off her in waves. "Wait for the love of your life, even if it's the scariest thing you've ever done."

I stared back in disbelief. "Look at you, Mom. Since Dad died, you've been a ghost. Why would you want that for me? To give my entire self and then lose him and be like you. Alone and lost and so damn sad." Tears choked me, but I fought them back, done with this whole conversation. "No, thanks. I like exactly where I am, and if you can't accept it, I won't bring him over again."

"Aurora, don't go. Let me try and explain."

"No, it's okay. Just respect my decision. Maybe not everyone is meant to have some great love like you. Maybe choosing someone to build a life with is enough."

I left, hearing my name echoing in the air, but I ran fast, certain she was wrong.

My fingers shook from the blast of raw emotion. Everything my mother had said now made a horrible kind of sense. She'd been warning me about Jason, but it was her own story that drove her. Mom sacrificed her entire world for my father and still held no regret. They'd loved each other that much.

Did loving someone like that mean an ultimate sacrifice? Because Jason and I simply did not have that type of relationship. I wasn't like Mom.

I'd rather be safe.

I pushed away the memory. Jason was a good man and worth fighting for. But I was afraid we were growing further apart and I wasn't sure what to do. I'd talk to Dr. Sariah, but maybe for now, the best thing to do was focus on myself. I needed time with my new family, time to process the truth about Mom. When I returned home, Jason and I could have a serious talk and see how we could fix things.

I finished my coffee and tore myself away from the amazing scenery. Okay, first, work. I needed to do some things for the podcast, contact clients, and open my manuscript. Then I'd reward myself tonight by doing some exploration.

My phone jumped again and I smiled. "Hi, Catena."

I heard the clatter of glasses in the background. "I cannot stop thinking about your mom and what happened. Come to the pub tonight. Everyone wants to see you."

I perked up. It was nice to think of the pub as mine, in a roundabout way. A true *Cheers* place where everyone would eventually get to know my name. "I'd like that."

"Good. Oh, my *mamma* is texting you later. After church tomorrow, she wants to go to the pizzeria and show you around Lucca."

Surprise hit. I hadn't been to church in years. "Church? Tomorrow?"

"Yes, we all go every Sunday together. It is important here. You will come, right?"

I remembered my mother begging me to go with her, and my snarky answers. I'd pushed back in my teen years, torturing her by commenting on my doubts and criticizing the Catholic religion. As I got older, I canceled regularly, until I just stopped showing up. Guilt stirred and twisted in my belly. What I'd give to be able to go back and sit with her in the pew on Sunday, watching her fingers nimbly count her rosary beads as she prayed. I swallowed past the knot in my throat. "Sure. I'll go."

"You will make everyone so happy! I will see you tonight."

I walked home, my worries about Jason fading. I liked the idea of having somewhere to go tonight, and people who looked forward to seeing me. I'd forgotten the simple joy of being with people who had nothing to do with work and only wanted your company.

After a quick shower, I settled in to deal with my growing workload. Wincing, I listened to the voice mail from Jason's client, his voice cold as he explained I didn't have to call him back and that he'd found another life coach. There were emails from Eliza, and another cancellation from a sponsor. Trying to keep a positive attitude, I responded to emails and put a Band-Aid on several tasks that had to be completed. Within the hour, I was exhausted. I stared at my laptop with a sense of frustration, wondering how I'd been able to keep up such a blistering pace without burning out.

Guilt leaked through me. I owed my clients more than this. They were waiting for me to call and lead them, but the thought of reaching out made me nauseous. Because for the first time in my life, I had no answers. If I couldn't fix myself, how could I fix them?

Taking a deep breath, I forced myself to do what I could in the next few hours. By the time I'd opened the manuscript and begun to write, I found myself journaling about my trip and meeting my family. I kept going, hoping that the story would lead into a teaching lesson for motivation and embracing change, but by the end of the section, I couldn't use any of it. I stared at the words in frustration.

I had to get out of here.

Checking my watch, I realized I could take a long walk before heading to Bar Sciacca. Maybe I could post some social media shots. People needed to know I hadn't disappeared completely or my platform would begin to disintegrate. Tension knotted my shoulders as I thought of all the ways I could fail not only myself but the people who relied on me. Meanwhile, I was in Sicily, eating in pubs and strolling in the sunshine. Yes, it was only for a few more days, but if I continued to spiral, I'd lose everything I'd worked hard for.

Maybe Jason was right to be angry.

I grabbed my purse, some water, and my sunglasses and headed out, hoping to find answers or at least inspiration.

TWELVE

THE MOMENT I stepped into the pub, a chorus of voices rose and sang my name.

Blushing, I grinned and greeted some familiar faces along my way to the bar. Catena, Theo, and Quint were all busy pouring and serving drinks but stopped immediately to welcome me. The place was packed with a healthy Saturday night crowd, but Quint pointed to the bar stool on the right, which they'd saved for me.

"*Grazie. Come stai?*" I'd been looking up Italian words and committing phrases to memory. At first, I figured everyone spoke Sicilian here, but it was mostly Italian and English.

Quint's golden eyes sparkled. "Ah, *sono molto occupato e ho bisogno di andare in bagno*."

I wrinkled my nose. "I only know *va bene*."

Catena appeared beside me, kissing both of my cheeks in greeting. "Ignore him, *cugina*. He is teasing you. He said he is very busy and needs to go to the bathroom."

Quint laughed and I joined in. "I'll remember that for next time."

"Would you like to learn Italian?" Quint asked curiously.

I nodded. "I took Spanish in high school but never really spoke it. I think it would be wonderful to be able to have a conversation with my family. Even if they speak English. I expected to hear Sicilian dialects."

"We are taught English and Italian when we are young. It is much harder in school when you do not hear it spoken around you," Catena said, gathering up some empty plates. "Nonna and Babba will sometimes use a Sicilian expression but mostly speak Italian."

"Mom never spoke Italian in the house," I murmured. "I didn't even know she knew the language."

Catena patted my hand sympathetically. "Your *mamma* hid many things, but so did our parents. I am shocked we did not hear about it through gossip. All this time, Theo and I had no idea."

Quint slid a glass of red wine in front of me—the same I'd liked before. "We do know how to keep our family secrets," he said quietly. "I'm sure your grandparents made sure no one would mention it. They take care of their own here."

I thought about his statement, which made me immediately imagine the Mafia, but I knew he meant it differently. For my mother to disappear and my cousins not to know about her existence must have required a big production of a cover-up. And they'd pulled it off.

I bet my grandfather led the entire process.

Theo came over, along with one of my second cousins,

whom I'd met yesterday. A plate filled with mini fritters and a side of asparagus was placed in front of me. "What's this?" I asked.

"Just a light dinner," Quint said, resting both arms on the bar. His biceps stretched his T-shirt, but he wasn't bulky like Jason. His muscles were leaner and more defined. I tried not to notice how perfectly he filled out his tight jeans. "Chickpea fritters with wild asparagus. I won't bring out the bread."

My lips twitched. "*Grazie.* I'm still recovering from yesterday."

He cocked his head. "Did you follow all my rules?"

"Yes. My grandfather yelled at me, so I ate the bread, too."

One dark brow rose. "Ah, you did the right thing. Was it horrible, eating the bread?"

I shuddered at the memory of the firm crust and warm dough, which was almost orgasmic. "Yes. It was very horrible. I need a safe word if I ever go back there for dinner."

Laughter danced in his eyes. "I will give you one, but you must only use it in emergencies. *Capisci?*"

I couldn't help it. I propped my elbows on the bar and leaned in. "Tell me."

The energy charged between us. "You say, *basta*."

I blinked. "I heard that word! One of my cousins yelled it."

Quint nodded seriously. "You do not take this lightly. It means 'no more,' but you may only use it sparingly."

"Got it. What do I owe you?"

He pulled at his beard and regarded me. "A favor. I will let you know when."

I opened my mouth to give a smart retort, but someone

called his name and he drifted to the other end of the bar. Shifting in my seat, I tried to make sure I wasn't blushing. I didn't mean to be flirting, but I thought I was. There was something about his masculine energy that pulled me in; the lazy warmth of his eyes and mischievous smile made my knees a bit weak. I watched him engage with a beautiful woman, pouring her some wine, and knew I was one of many among his admirers.

I ate my meal, drank my wine, and talked with everyone. I noticed my purse shaking a few times, so I checked my phone and found a stream of anxious texts from one of my clients.

Aurora, where r u? I need to talk. Now.

Please call me back. I need to make a decision and can't do this alone.

It's an emergency! I've emailed and left messages and can't find you!

My stomach flipped and I got up from the stool. "Be right back. It's a work call," I said, stepping outside. I walked past the patio to a small grove of trees that lent some privacy. I took a deep breath and settled myself before calling her back.

"Desi, are you okay? It's Aurora."

The whimper on the other line was full of distress. I'd had a complicated journey with Desi for the past two years but had been happy with her recent results. She was high-maintenance and high drama and had very high standards. Most of her issues revolved around her insistence on perfection, from her physical looks and weight to her need to stand out in her career as an art curator. I never minded working with her, because she embraced my advice and any actionable direction. But in the past few months, I'd relied on texts and emails rather than face-to-face dialogue. I couldn't seem to get super excited over her gain of three pounds or worry she wouldn't fit into her new Gucci dress.

So I had been doing the exact thing I counseled my clients not to do.

Avoidance.

"I've been desperate to reach you. Thank God you're finally getting back to me. Where have you been?"

I winced at her accusation. "I'm so sorry—I'm in Sicily on family business. Reception has been difficult, so I must've missed your calls," I lied smoothly.

"I have a terrible problem that I need help navigating. I told you about my new boss, right? He's straight from Switzerland and thinks he knows what art sells in New York. It's ridiculous, but the gallery won't listen to me."

"Yes, I remember. What happened?"

Her voice got choked. "It was terrible. I don't even know how to say it!"

A chill skated down my spine. "Desi, is he harassing you? Did he hurt you or threaten you?" I swore I'd do anything to help her in such an overwhelming situation, my mind already jumping through various responses.

"No, not that. But, Aurora, I spent hours setting up the new display for our art show, and he marched in and changed the whole thing! I was in shock. True shock. And when I began to correct him, he said I needed to trust him to try it his way.

Honestly, I think he was humoring me! As if I were some type of minor assistant rather than the assistant director. I'm so upset, I can't even breathe. I need to sit down."

She panted into the phone. It took me a few moments to switch perspective and realize it was about the placing of paintings. I'm sure it was hurtful, though, to be questioned in her role. Many women had confidence issues, and a man demanding a task be done his way could cause real challenges. "I'm so sorry you're going through this," I offered. Accepting each client's problem was key in establishing connection and trust. "Do you usually set up the shows? Is he trying to take over your responsibilities?"

"Well, no, it's not technically my job. But our last director gave me free rein, and now this man suddenly wants to take it back. And then something worse happened, Aurora. I have to admit it to you. I got upset and I couldn't reach you and I—well, I—"

"You can tell me anything," I encouraged her, pacing back and forth.

"I ate two Oreos. Not just one. I had two, and even after I washed my hands and brushed my teeth, I still tasted the chocolate. It was awful. I opened up a portal and I need you to help me close it."

I blinked. Had I once believed this was important? I vaguely remembered having a passionate in-depth conversation about her downfall at Dairy Queen when the new Blizzards came in and she'd eaten a mini. We worked out an action plan that began with forgiving herself, then moved to slowly increasing her workout by five minutes and upping her magnesium for the sugar cravings.

Now? Part of me wanted to tell her to just enjoy the damn Oreos and start again tomorrow. Because eating that bread at my grandparents' house?

It had made me happy.

"Aurora? What should I do?"

I pulled out my tried-and-true lecture cornerstones and inflected passion into my voice. "Desi, one failure does not make a life. Success relies on multiple small steps that lead to finishing a goal. When did you eat the cookies?"

"Yesterday," Desi said miserably. "After seven p.m.!"

"First, you're going to increase your water intake today and flush out the remaining toxins. Then you're going to forgive yourself. Would you yell at and punish a friend who'd had a bad day and indulged?"

"No. Never."

"Then you will not do that to yourself. Are the Oreos all gone?"

She hesitated. "No."

"You're going to take the rest of the bag and throw it in the garbage. Then you will take the garbage bag out and put it in the trash can so it's no longer in the house."

"Yes. Yes!"

"When you go back into work, you are going to have a calm, rational dialogue with your new boss. You will smile and explain to him that you had gotten used to being responsible for the setup and would still like to keep the job. You will thank him for giving you new ideas that you will implement. If he disagrees and still wants to do it, you should remain open to his viewpoint and take pictures of the setup. After the event, it will be easier to track flow and see if it was a success. A winner allows herself to admit others may do it better. There's nothing wrong with that—it's how we learn and become the best."

"Yes! I can do that. I'll wear my pin-striped Vera Wang suit in Barbie pink for power!"

"Excellent." I wrapped up my motivational speech, whipping up her confidence and taking her through a visualization. Finally, I hung up, knowing I had done my job and done it well.

I tapped into that place of satisfaction and joy at knowing I was doing exactly what I was born to do.

And still I felt . . . nothing.

I pressed my hand to my stomach and wondered why helping her had left me empty. As if I were putting on a show and not really connecting with Desi or her problems. Talking with Dr. Sariah was reminding me I wasn't a therapist and that my obsession with action might not be what all my clients needed after all.

Maybe my entire career was fake.

I lowered my head and fought for breath as the realization crashed down around me.

"Aurora."

The low, sexy voice pierced my panic, and I looked up to see Quint in front of me. He slowly reached out to gently grip my upper arms as I swayed on my feet. My skin tingled and I had a sudden craving to step into his arms, but he dropped both hands to his sides as soon as I steadied.

"Are you okay?"

I gave a quick nod. How embarrassing. I wondered how much he'd seen. I must've looked ridiculous having a panic attack over a simple conversation about Oreos and painting placements. I forced a smile. "Yes, sorry. It was just a client. I'll get back inside."

"No need. Everything is good. I'm on a break—want to sit with me for a bit?"

"Oh, um, sure."

I followed him to a quiet bench away from the busy tables and sat beside him. The shadows closed around us, and after a few moments of comfortable silence, I began to relax. He gave off a calm energy, and weirdly, I didn't feel the need to reach for conversation.

"How are you doing with everything?"

I tilted my head, wondering about his question. "Good."

He turned. A smile tugged at his full lips. I tried not to focus on his mouth and to ignore my heated cheeks. Lord, I felt like a hormone-ridden teenager. "I do not think I would be good. It must be very difficult to face so much change in a short period. Losing your mom. Finding relatives you never knew about. Traveling to Sicily to learn the truth. It is okay if you are struggling."

I wondered about the last time I was honest about feeling overwhelmed. With Jason, I'd tried explaining, but he was disappointed in my lack of strength. The public wanted to use my story to twist their own narrative of me as a popular figure, not caring about me as a person. And with Dr. Sariah, I was paying her so I could vent. Crying with my family had helped me release some of my loneliness from losing Mom, but I hadn't confessed my fear regarding my career path. How everything seemed to be slipping away and I wasn't sure how to get back to the person I once was.

Or if that was even possible.

I managed to sound light and teasing. "Are you offering to keep my secrets safe?"

He grinned. Warmth threaded his voice. "I'm offering to be a friend. *Sì.* I will keep your secrets."

A shiver crept down my spine at the intimacy. A sudden impulse to share with a stranger in the shadows overcame me. "I'm having a hard time with my job. Everything was going so well, and then I lost my mom, and suddenly, I was unable to do anything. I figured with some time, I'd be back to myself, but it's already been six months and I'm still a wreck."

"Six months is not a long time," Quint said. "Not when you're mourning a parent."

"I know." Frustration curled in my belly. "But work used to be my safe place. I figured I'd lose myself there while I heal, but it's been the opposite."

"You are a life coach? Your job is to help people do certain things?"

"Yes. They state a goal they want to attain, and I help them get there. I also run a podcast, and I had a mini breakdown during one of the tapings. Now I've lost guests who were scheduled and sponsors, and I had to delay new episodes."

"Catena said you are also writing a book?"

"Yes, but I can't seem to write. The publisher delayed its publication, so I don't even know when it will be released. I haven't been able to finish it. I'm failing at everything I used to be good at."

I waited for his good-intentioned advice, or a soothing gesture to show he was sympathetic. Poor guy was probably dying to run back inside and escape the ridiculous American who had her life tied up in knots. Strangers didn't go around dumping their messes on one another. I figured whatever he told me, I'd accept with a grateful thank-you and go back inside to forget the whole encounter.

"Sometimes, failing is good."

I blinked. "No, it's not. I mean, sure, you need to fail while you're learning, but I've invested plenty of time and effort specifically so I wouldn't fail. I have no excuse. Don't you think I should be pushing forward rather than giving up?"

Quint didn't seem bothered by my rant, but he also didn't brush it off. "I think there are different types of failures. Some can be used as tools to ask better questions. Go deeper. If we never stop to question ourselves or our happiness, how will we ever know we lost our way?"

I bit my lip and considered his comments. "Are you saying this may have happened because I'm not supposed to be a life coach anymore?"

"No. Not if you love being a coach. Or being big on social media. Or writing a book. Maybe this grief was a gift rather than a punishment. It has forced you to see all the things you have kept hidden. It has made you pause so you can choose again."

Oh, this was a lot. I stared at the man calmly giving a speech that rivaled a TED talk. Even Dr. Sariah had never challenged me on this. I thought about my mother questioning how I used my time, afraid I had lost my way. I thought about Jason and me constantly racing toward our next goal without stopping along the way to breathe. All the pressure throbbed in my head and my body.

A confession ripped me apart. "I don't believe in my ability to help people anymore. I used to think I had all the answers, but I realize I don't. Honestly, I have no idea what I'm doing lately. But what's worse? I'm questioning whether everything I worked so hard for is no longer what I want, and it scares the hell out of me."

The weight on my chest eased and my lungs opened to allow in more air. Saying the words aloud was terrifying but also freeing.

Quint slowly nodded, and his hand reached out to snag mine. I caught my breath at the shock of his skin, at the rough weight of his fingers entangled with mine, the strength of his grip. It wasn't a sexual gesture but one of support and security. "Do you feel you should always have the answers?" he asked.

I bit my lip. "Usually? Yes. I need to know the right steps so I can help my clients. But here I am, unable to advise anyone. Quint, I haven't written a word of this book I swore I'd finish by end of summer. I've lost interest in motivational videos and my podcast. Everything I worked for and believed in is slipping away. What's going to happen to me? To my business?"

His gaze met and held mine. His eyes burned with an amber light that made me want to linger and look deeper. To know his secrets and what made this man who he was. Quiet confidence vibrated in his tone when he spoke. "Sometimes, events change us. Losing your mother forced you to look at things in your life differently, and you are making new choices about what feels right. There is nothing wrong with this, *cara*. You are growing."

I sifted through his answer and realized it was the first time I'd heard my breakdown termed in a good way. Dr. Sariah had mentioned the same concept, but I'd been too busy berating myself to listen. Jason had only exacerbated it, though blaming him for trying to help wasn't fair.

"How do you know?"

His sigh disappeared into the night and wafted away. "Because I have lived this. I lost my mother, too."

I sucked in my breath and automatically leaned toward him. "I'm so sorry. I didn't know."

"She was sick for a while, but it did not make things easier. My father worked in the fields and we were never close. He was a hard man, but I know he loved us." Quint paused as if searching for the rest of the story and how to explain. "My sister, Carmella, was young. One of my aunts would come and take care of us, but Carmella had trouble. She became difficult. Acted out."

I was a full-blown adult and had fallen apart. I couldn't imagine dealing with such grief at a delicate age. "It must've been extremely difficult."

"*Sì*. I decided I would be the one to care for her. I was in university when this happened, so I came home and stayed to help. All of my plans were gone. I was going to study business and travel. Maybe move to the US or somewhere new." His eyes flickered with the memories. "Instead, I gave it up and raised Carmella. Worked in the local restaurant and learned a new trade. I'd always liked to cook, so I did more of that. Eventually, I was able to join Catena and Theo and have something of my own."

I thought of him alone with his sister. Abandoning his own dreams for his family and an unknown future. "Carmella is lucky to have you."

A ghost of a smile touched his lips. "I am lucky I have her. I think you are too hard on yourself, Aurora Rosa York. You have not allowed time for the empty spaces to be filled again. This takes time and patience."

"I'm stubborn."

He chuckled. "That is good. It means you are a fighter."

"So I should just stop worrying and let the universe guide me? Trust in the unknown and all that good stuff?" I frowned. "I don't like that at all. I work better with being the master of my own fate."

"Maybe you are forcing yourself to be who you were, not who you are now."

His thumb pressed into my palm. I studied his face: the rough lines of his features, the fierce dark brows, the sexy scruff of his beard hugging sensual lips. My entire body surged with heat and a deep understanding of what this man had gone through. How he'd chosen to live after tragedy. How he'd sacrificed to take care of his sister and was proud of it.

"Quint?"

"Yes?"

"I feel better."

His smile made breath gush into my body in one big rush, making my head spin. "I am glad." Quint released my hand and I mourned the loss. "You have family and friends who care about you."

"Are you my friend?"

I opened my mouth to take it back and say I was joking, but he nodded, his gaze serious and intent. "*Sì.* I am your friend and am here if you need me. *Capisci?*"

"*Capisco.*"

We walked back into the pub. Back to the laughter and light and revelry. But for a long time, I replayed our conversation in the shadows and wondered why his offer of friendship seemed like the best gift I'd been given in a long time.

THIRTEEN

SCIACCA WAS AN experience for all the senses. The smells, sights, tastes, touches, and sounds rose in perfect symmetry, creating an opera of richness that delighted me from all angles. Lucca gave a different aura—one of grit, simplicity, and a depth of generational understanding I'd never experienced. As we walked the narrow streets heading toward church, my cousins chattering beside me, residential neighborhoods intermingled with shops that were less touristy and more familial. Children ran and played without care, people lounged on balconies and called down to one another, and ancient buildings in faded Tuscan colors pressed tight against one another in long rows.

The place my mother grew up was steeped in tradition.

The Holy Mary Immaculate was the patron saint of the town, and people flocked to celebrate her with Sunday Mass. The outside of the Chiesa Maria Santissima Immacolata was simple—a battered tall stone structure outfitted with a bell tower and clock. As we filed in, I noticed the inside was quite beautiful, with curved, graceful marble arches soaring high above the altar. Religious sculptures overlooked the congregation, surrounded by fresh roses. As I sat on the hard wooden pew next to my grandmother and cousin, I thought about my mother attending weekly, head bowed in prayer, while fire burned bright in her heart for a man she loved and would leave everything for.

I'd never thought of my dad as a passionate man. I'd grown up watching their intimacy with the usual roll of my eyes or ick factor, but it wasn't as if they were publicly demonstrative or kissed all the time. Still, I always sensed a deep connection, as if they only had to look at each other to communicate. I'd imagined it came with all successful marriages, but now I wasn't as sure. I thought it was a gift I'd overlooked because they belonged to me. Here, sitting in her childhood church, I had a new respect for my mother's bravery, following a relative stranger across the ocean to build a life away from everything she knew.

I saw my cousins and aunts and uncles and understood the draw of the life they chose. One of respect, duty, work, and family. And faith. But my mother had all of that; she'd just chosen to share those qualities and traits with my father.

I listened to the priest say the Mass in Italian and studied my family surrounding me. I wished I could have asked my mother if she had ever regretted her actions and wished she'd stayed. The question burned and hurt, because her saying yes would have meant I wasn't born and my father hadn't been chosen. Either path caused pain. I sat with the uncomfortable emotion while Communion was bestowed under the Virgin Mother's peaceful gaze, and the faint scent of incense and roses drifted in the air.

My grandfather greeted me with polite aloofness, and I noticed my grandmother wringing her hands, glancing back and forth between us. I could do nothing to soothe her worry. I had no intention of knowing him well—he was just part of the bigger family I did want to concentrate on. Being around my aunts and grandmother for the second time was less awkward, and my cousins and I bantered with ease now, from the nights spent at the pub.

Once Mass ended, I met and spoke with the priest after my grandmother introduced us. He was kind as he asked questions with a tentativeness that warned of poking old wounds, but I learned he remembered my mother, and he offered a prayer service since she had been buried in New York. My aunt and grandmother cried, and I blinked my own tears away. The usual loneliness eased with their company and shared grief. It meant everything to have other people mourning her loss with me.

"We will eat at the pizzeria," Aunt Philomena said, tucking my arm in the crook of hers. "Having you at Mass today was special. You must come every Sunday with us."

Catena practically skipped along, emanating bubbly energy. "Babba, did Aunt Serafina behave at church like I do, or did she throw tantrums like Theo?"

Theo groaned and threw something at her that looked like a balled-up napkin. Catena twisted around and stuck out her tongue.

Aunt Philomena gave them both smart swats and berated them in Italian, though they were laughing.

My grandfather was quiet, and when I snuck a glance at him, he stared at me, fierce brows lowered in a frown. Tired of being afraid of him, I glared back. His voice was rough like gravel when he finally answered. "Sera did not disobey us. She would sit and say her rosary while Philomena and Agosto made faces behind my back."

Aunt Philomena gasped. "How did you know? You always had your eyes closed!"

My grandmother gave a snort. "Parents see all. Remember that, *mia nipote*."

My stomach lurched. I remembered my mother holding rosary beads, her lips moving as she prayed on the weeks she dragged me to church. Had she prayed for forgiveness? Offered prayers for the family she left? I wished I'd known what was in her heart. I wished she'd trusted me enough to share.

Aunt Philomena must have seen my distress, because she clucked her tongue and squeezed me tight. "Your *mamma* was the oldest, Aurora. She treated me and Agosto like her own children. She was in charge and we looked up to her."

I heard my uncle behind us; he laughed, but there was a tinge of sadness. "*Sì*. She never got in trouble like Philomena and I did."

"But I thought she ran wild," I said, trying to put the two images of her together. "I got the impression she didn't behave."

My grandmother spoke up. "It was when she turned sixteen she began to rebel. Before, Sera always did what she was told. But she was a dreamer—always had her head in the clouds. Remember, Gio?"

He gave a short nod, his attention on the road ahead. Agosto sped up and fell in step with him. They were both dressed in nice dress pants, loafers, and white short-sleeve button-down shirts. Each wore a cap, which looked stifling in the sun, but they didn't seem bothered. For a brief moment, I wished I could be the one next to my grandfather, listening to stories about my mom. I'd always dreamed of having a grandpa. He was right in front of me, but the awkward tension between us was obvious to everyone.

"Did you bring pictures?" my grandmother asked softly. Her eyes squinted behind her glasses, and we automatically shortened our steps so she could keep up. "I would very much like to see them."

"Yes, they're in my bag." I'd never shown them the photo album Friday night, so I'd scooped up a pile at the house and put them in my purse for later.

Her voice broke. "Good. I need to see her face."

I patted her shoulder and we all walked the rest of the way in silence.

When we arrived, I was overcome by the liveliness in such a small restaurant. It was packed with family members I'd met, along with some friends who were obviously curious to meet me. Tables had been pushed together, and the kitchen overflowed with sounds of dishes clattering and people yelling at one another. Scents of garlic and bread filled the air. The humidity was awful, drenching me in sweat that the fans couldn't break, but no one seemed bothered, so I refused to complain. I quickly twisted my hair up with a clip to get the strands off my neck.

Bottles of Coke came out for the children, along with red

wine and limoncello for the adults. Once again, I was unprepared. I'd expected a huge meal at my grandmother's, but here?

I literally thought I'd have a slice of pizza.

Eyes wide, I couldn't help but stare at the extensive line of pizzas that were being prepared, trying to memorize the names of the people working behind the counter as they introduced themselves. Teresa and Emilio immediately fell into work mode, donning aprons, and motioned me over.

"This is *tabisca saccense*," Teresa explained as Emilio served up an oval piece of doughy bread soaked in red sauce, cheese that didn't look like the classic mozzarella, and a sprinkling of fresh veggies. "It is our pizza here!"

I forced a smile, looking at the delicious, rather large slice that vaguely resembled a New York Sicilian but tweaked. Jason's face flashed in my mind, and I had the impulse to giggle out loud. This was his hell on earth—unlimited carbs and cheese and sugar and alcohol available in every delightful form, pushed by well-meaning Italian relatives.

My cousins watched while I took a bite.

The sharp cheese and soft dough melted in my mouth. The crispness of the veggies and the salty sardines rounded out the flavor and texture to perfection. "Is this mozzarella?" I asked.

Teresa shook her head. "It's caciocavallo. Good, no?"

"Superb."

My cousin beamed. I quickly googled the term and found it was raw cow's milk that was pretty expensive. I guess I was a new fan. I'd become a pickier eater as Jason's stringent restrictions morphed into mine, but he wasn't to blame. Jason had good intentions, but I'd made my own choices. Maybe it was time to reconnect with my adventurous side, starting in the kitchen.

From there, it went downhill in a repeat performance. Baked pasta dishes were brought out piping hot, bubbling cheese with cavatappi, peas, and some smoked meat. Various pizzas followed in a dizzying array, taken from the brick oven and thrust on the scarred wooden tables, servers bobbing and weaving amid the children screeching with happiness and playing tag.

I had just managed to escape the endless plates by running to the restroom, but when I returned, my grandmother was waiting. "Aurora! Try the *scacciata*. We make it special here and Emilio has made the recipe *perfetta*." She smiled and kissed her fingertips, then pushed another plate into my hand.

"Um, I'm so full, though. Maybe later?"

Her face fell. Disappointment seeped from her body language, and she slowly dropped her chin like I'd announced a fatal tragedy. My gaze fell over her shoulder to where my grandfather sat, surrounded by my uncles, watching the scene with full disapproval.

Dammit. I did not like him. But I did love my grandmother even after such a short time, so I took the plate and bit into the stuffed bread. I groaned with approval and nodded. "Delicious!"

My grandmother came back to life. "*Sì!* It is made for you. For America. We put hot dogs in it!"

I stopped chewing and stared. "Hot dogs?"

My cousin Emilio overheard and came over. "It is a surprise! We looked up the most popular American food, which is hot dogs, so we made this special *scacciata* for you. You like?"

I wanted to yell *basta*. My safe word. But Quint had warned me to use it only in extreme circumstances, and the stuffed bread was tasty. Maybe hot dogs in Sicily were like sausage instead? Better not to wonder where it came from and just enjoy it.

I stuck my thumb up, which they seemed to understand, and everyone's attention diverted to their own plates.

By the time a few hours had passed, the afternoon was gone. Eating really was an entire social event that took up most of the day. I loved the intimacy around cooking and food my family cultivated. So much more than ordering an organic vegan meal like it was a test to ace rather than an experience to savor.

I'd been in Sicily for less than a week and I was already looking at things differently. I tucked the information into the back of my mind to ponder later.

Suddenly, firm weathered fingers clasped around mine. I looked down at my grandmother. "Come with me, *nipote.* We shall talk."

Surprised, I followed her outside and we walked a bit until we came to a bench. It was set away from the main square, so we could overlook the groups of old men sitting together smoking cigars, and children playing ball. Couples strolled together eating gelato or small puff pastries. Women sat on their balconies sipping from tiny cups behind blooming flowers, staring down at the square as if it were their television episode of the early evening. I played with the chain of my necklace, thinking of my mom being brought to this same bench, so many years ago. My fingers smoothed over the metal disc as I untucked it from my shirt.

"What are you wearing?"

I turned at the sharpness of Nonna's voice. "Oh, it's a medal. It was Mom's. She used to wear it all the time." I stretched out the chain so she could see it, and her withered fingers touched the silver gently, eyes narrowed behind her glasses. She whispered something I couldn't quite make out. "I gave her this necklace."

I blinked, staring in shock. "What?"

Her face was ravaged in a combination of pain and pride. "St. Lucille. She is the patron saint of Sicily. Protector of the blind, gifting her sight so we are able to truly see. Gifting us the bright light of knowledge, truth, and the soul."

My entire body shut down, then ramped up again. I heard my mother's voice, full of faith, telling me the medal was her guiding light. "She wore it every day, Nonna. Never took it off. She told me it was her white light and guidance."

Her fingers shook, so I grabbed her hand and we held on to each other as the truth exploded between us. "She always carried me with her," Nonna said. A strange peace glowed from her eyes, as if she'd gotten an answer to a long-held question. "She never forgot about us. And now St. Lucy will guide you."

The lump in my throat made me unable to talk for a while. We sat on the bench, clasping hands, until we both felt stronger.

"You brought pictures?" she eventually asked.

I nodded.

"Can I see them?"

I reached into my purse and lovingly ran my fingers over the sharp corners, staring at the familiar images of my lost parents. A smile curved my lips as the precious memories of our time together pressed into my brain. "This is when I was born," I whispered, handing her the first picture. Mom was in the hospital, obviously exhausted but beaming. My tiny body was wrapped in a blanket and she held me close. The camera caught my dark curls, open mouth, and pissed-off expression.

Nonna rambled in Italian, but I caught my mother's name as she studied the photo. Her eyes grew wet. Slowly, I handed her each one as I set the stage. Our first vacation to the beach. My parents' anniversary. My fifth birthday party. Graduation. Mom in the kitchen on Thanksgiving, laughing as she held a giant turkey. Finally, I placed one of my favorites in her hands.

I heard her sharp intake of breath. She brought it up to her face and squinted, studying it as if she wanted to memorize the image. It was Mom and Dad, locked in each other's arms. The light from the living room lamp played over their figures to cast them in a golden glow. Mom tipped her chin up, laughing at something my dad said. His arms snagged around her waist and he stared into her eyes as if she were the sun and the moon, as if she were his everything.

"I was asleep and I'd gotten up to get some water. I found them in the living room, playing some old vinyl records, dancing. I know it was a private moment, but I wanted to capture it. There was this sort of magic when I saw them together. I got my phone and snapped it. They never even noticed."

This was the love I wished for one day in my secret heart. It was also the love I didn't think I could find, so instead, I sought out the type I could control. Respect. Trust. Honesty. Similar interests and goals and beliefs. I settled on a partnership rather than a passionate love to fill my soul.

Why?

After Dad died, I watched Mom fall apart. The pain of loving so deeply and losing haunted me. Now I'd lost her, and I was experiencing the same agony all over again. When was it enough? Wasn't it easier to be practical?

Hearing that she'd given up everything to run away with

my father made the last missing piece slide into place. No wonder they had such a connection—Dad had known the truth. Mom didn't just love someone with words. She'd sacrificed it all. For him. And he'd cherished that decision every day of their marriage.

The picture was now my proof of what had been true. Of why Mom left a loving family. I'd been the witness to an epic love story, played out in the quiet day-to-day of marriage and duty and parenting with no other audience.

Wasn't that type of love the most romantic thing of all?

Nonna tugged a handkerchief from her dress pocket, dabbing away the tears. Her hands shook as she gave the photographs back to me.

"I understand now. Thank you, *nipote*. You have helped me see now."

My voice came out hoarse. "Did you have any idea? That she could love him like that? That if you challenged her, you'd lose her forever?"

Slowly, she shook her head. "No. I thought she was young. Infatuation with a handsome foreigner that would quickly pass." Pain settled deeply in the wrinkles of her face. "If we had known, things might have been different."

"Did he—did my grandfather make the decision? Was he the one to decide to give her an ultimatum? To push her away like that?"

Her sigh drifted and disappeared in the hot wind. "Like me, he did not know how deep these feelings were. How could we? But when Sera disappeared, your *babba* was never the same. Something shut down his heart forever, and it has never returned. Your mother took that piece with her."

I hardened myself against her soft words, sensing my grandfather had not been that tender. Nonna caught my stubborn expression and cupped my cheek. "My Aurora, *la mia dolce nipote*. You do not know your *babba*, but you must. Things are not always so easy as you like to make them. We all made mistakes. You are our second chance to make things right. You must speak with him."

I shook my head hard. "He doesn't like me."

"He loves you. You are his *nipote*."

"No. I am a reminder of his mistake. He will always resent me." Nonna tilted her head as if trying to understand my words. "He will always be mad at me. Because of Mom."

She let out a rapid stream of Italian. "No, no, no. You must get to know each other. It is important for both of you."

I didn't want to be rude, but I was going to leave soon and I had no intention of wasting precious time trying to get him to accept me into the family. I'd found what I needed—my cousins and aunts and uncles. My *nonna*. I needed nothing more.

She groaned and rocked back and forth in distress. "Both so stubborn! Like your *mamma*. I beg you to stay, Aurora. Stay longer and be with us. There should be no more regrets."

I forced a smile and zipped up my purse. She was old, and I refused to get her upset. "I will think about it," I lied, knowing I couldn't extend my vacation. I had a life and responsibilities and a fledgling career to resuscitate.

"*Bene, bene!* You will think on this and we will fix things. Let us go now."

We walked slowly back to the pizzeria. Everyone drank espresso, wine, or limoncello. Warm ricotta fritters dusted with cinnamon sugar were passed around for dessert. They laughed and chattered as if there were nothing left to do with the day but exist in the moment.

La dolce vita.

It was a term I'd use to mock things before. Today, surrounded by the family that had welcomed me in, my mother dancing in my memory, stamped forever on the photograph I'd shown Nonna, I was beginning to think differently.

FOURTEEN

I COULDN'T STOP thinking about my grandmother's plea.

I talked with Dr. Sariah about it, and instead of agreeing that extending my time here was a ridiculous idea, she urged me to consider the option. Dozens of excuses immediately flew from my lips, until I became my own defense lawyer. She only listened and gently reminded me I got to choose my path. I was beginning to realize all my decisions began with responsibility, duty, or logic. Sicily kept showing me there was another way, but I was leaving soon. There was no time to really listen.

My vacation was almost over.

I hadn't talked to Jason and there were no missed messages. I kept telling myself he was busy and that the old me would have understood, but things felt off. I hated the doubts that assailed me. It was easier to blame the distance than probe the lack of emotional connection I was feeling with a man who was supposed to love me.

I tried to ignore my brain spiral and focused on work for a

few hours. I needed to check on Desi and some other clients. My podcast producer was frantic about the schedule and needed approvals on filler guests to make up for the big ones who'd canceled. I hadn't posted anything motivational other than a few of my Sicily pics, but at least they got good engagement. Everyone loved a travel post, so I'd allowed myself some fun, doing a few Reels and loading a YouTube of the pizza last night, showing off the amazing food and loud, laughing family members.

Holding back a sigh, I made the necessary phone calls and sent the emails on my to-do list. I tried drafting a post regarding Desi's Oreo incident and how to forgive yourself and move on when it came to obstacles, but I ended up deleting it. The words rang false, like I was patronizing rather than honestly engaged.

I kept remembering Quint's words.

Maybe you are forcing yourself to be who you were, not who you are now.

There was no joy left in my work. No motivation or enthusiasm. How could I show up to be my best authentic self when it had become a lie?

I stared lackadaisically at my computer, then out the window. Maybe it was best to push off all this work until I got home. I didn't have much time left here. I needed to use it to heal and get a true restart. Expecting to do all this work in Sicily didn't make sense. I knew Jason would be disappointed, but the thought of tackling any more of the tasks on my list was depressing, not motivating.

Screw it. I was going rogue. I wouldn't work. I'd take the next few days completely off and worry about the end result later.

Immediately, lightness danced through my body. I snapped the screen closed and then asked a question I hadn't in years.

What did I *want* to do right now?

Dr. Sariah had told me to listen to my intuition. The same voice that had counseled me to go to Sicily.

I dialed in to the silence, trying to ignore my brain, which was yelling at me to stop being weak and get back to accomplishing things that mattered. Feeling silly, I waited for an answer from another part, a part that had been shoved deep down and gagged so it wouldn't get in the way of my path to success. The very part I tried to counsel my clients to ignore and silence in order to spur them to action. I'd heard it for the first time in Dr. Sariah's office, telling me I needed to go to Sicily. Was it still around and available? Or had I imagined the mystical voice to give me a damn good excuse to run away from my life?

Go for a walk.

Startled, I looked around, but there was only empty space. Holy crap, it was working! It—she—spoke, and now I needed to . . . well, I needed to do something before I went out. I planned to meet Catena later to do some touring, and I needed to make a list of groceries that gave me some lighter, healthier options since I'd gone carb crazy yesterday. And—

It took a few moments for the realization to hit, and then I was shaking my head, laughing at myself.

I needed to do nothing right now except listen. I needed to go take a walk.

I wished the voice had told me where to go, but at this point, I'd take what I could get.

Grabbing my cross-body purse, water, and sunglasses, I left all my work behind and headed outside.

The sun hit like an explosion, scattering light around me. I gave a satisfied sigh, walking toward the marina. I noticed some fishermen selling their fresh catches, surrounded by small groups of people who seemed to be shouting and waving their hands with anger, but now I knew it was all normal. I knew the market took place early in the morning but noticed there were a few times throughout the day when fishermen would sail in with a fresh catch and offer it up on the spot. I must've gotten lucky and they'd just returned from a haul.

Hanging back, I watched the give-and-take of products and obvious haggling in Italian. An array of seafood was packed in ice, and it reminded me a bit of an auction. My nose tickled with the scent of fish and brine. It seemed the fishermen were evenly divided, as if they each had a group of regular customers. I wondered why people wouldn't take advantage and try to pit the fishermen against one another to get the best competitive price. Maybe Italians were more polite? Or loyal? It was a question I'd ask Catena. She'd mentioned taking me to the market for one of her purchasing trips. I'd remind her.

My legs stretched into longer strides as I walked past the boats. It was early enough that the shops were all open, so I popped in and out, lingering over the gorgeous hand-painted tiles and linens of Sicilian lemons and blood oranges. I bought half a dozen towels, a brightly colored majolica of the Sciacca landscape, and an apron for Jason.

I got lost within the narrow zigzagging streets, climbing the levels of the town now that I knew a bit of the layout. I snapped pictures at leisure. Then I bought a lemon ice and ate it while I looked out at the sea, my mind settling into a peaceful quiet. I thought about my mom and my grandfather. I thought about my cousin's wedding and how she'd begged me to extend my trip in order to attend. I thought about how Quint's touch made me shiver and how happy I was hanging out at the pub, being welcomed by strangers as family.

Soon I took out my phone and began typing random thoughts, wanting to capture them in words for later. The tart stickiness of the ice lingered on my tongue. Time spun away as I wrote freely, not worried about deadlines or a publisher's expectations or trying to grow my following. I wrote for me, untangling the knotted spool in my head, making sense of it on the page.

Catena called and I had to shake myself out of a happy fog. "*Ciao.*"

"*Buongiorno!* Aurora, *mi dispiace*, I cannot pick you up later. I have to meet with distributors and do a few things for the pub. Theo is also working, but do not worry, Quint will take you anywhere you want."

"Oh, no, Catena, I don't want to impose."

"What is impose?"

"I mean, it's okay, Quint doesn't need to come. I'm fine on my own—you need to take care of your business and I don't want to bother him."

Her laugh was full of her usual robustness. "Do not be silly! Quint cannot wait to take you out exploring! He has been excited about spending his day off showing you special places. *Va bene?*"

I bit my lip, torn. It was sweet of Quint, but I was a bit wary. I hadn't expected to react so strongly to another man, a man who wasn't Jason. It threw me off. But I was sure it was one-sided. He probably had a ton of women he dated and saw me only as a friend. Since our last conversation, I'd felt a bond with him. As if he understood my confusion and accepted me exactly as I was.

"*Sì, grazie.*"

"He will get you at three p.m."

We hung up. I looked down at my grubby shorts and sticky hands. My T-shirt clung to my skin, damp with sweat. My hair felt two times its normal size with frizz, and I wore no makeup.

I got my ass back to my rental as fast as I could. Whether or not we were just friends had nothing to do with it. I was not about to allow a handsome Italian man to see me like this.

I had my pride.

By the time he picked me up, I'd changed into a casual summer dress that floated above the knee. It had a happy floral pattern with bright red roses, and I matched it with cute red flats that were actually comfortable. I'd straightened my wild curls so now the tamed strands fell sleekly against my cheeks.

His eyes widened with appreciation when he greeted me. Pleasure rushed through my veins, along with a heady sense of excitement. Nothing would happen between us, but I intended to enjoy my time with Quint, along with my purely feminine reaction to his compliments.

"You look beautiful," he said, opening the car door.

"Thank you." I regarded him seriously. "Quint, I hope you didn't cancel important plans to drive me around. I could have done this myself."

His gaze reflected puzzlement. "What else would I have to do on my day off? It is an honor to be your company today."

I smiled and surrendered. "*Grazie.*" I slid into the seat and he shut the door. I watched him climb into the black economy car, which resembled a Matchbox toy. "What are the plans?"

"I will be your personal tour guide and show you our main sights. But I have a few surprises set up. Is that okay?"

"I love surprises."

"Good. We will do much walking since there are many roads we cannot drive on in Sciacca."

I gave a snort. "Walking doesn't scare me."

Quint laughed. I watched his tapered fingers confidently grip the wheel as he maneuvered down the clogged, narrow street. He was dressed in khaki shorts and a kelly green T-shirt that hugged his chest and shoulders. His hair looked freshly washed, spilling over his forehead. The car smelled like him—soap, and musk, and cinnamon. The color of his shirt brought out the green flecks in his eyes. "What does scare you?" he teased.

I shrugged. "Not sure. You?"

"I do not like bugs."

I pressed my lips together. "All bugs or any specific ones?"

"Flying bugs are okay. Crawling ones are not."

"What if you saw a spider? Would you kill it?"

"Yes, but I would not like it."

I liked the idea of this sexy, confident man afraid of creepy-crawlies. It evened things out for me. "I don't like red balloons," I suddenly admitted.

His brow rose. "Why?"

"I saw the horror movie *It*, and this killer clown haunts kids in this small town. They know he's coming when they see a red balloon floating by. It's horrible and now I can't even look at one without screaming."

"That sounds scary."

"It is." He didn't mock me or call me silly. "Anything else besides bugs?"

"Not having enough money."

Surprise shook through me that he'd share something so personal. I nodded, my voice soft. "I don't blame you. It must've been hard trying to take care of Carmella when you were so young."

He shot me a grateful look, then refocused on the road. "Now that I have the pub and savings, I'm not as scared. I'd like to invest in another restaurant and expand. When I'm ready."

"Sounds like a great plan. Now that your sister is more independent, do you think of moving somewhere else?" I asked curiously.

"No. This is my home and I am happy. I'd love to travel more—go on food tours and visit some big cities." He gave me another smile that made his eyes squint and my heart speed up. "I know it's not as exciting as you. I'm sure you've seen a lot of places with your job."

"I actually haven't traveled much. I've been focused these past years on building my career and have had no time."

"Then today is even more special because it's rare."

I loved how he refused to judge me, no matter what my responses were. It made me feel . . . safe.

We drove out of town, away from clogged streets and up into the hills. "We will take a walk around Castello Incantato, then I will show you the thermal baths."

"It's called the Enchanted Castle, right?" I asked. I'd read about it in the tourist guidebook as one of the main sights.

"*Sì.* It is an outdoor art world created by Filippo Bentivegna. He is famous in Sicily. Many called him a madman."

We paid for the tickets and joined another group of tourists who were exploring the gardens. I was overwhelmed by the sheer number of sculptures carved in stone amid walking paths of lush greenery. Olive and almond trees created a natural oasis. It was like exploring a giant maze with treasures hidden behind every twist and curve. There seemed to be endless heads in various shapes and sizes, eyes staring back from the hard stone in an effort to communicate with each visitor. The result was both beautiful and eerie.

"There are a lot of heads here," I said.

Quint grinned. "He carved over one thousand heads while he was on the property. It took thirty-five years. Would you like me to tell his story?"

"Please."

He flipped the sunglasses on top of his head and tapped his lip as if wondering where to begin. "Filippo was very poor, so he went to America and joined the navy. Unfortunately, he had much trouble when he fell in love with an American. He was beaten severely by a rival for his lover's affection and returned to Sicily a changed man. He bought this property and began sculpting the rocks and trees into heads. They are known to be people he met throughout his life in the States and here. He was a strange man to the town and would walk around with a stick, acting like it was a scepter and insisting he be called His Excellency."

I shook my head, fascinated by the story. "He spent his life on this property, steeped in his art? And never married or had children?"

"That is right. His work was not appreciated until after his death, when his family opened the estate to tourists. He also painted. There are frescoes in the main house to also enjoy."

"His work is beautiful."

Quint tilted his head, regarding me with interest. "You think? Many say it is . . . strange. They wonder why he wanted to only sculpt heads."

"They say the eyes are the windows to the soul. Maybe for him it was faces. Or maybe he was searching for something special, and in each person, he found one tiny thing, so he kept looking, hoping for completion."

"You have an artist's soul," he said softly.

I laughed, startled. "Oh, no. I'm too logical. I need things to make sense, which isn't very creative."

"You do not see yourself as I do."

I sucked in my breath at the comment, trying not to blush as warmth hit my insides. He didn't say it in a flirty manner, which made it more special. I wondered what Quint did see when he looked at me. I wanted to ask, but it was too intimate, so I kept walking and didn't respond, just smiled.

We took our time exploring, having fun making up stories for each sculpture, getting more outrageous in our descriptions of how Filippo knew them and transformed them into a stone legacy from their interaction. At the top of the hill, we stared down at the Mediterranean in all its glory, a stinging blue that seared my eyes in pleasure.

"What do you think? Was he a madman or a genius?" Quint asked.

I breathed in the sea air until my lungs filled to bursting, dizzy with oxygen. "He was both. Most artists are. How can you remain sane when a part of you is not human but mystical?"

My hair whipped into my eyes, and he slowly tucked the

wayward strands behind my ear. A strange longing edged his deep voice. "As I said, you have an artist's soul or you would never be able to see such truth."

I blinked, caught up in his spell. "And you? Ever created anything that put you into the mad genius category?"

"Only my food, but that is more to comfort than impress. I like the idea of making something that fills one up. To nourish and give pleasure at the same time. That is enough."

How wonderful to simplify his gift rather than chasing fame and fortune. Quint didn't need validation from anyone but the ones who ate his food, who sat in his bar and shared stories and laughter. It was the connection that he gave and received.

I thought about what I did and realized I'd been looking at it wrong. Like a teacher who lectured students, I force-fed information that was helpful but had never truly connected on a personal level—story to story.

"Are you hungry yet?"

I shook off my thoughts and gave a chuckle, putting out my hands. "No. Yesterday ruined me. They made hot dog pizza!"

His eyes twinkled. "Your family honors you. Are you ready for our next stop?"

"Ready."

We got back in the car and drove by the famous spa known for healing many health and skin conditions. The sprawling Greek building displayed classic columns, large wooden doors, and terra-cotta roofs. "There are three different sections that make up our famous baths. A main pool is housed in there," he said, pointing to the building, "and there are three large pools we call the Piscine Molinelli. There are springs close by that supply the water. It is very big and has a view of the sea. It was a beautiful place to visit if you did not want to go to the beach and liked to sunbathe. We are very sad it has been closed for a while."

I looked down at my very tanned skin from the blistering July heat. "I think I've had enough sunbathing anyway. I read about the hot springs in a cave. Can we see those?"

"Unfortunately, the vapor caves of Monte San Calogero are closed. We do not know when they will reopen, but they are very special. People flock to use the water to heal all sicknesses of the skin."

"Have you been? What does it feel like?"

Quint scratched his head. "There are five separate caves, but only three are in use. They call the vapor caves the stoves of San Calogero—the temperature gets to thirty-eight degrees Celsius. Very, very hot. The steam—vapor—rises and surrounds you. It smells. The sulfur."

I imagined Romans wrapped in glorious robes sinking into the steamy water to soothe all their ailments. "In Sedona, Arizona, they have special hot springs that are supposed to be centered on Earth's meridians. People from all over go there for healing."

He lit up with interest. "I would like to see this. Maybe that will be my next travel adventure."

"I thought it would be New York. To see me."

The words popped out before I could stop them, and then I tried hard to seem nonchalant. He laughed. "You are right. I'd rather come see you."

"Well, we don't have healing springs, but the Mandarin Oriental hotel is pretty sweet."

We took our time walking the grounds. "Is Sciacca a big tourist attraction? I'd never heard of it before."

"We are in the southern region, Agrigento. As a working fishing village, we don't offer as much as other tourist places. But I believe whoever is meant to come here will receive a great gift. We are small but we have heart. Our people work hard and it is unspoiled, with some of the most beautiful beaches, olive oil, and food."

I loved the passion ringing in his voice when he spoke about his home. I enjoyed living near the city, in a bustling, eclectic town that had prestigious shops and vegan cafés. Where the roar of the Metro-North train echoed in the air and everyone bumped into one another on the streets because they were all on their phones. But I never questioned whether there were other choices.

It was so much simpler here, stripped down to family, faith, and land. But was it something I could do long-term? Would I miss the rush and adrenaline of the race to success? It was what I'd lived and breathed for the past five years. Would I eventually heal from this grief and be ready to dive back into my busy life?

I wondered why I was even questioning myself. It wasn't like I was staying in Sicily. I was going home soon.

"You're lucky, Quint," I said. "Not only for where you live but how you appreciate it."

He tilted his head and regarded me over his dark lenses. "Right now, it's hard to appreciate anything, Aurora. You are still in grief over your mother."

I nodded, my throat tight. "Was it like this for you? Were you different afterward?"

He reached out to touch my cheek, then dropped his hand. "*Sì*. But I liked myself better. I believe that with each loss, our heart grows bigger, not smaller. Let's go eat."

His words haunted me as we left.

WE DROVE AND chased the dying light. I watched the fiery colors of dusk soak the landscape in a rosy glow, content to let Quint choose where we were headed. We pulled into a magnificent vineyard with a stone castle-like structure snuggled in the midst of twisted grapevines and olive trees. The building soared high like a mini fortress.

"This is De Gregorio Winery," Quint said. "I know the owner, so I thought it would be nice to eat and taste some wine."

"It's stunning," I said in an awed whisper. We parked and walked up the winding paths, surrounded by a natural beauty that my time in Italy was showing me I rarely stopped to notice. I knew the mountains in the Hudson Valley were special. I knew when the leaves turned to golds and vibrant reds in the fall, crowds flocked to witness the spectacular views and shop at our farm markets for apples, and pumpkins, and cider doughnuts. I knew all of this, always smiled with pride, and hurried past, intent on my phone or needing to get to the next event.

But as we walked into the winery, a hush overcame me, a sense of gratitude and humbleness for being allowed to enter such a gorgeous setting. My eyes were finally opened and I never wanted to close them again.

I followed Quint inside, where he spoke briefly to the woman who came to greet us. She nodded, glanced at me with a big smile, and brought us out to a sprawling terrace. Tables and chairs were scattered along the ceramic floors, and rows of vines stretched out over the valley in front of us. Fairy lights weaved in and out of the crooked tree branches and added a romantic atmosphere.

"Would you like me to order some food for us?" he asked. "Liz said my friend isn't here, but she's happy to host us. They have wonderful wine, and the chef is very good. But I do not want to force you to eat anything if you prefer to order yourself."

I melted at his considerate charm. Quint displayed a gentleness and depth I'd never seen in a man. I tended to go for the driven alpha type who excited me. I was beginning to realize there was an entire level of attraction with him that was a bit dangerous. "I'd like that. Just don't make me waste my safe word."

He laughed, a deep, booming sound that created flutters of pleasure in my stomach. "I promise. You are in my hands tonight."

I pretended to ignore the intimate statement and fought my blush.

I sat back and enjoyed watching Quint chat with Liz, ordering food and wine while she nodded and stared at me with interest. Probably assuming I was the new girlfriend or a first date he wanted to impress. I wondered if he was dating or if he had someone special in his life. I wondered if she'd be jealous knowing he spent the day with me.

I wondered why I cared so much.

Liz drifted away and I tried to refocus.

"You didn't mention how Sunday was. With your family. Did you enjoy going to church?" Quint asked.

"Yes. I haven't been in years. Mom used to beg me to join

her, but I always said no. It was nice to be surrounded by relatives in a peaceful place."

"Church is part of our routine here. I have found it is a place to come back to when I am lost."

"I like that."

"Do you have a safe place, Aurora?"

His gaze was thoughtful, but as I fell into his golden-brown eyes, I realized the truth. "It was my mom. And now I have to find a new one."

He reached out and took my hand. I was enveloped in warmth and understanding, like a fluffy fleece blanket for my soul. "No. She will always be your safe place. I listen to my *mamma* all the time. I talk to her in church and when I need help. I believe they are part of us. How can someone we love so much ever truly leave?"

I smiled. "I've never met a man as open as you," I admitted. "Is it all Italians? Because in America, it's almost looked down upon to show so much emotion or speak your heart. Especially for men."

He tilted his head as he considered the question. "Why would I be afraid? It is only feelings. It is part of being human, no?"

I wondered how freeing it would be to embrace the mess in my life. All I knew was that I'd had a major breakdown in public and was made to feel ashamed. Grief was a funny thing. It shoved you straight into the discomfort of chaos, ripping away blinders and walls carefully built over too many years. You couldn't argue with it, tame it, or deny it. You could only ride the wave and do your best not to drown.

But I finally realized the piece of the puzzle I had been missing.

The people you loved became your life jackets.

Or they watched you sink, shaking their heads with sympathy but never reaching out their hands.

"How do you feel about returning home?" Quint asked, startling me out of my lightbulb moment.

"I'm not sure. I have all of this work to do and big decisions to make. I guess if I'm honest, I don't know if I'm ready."

He nodded. I realized he hadn't pulled his hand away. His thumb absently rubbed my palm, and the simple touch set a fire that simmered under my skin. "I am amazed at your strength, Aurora. Maybe you need some time to figure out if you want to go in a new direction. Have you thought of extending your stay?"

I blinked in surprise. "Actually, my grandmother asked me the same thing. Magdalena, my second cousin, is getting married and she wants me to attend the wedding."

"*Sì*, I am going. It will be a wonderful celebration."

"I'd love to be a part of it." Funny, a few days ago, I would have never imagined myself being comfortable enough to be at a family wedding. I'd just met my relatives and was an outsider. But they'd welcomed me as one of their own, and the idea had reshaped my mind. "Except running away from my life for three more weeks doesn't sound very responsible of me. I have things to face in New York. My podcast and clients. My . . . boyfriend."

I stumbled over the word, but I needed to say it. Catena said she'd mentioned Jason to Quint, but we'd never actually spoken his name between us. Of course, I was probably being ridiculous. Quint had his pick of women and I didn't even live here. I was sure he only saw me as a friend, even if there was mad chemistry between us. At least, from my perspective.

He didn't flinch or look away. "These things are important, I know."

"There's another reason, though. My grandmother wants me to have a talk with my grandfather. Get to know him better. We've been a bit prickly toward each other."

"Prickly?"

"Sorry—we have been avoiding each other. I resent him for forcing my mom to leave. I think he was the reason she ran away, and he knows more about what happened with Mom than anyone."

"Ah." A tiny frown creased his brow. "I did not know. Has he spoken to you?"

I shook my head. "He avoids me or glares. I do the same. I don't think we like each other."

His lower lip twitched. "He is scared of you."

I burst out laughing. "I doubt it. He yells at me if I don't eat."

"All Italians do. I know I'm not family, Aurora. I know I cannot imagine the responsibilities you have waiting back at home. But staying in Sicily does not mean you are trying to escape. Perhaps it is the very opposite. You are here to find all the answers of your past, so you can return in your full power."

A waiter appeared at the table and Quint's hand released mine.

I refused to mourn the loss.

The dishes began to flow with the graceful choreography of a ballet. Tuna amuse-bouches, stacked on cucumber slices and layered with avocado and crispy black sesame seeds, paired with a fruity white wine that danced on my tongue.

Oysters cracked open, tiny tender treasures with a slight sting of ocean saltiness. Gnocchi drizzled with rosemary oil, served with wild boar ragù. Thinly sliced beef with artichokes and potato croquettes soaked in a creamy citrus sauce. Grilled sea bass, oily and flaky, poised atop blistered tomatoes and spinach, the crisscross of yellow sauce an explosion of color against the white plate. We moved from white to red wine, the full, bold tannins settling heavily against my tongue, hints of blackberry and currant highlighting the rich meat.

We spoke of our childhoods and our mothers, of dreams and realities, as time fell away and the olive trees and twinkling stars were our only witnesses. I became drunk on our closeness, my head spinning more from the musky scent of his cologne and the fragrant flowers than from the alcohol. As I ate without a care about carbs and spoke without worry of judgment, I unraveled a piece of myself I'd missed.

After dinner, he spoke to Liz and we got free rein of the property. We walked through the stooped archway of olive trees, meandered deep into the vineyard where the dark sky stretched open and our steps fell silently on the soft ground. Insects chirped and buzzed a distant melody. Then he led me inside the tower, through stone tunnels, up the stairs to the rooftop, where I took in the stunning scene before me.

Endless acres of trees were glowing with soft light all the way to the outline of the sea and mountains in the distance. I felt so high up I could touch the stars, and the building reminded me of a scene from *The Lord of the Rings*, a medieval fortress to fight off approaching enemies.

Emotion stuck in my throat. It was all too much. I wasn't used to it.

"I feel more myself here than I have in a long time," I confessed, my shoulder lightly brushing his. The comforting strength of his presence allowed me to open up. "The last time I saw my mom, I was irritated. She had issues with her television, and I was busy, so I resented being there. Since my dad passed, she needed me more, and I hated it. I wanted to live my own life." A humorless laugh escaped my lips. "I literally got mad because she was still lonely without him. I figured five years was enough time to recover. After all, I'd managed. I judged her for being weak. Isn't that terrible?"

He didn't seem disgusted by my admission. "It is human. If we were told it was our final chance to see our loved one, we'd act differently. Speak from the heart. But it is not that way."

Quint was right. "I know. I guess it's hard not to remember the mean stuff." I thought about the things she'd said the night we fought about Jason. "Mom said she worried I was using busyness as a mask so I didn't have to probe deeper. I disagreed. I told her she'd never had a goal she wanted to achieve that required action. I made it sound like an insult."

"I said many things to my mother I regret. She knows you loved her, Aurora."

"Yeah, but what if she was right?" He waited as I struggled to gather my thoughts. "I'm starting to see things differently. All of my achievements I believed were so important? I wonder if it was a convenient excuse not to really take stock of my life."

He took his time answering. "Sometimes, the most powerful changes in life happen within the silence. In between breaths. In between actions." He regarded the sea, lids hooding those beautiful golden-brown eyes. I studied his strong profile, the slope of his jaw, the bump on his nose, the beard hugging his chin and framing his defined lips. "We must listen to the breeze, to the crash of the waves over rock. Answers are hidden there, given by God, but we are too busy being distracted to see the solutions."

I nibbled on my lower lip, moved by his words. "But dreams don't work unless you do."

A faint smile touched his mouth. I wanted to catch it with my fingers and savor the fleeting warmth from the gesture. "What is work? Tasks? Money? All are important, yes. But those things do not contain the meaning we really search for. The joy that stays even when the work is complete or the tasks done or the money spent. *Sì?*"

My mind grabbed on and tried to figure it out, sifting through his statement as if sifting for gold nuggets amid rocks. I was beginning to see things I never had before. Here, in Sicily, work was cooking for family, conversation with friends, sitting in church. It was in the subtle moments that I'd always glossed over, deeming them unimportant and unworthy of my attention.

"I don't understand that type of life," I admitted, a bit sad I wasn't genetically disposed to enjoy the work of leisure. "I've built a career that's focused on action. Not emotions."

He nodded. "That is not a bad thing. I only wish for you to see there are other ways to live and be happy. Other dreams you do not have to work so hard for if you are brave enough to let go."

It seemed that was the theme I was learning here. Let go. Of expectations. Of my old life and relationship. Of my old ideas and limitations.

Not once had I ever counseled a client to let go. They hired me to help them make changes, all proactively. The idea of advising someone to sit back and wait for answers made an innate protest rise from my lips, but I bit it back, wondering what would happen if I experimented.

If I tried things Quint's way.

"Do you want me to stay?" I almost gasped as the words shot out of my mouth, and I quickly backtracked. "I mean, do you think I should stay?"

I loved the chuckle that warmed the air and my ears. He turned to face me, reaching out and touching my warm cheek, tucking the hair behind my ear in a heartbreakingly gentle gesture. "Oh, I want you to stay."

My breath caught. He'd gone right to my original question. What did that mean? What were we doing?

He continued in a careful tone. "But will your boyfriend feel differently? Does he not want you home?"

His gaze probed mine. I sensed his questions regarding the line he refused to cross since I'd told him about Jason. Things felt . . . confusing. First, Jason wanted to take a break, then he said we were together, but after I left for Sicily, he hadn't reached out. His work took priority over me all the time. I'd never questioned our relationship before because we'd wanted the same things, but I'd begun to wonder if I was shortchanging myself. Wasn't love supposed to come first? And if I would always be the sacrifice, maybe I was wrong in thinking this was a healthy connection.

Maybe Jason wasn't the man for me.

"I don't know," I said honestly. "I need to figure some things out with Jason and my grandfather. On my terms."

He nodded. "I understand." A smile touched his lips. "I can wait."

A thrill shot through me at his words, even though a part

almost wished he'd pushed, or given me a clear statement that he was interested in me other than as a friend. But I also respected his honor. This was my choice. His words told me he cared and was dancing on the edge of acceptability. I had no idea what three more weeks in Sicily would bring, but it was time I began to engage in my relationships differently and stop being afraid. I deserved to feel worthy and accepted for who I was. Not who I should be or could be. I wanted to try with my grandfather, for my own sake. And for my mom.

The air cooled. I shivered.

"Come. I will take you home now."

I wanted to say much more, but words tangled inside me and I had no idea how to work out the knots. So I nodded and followed him out.

FIFTEEN

I LOOKED AT the email requesting I check in for my return flight and paused on the confirm button. My conversation with Quint the other night had been spinning on repeat in my mind. Afterward, I'd texted Jason and asked him to call me back.

I still hadn't heard from him.

Yesterday, I shared the day with Catena, Teresa, Magda, and Aunt Philomena. We spent hours popping in and out of local shops as I went on a buying binge I refused to regret. Stocking up on future holiday gifts and treasures for my home, I steeped myself in the Sicilian crafts of ceramics, paintings, and jewelry. I indulged in delicate hand-stitched table linens and a set of gorgeous plates with fruits swirled at the bottom, colored in bright yellow and orange. We relaxed with a two-hour lunch at La Lampara, drinking sparkling wine and nibbling on tasting plates of spaghetti with smoked sea urchin, grilled vegetables, and a bright salad seasoned with olives, anchovies, sweet onion, and delicate Parmesan cheese crisps. We finished with soft, fragrant pears with ricotta, blood oranges, and dried apricots.

I'd been afraid of the sea urchin, but one taste silenced my inner skeptic. This time, I didn't flinch when bread was served and took a few precious bites swirled in fragrant olive oil. My aunt and cousins looked on proudly, as if I had finally been allowed secret entry into their food club. It wasn't my foray into daring culinary dishes that impressed me.

It was my refusal to criticize myself while I enjoyed every morsel.

Catena took me to the fish market and schooled me on the mechanics of negotiation. Her wicked-fast Italian was hard to keep track of, but I studied the fishermens' body language to know what was going on. They screamed back and forth. They whipped their hands into a frenzy. They glared with stony stares and deep frowns. Thank goodness Catena had warned me not to panic, because it was all par for the course. We ended up with prawns, octopus, and sea bass. Catena was happy with her prices and wore a satisfied grin on her face. I was reeling from her feminine fierceness. It was even better than the hoot I'd taught my clients.

I'd never bargained with anyone before. When someone told me the price, I just paid it. The idea of such negotiation both thrilled and scared me, but I tucked the new experience away to be pulled out at a later date, if needed.

I wondered if I could use my cousin's talent to get discount designer clothes. That'd be cool.

Later that day, I gathered at Bar Sciacca with my new friends and ate the fish, cooked by Quint's skilled hands. Even though he wasn't the official cook, Catena told me he involved himself with every meal, sometimes joining the chef to create a special side dish or change the menu. I loved how passionate he was about not only the pub but the food served. He'd told me at the winery his goal was to impart pleasure and comfort in every bite he served. But he didn't want to be a full-time chef. He said it was too stressful, and he preferred to assist, bartend, and be involved in the business side with Catena and Theo.

Quint knew exactly who he was and what he wanted. Once, I'd believed the same thing about myself, but now I was beginning to accept I was still on my journey and had been forced to the side of the road.

With a hell of a lot of potholes.

Jason called me later that night, a full twenty-four hours after my text. When I picked up, I tried hard not to be resentful or open the conversation with accusations.

"Hey, babe. I've been so busy here. The new gym was written up in the paper and I got a ton of client sign-ups. Oh, and I decided to expand the health bar. When we started offering shakes, I figured it'd barely break even, but a ton of profit is popping from clients wanting to hang and socialize after. We're going to begin offering more items, but it's a lot to take on."

I stared at the FaceTime screen and wondered if he even saw me. He was home, but walking around his house as if trying to talk to me and straighten up at the same time.

WTF?

I couldn't help the sharpness of my tone. "Jason, can you do me a favor and sit? I'm getting vertigo bouncing around your place."

"Oh, sure, sorry." He positioned himself on the black sofa and smiled into the camera. "Better?"

"Yes."

"How is Sicily going? Aren't you coming back on Friday?"

"Yeah, I'm surprised you even remember. Miss me much?"

He jerked back and gave me a hurt look. "Of course I miss you, Aurora. I'm just in a bit of a time warp. I've been working sixteen-hour days and need to catch up on sleep."

"The last thing you sacrifice when things are stressful is healthy rest," I quoted back. "Remember?"

"Sure. But as you know, giving advice is sometimes easier than taking it." His jab back was deliberate, his gaze narrowed as he stared at me.

Ah, he did have a mean streak. Jason and I had never fought. Not once. We agreed on everything, and if we didn't, I usually decided he was right, and I deferred. It had never bothered me before—I had actually bragged about our easy relationship—but now I wondered if it was only because I'd never challenged him. Or we never dug deep enough in our dialogue to find something meaningful.

I breathed in and reminded myself he had no idea why I was angry. Maybe we were overdue for a true heart-to-heart talk. "I don't want to fight."

Relief crossed his face. "Me, either. I'm sorry, I should have called earlier. Have you enjoyed spending time with your family?"

"It's been life-changing," I admitted. "I can't believe I finally have cousins and aunts and uncles. I adore Nonna, but my grandfather is acting distant. I'm thinking of trying to talk to him tomorrow."

"You should. Get things wrapped up before you leave so there's no regrets. I'm happy for you, babe. You can Zoom with them and keep in touch. Maybe we can even take a vacation to Sicily together one day!"

Unease stirred within me. Everything with us seemed forced. As if we were trying to be a picture-perfect couple, but underneath things were rotten. I softened my voice. "I wanted to talk to you about some things. I mentioned it before, but my cousin Magda wants me to stay for her wedding. It would mean I extend my time here by another three weeks."

"Yeah, but we both agreed it was ridiculous. That's too much time away from your business."

I firmed my lips. "Well, I'm rethinking my decision. I'll talk to my grandfather tomorrow. We're going to my uncle's olive oil farm. Depending on how things go, I may decide to stay and give us more time to know one another. It may be nice to attend her wedding, too."

His easy manner turned fast. Letting out a humorless chuckle, he shook his head with obvious irritation. "Aurora, you're not making sense. You cannot stay in Sicily for three more weeks."

"Why not?"

His eyes widened. "Because you have too much shit going on in New York! You're running away, if you want the truth. Making excuses to avoid reality. There is nothing to gain and everything to lose. You spent years building your client base and podcast. Are you ready to let it all go because you're afraid of doing some hard work?"

His words were so out of touch with my real emotions, I wondered if we were on different wavelengths rather than just time zones. "I'm not afraid. I'm drained. I've lost my passion for counseling and parroting motivational speeches to people who want to make more money and lose weight."

"What's wrong with those goals?" he demanded.

"Nothing. They're worthy goals. I'm just not invested like I was, and I need to take a hard look at what I do want. Maybe time here will help give me the space to figure that out."

"What about the book?"

"I haven't finished it. I stalled out a while ago and my publisher pushed back the delivery date. I was afraid to tell you before."

"I can't believe I'm hearing this," he muttered, dragging both hands through his thick hair. Irritation exuded from him and pressed through the screen, as if I was ingesting his aura. "That book was critical to leveling up your platform. You want to give it all up for carbs and wine and naps? No one tanks a rising successful career because she wants to eat, pray, and love through Sicily! You are no Elizabeth Gilbert, and the time to find yourself was five years ago." A curse whizzed from his lips. "And what about us? I thought we were trying to build something together."

I swallowed past the lump in my throat and asked the hard question. "What about us, Jason? Do you love me because it's easy? Because I fit in with your goals and future plans? Or are you truly passionate about me? Am I in your mind or in your heart?"

His jaw dropped. "That's the stupidest question I ever heard. We talked about moving in together. We've been together over a year. I gave you a hell of a lot of my time to build a solid, healthy relationship and now you're questioning me? You're the one who left!"

"Yes, I did. Because my mom died and everything fell apart."

"I supported you like I was supposed to. I gave up a lot to be there and hold your hand."

"Supposed to?" I asked. "What does that mean? Are you trying to win the best boyfriend medal?"

He groaned. "I didn't mean it like that. Right now, I feel attacked. I've done nothing wrong, but I'm supposed to happily accept that you don't want to come back and be with me. I'm supposed to apologize for working hard to build my company. I'm supposed to allow you to throw your entire business away because one bad thing happened to you."

His words weren't technically wrong, but they hit me in all the wrong ways. I stared at his handsome face on the screen, obviously frustrated, and slowly came to one realization.

Jason no longer made me feel safe with him.

It was simple. A bit ridiculous that it took me so long to see it. After all, I was a grown-ass woman who could take care of herself. But I was always on guard with him, afraid to be my true self in case he judged or criticized. What began as exciting and motivating had pivoted to an emotion I didn't want to feel anymore.

Like I'm not enough.

I studied him and wondered why my heart didn't squeeze or long for him the way it did for Quint. I'd thought Jason was the one, but now I knew I'd been lying to myself because I didn't want to face the truth. I'd fallen for the man who looked good on paper, the man who made sense and fit into my life. With him, I'd never had to fully risk a broken heart because mine had never been truly his.

One day, I hoped I'd be brave enough to do that. Like my mother.

My eyes burned, but tears didn't fall. "I don't think this is working anymore, Jason."

His gaze narrowed and I caught a flash of anger in his blue eyes. He dragged his fingers through his hair and gave a derisive laugh. "Maybe because you're blowing up your career to hang out in Sicily on a whim. I can't help being disappointed, Aurora. I don't know who you are anymore."

I smiled tightly. "Funny, I'm just beginning to find out who I am."

Jason's face morphed from boyfriend to stranger. "You're right. This isn't working. I tried to support you through this difficult time. I thought it was temporary, so I was patient. But I can't be expected to accept a completely different person from the one I fell in love with."

I couldn't help the smirk. It was so obvious now. Everything needed to work for Jason to be fully engaged. He wasn't the person I wanted to depend on when things went to shit. He expected me to be a certain type of woman, and if I changed, I'd be lectured or counseled. I'd be punished.

Maybe I needed to be grateful this happened. In the end, Mom had proven to be right.

Jason was selfish and unworthy of my heart.

"I think it's over between us."

He jerked back. Had he honestly expected me to fight? To beg? To promise him I'd be better in order to keep him? I wasn't even angry at his reaction. Just sad I'd lied to myself about who we were to each other. "You don't even want to try to salvage this? I thought we loved each other."

I almost smiled at his immediate backpedaling. When it came to personal relationships, Jason liked to be in charge. "I don't think we loved each other, Jason. Not the way we should."

"That's a crappy thing to say." He bristled with irritation. "I tried to make this work, Aurora. If you want to give up, you can't blame me. Are you ready to walk away? Because once we hang up, I'm done. I won't be at your door, chasing you, when you get back from your vacation and suddenly realize you made a mistake."

I took a deep breath. "Jason?"

"Yeah?"

"I've never been more certain of anything. I'm sorry it had to end like this. I only want the best for you."

He made a noise and shook his head in mockery. "Sure you do. Your choice. Good luck."

The screen went blank.

With slightly shaky hands, I clicked off my phone and leaned back into the cushions. I'd broken up with Jason. I should be sad to lose a man I'd spent a year with, after making plans together, building dreams, chasing a happy ending.

Instead, I experienced a sense of relief. I was the only one crafting my future and taking charge of my happiness.

And God, it felt damn good.

Coming to Sicily had shown me that even though I was scared, I was more ready to discover all the things I'd been missing.

Love. Failure. Growth. Grief. Family.

I squeezed my hands around my middle and reminded myself I was brave enough to try.

On my own.

ACCOMPANIED BY MY grandparents, Uncle Agosto, Aunt Philomena, and my cousins, I greeted Uncle Tony—Magda's father—

at his olive tree farm; he came to meet us with welcoming smiles and hard hugs. His wrinkled face was tanned and brown, but he seemed strong and more fit than some of Jason's clients. Muscled arms, weathered hands, and tree-trunk thighs showed that this was a man who lived off the land and had made peace with the bargain. My aunt Lucia came out to welcome me, then urged us to go on the tour while she finished preparing lunch. Aunt Philomena and my grandmother immediately joined her, waving us away.

The house was average size but stood upon a high hill that overlooked plentiful groves of trees, stretching out for miles. As I took in the magnificent view, my gaze swept over the dusty brown mountains that framed the farm. Sunbeams scattered and bounced off the leaves, and the sticky air seemed cooler on my skin so high up. "I feel like I'm in a movie," I said to Magda. "Did you grow up here?"

She nodded. "My two brothers and I learned how to pick olives very young. They stayed as part of the business, but I wanted to work in Sciacca like Catena. Papà was not happy at first, but now he sees I can help him with the finances."

"Magda is very smart with numbers," Teresa said. "She was the top student at university in her classes and got a job with a financial company."

I shook my head, impressed. "That's amazing. I'm so happy your family ended up supporting you."

"*Sì*. I was very lucky. But this farm is my home, and I love it. I will always return."

My heart squeezed at the sincerity that rang in her voice as she spoke. The image of my mother's face floated before me, and I sucked in a breath at the smack of pain that followed.

God, I missed her. I realized too late she'd always been my safe place in life, and now I was alone.

As if they sensed my distress, my cousins closed ranks around me, and I leaned in, allowing myself to accept the comfort.

"I know it is hard," Catena whispered. "But you have us now. And though we never met your *mamma*, she is part of our family and our history. We will not forget her."

"Come," Uncle Tony called out. "Let us show Aurora the farm and how we make the oil."

I smiled at my female crew, heart eased, and followed the men down the path. Gnats and bees buzzed around us, and my shoes kicked up dust as we walked through the olive groves. The scent of citrus and earth drifted in the air. "Picking season is fall, and we do much to get ready for the olive oil festival in October," my uncle said, occasionally stopping to check the olives or adjust branches, muttering to himself as if making mental notes. "Russo Farms is a large supplier in Lucca, and we have just begun to ship products out. We even purchased a bottling machine!" Pride vibrated in his tone. "We will now sell our oils to bigger markets."

Magda bumped my elbow. "I helped him with the financial plan," she whispered.

My grandfather said something in Italian, then went back and forth with Uncle Tony.

"Babba, English. Aurora is here!" Catena admonished, though she was smiling.

I stilled as he glared at her, then me. His lips tightened with disapproval. Oh God, what if he began yelling? I threw my shoulders back, ready to defend her, but my grandfather said something else and my cousin laughed in delight, then blew kisses to him.

"What did he say?" I asked.

"He called me a chattering magpie who will get you into trouble. He likes to tease."

I stared at his frown, which seemed to be permanently creased between his brows, and truly doubted it. I couldn't imagine him laughing or teasing me. The idea of having a private talk with him later twisted my stomach with nerves.

Uncle Tony continued. "We grow two types of olives here. Biancolilla and Nocellara del Belice—one makes lighter, one makes very *robusto* oil. We call it the yellow gold." I loved the sound of the term, like a queen bestowing her riches on the patrons. "We harvest by hand. We lay out *lenzi* to catch all the olives. They wrap around each tree like a blanket."

"Nets," Catena murmured.

"Many pick by hand, and others use rakes to reach the tops of the trees. We gather the olives up and bring them to the mill. We also have almond trees, oranges, and lemons. We are able to use all to make beautiful oil."

I loved his lyrical accent and the passion within his words. I asked a bunch of questions and fell into step with Uncle Tony. I was introduced to my other two cousins—Magda's brothers—and they showed me how to spot an olive ripe for picking, carefully detailing the process of harvesting and what they looked for. I tried an olive fresh from the vine, noting the bitter taste to the hard flesh. When I shuddered with distaste, everybody laughed.

"We go to the mill and see where the magic happens!" Uncle

Tony boomed out, patting Uncle Agosto on the back with affection. I noticed they slowed their pace to walk with my grandfather, who took his time, head tipped up as if to gather the scents and sights of the day. His cap perched on his head with a dash of style. I noticed even though it was hot, he wore a collared polo shirt and long brown pants with sensible shoes.

The mill was a large building to the side of the house. It was full of equipment that looked industrial and important set up in various stations. The pungent scents of olives and brine and oil soaked the air. "Let us go on the journey of our olive!"

The girls looked at one another, lips tugging in smiles, but Magda's gaze held only affection. "Sorry, Papà loves an audience," she confided. "He is like a . . ." She trailed off, searching for a word.

"A big ham?" I suggested.

She blinked. "A ham you eat?"

I gave a half giggle. "It's an American expression. One who likes attention and to show off."

"Yes! He is a ham. I will remember this term."

Uncle Tony held up an olive and headed to the first machine. "We used to clean all the olives by hand, but we now have a machine! It removes all the twigs and dirt. Then they are cleaned and go through the crusher until it is pulp." He moved down the line and pointed out each piece of equipment as if they were his children. "Finally, the olive enters the *trapito*, to extract all the juice, and this centrifuge separates the oil from the water." He patted the end of a metal monster. "Over here, the oil is filtered and collected in these bins." He pointed to large plastic jugs.

"I want to see how the bottling machine works," Catena said.

"Ah, watch! It is a joy to see our product for sale. We even design our new label!"

"I did that, too," Magda whispered.

Her brothers rolled their eyes and said something in Italian. She shot something back and they got into a loud argument. No one seemed to care, but Uncle Tony shouted "*Zitto!*" to the boys and they all stopped. His voice returned to normal. "Watch how nice this works. I saved some just to show you."

Magda stuck out her tongue.

Her brothers whispered something and grinned evilly.

Lord, maybe I was glad I didn't have a sibling.

Everyone gathered around for the demonstration. Grabbing a container of oil, Uncle Tony clicked on a series of buttons, and beautiful glass bottles began to fill with pale yellow liquid. Once it reached the top level, the bottle was capped, and another robotic thing came out and pressed a label over it.

Uncle Tony took it off the assembly line and held it up. "See?"

We oohed and aahed and my uncle handed me the bottle. The label had **Russo Farms** in a bold red font, with olive trees sketched in the background. My fingers scrolled over it. This was something tangible, made by my family's own hands, made for people to love and enjoy. This bottle would be on tables across the world, surrounded by conversation and laughter and good food. And I was a part of it, in a very small way, because of my mom.

"Now we shall taste the oils and eat!"

I was eating. Again. A laugh bubbled up from my throat

when I thought of Jason's reaction. I'd already gained a few pounds, but I felt good. I guessed carbs, wine, and fresh air were the winning combination.

We returned to the main house, where the long wooden table outside had been set. Pitchers of water were poured alongside wine. Plates of various olive oils were scattered alongside crusty homemade bread. Smoked meats and fish, caponata, cheeses, and grilled vegetables filled the table from edge to edge. Juice freshly squeezed from the farm's blood oranges was distributed.

My grandmother led a prayer of grace as we bowed our heads. A peaceful stillness settled over us as she spoke. A bird sang. The trees rustled in the breeze. The sound of breath and shifting bodies only added to the sense of closeness. We said amen and began to eat.

Uncle Tony kept up his tutelage, to my delight. "The oil on your right is extra virgin. One percent acidity. See the color? Goldish. Different from the oil on your left, no? That is two percent acidity and a straw yellow rather than lemon. Now—you must pair with some herbs. And the one in the corner has been pressed with blood orange—it is *delizioso*!"

My uncle rambled and instructed me to pair different foods with the oil. I was astonished I'd never truly noticed the subtle shift in flavor depending on how the oil was prepared. The men got in a lively discussion regarding what product Uncle Tony should sell next, while my grandmother and aunt spoke of local church gossip and the children. My cousins talked of the wedding and Catena's last disastrous date. Uncle Agosto heard the tail end and interrupted.

"You will not see him any longer," he demanded. "He has no respect."

Catena sighed patiently. "Papà, it was only a first date. He was late because of work. I want to give him a second chance."

"Work is important, but there is no excuse to leave you waiting in a restaurant. If he wants forgiveness, you bring him to the house to meet us."

Fascinated, I glanced back and forth at the daughter-father argument. "No. The last time I brought a man home, you were very mean and scared him."

Uncle Agosto slammed his fist on the table. "I ask him normal questions and he refuses to answer! That is disrespect. It is not allowed in our house with my daughter."

"He did not understand. He was not from around here."

"I know. If he was, he would know the proper way to meet us."

Catena groaned. "Well, he's gone now, *va bene*?"

Aunt Philomena clucked her tongue. "Can you not try with Michael again? He is so lovely! A perfect husband."

"Michael doesn't like me, Mamma. He says I'm too headstrong. He wants a wife who will be sweet and do what he says."

Aunt Philomena's face fell in disappointment. "That is not you. That is very sad."

Uncle Agosto yelled again. "Why can't you be nicer, Catena! You are getting old!"

I clapped my hand over my mouth to stop from laughing.

Teresa spoke up. "My cousin needs time to find herself. Look at Aurora. She's much older and is not married."

Everyone stared at me. My cheeks reddened. Well, that took a bad turn. I figured I'd be thrown to the wolves, but surprisingly, my grandmother came to my defense. "Aurora is in New York. It is different. She knows no better."

"She has a serious boyfriend," Magda pointed out. "They're practically engaged."

Aunt Philomena beamed. "Wonderful! Can we come to America for the wedding? Or maybe you will get married here?"

Oh my God.

I almost choked, then grabbed for water. Was now the time to confess we'd broken up? No, I'd do it later. In a more private setting. I tried to keep my voice casual. "Um, Jason and I are just dating. Not engaged. Sorry."

My family looked sad, like I'd broken their dreams. I wasn't used to such familial involvement in my personal life and wondered how my cousins managed. The other part of me liked the attention, the poking and prodding and refusal to back down. The right they believed they had to pry.

They treated me like one of their own.

The yelling stopped and the conversation turned and the subject of marriage disappeared. We finished lunch and nibbled on pistachio cannoli with crisp homemade shells and creamy, nutty cheese. Joy pinged in my veins as the food nourished and the company warmed me from within.

The women cleaned up while the men sat outside talking. "Aurora, when are you leaving?" Magda asked, stacking dishes. "Is this the last time we shall see each other?"

I swallowed back the tightness in my throat. "I think so. I leave Friday. Catena said she's asking everyone to come to the pub to say goodbye tomorrow night."

Magda sighed. "I cannot come—I have wedding appointments." She paused, biting down on her lower lip. "I know I asked before, but I would do anything to have you stay. Can you extend your vacation? Work from here? It would mean so much to all of us."

Her honest entreaty touched me. Everything seemed to merge, forcing me to see all the sharp angles butting together. My crumbling relationship with Jason. The memory of Quint's words reminding me I had changed from who I used to be. The pull of Sicily and my family against the pull of the familiar. But most of all, the warring emotions regarding my grandfather.

"*Grazie.* I'm so grateful to be wanted," I managed to say. "Can I—can I just think a bit more?"

My cousins all gasped. "You will consider it!" Magda screeched.

I smiled and nodded. "*Sì.*"

Suddenly, my grandmother appeared, shooing them away. "Get back to the dishes. We have much cleanup."

Catena muttered something about the men not helping but trudged back to her drying duties. Nonna gently took my arm and guided me to the window. I looked out at the men talking quietly. My grandfather had moved from the table and stood on the outer edge, staring over the hills, obviously lost in thought.

"You can talk to him, Aurora."

I swallowed past the lump in my throat and nodded. Then, after pressing a kiss to her cheek, I walked outside and over to my grandfather. My heart pounded and my palms sweated, but I managed to stand next to him. I knew he sensed my presence, but he didn't glance over. His stubborn refusal to even acknowledge me gave my voice an edge. "Nonna thought we should maybe talk."

No response.

My skin immediately itched and I fought the urge to scratch. Stupid hives. I tried again. "Um, it's been a nice visit. Meeting everyone. I'm supposed to fly back home Friday."

"That is good."

I waited for more, but he seemed entranced by the view and had no desire to converse. I turned to walk away, but the memory of my mother's face froze me in place. I owed her and my grandmother a fair effort. Suddenly, the words burst from my lips, raw and vulnerable. "That's all you have to say? I know you don't want me here. Everyone has shared memories of my mother, but you haven't said a thing. You act like you're still angry at her, and me, and wish I'd never come. Instead of ignoring me, why don't you just tell me the truth? Did you drive my mother away? Do you hate the idea she had me and made herself happy without you?"

This time, his head turned. His gaze pinned mine, and a wave of emotion flickered over his hard features. I stood my ground, ready for him to yell or dismiss me and call me impolite or any type of derogatory Sicilian term. My cousins said over and over how elders were respected here, and grandparents were revered. But I couldn't pretend any longer. I needed to know what had happened between them.

"Let us go for a walk."

Without waiting, he began trudging down the pathway toward the olive grove, not looking back to see if I followed. Slightly shocked, I fell into step with him and matched his pace. I waited for him to lecture me, but after a few tense minutes, he remained silent and I relaxed. The wind played with my hair and the sun shone bright and strong. The fields spread in front of me in a mix of earthy colors. He led me up a hill where there was a bench hidden under a large twisted tree. He took a seat in the shade, and after a brief hesitation, I joined him.

"I am not mad at you. And I am glad you are here."

I couldn't help but snort. "You sure don't act like it," I muttered. "I could tell you don't like me."

He rested his fingers on his thigh and gave a half sigh. I studied the gnarled knots of muscles in his hands, the wrinkled brown skin of age, the simple gold band of his wedding ring. My heart ached for something from him I couldn't define. Acceptance? Love? Pride? The emotions stuck in my chest as I waited for him to speak. "You look like your *mamma*. Like Serafina." His voice broke a bit on her name. "I was not ready for it. To hear about my daughter's death too young and be the last to know."

This, I understood. While everyone had grieved and cried with me, my grandfather had stayed aloof, so it was easy to assume he didn't care. Especially with his reaction toward me. "I understand. You were her father. I was in shock when I heard about all of you. We were both cut out from parts of Mom's life."

"I thought she'd come back. I waited for a call, or letter, or for her to walk back in the house and say she was sorry. I waited but nothing happened. Then I knew I had lost her."

His last statement held threads of a deep loss I recognized well. "What was your relationship like?"

He took a deep breath. "Sera and I were close. We spent much time together. She liked to go with me to work at the pizzeria." A faint smile touched his lips. "She always said—"

"—pizza makes people happy."

He looked at me in surprise, then nodded. I almost choked

on the tears as I remembered the familiar phrase that used to drive me mad. I'd insist on cauliflower crust to avoid calories and bitch about why we had to eat pizza a million different ways until she backed down and finally began cooking fish, steamed veggies, and all the things I insisted were healthy so I could tame my curves and be what I thought everyone wanted me to look like. How many times had Mom begged me to accept my body and love it the way God created? How many times had I interrupted her joyful singing as she created versions of pizza that made her happy and me furious?

Mom was right. The joy of eating pizza was a reminder of childhood and its gorgeous simplicity. The purity of a few ingredients that can beckon us to sigh in pleasure. Hearing my grandfather say she loved their restaurant broke my heart because she'd never shared the loss of it with me. Or helped me to understand why she'd left a loving family behind.

My grandfather spoke softly. "*Sì*. She was a good girl. Happy and obedient and loving. But as time passed, she grew restless and unhappy. I did not understand, so I believed this was a phase. She would return to her sweet self."

Confusion and sadness resonated in his tone. I didn't interrupt, so he continued. "I did not know how serious it was with your father. When Sera asked for me to meet him, I found out she had been sneaking around because she was afraid I would forbid it. I got angry. I did what any father would and tried to stop it. I locked her in the house so she could not see him. He was going to leave and I would have my Sera back."

"But it didn't happen that way. Mom disobeyed."

He didn't answer for a while. "Sera said she loved him. A man she'd known only about a week. A man who lived in England and knew nothing about our ways or respect for our family. She threatened to leave with him, and I told her if she walked out, she would lose all of us forever. I told her she would never be welcome in my house again. That she could never come back. I knew if I scared her enough, Sera would obey and this infatuation would pass. It could not be real love."

A tense silence fell. "But it was. They got married and had me."

"I was her father!"

I jerked as he boomed out the sentence, shaking slightly. I bit my lip and watched him through lowered eyes. My heart thundered in my chest as I asked the question I dreaded. "So you blame my dad? Do you think he tricked her or something?"

He pushed his glasses up his nose and muttered in Italian. "Your father tried to speak with me. I refused. He told me he wanted to marry her, but I did not believe it. I had seen men before come to our town on vacation and ruin our daughters. I sent him away."

The horror of the situation hit me full force. I pictured my mother at nineteen falling desperately in love. I imagined my grandfather trying to save her from a life he believed would ruin her. Romeo and Juliet were never romantic characters. They were pure tragedy.

"Do you regret your decision? Do you believe it could have all ended differently?"

My question was desperate, but I needed to know if his heart was cold. Had he cut her off easily? Had he mourned or just pretended she didn't exist?

"She left. She made her choice."

I stared at the gruff man beside me. Hat tilted low on his brow. Lips firmed and pressed tight together. Fists clenched. There was no softness or vulnerability there. His entire body screamed anger and tension, but the moment I began to turn away and dismiss him, to hide from the agony of having him reject me like he had her, I lingered. Looked deeper. And found what I was searching for.

Pain.

So much pain throbbed from his very aura, and I lost my breath as the truth slammed through me.

"She broke your heart."

He gave a slight jerk at my words. I waited for him to yell in Italian, to wave me off, to walk away in pride and dismissal. "*Sì.*" A terrible pause. "She loved him more than me."

The words fell into the silence between us and landed like a rock, creating ripples in the air. I bit my lip and struggled to understand him. The wall he'd erected to keep me out, along with my mother, seemed built from bricks and stone. Anger hit. He was too stubborn. If he'd bent, if he'd stifled his pride, maybe he could have tracked her down and made things right again. Now it was too late.

My accusation spilled hot from my lips. "You broke her heart, too. You never tried to find her."

He remained rigid, shoulders erect, chin up. But I caught the shake of his fingers and the full-body shudder that he couldn't hide. I waited and hoped. I'd come to confront him with no plan or speech. I only wanted to talk from the heart and allow him to make my decision.

"*Sì.*"

Slowly, his gaze swerved to me. I looked into his hazel eyes and clung to the glint of emotion I spotted. I knew I had two choices right now. I could hold on to my own anger and resentment and walk away. Go home and take the gifts I'd been given by the family members who'd opened their hearts. My grandfather and I wouldn't talk again. He'd be a distant figure in my life and my mother's past.

Or I could stay and fight. See if there was any type of relationship worth exploring, not only for me but for my mother's memory as well. To close a loop that had been ripped open and left vacant.

"Do you want me to stay, Babba?"

I used the Italian term deliberately, testing it out on my tongue, the comfort and intimacy of the word filling me up. The horrible vulnerability of waiting for his answer was a risk, but I sensed it was important for me to be brave.

His gray brows drew together. His gaze narrowed behind his glasses. "You would stay?"

I nodded. "For Magda's wedding. To give both of us . . . a chance. If you want."

I'd slid my heart over to him on a platter, and he had the weapon to smash it. But I thought of Quint and how he believed I was brave and owned an artist's soul, and I wanted to be better. For him to be right.

"*Sì.*"

There was no emotional outburst. No hugs or kind words. But the yes was special and I knew it. He wanted to try.

Tears burned my eyes, but I blinked them back. I cleared my throat so I wouldn't sound hoarse. "*Va bene.* I will stay."

He nodded. His hand reached out to awkwardly pat my shoulder. Then he slowly rose from the bench and began to walk. I joined him, and we crossed the olive grove in silence, but this time, a new gentleness flowed between us, like a light, warm wind skimming the waves of the sea. I had forgotten the power of quiet. Of waiting. My father had shown patience in conversation and action, and I saw my grandfather owned the same quality.

I wondered if they would have been good friends if things had been different. I bet my mother thought so.

We returned side by side to the house, and I told everyone I was extending my trip for another three weeks.

SIXTEEN

I CANCELED MY plane reservations and was lucky to be able to extend my Vrbo stay. I left a voice mail with Dr. Sariah's office saying that I needed additional Zoom appointments since I was staying a bit longer. Then I spent a few hours on my laptop trying to decide what to do with the mess.

I was lucky. My mother had a hefty life insurance policy that easily took care of the bills, and I'd been able to save a nice nest egg the past few years. For now, I didn't need to work. The thought made me feel a bit lost, as if my career had been my main tether to a sense of self-worth, and without work, I'd be useless. But I was learning other things about myself that I deserved to delve deeper into.

Some of the work lit me up, but other parts rang false. I needed to figure out what I wanted to give up or change. After a long conversation with Eliza, I made a hard yet radical decision.

I canceled the rest of the season of the podcast.

There was no way to bring true authenticity to listeners and respect my guests when I wasn't fully emotionally invested anymore. The idea of pushing through to finish the book also had to be set aside. My outlook had changed, and I was no longer qualified to tell the world how to handle problems when I was struggling through so much myself. I needed to be a student again before picking up the role of teacher, adviser, or coach.

My clients were trickier—I couldn't disappear, and I owed them the care they paid for and expected. I decided to talk with each of them personally. One by one, I shared with them my vulnerability regarding my mother's passing and asked to put most of them on hold. Some I kept, because I believed I could still help. By the time afternoon fell, I was exhausted but elated.

For the first time, I was facing things head-on and making hard decisions that I'd tried putting off for too long. My entire body seemed lighter and more open. Even better?

The world suddenly held limitless possibilities. Scary? Hell yes. But hopeful. I'd practiced the meditation Dr. Sariah had set for me to tap into my intuition and strengthen that inner voice that popped in and out at various times. I guessed the voice was my truth teller.

I began a new routine.

Each morning, I'd write in my journal, then walk. At first, I felt lost, untethered to the world I'd created and believed in. I couldn't remember the last time I wasn't pulled toward a task or pushing myself to do more. Be better. Achieve. Here, under the warmth of my family's company and the laid-back manner of Sicilian culture, I was beginning to change, shedding my old self like a snake shed its skin.

I toured all the iconic sights of Sciacca, lingering over the hidden histories and details of the churches and monuments. I snapped pictures that called to me, captioning them with *My Sicilian Summer*, sometimes doing videos that were all about sharing my discoveries and had nothing to do with followers or courting clients. I became addicted to the traditional Sicilian breakfast consisting of day-old bread soaked with espresso and served as a cereal. I drank freshly squeezed blood-orange juice that reminded me of Russo Farms and ate gelato every afternoon during my sightseeing. I haunted my favorite *pasticceria*—La Favola—and chatted with the owner, Maria, who always welcomed me. Each day, she'd recommend a new treat, and I'd sit and sip a cappuccino, nibbling on puff pastries filled with cream, apple tarts with caramelized burnt edges, and cannoli baked perfectly crisp yet tender, overflowing with salty ricotta and nutty pistachios. My favorite was their famous *ova murina*, a soft shell filled with cream, almonds, and cinnamon.

I ignored the scale, blossomed into my natural curves, and embraced my new physique, which was strong from the daily hiking and hill climbing.

I sat on benches and eavesdropped on conversations in Italian, spending time listening to audio lessons on the basics of the language. I saw my family every day—either at the pub in the evenings or at my grandmother's house. Sometimes, I visited the pizzeria, where Teresa and Emilio taught me how to make the dough and some unique signature dishes.

We held a simple memorial for my mother, where the priest blessed us and we offered candles and prayers for the safe passage of her soul. When I wept, I was never alone, and somehow, the grief was manageable. My grandfather stayed close to my side, a silent support of solidarity that soothed my soul. Afterward, we walked, and I shared memories of Mom, enjoying the surprise of his smile when he heard a story he liked.

I slept easily and dreamlessly. I woke up energized and smiling.

And I began to fall for Quint.

The connection between us grew slowly, subtly, as everything good here in Sicily did. He helped me when I practiced speaking Italian, quizzing me on simple sentences and correcting my mispronunciations. When I arrived at Bar Sciacca, Quint always had a special dish for me to try, made by his own hands. There was something beautifully intimate about eating the food he cooked, and I enjoyed his teasing when I ate carbs without a fight and moaned over a delicious dish.

Every evening, we walked outside and sat on the bench shaded by a cluster of trees. Each day that passed, a closeness developed between us, a blurry line of friendship and something deeper. We never crossed the divide. I'd told my cousins and family about my breakup with Jason, but I hesitated with Quint. Somehow, my saying aloud that Jason was out of my life was an invitation to change things between us. And as much as I craved a deeper intimacy, I was scared. It was easier to live in this shadowed middle ground where all kinds of possibilities existed. I thought of indulging in an affair until I returned home, but the hollowness in my chest confirmed I wasn't looking for a fun fling. Not with him.

God, I was confused, and his continued silence made me afraid to push the issue.

"Your thoughts are serious tonight, no?" Quint asked with a bit of teasing. He sat on the bench next to me, obviously studying my face as I chewed away over my analysis of us.

I was glad he couldn't see my cheeks burn. How embarrassing to think I was tangled with longing for him, when he most likely went home to a woman each night to warm his bed. Which was his right, because I'd come here having a boyfriend. I shifted in my seat and forced a smile. "Sorry, I guess I was thinking about work."

"Are you worried about what you left behind?"

My gaze crashed into his and shivers skated down my spine. The question burned in his eyes, but his meaning seemed deeper. The scent of spice and citrus swarmed me. I ached to touch him, so I curled my fingers into fists. "Not anymore," I said softly.

He reached out and dragged the backs of his knuckles across my cheek. My breath stuttered in my chest. "You have had so much change to deal with. I understand if your heart has ties to the past."

Now I knew there were undercurrents, and I had a choice. It was then I made my decision, in that moment, under the moonlight, with a man who had begun to stir things up inside me I'd never experienced before. "I'm figuring stuff out about work. I want to go in a new direction with my career, but I'm not clear yet. As for my heart?"

He cocked his head, waiting for me to finish. I still felt the imprint of his hand on my cheek, the rough warmth lingering.

"I told Jason I don't want to be with him anymore. We broke up."

A wave of emotion flickered across his face. I couldn't pinpoint anything specific, though I hoped he was pleased. The air was charged between us, full of possibilities, but his tone was mild when he finally spoke. "I see. And how do you feel about this?"

The question held undertones I didn't know if I was ready for. Yes, I'd been with Jason for more than a year, but looking back, I knew my heart hadn't been completely invested. I didn't feel like I was broken and looking to soothe a gaping wound. Instead, it was as if a lock had been opened and I was ready to leap.

But Quint didn't know anything about my relationship with Jason. Once again, I admired his restraint and care as he navigated my announcement.

"Relieved," I said honestly. "It wasn't working for a while. We weren't right for each other, but it took my mom's death for me to realize everything that was wrong with us."

"Sometimes, a tragedy does this to us. Forces us to confront things we hid."

I loved the way he shared his thoughts without hesitation. It was a strength that made him even sexier to me. I ached to be impulsive and lean into his arms. To see what happened next. But there was too much to process, and I needed more time before I made a move.

I remembered our last talk and the words sprang from my lips. "Sometimes our pain is a gift of growth."

His eyes warmed. We sat in silence together, shoulders touching, staring into the night. Slowly, he clasped my fingers with his. Giddiness sparked through my veins.

"I have tomorrow off. Would you like to go to the beach with me?" Quint asked.

"Yes. I'd like that."

"Then it's a date."

We smiled at each other, still holding hands.

SEVENTEEN

QUINT PARKED THE car and I stared out at the stunning view from the top of the hill.

A long strip of sandy beach snaked a trail, hugging the blue waters of the Mediterranean, then morphed into a giant cliff of blinding white rock. As I blinked, I noticed there were striations carved into the sandstone that made it look like steps rising to the top. Blue swirls in the sandstone reflected the stinging blue of water and sky, all merging into a dazzling vision. I turned to him, jaw unhinged.

"This is not like the Jersey shore."

He smiled. "What is that like?"

I gave a snort. "It used to be paradise, but now I'm ruined. This is stunning. What is this beach called again?"

"Scala dei Turchi. Many tourists flock here. I knew you'd enjoy."

"*Grazie.* I'm so happy."

His grin was as dazzling as the view, a flash of white teeth against his sexy dark beard and full lips. "You may not be once you see the hike."

"Don't you remember? I'm not afraid of exercise."

"Ah, *sì*. At least it is not a mountain of bread. Or red balloons."

I laughed long and hard. "Or a mountain of spiders."

He laughed with me and tugged my hand forward. "Come."

We started down a long, twisty staircase, making our way to the beach. There was a small building with drinks and snacks for sale, and we greeted a few people as we passed them on the way down. When my feet hit the powdery sand, I immediately flung off my sandals, tugging Quint forward in my hunger to feel the water.

We dropped our towels and bag, then stripped down to our bathing suits. One glance at his tight black briefs had me momentarily speechless. Lord, he was like an Italian god. All toasty brown skin and carved pecs with tight abs. I had a moment of shyness in my red tankini, but I caught the light of appreciation in his eyes and shrugged off my modesty. I was tired of worrying about my body and how Jason judged my diet and fitness routine. Funny, I weighed more now but had felt more myself in the past few weeks than I had in years. I refused to backtrack.

The water was cool against my heated skin and crystal clear, easily showing the path forward amid the various rocks. Throwing my arms out, I tipped my head back and smiled up at the beaming sun. The beauty of the natural elements surrounding me sank into my core, bringing a buzz of energy. I breathed deep, smelling salt and earth and sunscreen.

When I glanced to my side, I froze at Quint's look. "What?"

He shook his head. Emotion flickered over his face, along with a touch of longing. He said something in Italian I tried to decipher. "*Grazie?*"

His bottom lip quirked. "*Prego.*"

I blinked. "Wait—what did you say?"

Heat surged between us. I was glad I was in the water to cool off. "Maybe I will tell you later."

I didn't push. Instead, I splashed him, then he rewarded me with a masculine roar, and we played in the surf like children.

I didn't even care about ruining my hair.

After our swim, we donned our cover-ups and began the trek across the beach. "How is it going with your *babba*?" he asked. "I know it has been difficult. I'm sure it meant a great deal to him that you stayed."

"I don't feel like he hates me anymore. It's strange sharing stories about my mom. He knows her only as a child, and I know her as an adult. It's like we're trying to fill in all the blanks for both of us."

"I feel that with Carmella sometimes. She is eight years younger and does not remember my mother as well. I have trouble explaining how good she was. How her hugs made me feel like I was safe. How she pushed me to do things that scared me, and when I did, whether I failed or not, she smiled so big I knew I'd made her proud." His sigh was full of wishes. "She smelled of baked bread and wildflowers from the garden. And when she lost her temper she dropped terrible Sicilian curse words, but if I repeated them, she'd smack me."

I smiled at the vivid picture in my mind. "You describe her so well. It's not fair that Carmella didn't have more time, but she has you. You can be her memory."

"I like that thought," he murmured. "Like you and your grandfather."

We reached the bottom of the massive carved sandstone and began the climb. People stopped at various levels to take pictures, slipping sometimes on the stone and laughing with their group. "How did it get like this?" I asked.

"It's built-up minerals, mostly shells. Centuries of water and wind wore the rocks down to a smooth surface. It is called the Turkish Steps. You can also find many hidden belvederes to explore and sneak off to. I will show you my favorite, where it is best to take pictures."

My sandal slid and I fumbled for balance. He grabbed me, tucking me against him, his bare thigh brushing mine. "Careful, *dusci*."

"What is that term? I haven't heard it before."

He glanced away. I noticed a red stain on his cheek. "Ah, 'sweetheart.' *Mi dispiace*, it just came out."

I touched his arm gently. "No, I like it."

This time, he met my gaze and nodded, pleasure gleaming in his golden-brown eyes. "*Bene.* Me, too."

We resumed our climb until the spill of rock sloped beneath us. Some people were trying to walk to the summit, a high angle that looked dangerous. The lifeguard's calls and sharp whistle warned them to get down, and Quint shook his head.

"Silly tourists. They will do anything for a picture."

I grinned. "Me, too. Shall we take a selfie?"

"*Sì.*"

I took my phone out and we put our heads together, smiling giddily into the camera. Then I snapped a couple of different shots to capture the idyllic beauty of nature in the wild. It made me feel both giant to be poised so high and tiny as a small part of the universe and its many moving parts. Right now, all the things that used to worry me dissolved like sand spilling through open fingers. This was important. These moments of clarity and quiet shared with people who mattered.

A walk in the olive groves with my grandfather. Making pizza with my cousins. Sharing a meal with my family.

I had a primal urge to pick up a pen and write down all the thoughts and feelings spilling from within and overflowing. Later, I would sift through today and try to piece together the images and emotions with words.

"Let me show you my spot."

We made our way back down, and then, by the entrance to the steps, he led me through a hidden space that overlooked the opposite side. I caught my breath at the panoramic view. Sunlight bathed the white sandstone, surrounded by every shade of blue, from turquoise and azure to cobalt, setting off the pebbly beach and rocky outcroppings kissing the coast.

We stood together, shoulders touching, lost in the moment. "No wonder you never want to leave Sicily," I murmured.

"What does your place look like?"

"It's beautiful in a different way. I'm not around any beaches but surrounded by mountains. It's a small town with shops and cafés near the Hudson River. Most people own a dog and eat vegan or vegetarian. Many commute to Manhattan for jobs. I love it, but we run at a fast pace. New Yorkers are proud of the ability to push hard and push often. We like money and achievement, and even creativity needs to fit into a certain niche to make a profit."

He cocked his head. "You have always lived there?"

"My parents lived farther south, closer to the city in Westchester. I wanted to be a bit more rural, so I ended up in Cold Spring. But, yes, we've always been in New York."

"I believe we all end up in the places meant for us. Later, we get to choose in order to fill in the missing pieces."

I loved the way his statements held profound thought and deeper meaning, making a casual conversation so much richer. "What do you think you learned from Sciacca?"

Quint stroked his beard. My fingers tingled to see if it felt silky against them. My lips. I'd never kissed someone with a beard, and now I couldn't stop fantasizing. "Hmm, I believe I have learned that not much is needed for happiness. Family. Friends. A beautiful view. A meal made with intention." Transfixed, he slowly turned to gaze at me, pulling me into his green-gold eyes and holding me there with intensity. "And love. Sicily has taught me about love."

Time stilled as seconds ticked by and we didn't break our eye contact.

"What did you learn, Aurora?"

His voice was deep and gravelly, stroking my ears like a caress. I breathed in his scent and offered my own truth. "New York taught me to dream big. To work hard. To believe in myself. Most of all, it taught me grit and the power of moving forward."

His smile lit me up from the inside. "A worthy gift."

"Yes. But what you said about the missing pieces? I think I've filled them in Sicily."

He reached out and I stepped forward into his arms.

A clatter broke the quiet, and we turned to see a young mother with two children burst into our space. She caught sight of us and chattered brightly in Italian. Quint moved toward her, conversing easily, kneeling down to talk to the two boys, who seemed to brim with energy and excitement. I watched the interaction, enjoying the way he acted with the children and his gentleness.

And I wondered what would have happened if we hadn't been interrupted.

We finished up at the beach and headed home.

"Do you have plans for tonight?" he asked.

My heart beat faster. "No."

"Carmella is home from school and asked to meet you. Would you like to come to my home for dinner?"

My grin was so wide it hurt my cheeks. His sister wanted to meet me. Which meant he'd mentioned me enough to make her curious. "I'd love that."

Quint nodded. "I will drop you off so you can change and nap. Then pick you up later."

"*Grazie.* I'm looking forward to it."

I noticed he was smiling, too.

QUINT'S PLACE REMINDED me a bit of my grandparents'. It was a tall town house–like structure in burnt umber, with a wrought-iron balcony. Brightly colored bougainvillea spilled over the railings along with pots of fresh herbs. The arched door was a heavily carved wood, and when I stepped inside, I was struck by the warm Tuscan colors and delicious smells scenting the air. "*Sei molto bella,*" Quint murmured, leaning down to kiss my cheek in greeting.

My breath caught at the gesture and compliment. "*Grazie.*"

Catena had called, and when I told her I was going to Quint's, she said she could drop me off since he lived close to the pub. I'd dressed simply, in white shorts and a matching lace top. I'd twisted my hair up and paired the look with fun accessories, from dangly earrings and stacked bangle bracelets to my delicate gold daisy anklet. My necklace was a beaded evil eye I'd purchased from one of the shops in town. I'd spritzed myself with a floral perfume—another indulgence from a local vendor. Quint was also dressed casually in jeans, a pink T-shirt, and sneakers. He looked freshly showered, and his hair curled around his neck, slightly damp. "Oh, I brought wine."

"*Grazie*, come to the kitchen." He led me through the house, which was small but cozy. There was just enough clutter to make it homey, with photos, colorful mosaics, and books sprinkled around. His laptop and workspace were set up in the corner. The furniture was dark wood, but the couch and chairs were a deep blue with pale lemon cushions.

I smiled as I stepped into the kitchen, obviously his favorite place. "Oh, I love it," I breathed out, walking over to the butcher-block island and updated appliances. It was a great mix of traditional and modern, and I could tell Quint liked his machines. There were espresso makers, juicers, mixers, and an impressive variety of pots and pans. Ceramic bowls were filled with lemons, blood oranges, loaves of bread, and bunches of garlic.

Quint opened the wine and poured three glasses. "Carmella should be down any minute—she changed her outfit three times."

I blinked. "Why? It's just me."

He grinned and pushed the glass toward me. "You're a bit of a celebrity. She got a hold of your social media stuff and watched all the videos. I think you have an admirer."

I bit my lip, hesitant. I was flattered, but I had nothing to offer in that vein lately. All of my current stuff was focused on Sicily and I'd stopped most of the motivational videos. "That's so sweet, but she certainly doesn't have to impress me."

"You're right. Being related to me should be enough."

I rolled my eyes, incurring a laugh, and then a young woman rushed through the door and stopped before me. "Aurora? I am Carmella—it's so nice to meet you," she said in perfect English. "My brother has told me so much, and I can't wait to hear everything!"

I laughed at her warmth and enthusiasm, which reminded me of my cousins. Her features resembled her brother's—the same defined nose, sharp cheekbones, and generous mouth. She was tall and willowy, with gorgeous olive skin. Her eyes were darker than Quint's, a rich chocolate brown, and held a clear-eyed intelligence. But that was where the resemblance ended.

Her wavy hair was a bold mixture of golds and red. A diamond winked from her nose. Long black-tipped nails gave off a vampy vibe. She wore a short bloodred dress that accented her figure but wasn't classically tight. Seemed Quint's sister liked pushing the edge of style, and I immediately related. It must be difficult without her mom, but I bet Quint worked hard to fill both roles.

"No, the pleasure is mine. I've heard so much about you. I'm honored to be here. And I love your outfit! Red is your color."

Carmella beamed and my heart melted a bit. "*Grazie.* I can take you to the shop in town—Ava makes the most beautiful dresses and they are affordable. I will tell you what places to avoid—they are tourist traps. They double their price if you speak English. It is bad."

Quint poured another glass of wine and shook his head. "Carmella, that's not nice. Who are you talking about?"

She wrinkled her nose and the diamond winked. "Georgina, that hag. She told me when she sees a bunch of tourists, she doubles everything, then brags about it."

"Isn't that Jordan's mom? The girl who dated one of your ex-boyfriends?"

Carmella glowered. "*Sì.* She is like her *mamma*—not to be trusted. *Lei è una faccia di culo.*"

I couldn't help my excitement. "I know that curse word! It means assface, right?"

Carmella winced and Quint sighed. "Very good. I'm teaching Aurora Italian, Carmella. Thanks for helping her with the bad slang."

"*Prego!*"

I pressed my lips together to keep from laughing. Quint pointed to the bottle. "Do you want wine? Aurora brought it."

"Sure!" She took the glass and slid into the chair while her brother began putting food on a plate. "I cannot believe you came to Sicily to meet your family. I am so sorry about your *mamma*. When I lost mine, I was sad for a long time."

"Thank you. It's been hard, but I think you had it worse. You were so young." Carmella nodded. I caught the flash of pain on her face and realized grief wasn't a passing thing that eventually left for good. I'd always feel the sting, but I sensed it would be in varying degrees. "Discovering all these new relatives has been a gift. I have no one back home."

Carmella gasped. "None? No aunts or uncles? Cousins?"

I shook my head. "I was an only child. But not anymore."

"I cannot imagine having no one. Of course, sometimes I wished my brother would go away for a little while."

"Sure. And you were always a joy to live with," Quint retorted.

Carmella laughed, loud and full like her brother. "Please tell me all about New York. I love your videos so much—they inspire me. You have so many followers and you are beautiful and famous. How did you do it?"

I shifted in my seat, already uncomfortable. "That's so nice of you to say, but honestly? I'm going through an identity crisis at the moment."

"What is this?"

"It means I think I may want to do something else. After I lost my mom, I fell apart. But I think in some weird way, it was a good thing, because I realized I wasn't really happy. While I'm here in Sicily, I thought the time might help me figure it out. See what I'd really like to do with my life."

Carmella studied me with the same intensity as Quint. And though she was young, and in her own world right now, I felt completely seen and understood. "Are you scared you may lose what you have?"

I smiled. "I think I'm more scared of not trying to be truly happy. Have you felt that way?"

She nodded. "*Sì.* I wanted to work in fashion and go to Milano, but Quint convinced me to go to school first."

Quint laid down a platter full of sandwiches with grilled eggplant, along with a salad and chickpea fritters that I was becoming addicted to. "Carmella was not happy with me for a while."

His sister grinned cheekily. "I hated him. Called him very bad names."

"But I was right."

"*Sì*. This time."

Quint sat down at the table with us. "Now she is going to be a teacher. She is very smart with languages and loves children."

"Only the well-behaved ones." We laughed. "I will be the most fashionable Italian teacher ever."

Quint sighed. "Maybe you take out the nose piercing?"

"Maybe not."

I grinned at their easy banter. We said grace and began to eat. I'd learned dinner was a lighter meal than lunch, and I found myself embracing the change. Indulging early left more time to digest and exercise and I was beginning to adjust. The sandwiches were drizzled with oil, full of fresh vegetables and creamy cheese. The fritters were crispy on the outside and tender on the inside. Carmella chatted about school and about her dream to meet the right boy and fall in love after she started her career. I realized the younger women in Sicily were like Americans—they wanted it all. We truly were all connected with the same dreams of love, family, and fulfilling work. We just went about getting there in different ways.

Afterward, we nibbled on almond cake, drank coffee, and helped Quint clean up. Seeing him in the role of protector and parent made me fall even harder. Carmella obviously adored him, and though it seemed they'd had some bumps along the way, they both loved and respected each other. It took a good man to give up his own needs for someone else quietly, allowing Carmella the dignity of carrying no guilt. Too many people I knew needed praise and pats on the back when they made a sacrifice.

Not Quint.

Finally, I said goodbye to Carmella, and Quint drove me home. We were quiet for a while, the hum of energy between us occupying my thoughts. Meeting his sister had tightened the bond between us.

At least, from my view.

Except Quint hadn't made a move today. Maybe he was being careful since I'd just broken up with Jason. I sensed he wanted more than friendship, but I was also used to American men who played games. My past relationships had not been stellar, mostly because of my focus on work and my inability to commit fully.

Now things felt different.

Tamping down my spiraling thoughts, I spoke. "I loved your sister. Watching you together made me happy."

I caught the flash of white teeth in the shadowed car. "She loved you. I respected the way you talked to her. Being open about figuring things out. I think it was important for her to know even the people she admires are always growing."

"I never wanted to admit it before. Someone once said the moment you admit you know nothing, wisdom truly begins."

"That must have been me."

I laughed. "Definitely you."

When he got close to the marina, he parked and cut the engine. "Would you like to walk a bit?"

My voice came out in a squeak. "Sure."

I was over thirty years old, and my palms were sweaty when he came around to open my car door. Nerves jumped in my belly with every step we climbed, standing close, our fingers occasionally brushing. The ocean was quiet at this hour, with the occasional echo of chatter drifting in the wind. We reached the top and stood by the rail, looking at the spill of boats and lights, of stars and moonlight, of dark sky and crescent moon.

"Are you looking forward to the wedding?" he asked.

"I can't wait. I'm going dress shopping tomorrow with Catena and Teresa. Then eating with my grandparents."

"I was also invited to your grandparents' house."

I tilted my head and stared at him. "You were?"

"I go there often, sometimes with Carmella. I've stayed away because I thought it was important you have time alone with your family. But I think it is okay to join you tomorrow, no?"

"Yes! *Sì!* I'd . . . love that."

My cheeks grew hot as I stumbled over my words. A few strands from my topknot escaped and whipped across my lips. He reached out, carefully tucking them behind my ear, leaning closer.

My breath seized as I waited for his next move.

"Have you been practicing your Italian?"

I blinked. His rumbly voice was seductive, and I had to focus hard on the question. "My Italian? Um, yes. When I can. I did catch your sister's curse word and am proud of that."

"You are my star pupil." I felt like drowning in his eyes—the swirl of rich green and whiskey brown. "I should quiz you on a few terms, though."

I frowned. "Now?"

"Tell me if you know this one. *La notte è bellissima.*"

"The night is beautiful!"

He smiled and my gaze dropped to his mouth. "*Molto bene.* How about this? *Grazie per essere venuta a cena.*"

I concentrated really hard to figure it out, but the view of his gorgeous face was distracting as hell. "Um, thank you for something dinner?"

"Thank you for coming to dinner."

"I was super close."

"Last one. *Voglio baciarti.*"

His breath rushed over my mouth as he whispered the words, and I shivered. "I have no idea."

Slowly, his hands reached out to cup my cheeks. His forehead pressed against mine, nose close, mouth an inch away. Everything inside and outside stilled.

"It means I want to kiss you, Aurora."

My entire soul sighed with longing. "*Sì, per favore.*"

His mouth took mine, sweetly, gently, sipping at my lips like a precious drink of water in the hot desert sun. I bloomed under the leisurely slide of his lips, the silkiness of his beard against my skin, the press of his body against mine. Leaning in, I slid my hands up and around his shoulders and let go of any thoughts.

He kissed me for a long time under the moonlight. The taste of him made me dizzy, so I clung tighter and he held me like a gift he refused to let go of.

When he pulled back and gazed into my eyes, I knew everything had changed.

At least for me.

"Did you love him?" he asked, a tiny crease between his brows.

I didn't have to pause or think. I answered from my heart. "No. I know that now."

The frown disappeared. I reached out and stroked his beard. "I've been wondering how it would feel if you kissed me."

A grin lightened his face. "Am I keeping it or shaving?"

My voice felt thick in my throat. "Definitely keep."

He lifted my hand and pressed a kiss into my palm. "Come."

I followed him to my door, hesitating. Did I invite him in? Was it too soon? How had it been only a few weeks, yet I felt as if I'd known him forever? It was as if just his presence filled a part of me I didn't realize was empty. Was this what my mother had experienced with my father? Or was it just part of my journey here, leading me back home to where I could make a new start?

The questions whirled in my head, but I had no time to sort through any answers.

"*Buona notte, bella.*"

His voice was achingly gentle, but his eyes burned like fire, confirming he wanted more, but not tonight. I watched him go and then let myself inside to slump against the door.

Oh Lord, this was getting complicated.

But it was too late.

I already needed to find out what happened next.

EIGHTEEN

I DECIDED TO surprise Catena, Theo, and Quint.

Each morning, I'd walk to the marina and the fish market and watch the fresh catch of the day be snatched up by various restaurants and locals. There was always a different group of fishermen at the tables, but I knew that Catena and Quint liked to get there for the earliest catch so there was plenty of time to prepare the specials.

I'd accompanied them twice before and felt ready to test out my Italian and sales skills. When I texted them both that I was going to bring back the fish today, they didn't try to fight me, just easily accepted I'd be up to the task.

I set out to arrive before the crowds, but the market was already bustling with activity when I made my way onto the wharf. As I looked around, the scene reminded me of controlled chaos.

The sharp scents of seawater, salt, and fish filled the air. Boats were docked, and fishermen shouted back and forth in

Italian to one another, haggling with different people. Big plastic crates of seafood practically overflowed, and I winced as I saw lines of creatures' faces all staring back at me.

I shuddered and tried not to think of *Finding Nemo*. Or Dory.

There were giant prawns, octopuses with squiggly legs, slippery long eels, and fish in a variety of colors and sizes, all packed on ice and displayed proudly for their audience. The fishermen yelled, shook their fists, laughed heartily, or greeted their customers with open affection. The nerves in my belly tightened and I went over my Italian phrases again. I'd been practicing for this moment and really wanted to do well.

I noticed Antonio, the man Catena and Quint always went to, had a big array of fish out, but there were at least three people ahead of me, waiting to talk to him. I squinted and studied him, a stout man with a stained apron, white mustache, and grizzled face. I figured he'd recognize me since Catena had introduced us both times, and he'd nodded and pretty much sung to me in Italian like we were on a gondola in Venice rather than at a fish market.

I glanced to my right, and another man was staring at me. He had no customers, and when he caught my eye, he began gesturing me over, speaking loudly. I bit my lip, figuring Antonio would be busy and it wouldn't hurt to just get what I needed now. Especially since it looked like the batches of seafood displays were similar.

"*Signora, buongiorno! Guardi i gamberi!*"

The other man held up giant prawns and I nodded with enthusiasm. He seemed thrilled with my response and launched into a long litany in Italian, picking up different types of fish and holding them up. I refused to look into their dead eyes and tried not to gape at a huge swordfish hanging by the side, where another fisherman looked like he was about to begin cutting it up.

Better to do the job and get out before I had to see the butchering.

I spoke slowly, pointing to the prawns, clams, and a light blue fish that Quint had snatched up before that I loved. He'd cooked it with lemon and garlic and tomato, simple and light, with a flakiness that melted in my mouth. I think it was simply called bluefish. I pointed. "That!" I shook my head and repeated the phrase in Italian. "*Posso averlo, per favore?*"

He beamed and began laughing, waving me closer. He asked me something twice, and I figured out that he wanted to know how much fish I wanted. I'd studied the numbers in Italian and knew it was by kilogram. I told him to give me three kilograms, the fish was packed up for me, and I tucked it into my overlarge bag to take to the pub. I paid the fisherman, who seemed so happy, he came around and practically hugged me, so I hugged him back, nodding, and used a few casual phrases I knew to say thank you and goodbye.

I turned to leave and noticed Antonio's intense stare. I waved, glad he'd recognized me, but he was suddenly glaring, a fierce furrow dipped in between his brows. He shouted something at me in Italian and shook his fist, which spooked me enough that I hurried my pace and left.

Geez, I wondered what that was about.

I pushed the scene from my mind and grabbed a ride to the pub. It was a silly thing to feel excited about, but I loved being able to help in a small way. Of course, I'd done a few media posts about Bar Sciacca, touting it as the best local place to eat. I'd also given Catena, Theo, and Quint a marketing strategy session and gone over some highlights to hook patrons into choosing their restaurant over Murphy's Pub. I thought adding a fun weeknight game, trivia, or contest would help, and they'd loved the idea.

But bringing actual product into the restaurant was more satisfying. I hoped they liked my picks.

I reached the pub and went inside. It was dim, and prep was already beginning for lunch. I greeted one of the cooks and the waitresses, then moved toward the bar, where Catena and Quint were unpacking boxes and setting out bottles of wine and liquor.

"*Buongiorno!*" I said brightly. "I have a present for you."

Catena squealed and hurried around to give me a hug. "You did it! Oh, Aurora, thank you for doing this—it gave Quint and me some extra time to get stuff done. Bluefish!"

Quint joined her, wiping his hands on a towel and smiling intimately at me. I became a bit breathless when he neared, and then he kissed my cheek. "*Buongiorno, bella,*" he murmured against my ear. His beautiful eyes danced like we held a secret.

And we did. That kiss had kept me up all night like a teenager. I'd gone over it in my mind, finally settling into sleep with a dreamy sigh. I caught Catena's look as she glanced back and forth between us. It was as if a lightbulb had gone on in her brain. Her eyes grew wide and she made a little gasp of discovery.

I'd intended to tell her about my crush on Quint, but now it was too late. Catena shook her head and bumped Quint's arm. "You two have something to tell me?" she demanded.

Quint and I held matching innocent expressions. "No," we said at the same time.

She pointed at me. "I will get the full story when we go dress shopping later. Be prepared."

I blushed, which made her laugh. I'd gone from a hive problem to a blushing problem since I arrived. Ridiculous.

"Let us see what you brought," Quint said. They both approved of the fish and giant prawns and immediately began discussing how to use the clams for *spaghetti alle vongole.*

"Did Antonio take good care of you?" Catena asked.

"Oh, I tried to go to him, but his line was long, so I went to someone else."

Catena and Quint froze. Slowly, my cousin's gaze swerved to me. "Wait. You didn't buy this from Antonio?"

I shook my head. "No, there was this other guy across from him who waved me over, so I bought it there. I did good with the price. I'd taken notes from our last visit."

My cousin paled. Quint cleared his throat and muttered something under his breath.

"What? Did I do something wrong?" I asked.

"*Merda,*" Catena said. "It's my fault. I forgot to tell you."

Nervousness flowed through me. "Tell me what?"

Quint's voice was gentle as he explained. "We've been going to Antonio forever. You never switch suppliers at the market—it's a great insult. Did Antonio see you?"

I buried my face in my hands. Suddenly, his reaction made

sense. "Oh God. Yes. I didn't understand, but he looked really mad and shouted at me. I just left."

Catena nibbled on her lower lip. "We need to fix this right away. I have to go see Antonio. I'll explain that you misunderstood and I will apologize."

"Is it that bad? What could he do to you?" I asked.

Quint hesitated. "He can refuse to sell to us again. He could spread the word that we have betrayed him and cause a lot of issues."

I blinked. "A fisherman can do all that? What about healthy competition?"

"This is Sicily. There is no such thing," Catena said.

My expression must've shown my misery at screwing this up for them, because Quint reached out and squeezed my hand. "We will fix it. You didn't know, Aurora."

I snapped up to full height. "I'm coming with you. I want to apologize in person."

"He may yell at you," Catena warned.

"I can take it. Let's go."

Quint gave me a look of admiration and nodded. "*Va bene.* We will go together. Let me get this fish to the kitchen first."

We drove back and I tamped down my anxiety. I was a grown woman and I could apologize with dignity for hurting Antonio's feelings. Even if I felt like a toddler being dragged by my mom after mistakenly insulting someone. The moment we approached Antonio, he came around his post and threw his hands up in the air, yelling something at Catena.

And then it began.

Quint got involved, and the three of them began fighting,

while I stood outside the circle. The guy who'd sold me the fish crossed his arms in front of his chest and watched the whole debacle with a huge grin. When he caught me looking, he beamed, nodding proudly. A crowd had gathered around us, nosily listening to the fight and studying me with frowns and disapproving looks.

Dear Lord, I'd started a fish war.

Finally realizing I needed to do something, I dragged in a breath and shouted at the top of my lungs. "*Basta!*"

At least the emergency word made them all stop shouting. The three of them stared at me in surprise.

I faced Antonio with my hands out in supplication, palms up. "*Mi dispiace*, Antonio," I said, holding his gaze. "I did not know. I am *Americana.*" I paused. Pointed to myself. "*Stupida!*"

It felt as if the entire wharf was silent, waiting for Antonio's response.

He glared at me for a while, then his face dropped into a neutral expression. He nodded. "*Sì. Va bene.*" He rattled off something long in Italian to Catena and Quint, and then they all got in a tight circle and kind of hugged.

I couldn't help it. I stepped in and joined them, and Antonio patted my shoulder.

And I'd never felt so good about belonging.

"TELL ME EVERYTHING."

We were at my second cousin's friend's shop looking for the perfect dress. Teresa and Catena flanked me as we worked our way through displays of various dresses in silk and lace. Many were handmade, with gorgeous stitching. The owner chatted for a bit, then left us to browse and gossip.

My cousins immediately pounced.

Catena faced me. "I saw the way Quint looked at you. How could I have missed it? When did this start?"

Teresa had a big-ass grin on her face. "Quint is H-O-T. And sweet. He has not been able to find a good connection and I think you are perfect together."

I tried not to groan. I guessed I wasn't used to being teased or pushed to give information. Even my acquaintances were more work-oriented and rarely probed for any intimate details about Jason. "Jason and I were having issues before I came here, but I wasn't ready to deal with them. Things got worse during this separation, so we broke up. I felt good about my decision. Not sad or depressed. Honestly, I think I was mostly relieved."

"Good! Then this will not be your rebound," Catena said.

I grinned at my cousin's knowledge of girl code. "I found Quint attractive the moment we met, but it's more than that now. Each conversation has brought us closer. What he did for Carmella was special. I . . . like him."

My cousins shrieked and I laughed. Pleasure flowed freely through my veins. My mother had given this up—the close bond of siblings and cousins joking and having fun together. I felt an odd warmth as I imagined her face and her smiling at our interactions.

"Now that you're staying for the wedding, you will have more time together," Teresa said. She lifted a dress in black, frowned, then replaced it. "Maybe you will fall in love."

Catena sighed. "Quint has been in a great mood lately. Have you kissed?"

I turned and pretended to study a beaded gown.

"You have! How was it? Better than Jason?" Catena asked.

Teresa jumped in. "Open mouth or closed? Long or short? Were you touching?"

I groaned. "Stop—this is painful."

They shot me mischievous looks. "We can always ask Quint instead," Catena said.

I gasped. "That's plain mean."

Teresa shrugged. "Welcome to the family."

I half closed my eyes, then steeled myself. "He drove me home after we had dinner at his house. We took a short walk, and he kissed me while we were looking over the water, in the moonlight." They kept up their hard stares, expecting more. "He put his fingers on my cheeks and in my hair, and it was one of the hottest kisses I've ever experienced. Then he politely walked me to the door and left."

Finally, they looked satisfied. "Much better," Catena said. "He is coming to Nonna and Babba's tomorrow, right?"

"Yes."

"And he introduced you to Carmella?" Teresa asked.

"Yes. She was sweet—I really liked her." My cousins shared a knowing look. "What?"

"He is serious about who Carmella meets. Quint is known to date many women but for only a short time. He is acting very different with you."

My heart sped up, but I tried to remain cool. After all, I wasn't sure how this whole thing would work. I'd return to New York and he'd remain here. Did a long-distance relationship have the capacity to work? I couldn't see how we'd be able to continue if we were separated by so many miles, even with technology.

The thought depressed me, so I pushed it aside and tried to enjoy the fact that I wasn't alone in my feelings. I might not have Mom anymore, but my cousins were here for me, and that meant everything.

"I'm not sure how this will end," I admitted. "But we'll see what happens."

"Love works its way if it is meant to be," Catena said confidently.

"*Sì*. I believe— *Merda!* I found it!"

I jumped at Teresa's shout and stared at the dress she'd unearthed from the pack.

Oh, it was perfect.

The dusty rose lace dress had delicate stitching, a modest hem, and cap sleeves. The neckline was a deep V, but more of a tease than a reveal. My usual style was modern and sleek, perfect for work and after-hours events.

But this? It was a dress made for a dream. The color was rich enough to flatter my dark complexion, and the cut would emphasize my curves rather than conceal them. It screamed romance and I touched the lace with awe. "Stunning. My size?"

"*Sì*, try it on," Catena urged. "We will look for jewelry."

"And shoes!" Teresa added.

I went to the dressing room, changed, and stepped out to look in the full-view mirror.

It was everything I'd ever want for a wedding in Sicily: modest yet sexy, classic yet unique. My cousins heartily agreed, and we spent the rest of the time matching up accessories. Nude pumps in Italian leather. A delicate gold chain choker. Earrings in bold beading that dangled playfully.

We left the store, giggling and linking arms. I couldn't wait to be part of the wedding and stand beside my family in a beautiful dress.

I also couldn't wait for Quint to see me in it.

NINETEEN

THE NEXT DAY, I left my grandparents' table dangerously stuffed, but I was beginning to get used to it. After several courses, I'd tried to say no to the *zucca in agrodolce.* I shook my head politely but caught my grandfather's disapproving look. He stared at me in warning, as if rejecting any part of my grandmother's cooking would be a personal insult. After the debacle at the fish market, I smiled weakly and accepted the food on my plate.

It was delicious. The thinly sliced pumpkin was seasoned in a sauce that had a sweet-and-sour element, sprinkled with mint. I caught my grandfather's nod and relaxed. I was becoming more adventurous in my palate and was writing about my new experiences in my journal. Quint teased me that he was going to take me on a food quest where he showed me every local specialty I'd been missing.

I laughed but I was a bit scared. I'd learned Sicilians really liked to cook with organs. It was a taste I wanted to avoid.

I watched Carmella and Quint be enfolded easily into my family's arms and marveled at the power dynamics of connection. People might not have a lot of money here, but they were rich in ways I never imagined. There was always someone to welcome them, to touch and hug and listen. Even the fights were part of communication, as I became more familiar with the shouting and frantic hand gestures that only faded minutes later with a gruff humph, eye roll, or frown. Then the argument was officially over, and I waited for the next explosion.

My family was comfortable with their feelings, including outbursts. I'd never felt as if I had to hide my true self from my parents, but in my work, I'd valued what the world saw on the surface. Here, I'd begun to question whether any of my reservations had mattered. Who cared if there were cracks in my armor? Who cared if thousands of random people followed me if they didn't know the real messy stuff I never shared? I'd believed I was helping, but now I knew it was a ruse—something I told myself, to feel good about fame and wanting more of it.

My ego had been fed. Not my soul.

Yet I'd begun to find hidden pieces of myself here I hadn't known existed. By sharing a meal. Taking a walk. Writing what interested me rather than to make a point. Sitting in the sun and daydreaming.

How did doing nothing make me feel more productive than I had in ages?

Quint appeared by my side. I'd been drying dishes but evidently had stopped to stare off into the distance, lost in my thoughts. "What takes you away from here?" he asked, gaze curious. "You have a look on your face I've never seen."

Surprised he studied me that deeply, I smiled. "Comparing

this life to the one back home. I'm figuring stuff out. What I want and what I don't."

"Me, too."

I loved the creases around his eyes when he grinned. I tried not to look at his mouth but kept replaying the silky feel of his beard against my cheeks when he'd kissed me. "Oh. Quint—"

I didn't know what I was about to say—his name alone was a harmony on my tongue—but suddenly my grandfather stormed up behind us and gave us his very familiar dark look. He said something in Italian to Quint, then turned to me. "Let us walk."

I blinked. Quint took the dish I'd been drying. "Go ahead. I'll finish up."

I felt the heavy gaze of my grandmother on us as we walked outside together.

We'd definitely gotten closer in the past week, but it was still a tentative dance between us as we tried to figure each other out. He still intimidated me, and I obviously still irritated him with my behavior. Now he seemed mad at Quint, which was distressing. Had I done something wrong by flirting with him? Was my grandfather pissed that his new granddaughter was trying to date a local? Or did he think I was like a . . . harlot?

God, I was such an idiot. I didn't think anyone used the word *harlot* anymore, even my grandfather.

As usual, he didn't speak for a while. I slowed my pace, and we headed toward the town square. The streets were quiet. After lunch, many stayed indoors, closed businesses, and relaxed or napped. The town would pick up again in an hour or two for the second half of their day, buzzing with activity.

I decided to break the silence since I had no idea what he

wanted to talk about. "I found a dress for the wedding. I went shopping with Catena and Teresa."

A pause. "What does it look like?"

"It's lace and a really pretty rose color. We had fun. They helped me pick out jewelry, too."

He nodded. His shoes scraped against the pavement. The sun was hot, but he still wore a formal button-down shirt with long pants and loafers. His derby-type cap was perched low on his head. We passed another gentleman sitting on the steps, smoking a cigar. He called out a greeting, which we both responded to. "That is good. I am glad you are spending time with *i tuoi cugini*."

"Me, too. I went to the fish market yesterday to help out. I wanted to surprise them by buying the seafood for Bar Sciacca."

"How is Antonio? Did he take care of you?"

I winced. "I had a problem." I launched into the story, surprised when I saw the little grin spread across his face.

"You did not know. It is good Antonio forgave. Catena and Theo would have been banned."

I relaxed and began to chat more. I told him about my walks in the morning and writing in my journal. He asked about my book, and I shared that my publisher had delayed publication and that I was relieved. I had no idea if I bored him, but he seemed to listen intently, nodding. Warmth washed through me at his full attention.

We got to the square and sat down on the bench. A few kids ran around us, playing. Some men, also smoking, sat in small groups, acknowledging us with a nod. Buildings encircled the space, a display of peeling paint and architectural beauty in fading colors. A fountain spurted out water, the sculpture cracked at the top. Flowers burst from balconies. The echo of Italian drifted in the air from houses with doors flung wide open.

"What else did you do this week?"

"Quint took me to the beach." I launched into the details of our day but left out the kiss. "I was happy to meet Carmella. He said they usually join you for dinner, but he wanted me to have time alone with all of you until I was comfortable."

"Quint is a good man. He treats you well, no?"

"*Sì*. Very well."

"And you like him."

Holy crap, was my grandfather asking about my intentions? Immediately, my skin prickled and I gave a quick scratch. Did he think Quint was too good for me? Did he want me to leave him alone? I bit my lip and considered my answer. "*Sì?* He is—he is only being nice. To take me places. To make me feel comfortable." When my grandfather didn't answer, I struggled to translate in Italian so he would understand. I didn't want to upset him if I'd done another thing he disapproved of.

His rough hand patted mine. "*Bene, bene.* I am glad. He took care of Carmella when his *mamma* died. He helps Catena and Teodoro. Quint is a good man," he repeated.

I waited. Squirmed in my seat. "Would you be mad if I wanted to . . . date him? I mean—I'm sure you heard I broke up with Jason. My last boyfriend. I didn't love him." I gave a nervous laugh. "I thought I could love him, but didn't, and I'm not sad about it like I thought I'd be. I'm actually happy. But Quint is very . . . nice."

Oh Lord, I couldn't stop babbling!

He stared at me. I peered into his eyes, which delved deep and assessed my comment. Gray brows lowered. If he said no, how could I disappoint him? After my mother ran off for a man and broke his heart, I had no right to get my grandfather upset. My breath seized in my chest and I scratched the back of my neck again.

"No."

I stilled. "No?"

"No. I would not be mad. Quint is a good man." Since he'd said it three times, I imagined Quint had his full approval and respect. And if I was okay to date him, maybe my grandfather held the same emotions for me.

"*Grazie.*"

"Did you like the *zucca in agrodolce*?"

I was grateful for the swift change of subject and relaxed. "Yes, I've never had pumpkin like that before."

"You will try *pani ca meusa* next. It is a Palermo food you will like."

"Oh, that sounds good. Is it meat?"

"*Sì.* Spleen and lungs."

Horror washed through me. I swallowed hard. "Um, I don't think I like organs. Maybe I will skip that one."

In seconds, his face transformed into that of an angry old man. "You will like if you try. *Va bene?*"

I wanted to challenge him, but I couldn't. "*Sì.*"

"We go now."

I followed him back to the house with one Italian word replaying in my mind.

Merda.

TWENTY

LATER THAT WEEK, Quint took me on a special shopping trip.

I knew Sciacca was known as the queen of Sicilian coral and had dedicated fishermen to extract the rare treasure. The art of creating jewelry from the red-orange coral was a dying art, and I was already mesmerized when I walked into the small shop at the end of a narrow street, deep in the historical part of town.

Quint introduced me to Patrizia, the curator and shop owner. She greeted Quint with a kiss and hug, then spoke to me in perfect English. "Welcome, *signorina*! We are so happy to have you here to create your own special jewelry."

"I appreciate your showing me your beautiful shop," I said sincerely. Patrizia could have been from New York. She was impeccably dressed in tailored pants and a silk blouse in neutral tones, with her tawny hair twisted up in a knot. It was as if she were a canvas for her own product, and I couldn't help but appreciate the savvy marketing. Gorgeous teardrop coral accented in gold hung from her earlobes. A coral cross encircled her delicate neck, and a bracelet of coral beads in rich salmon looped in three long ropes.

I immediately wanted all three pieces.

"Let me introduce you to our master jeweler, Stefano. He is the one who takes our ocean treasure and turns it into an art piece."

I turned to see an older man with a bushy white beard and eyebrows. His tufts of white hair sprouted from his head in a parody of Einstein. He wore yellow-framed glasses, a bright blue button-down shirt, and blue pants. His smile showed off crooked teeth. He exclaimed a string of Italian, motioning around the store with enthusiasm.

Patrizia nodded. "Stefano does not speak English, so I will translate. He is happy to meet you. He will show you how he makes the jewelry and then you can decide what you would like. Right now, he is finishing up a cameo necklace."

"*Grazie. È un piacere di conoscerti. Mi chiamo Aurora.*"

I bloomed under Stefano's delighted beam and Quint's respectful gaze. I tried studying Italian every night and had fun with Quint as he taught me phrases.

Stefano led us over to his workstation, and Patrizia pointed out the various pieces of equipment used to cut the coral. I was fascinated by the patience and care it took to turn the stone into something wearable. Patrizia showed us the different shades of color to the coral and how each piece demanded a specific skill set to reveal the finished product.

The cameo Stefano worked on was a delicate square with the facial impression of a girl's profile. He wielded a sharp metal tool called a burin to painstakingly cut out the details of the features and coax the delicate face from the coral. He polished the piece with oil and pumice, finishing up with a simple wash and dry. His final step was attaching the gold chain.

Breathless, I traced my fingers over the high shine of orangey red, where a young girl's face was imprinted on the stone for a piece of immortality. I imagined wearing my mother's cameo after her death and what it would mean to me. This type of jewelry was so much more than a pretty bauble to take home. It had meaning, from the fishermen who found the rare coral, to Stefano creating the trinket, and Patrizia matching it with the right customer. Hearing the history of Sciacca's queen jewel gave me goose bumps and a feeling of something significant.

I caught Quint studying my face, as if memorizing each of my expressions. His eyes held a glint of emotion that made me want to move closer to him. A smile touched his lips and he didn't hesitate to reach over and run a fingertip down my cheek. His voice held an intimate pitch, even with Patrizia and Stefano watching. "Pick something that calls to your heart, *bella*. Do not let it make sense here."

His words surprised me. They held no mockery or judgment, just a simple acceptance that showed Quint knew my tendency to use my head rather than any emotional impulses. I liked his being able to see my truth. It was a beautiful exchange, taking place quietly between us.

I walked around the store, chatting occasionally with Patrizia as I viewed the sample pieces. I got to choose the coral color and design, so there was a lot to consider. Finally, I picked out two I fell in love with. One was a cocktail ring with beads of coral arranged tight together. Diamonds were inserted between the beads. It was a bold piece I could imagine wearing on special occasions or when I needed to feel powerful. The band was a delicate gold, allowing the center stones to shine.

I also fell in love with a simple necklace in a darker coral color. Thinly braided ropes formed a crisscross shape that came to a V right at the base of my throat. A heart in filigreed gold nestled at the center of my throat. It reminded me of my mother—richly colored, elegantly simple, and full of history.

"This one," I finally said, lifting the sample up. "I love it."

"A beautiful choice. You'll see this piece is a bit more rare due to the darker color. This means the coral was dug beneath the surface—the deeper you go, the richer the hue," Patrizia explained.

Quint gestured to the ring. "I like that, too."

"Yes, but I won't wear it as much. I'm looking for a more everyday item."

Quint nodded. "*Sì*, the necklace is perfect."

We smiled at each other. Stefano explained the steps in creating my jewelry, and we spent a few hours watching him work in the shop. The steadiness of his fingers and the intense focus needed to cut and create gave me a new appreciation for the art of jewelry making. After checking with both of them if it was okay, I filmed part of the process and decided I'd write about the experience and pair it with a link to the video. How many people were able to see the intricacies of a master craft like this? Sciacca seemed to be a hidden jewel off the beaten path, and I loved the idea of sharing such a treasure.

I walked out wearing my necklace, a bit buzzed over the

excitement of the day and being around Quint. As we strolled, he took my hand in his. My heart sang at the touch of his fingers entwining with mine.

"How was your chat with your *babba*?" he asked. "I never got to ask you about it."

I remembered how afraid I was that my grandfather disapproved of me and Quint. I shook my head with a snort. "We're getting better. I find once I open up and tell him stuff, he's a good listener. I was a bit worried about you, though."

His eyebrow shot up. "Me? Why?"

"I think he saw us together and wanted to know if we were . . . dating."

Amusement danced in his voice. "Ah. And what did you tell him?"

"That it was none of his business."

His obvious shock made me laugh hard, and then he was laughing with me. "You tease me."

"*Mi dispiace.* I couldn't help myself. He said you were a good man. Many times."

"It is very important to have the blessing of family. I am glad your grandfather thinks of me so well."

The playfulness drifted away and I thought of my mother. I wished that somehow there had been a way my grandfather could have listened to my dad and had an open mind. I still felt resentful that neither of them had tried to bridge the gap over the years. After all, I had been the ultimate casualty.

But within this grief, I also didn't want to keep carrying the anger. What good would it accomplish? It was time for me to be the one to lay down the sword—to accept what was and find a way to move forward. The idea that my grandfather had blessed Quint and me felt right. Even if we were temporary.

Because, very soon, I'd return home. And this romance would be a distant dream.

Suddenly, Quint stopped. Cupping my chin, he turned me toward him, and I blinked in the sun, taking in his deep, dark eyes and carved features and sexy beard that framed his full lips like a gift. "*Mia bella*, do not look sad. We have today, and being in your company is . . . everything."

"Yes," I whispered. Our gazes met and locked. He lowered his head and kissed me, sweetly, thoroughly. His words threaded within the kiss, until I felt as precious as the coral in my necklace. When he lifted his head, we smiled at each other like teenagers, half giddy and desperate for contact.

"Let us go eat."

"To the pub?"

He shook his head. "I want you to myself for a bit. If that is okay?"

"Oh, yes. More than okay."

We stopped at a small café and sat close, knees pressed together, leaning in to keep the minimum amount of space between us. We drank red wine and ate pizza. I showed him some of my newer posts and shared what I was writing about. He talked about a property he might be interested in buying for his own restaurant—a small beachside café that had potential. The sun sank and we didn't move, switching to espresso and cannoli, desperate to hear each other's dreams and secrets and memories. It was late when we finally returned and he dropped me off at my rental, a déjà vu of the night of our first kiss.

How could time move so slowly yet feel so full? How could one day spent with Quint compare to a year with Jason? It made no sense. Normally, the obstacles ahead wouldn't allow me to move farther. There was no way to make a relationship between us work—I knew this in my gut. My home and life were in New York. His were here.

Yet . . .

He walked me to my door. I turned and stared into his eyes.

"Aurora?"

My name was a whisper, a prayer, a question.

I stepped off the ledge into the unknown and right into his arms. "Stay with me tonight."

His forehead pressed to mine. Slowly, he nodded. "*Sì.*"

I opened the door and he followed.

Butterflies danced in my stomach, but I acted calm as I moved to the kitchen. "Water? Wine?" I asked.

"A little wine if you're having some."

I grabbed the half bottle of red, poured two glasses, and walked toward him. His gaze locked with mine as he took the glass. "*Salute,*" he said in a low, gravelly voice.

"*Salute,*" I whispered back.

We stared at each other as we both sipped. The tension was like a fine-tuned instrument, held on the razor-thin edge of anticipation, ready to break into a soaring, gorgeous symphony.

"It has been a long time for me."

Shock barreled through me at his admission. He said the words with no apology or embarrassment, just a simple fact. I shook my head. "When we first met, I figured you were getting action every night of the week."

His laugh was rich and robust. "So, you thought I was a *donnaiolo*?"

My lip quirked. I didn't need to know the Italian word to gauge the definition. "A womanizer? Playboy? Don Juan? Um—yeah."

He shook his head, grinning. "No. I am careful who I involve myself with. I am no monk, but my focus has always been Carmella."

Knowing he'd taken me to meet his sister told me this was bigger than one night. "I like that about you." I shifted my feet. "I think you need to know that I'm not the type to just jump from one man to another. I've been unhappy with Jason for a long time, but it's not as if I'm afraid of being alone."

He set his glass down and closed the distance between us. Slowly, he plucked my own glass away and set it next to his. My heart beat rapidly, and I leaned forward so our bodies were inches away, and his masculinity shimmered in waves of heat.

"I know. You are strong, Aurora. But not in the ways you were probably told."

My breath eased from my lungs as I stared at his carved lips. His words felt important, and I sharpened my focus before I fell under the spell weaving between us. "How do you think I'm strong, Quint?"

His fingers cupped my chin, tilting my head up. Those golden brown eyes burned with a passion and care that made me feel both safe and wanted. "In your heart, *amore*. Where it counts the most."

And then he kissed me.

I surrendered to the embrace, opening like a flower under the golden heat of the sun, my arms wrapping around his shoulders to pull him close. His scent rose to my nostrils. His lips warmed mine, taking the kiss deeper until heat blistered between us and there was only a long, delicious slide into pleasure. There was no awkwardness, no hesitation or questions as we sank into each other, only a desperate need to be closer and learn his body like I was learning his soul, uncovering each precious inch and secret with joy and abandon.

It was that night I learned the difference between sex and making love, between physical arousal and giving myself to someone fullheartedly, with no regrets or fear.

By morning, I realized Quint was like my love affair with Sicily.

Slowly, he had healed my wounded heart and changed my entire life.

TWENTY-ONE

THE NIGHT BEFORE my cousin's wedding, I was invited to witness a beautiful tradition.

The rehearsal dinner wasn't the type I was used to. It wasn't extra fancy, and no one practiced their role in the ceremony, like how to walk down the aisle and whom to pair up with. Everyone gathered at a small local restaurant to eat and talk excitedly about the next day. I doubted I would've been invited to such a private event, but I was treated like royalty, a newly discovered relative whom the bride's family not only welcomed but insisted stay close.

I kept sneaking glances at Quint throughout the meal. We'd stayed together each night this week, locked in a world where only the two of us existed. Logically, I knew the first rush of a new relationship was heady and that hormones played a key part. I'd read all about oxytocin. I understood sex was not love. Yet being with Quint was unlike anything I'd experienced or even imagined. It was as if not only our bodies were in sync but our entire beings. We spent hours under the covers, talking and sharing. I felt fully seen for the very first time in my life. I craved not only his touch but his presence, and we'd been able to sneak in time together so he could show me everything about Sciacca and why he loved it.

Catena and Theo both knew about our blooming relationship and had happily told Quint to take time off from the pub. I didn't have many days left here, so we'd decided to make the most of the time we had.

After dinner, my cousins took me back to Magda's house, and all the men stayed behind, going off for a drink. Giggling, Teresa and Catena pulled me up the stairs to the bride's room, and I gasped when I entered.

The space was decorated with an enchanted, romantical charm. The bedsheets were pulled back and neatly folded, gleaming in bright white silk. Flowers filled the room in rich citrus colors, scenting the air with happy floral notes. Wedding gifts were spread around the room, a bounty of well-wishes for the bride and groom. Pressed, crisp linens; gorgeous ceramic platters and bowls; jewelry displayed in small velvet boxes—I spotted a coral ring and chandelier earrings—along with polished silverware and a shimmery lace negligee hung in front of the mirror.

Sugared almonds in pastel blue and pink were tucked within the sheets. As I stepped closer, I noticed a strange assortment of wheat, rice, and money.

Magda's wedding dress was laid out carefully on the end of her bed. The stitched white lace with sheer flowing sleeves and a dreamy train, along with her veil, seemed straight out of a fairy tale.

"What is this?" I asked Catena. "Does Magda know about this?"

My cousins laughed. "Of course! It is a tradition. The night before the wedding, the women in her family come to prepare the wedding bed. But only a single woman can touch the sheets," Catena explained.

"You could have done the job, *cugina*," Teresa teased.

Catena laughed. "Magda's younger sister stepped in to help. We gather her wedding presents to display, and on the sheets, we leave gifts to represent fertility and wealth and happiness. Then we lay out her dress."

"It's stunning," I said. I looked at the tight circle of women, old and young, crushed into the bride's room. Everyone was chattering nonstop, sharing in the excitement of the bride-to-be. "Why isn't Magda here?"

"She will come in a bit to see. Then we will distract her for the next part of the evening."

"Something else happens?"

Catena nodded, her eyes dancing with joy. "Ah, yes. My favorite part. Come—let's prepare drinks for Magda for when she arrives."

"Would it be okay to take pictures? For my posts?"

"Of course—Magda will not mind!"

I took out my phone and snapped a bunch of pictures. I loved the one with the older women in a tight circle, heads pushed together, talking in Italian and pointing to things in the room. Afterward, I joined my cousins in the kitchen, pouring wine and setting out snacks—even though we'd just eaten. When Magda arrived, her sister escorted her to the room, and I loved the cries and sounds of happy weeping from upstairs.

Time flew by as I settled into the chaos of my family, hugging Magda, who told me once again how glad she was I had stayed.

I didn't know how much time passed before a sense of anticipation rippled through the air, and my aunts began yelling in Italian. Catena jumped up and down and grabbed my hand. "He's here! Come outside and see!"

Having no idea what was going on, I followed her out the door and caught sight of a large group of men in a circle, standing under one of the windows. "What's happening?" I whispered, trying to take in the odd scene.

"*La serenata.*"

I realized the group of men were hoisting up a wooden ladder to rest against the house. Magda's fiancé tilted his head back and called her name loudly, followed by a long stream of Italian. I couldn't catch any of the words and tugged at Catena's arm. "What did he say?"

"He called her the lover of his heart and told her to come out to him."

"No. Way."

She grinned. "Oh—here she is!"

The lace curtains parted and Magda appeared at the window. She opened it and leaned over, resembling Juliet. Her long hair spilled over her shoulders and she laughed, her face beaming with joy. She said something to him, waving her hand as if to invite him up, and everyone in the crowd began to shout.

Her fiancé began climbing the ladder with a large bouquet of flowers clutched in his hand, as his support group stood in a line behind. The ladder looked rickety, so I hoped they'd spring forward to catch him if it went down. Step by step, he climbed up, reaching the top rung, which ended right at her window.

He whispered something. She whispered something back. They stared at each other in the moonlight, and for a few seconds, there was only silence.

I held my breath.

And then he began to sing. His deep, rich voice boomed out into the night with a passion that gave me goose bumps. His friends hummed in beautiful harmony for backup, but Magda had eyes only for him. I didn't understand the words to the song, but I remembered when I saw my first opera at the Met in Italian and realized I didn't have to truly know what they were saying to get the story. It was the same here.

The song was about love, and it was a gift offered to his bride.

The moon glowed and the stars twinkled, and for a few moments in the world, everything was perfect. Because we were all invited to step into their love story and share in their emotions.

Finally, he ended with a long, drawn-out note that was heartbreakingly tender, fading into gentle silence. Slowly, he pressed the bouquet to her chest in a parting gift.

She bent over and kissed him.

Everyone cheered and shouted. My heart expanded and my throat closed up. I'd never experienced this kind of feeling a part of something bigger and realized I'd cut myself out of any opportunity for this type of connection. Tonight was a gift, and I wasn't about to waste a single moment. I wanted to remember tonight forever.

Catena sighed. "I cannot wait to find a love like that. When I'm ready." I opened my mouth to agree, but she looked over my shoulder and gave me a mischievous wink. "See you later, *cugina*. Yours may be here now."

In seconds, she'd disappeared, and Quint was beside me.

"Did you enjoy the singing?"

I stared into his face and wondered why I suddenly pictured myself on the balcony, looking down as he sang to me the night before our wedding. Blinking, I tried to erase the image, but it stubbornly held. "Um, yes. It was very romantic. I didn't know about decorating the bride's room, either. I think we need to steal some of these traditions for America."

"Ah, what are some American traditions?" he asked.

"The usual, I guess. A bridal shower where gifts are given. A rehearsal dinner and reception. And of course, the bachelorette and bachelor parties."

He lifted a brow. "What type of party is this?"

I grinned. "The bride takes a bunch of her friends and travels somewhere fun. Or goes out to party for a night."

"Ah, I know this. We call it stag parties."

"The ones we hold usually have strippers."

His dark eyes widened. "I can't even imagine this."

"Same for the men. I guess we're a bit wilder. It started as a way to blow off steam before committing for life."

"Blow off steam?"

I loved the way he frowned intently when he didn't understand my expressions. How could a man that sexy be adorable, too? "Be a little bad. Maybe we don't have the best views of marriage in the US."

"We take it seriously in Sicily, but there are still many men who like to be . . . a little bad."

I laughed with him. Feeling the press of stares, I glanced around and noticed my cousins looking at us with big smiles, and my aunts nodding with approval. My cheeks heated. It was strange to have my dating life on display. I had an inkling of what it might be like if I was in love with a man everyone disapproved of. My mother was young and passionate. Would I have been so different if it had been me? I remembered the way she'd judged Jason and how angry I'd gotten. It was easy to blame a parent. I saw things more clearly now.

"I wonder if they are worried about my intentions toward you," I said.

He lifted my hand and pressed a kiss in my palm. His eyes twinkled. "You can use me as you see fit, *bella*. I can take it."

I bit my lip and shook my head, grinning. "You are very bad."

"Will you come home with me tonight?" he asked softly. "Carmella is staying at her cousin's."

His gaze turned heated. The memory of our bodies entwined, lips skating over my naked skin, his breath in my ear, his hands in my hair, all of it washed over me and I trembled with longing. For more. "Yes."

"And will you be my date for the wedding tomorrow?"

I touched his cheek. "*Sì.* I would love to be your date."

"Then let's go home."

He held my hand as we said our goodbyes, the sound of the word *home* echoing in my mind like a beautiful mantra.

THE DAY OF the wedding burned sunny and bright. I joined my family close to the church and watched the bride walk with her parents in a procession through the narrow streets. They strolled into the main square, where people lined up and waved, calling out *auguri* in booming voices. Magda looked stunning in her white dress, holding a bouquet of orange flowers, her veil and train trailing behind. As she reached us, she blew me a kiss, which I returned, and then we followed her in a group to the church, where the bells rang merrily and the town gathered to celebrate a local wedding.

The groom was already at the altar, and one look told me he was a nervous wreck. Still, he looked handsome in his black tuxedo, hair neatly slicked back, clean-shaven, and eyes brimming with anticipation as he watched everyone walk in to take their seats.

I sat in the pew, light beaming through the stained-glass windows, surrounded by my aunts, uncles, and cousins. As I glanced around, I noticed the majority of them I now knew by not only name but interaction. Somehow, in the past month, I'd bonded with dozens of people who all meant something to me in some way.

The music soared and we stood. Magda had only her two sisters walk down the aisle in front, their sky blue dresses a happy pop of color. When the bride appeared in the entryway, flanked by her mother and father, a hush and gasp came over the crowd. Her husband-to-be seemed in a trance as he stared, and with every small step, she edged closer to where he stood. Magda's parents placed her hand in his and stepped back.

And the ceremony began.

It was a full Mass, but after attending every Sunday, I was used to it now. I let each moment unfold and found peace in allowing myself not to rush to the finish. Seemed I'd gotten used to seeking the end and forgetting about the journey. It wasn't about the pronouncement of being husband and wife or rushing to the reception or wondering what happened next.

It was about this second, right now. And it was beautiful.

They became husband and wife. They kissed. They walked back up the aisle together, hand in hand, rings shining on their fingers.

I was so damn lucky to be part of it.

We took pictures galore and my cousins shrieked with excitement. "Let's go party!" Catena announced, linking my arm with hers and Carmella's. Quint joined in with Theo and we made our way to the winery for the reception. Tables were scattered on the deck outside, overlooking the vineyard, the mountains shimmering in the distance. A full band entertained, while wine and endless amounts of food were first passed around, then formally served at the tables.

It was a celebration of love and life and family. My sides hurt from laughing and my stomach hurt from overeating. Suddenly, the band launched into a fast song and everyone screamed with excitement, flooding the dance floor. The guests formed a large circle and Quint grabbed my hand. "We must dance. It's 'La Tarantella.'"

"I don't know the steps!"

"It won't matter. Just do what everyone else does," Quint said.

I joined the circle and held Quint's and Catena's hands. As the music geared up, I threw myself with enthusiasm into the dance, moving with the crowd right and left, lifting our hands, feet jumping to the rhythm, voices shouting the words in gaiety. I noticed the very young and the very old were part of it, catching sight of my grandparents dancing next to each other. The joyous grin on my grandfather's face made me stumble. I wondered if he'd once looked at my mother like that—with stars in his eyes and pure love in his heart for his precious daughter. Emotion flooded me at the thought.

After the dance, I staggered away for air, gulping down water. The sun soon set and threw the sky and grounds into a fiery color explosion. I watched the light get swallowed by shadows, inch by inch, and wondered how I was ever going to be happy alone now that I knew what I was missing.

I turned to find my grandfather walking up behind me. He looked handsome in a neatly pressed navy blue suit and red tie. I caught the scent of aftershave in a comforting spice. He'd gotten a haircut, and the strands were combed to the side. His hazel eyes scrutinized me behind his glasses, as if he were still unsure what he wanted to say. "Aurora. Do you enjoy the wedding?"

I nodded. His big smile was gone and replaced by his usual reserve. Knowing there was a deeper level of emotion residing within him that I was unable to reach hurt me. Which was ridiculous. I was being ridiculous, treating my grandfather's affection like a prize to chase and claim. I had no right to his love on my own. It was strictly from my mother's memory. He didn't know me deep enough to care like that. "*Sì*. It's beautiful. I liked the dance."

"'La Tarantella.' I have not done it in a while. Makes me tired."

"Me, too."

We stood in silence and watched the evening creep in. "What did you do this week?"

I gathered my breath. "Quint took me to see how coral jewelry is made. I bought this." My fingers brushed against my necklace. "I learned a lot—I had no idea how important coral was to Sciacca."

"After the coral was gone, many had to go back to fishing in order to make money. Craft is important here. Learning the old ways is not just for pride but to carry on our traditions."

"I can see that. I don't think there are enough crafts- and tradespeople anymore. Everyone wants to learn tech and sales, but no one wants to make anything. Here, art and wine and food are respected as highly as computers or social media."

He cocked his head. "Your job is this media, no? And . . . sales."

"It is. It was." I laughed self-consciously. "I've been writing a lot. Posts about Italy and how it feels to welcome change. Stuff about Mom and grief. I'm exploring."

"That is good. To be happy in life and in work."

"Were you?" I almost clapped my hand over my mouth as the question popped out. He narrowed his gaze, but I didn't back down. "Were you happy? With Nonna and your job and your family?"

Puzzlement flickered over his features. "It is different. I did what was needed. My father came from Lucca and worked on an olive oil farm. I followed in his footsteps. I did not ask if I was happy—I was glad to be able to support a family."

Fascinated, I probed a bit more. "How did you meet Nonna?"

"We were introduced by our families. She was a friend of my cousin's. I asked if I could court her and her father allowed me the privilege."

I couldn't help smiling at the idea of such a custom. "Did she get a choice, or did her father force her to date you?"

He looked affronted. "There was a choice, of course! I was very handsome."

A startled laugh escaped. My grandfather did have a sense of humor. "I bet you were."

He shifted his feet. "We had a good life. Good children. A house and jobs. Food and family. What more is there to ask for? This happiness you ask about. All of this should be enough."

I nibbled at my lip, assessing his sudden irritation. "Did you want my mother to do the same? Listen to you and do what was expected rather than running after my dad? Do you blame her for chasing what she thought would make her happy?"

A dark cloud settled over him and I regretted pushing. It was a beautiful day, the day of my cousin's wedding, and here I was playing with fire. I was like my mother—stubborn. I wondered if it was easier for him to forget about me and Mom and leave it in the past. Because talking about her and her choices was painful.

"Never mind," I said softly. "I'm sorry."

"No." He shook his head hard. "No, I do not blame her. I didn't understand. Your *nonna* did—she tried to explain, but I thought we were enough. Her family. I did not understand this type of love. The love she had for your father." I held my breath and prayed he'd continue. "But it was good. She was happy. I know this now."

"How? How do you know for sure she was happy?"

Understanding beamed in his eyes as he stared at me. Surprise threaded his tone. "Because of you, Aurora. My sweet *fragolina*. Your *mamma* had your father and you. She had the family she chose. And now you are here, a gift from above. You are here, my second chance."

My feet froze to the ground. I swayed, staring at my grandfather, who had said these extraordinary words without hesitation. My eyes burned and my voice came out like gravel. I said the only thing I could in that moment, when I finally realized what I meant to him. "Babba."

He blinked. And slowly reached out.

I stepped into his arms and hugged him tight. The scent of coffee and spice rose to my nostrils. His jacket was rough against my cheek, his bones solid yet fragile within my grip. Comfort and warmth surrounded me, burrowing deep into my soul. Our embrace brought in a solace that lingered. And stayed.

When we broke away, I brushed at my stinging eyes and laughed. A smile tipped his lips. "Come. We go back now."

I followed him back to the party.

TWENTY-TWO

I QUIETLY ROSE from the bed and walked to the balcony.

The night was still and humid. Boats rocked gently on the water. Insects screeched out their songs. The moon skipped beams across the glassy surface of the ocean. I sat down on the chair, bringing my knees up and wrapping my arms around them. I stared at the scene before me, thinking of my conversation with my grandfather. Of the wedding. And of returning home.

My last Zoom appointment with Dr. Sariah had touched on my inclination to keep myself in a controllable space. After I'd shared my story of being bullied years ago, and how I'd remade myself after Dad's death, she suggested that I'd learned to direct my life in analytical patterns with clear markers. I'd taken raw emotion that made me uncomfortable, broken it down into bite-size pieces, and found specific actions to feel better. It was kind of a breakthrough when I began looking at my past through that lens.

I also liked that Dr. Sariah had not labeled my behavior good or bad. It just was. If I was able to see my responses clearly, I could choose to react differently. Losing Mom had forced me to stay in full reactive mode and caused a mini breakdown. Coming to Sicily was something I'd probably never have done if my entire foundation hadn't been eradicated. It would've been easier to do what Jason advised: set up a few Zoom calls and chats and get to know my family from a safe distance.

The big question still haunted me. What would I now do differently when I got back home? I had no desire to be alone anymore. I wanted true connections. Could I make new relationships in New York? Or would I be forever longing to be with my Italian family?

I sat and thought for a while, until I heard the sheets rustling. Minutes later, strong arms wrapped around me. I sighed and cuddled against Quint's bare chest, enjoying the musky scent of his skin. "Is it a bad sign I didn't exhaust you enough to sleep?" he murmured in my ear.

Shivers raced down my spine even as I laughed. "It's not you. It's me."

"This keeps getting worse."

I turned around, loving his sense of humor, and ran my fingers through his mussed hair. He was sexy fresh from bed. A crease cut across his cheek from being mushed into the pillow. His eyes held a lazy gleam. "My grandfather and I had a moment today. After the wedding."

"Will you tell me about it?"

He sat down on the other chair and pulled me onto his lap. I leaned my head against his shoulder. "I called him Babba, and it finally felt right. It was the first time I felt like he loved me and that I had a true grandfather."

"I'm so happy for you, *bella*."

"I can't believe a month ago I had a completely different life. Being here, surrounded by my blood relatives, has changed me."

"You changed us, too. Brought us adventure and laughter and a new way of seeing things."

"I came with an intention to fix my brokenness. Losing Mom took away everything I'd put stock in. Stripped me of what I thought I knew." My sigh escaped into the quiet night. "How odd that so much loss could bring something good."

Quint stroked back my hair. "There's nothing to fix within grief. It just is. You accept the new part of yourself, and eventually you embrace it, because the world no longer owns a person you once loved. There is a new space that must be filled. Sometimes people want to do the work of filling it up too soon. They do not want to feel the empty place, but it is only in that pain that new things will come. Beautiful things. Such as this."

He waved his hand in the air at the scene before us. "Without your mother's passing, you would not have found family." Suddenly, his gaze swerved and pinned me tight. My breath rushed out of my lungs and my heart pounded in my chest at the intimate gleam in his beautiful eyes. "I would not have found you. Pleasure within pain, no?"

And just like that, I realized I was in love with Quint.

I knew now why I couldn't say the words back to Jason. I knew now why my mother could have felt brave enough to leave everything behind to follow the unknown. The realization didn't even terrify me, just revealed itself with a gentle awareness like a petal blooming under the sun after a long winter.

God, I wanted to tell my mom.

I closed my eyes and reminded myself she already knew. She would have loved Quint. He was a good man, as my grandfather said.

Trembling with wanting to share my feelings, I swallowed them back and sensed it wasn't the right time. I knew we shared a strong connection, but was it enough to sustain long-distance or obstacles after we'd only known each other for four weeks?

I wasn't ready to find out. Not yet.

Instead, I slid my arms around his neck and pulled him down toward me. Kissed him. Then whispered, "Why don't we concentrate on the pleasure tonight?"

His lips curved under mine in a smile.

He picked me up and brought me back to the bedroom.

My final days in Sicily were bittersweet. Each second took on a sharper, more emotional edge. I leaned into each moment, spending as much time with Quint and my family as possible. I allowed myself to bloom and give without worry about the future or getting hurt. I threw myself into my emotions full force, like flinging myself off the cliff to dive into the uncharted depths of the Mediterranean.

My gift was being not only caught by the water but embraced in a warm, comforting grip.

On the night of my final goodbye meal, we gathered at my grandparents'. The house was overflowing with relatives, spilling out onto the balcony and street until it became a bit of a block party atmosphere. My grandmother and aunts busied themselves in the kitchen like captains of infantry, barking orders to the younger women and directing a massive plate dispersion and retrieval.

I tried to help, but Nonna shooed me out, saying I was the guest of honor.

I took nonstop pictures, cataloging the beautiful gift of a meal cooked and planned with so much love, smiling with my aunts, uncles, and cousins, and laughing over bad selfies. I played with the children on the hot, dusty street and stole kisses with Quint in hidden corners.

When we finally sat to eat, I felt as if every day in Sicily had been training me for this particular meal.

Nonna brought out the very best. Platters of caponata on thick crusty bread and *sarde a beccafico*—baked sardines stuffed with breadcrumbs, spices, pine nuts, raisins, and garlic. Grilled swordfish dripping with lemon and herbs, potato croquettes crispy on the outside and fragrant tenderness inside. The pasta dish was *busiate al pesto trapanese*—baked with pesto sauce, ripe tomatoes, almonds, basil, and garlic. The simplicity and fresh flavors elevated the food beyond a five-star restaurant, and I told Nonna that through each dish and each bite of delicious, swoon-worthy carbs.

Finally, the platters began to slow and I gave a prayer of thanks. I was truly at my limit—afraid if I took another bite I'd get sick. And then Nonna appeared by my side with a dish of sliced bright red meat. I shook my head and smiled.

Nonna stopped and stared at me. "It is *polpette di cavallo*," she said. "*Delizioso.*"

I opened my mouth to say no.

Babba gave a loud humph. I glanced over to his usual spot at the table and found him glaring. I swallowed. "*Grazie*," I said weakly.

Nonna happily filled my plate. I stared at it for a while, moving my fork through. It looked extremely tender and fragrant, but my stomach was rebelling and there was an odd inner warning that told me not to eat it. When I looked up again, I noticed Quint watching me with a strange look on his face. Like he was waiting for me to take a bite.

Like he was waiting to see what I thought.

"Um, what exactly is this dish?" I asked. Everyone was talking loudly and yelling across the table, so no one heard me. Quint immediately involved himself in a conversation with my uncle, increasing my suspicion. Something was going on here.

"*Scusate*, what is this dish?" I yelled, not caring who answered me.

Babba frowned fiercely at my interruption. "*Mangia*," he commanded.

Normally, he'd scare the hell out of me enough to eat it, but I was braver now. "What is it?" I asked for the third time.

Catena pressed her lips together as if trying hard not to laugh. "Horse balls."

I stared at her in shock. "What did you say?"

"Horse balls," Babba repeated. "It is good. Your *nonna* has been preparing this dish for you. *Mangia*."

Horse balls?

I stared at my plate. I sensed an air of tension tightening around the table, in the atmosphere becoming charged around us, and I knew I had to make a decision.

Horse balls.

And I knew with crystal clarity that I couldn't do it. I just couldn't eat this dish.

My gaze swerved to Quint. A tiny smile played about his full lips. He was waiting to see what I would do.

I remembered my safe word. My voice burst out from my inner soul, passionate and desperate and stubborn. "*Basta!*" I yelled. "*Basta!*"

A gasp echoed in the air. Silence fell. Slowly, I met my grandfather's eyes, preparing myself for the battle ahead on my last day in Sicily.

Then it happened.

Babba began to smile, then laughed out loud. It was a deep bellow, a joyous sound that filled me with an overwhelming happiness and love for this man, my mother's father, the patriarch of the family, a man who'd made mistakes and had regrets but was here with me right now, loving me back.

I began to laugh and then everyone joined in. Nonna shook her head, grinning, and took my plate away.

Quint gave me a wink and mouthed, "Nice job, *bella*."

I shook my head at my ridiculous, chaotic Italian family and asked for more wine.

LATER THAT EVENING, I sat with Nonna and Aunt Philomena and leafed through the photo albums. We pored over pictures of my mother when she was young and shared stories that made us cry and giggle and hug. While I listened and told my own accounts, Mom came alive again, her presence shimmering around me. I'd told Dr. Sariah that I begged to dream about her or recognize certain signs, but she never appeared. I'd read that the harder you chase the ones you love, the less you find. Tonight, as I sat in her childhood home, she burned bright.

"How will we keep talking?" Nonna demanded, squeezing my hand.

"We're lucky, Nonna. We have the computers now. Zoom, FaceTime, WhatsApp."

"What's what?"

I smiled and hugged her. "You don't need to worry—Catena and Theo will set it up for you. Maybe we can schedule a day and time each week to talk?"

"*Sì.* I would like that."

I moved to each of my relatives to spend dedicated time, until most had said their goodbyes and left. A pat on my shoulder made me turn.

"We walk," Babba said.

I nodded and followed him out. We fell into our usual leisurely pace and headed toward the square. An easy silence settled between us, so different from how our relationship had begun. I greedily devoured the sights and sounds around me, tucking away the images to revisit later in my memory. We greeted the older men sitting on benches, nodded to families on their balconies, awash in the lyrical Italian chatter rising around us.

We sat down at our spot and surveyed the square. Children shrieked and played. Mothers strolled with their babies. Friends gathered in tight groups to gossip. Shops opened and the scents of baked bread and garlic rose in the air.

"When do you leave?" he finally asked.

"Thursday. Tomorrow, I'll pack and visit Bar Sciacca for my last night."

He nodded. "What will you do when you get home?"

I studied the stubborn set of his chin, wrinkled face, and familiar hazel eyes behind his black glasses. "I don't know. But for the first time in my life, I feel good about not knowing. I think something different. Being here has changed me."

A serious expression settled into his features. I frowned, sensing he was troubled. "Will you be alone?"

"*Sì.*" I paused. "But now I know I'm not anymore."

With slow, methodical motions, he reached into his pants pocket and removed a black-and-white photo. It was creased and battered, as if it had been viewed hundreds of times, lovingly tucked into a wallet or drawer or tight space. He handed it to me.

My breath caught. It was Babba with my mom. They were holding hands and she was probably about twelve years old. They stared at the camera, both smiling, both obviously being silly and happy. It was taken right here in the square, in front of this bench. My fingers traced over my mother's beloved face. "I love this picture," I managed to say.

"I had just gotten her gelato. She was sticky and dancing around the piazza, and when I called her name, she ran to me and jumped into my arms." Babba paused, and I sat still, willing him to go on. "She said, 'I love you, Papà, and I will never, ever leave you.' We had taken the camera out that afternoon, and your *nonna* saw us and told us to get together so she could take our picture."

My throat burned with emotion. "I could tell how much you loved each other."

"I did not tell her. Before she left. I yelled. I was very angry. I said bad things and I never saw her again."

His confession broke me apart. I hugged him hard and started to cry. "She knows that, Babba. And so do I."

"You will come back?"

I nodded, swiping the tears from my cheeks. "I will come back. I promise. You will never lose me."

"*Va bene. Ti amo moltissimo, piccolina.*"

"*Ti amo*, Babba."

We sat on the bench for a while, quiet, with no more regrets.

TWENTY-THREE

THE NIGHT BEFORE I left, Quint and I had dinner together. After the conversation with my grandfather, I realized that we'd been given a gift. To leave each other with everything said and no regrets. But with Quint? I'd run out of time. And as the hours ticked down to my departure, I began to get angry.

Quint treated our last day like every other. Instead of asking many questions about my intentions or our relationship, he remained quiet. I got up early to pack, then joined him at the beach. We ate lemon ices and swam. We kissed on the blanket and walked the shore hand in hand. We grabbed lunch at a café. Later, we cleaned up and changed, then headed for dinner.

And not once did he say anything about his feelings.

Not once did he seem worried about my departure or figuring out what the hell we were doing together.

By the time the food was served, I'd grown quiet and very pissed off.

Maybe I'd been completely wrong about us. The man didn't seem the least bit concerned about me taking off across the planet and not seeing him for weeks or months. We'd made no promises; we hadn't declared our feelings. And right now, I was afraid to admit maybe I was getting played.

Maybe I had fallen in love with someone who didn't love me back. Or want any type of future together.

Maybe I had assumed my emotions matched his.

The panic and unease built. The silence that fell between us during dinner wasn't comfortable. He asked me several times what was wrong, and I said I was distracted by having to leave. Then he'd just nod, saying he understood and that things would work out.

But how? How would things work out exactly?

Even worse? This was all my fault. I'd fallen in love with him, and there had been no clear rules.

I hated it.

Finally, we paid the bill and walked out. When he tried to take my hand, I shook it off. "Aurora? Talk to me, *bella*. What is wrong?"

I spun around to face him. "I don't understand what we're doing," I said. Frustration bubbled up and leaked into my voice. "Are you my flirty friend? A supportive honorary kissing cousin? Or something else that I can't seem to define?"

A glimmer of amusement sparked in his eyes. "I don't think we have kissing cousins in Sicily."

I glared at him, not in the mood for humor. The lightheartedness was slowly extinguished, replaced by a tiny frown. "Is this important to you? To define us?"

"Of course! We've been circling around each other for weeks

and I'm confused. I don't know what you want, so just tell me. What are we to each other, Quint? An affair? A really good friendship? Nothing?"

Quint reached out, burying his hands in my hair and tilting my head up to face him. "You can never be nothing, *mia bella*. Not to me."

My heart beat so hard against my chest I figured he heard it. The spicy scent of his cologne drifted to my nostrils, and the sound of music from the streets weaved a spell in the air. I swayed toward him, caught between yearning and fear, wanting to lean into his hard, muscled body but afraid it would be another mirage. I'd begun to think of myself as a gaping hole that needed desperately to be filled, which made me feel weak. I'd looked to satisfy the yearning with work, and success, and then Jason, but I always came up short.

"I can't do this." My voice broke and I turned, desperate to flee from this horrible vulnerability and need for another person. It couldn't be healthy, this type of hunger. It would be best if I walked away with my independence and strength and returned home alone. I was enough by myself. Wasn't that what I consistently lectured on and tried to convince my clients? I choked out a half laugh. "I'm going home tomorrow and you don't seem to care. Maybe we can be pen pals."

"I'm so sorry, Aurora. I thought you knew how I felt—it was so clear to me I thought we needed no rules."

Oh God, he was gently trying to let me down easy like Jason. I needed to get out of here with my pride intact. "No, it's fine. I'm fine. We're good, let's just leave things the way they are. I had a wonderful time with you. I won't ruin it." I tried to break out of the embrace, but he muttered something under his breath and held me closer, wrapping his arms tight around me in a full-body hug. His husky voice rumbled against my ear.

"I am very bad at this. I scramble my English words sometimes. What I am trying to say is you are everything to me. From the moment you walked into the bar, I knew you would be part of my life; I just did not know how. I did not want to move too fast because of your boyfriend. I wanted to respect your space."

"Ex-boyfriend," I automatically corrected. "And I understand, Quint, we can just be . . ." I trailed off as his words registered in my brain. "Wait, what did you say?"

"I said you are my everything."

Shocked, I tilted my head up to meet his gaze. Heat and gentleness poured from him, filling me up. He shook his head slowly, his palm caressing my cheek.

"Aurora, I prayed for you every night. I knew you were out there, but I had no idea when we'd meet. I have been lonely without you, but I kept my faith, and you are finally here, *amore*. And now you have my heart for whatever you want to do with it."

The cold lump that had been stuck in my chest since my mom died suddenly crumbled and broke apart, releasing my breath and all the emotion built up. It came in a messy rush, filling my eyes with tears and my throat with a sob, but it was too much to tame. As if Quint knew, he murmured my name and kissed me tenderly, over and over, brushing his thumbs over my wet cheeks, patiently waiting until I realized he wasn't going anywhere. That he was mine.

"I love you, too," I whispered against his lips, burrowing myself against him and allowing pleasure to overtake my body in waves, making me feel alive again. "I was so afraid I'd mess up. That you didn't care I was leaving."

"Never. I did not want to pressure you, *bella*. You have many decisions to make, and I did not want to make you confused. *Mi dispiace.* I have always been yours, since the moment you smiled at me." He gave me a crooked smile. "I was waiting to give you this, but I think now is the perfect time."

He took out a small wrapped box from his pocket. "You got me a gift?"

"Yes. Something I know you will like. Open it."

I got all melty inside as I unwrapped the box and opened the lid. My breath caught as I gazed at the coral ring I'd loved from the shop. The dark orange-red stones gleamed with high polish and the diamonds sparkled. "Oh my God. It's gorgeous, Quint."

"Try it on."

He pushed it onto my index finger, nodding with satisfaction at the fit. It was a ring for royalty. Bold and sophisticated and unique. "I can't believe it. I love it. You didn't have to do this."

"I wanted you to have something to look at and remember when you got home. To know how many people love you." His voice caught. "To know how much I love you."

I shook my head, a bit shaky at the rush of emotion from such a heartfelt gift. "What are we going to do? How will we make this work?"

"We will do what is necessary to be together. It may take some time. You have things to do."

I nibbled my lower lip. "But you want to open up a restaurant here and Carmella still needs you. And I'm not sure how I'm going to rebuild my job."

He smiled with a patience and knowing that immediately calmed me. "I will visit New York. You will come back here. We will write and talk every day."

"*Sì.*" I looked into his eyes and realized that there was one last thing I needed. One last lesson to learn.

Faith. Right now, we both needed faith to take the leap.

"I am yours, Quint," I whispered.

And then I kissed him.

The next day, I got on the plane and returned home.

PART THREE

New York

TWENTY-FOUR

"THIS IS A shitshow," I muttered under my breath, staring at my computer.

My inbox was a cluttered mess of questions and demands from clients, sponsors, and guests who still wanted to be on my podcast. Even though I'd canceled the summer season, there was an opportunity to resume recording. If I hustled and did the proper outreach, I'd be able to book enough speakers to fill the empty spaces. Then I could relaunch in a big way for winter and regain the footing I'd lost.

Eliza and the podcast team were pushing hard to move forward. We'd held a big meeting, where I was finally truthful. This time, I didn't try to make excuses or hide my conflicted emotions. I confessed my grief had overtaken me and I'd needed time away. Real time. I told them I was thinking of canceling the entire year and stepping down.

Everyone had surprised me with their support and understanding. No one tried to rationalize my decision out of me or convince me to push forward. They laid out the options, and I knew if I wanted to, I'd be able to rebuild and gain back my momentum. All the pieces were in place. I just needed to bring back my heart and soul and passion into the project.

I didn't know if it was there. But the decision needed to be made if I wanted another season.

As I moved through each obstacle of my blown-up life, I found something that surprised me.

I had a good support system. I'd just never used it.

My pride had been my biggest downfall. In setting myself up as an expert in solving problems, tweaking mindsets, and focusing on the endgame, I'd cut out any type of real human mechanics. When my client Desi ended up calling me again, in tears because she was halfway through a bag of sour cream and onion potato chips after a stressful time at work, I'd finally seen the real issue.

"Desi, I want you to tell me the raw, awful truth right now. Are you ready?"

"Yes." She was probably prepared for the terrible punishment I'd inflict on her for her weakness.

"Does eating those chips make you happy?"

Stunned silence fell over the line. "Does it matter?"

"Actually, yes. It does. Do you want to sit on your couch and watch *The Bachelor* and eat potato chips tonight?"

I could literally feel her shudder with longing and guilt. "Yes," she whispered, full of fear and self-recrimination and too much loathing. "But I had a bad day. It's an impulse. If I soldier through it, I can be strong. I need you to help me be strong, Aurora."

Regret coursed through me. I'd made mistakes, but I was

willing to learn and grow. To try to fix them. "Desi, I'm so sorry. I was wrong when I told you before to put down the Oreos and do more weight training."

"Should I have run a few miles instead? I heard cardio is coming back in a strong way for weight loss."

My heart broke at this woman's perspective on her body and the world around her. God knows, I couldn't fix it all. I could only use what I'd learned and move forward. I looked down at my very generous curves and realized it had to start with my own acceptance and love for my choices. "No. All I want you to do tonight is allow yourself to relax. Eat the chips if they are satisfying to you. Watch the show. Go to bed early. And do nothing else."

Her gasp filled my ear. "You can't be serious! It's the road to ruin!"

"No. It's the road back from ruin. By making junk food your mortal enemy and not allowing yourself any space to enjoy it, you set up your body and mind as a battleground. It's okay not to be perfect all the time, Desi. In fact, it's required."

"You're telling me to eat the chips. Right now. Tonight."

"That's right. Eat what you want, no guilt. No workout. And enjoy it. Okay?"

I waited to see if she'd fight back and refuse. I probably would have. But the woman surprised me, and I sensed she had desperately needed permission. "Okay."

"Good. I'll check on you in the morning. Try to walk tomorrow outside, too."

"Power walking?"

I tamped down a grin. "No. A leisurely pace."

"Aurora, are you okay?"

"I've never been better."

I hung up and began to realize what I needed to do.

What I wanted to do.

I called my team back into a meeting and pitched my new idea. Because it was such a radical change, I knew there'd be a learning curve. But once I presented the plan, with a list of prospective guests and topics, there was a new excitement in the room that was palpable.

"Is this something you can get behind?" I asked Eliza. "It'll mean a different segment. New marketing. We may lose all our numbers and momentum and have to completely start over."

She grinned. "Hell yes. Things were starting to get a little stale around here, Aurora. It's nice to see you back in full force." She paused, a flicker of pain crossing her features. "You know, I lost my mom about eight years ago, and I still miss her every day. It's a bitch. But I honestly think, if we do this right, the podcast can be even bigger than before."

My fingers automatically reached up to rub the medal around my neck. The gesture gave me strength. "I think so, too." I also knew I'd learned some hard lessons. Success wasn't always bestowed with kudos, gifts, and easy times. Success could be many different paths, it could be lots of different things for different people, and no one had a right to judge. Finally, I'd figured out the path I wanted. "Thanks. I can't wait to see what we can all do together."

Later that night, I sat on my bed and spoke with Quint. "I finally decided what to do with the podcast."

"Tell me."

"I'm moving forward. I realized I actually love talking with people. Sharing ideas and building community is important to me. It was my limited focus that didn't fit any longer." I told him I was keeping the name, but the format would broaden. "Everyone wants the secret answers to success, right? I'd hoped by giving out specific steps and plans, it would be a foolproof map to get there, but I forgot about emotion. I discarded the mess. I literally had a bunch of successful people calmly tell the audience what to do to get *their* life. But what if we don't want that particular road map? What if someone wants healthy relationships instead of money? Or joy in their body rather than weight loss? What if something bad happens and blows up all their expectations of who they were and they need to rebuild? The mess is where the magic is, Quint! That's what I want to dig into."

"I love it, *bella*. I think so many can relate. Because the mess is beautiful."

As the days passed, I spoke with Quint regularly. We shared stories about our days, texted funny videos back and forth, and fell into an easy rhythm. Sometimes, the pain of missing him hit so hard, I'd take out my ring, study the coral gems, and run my finger over the smooth, polished stones. I'd remember his beloved face as he told me I was his everything. And I'd remember my promise to have faith in us.

Slowly, I made some harder decisions. I decided to permanently close my life-coaching business. Maybe one day I'd reconsider, but right now, I was focused on two things I was passionate about.

The podcast.

And writing.

I wrote every day now, scribbling nonstop about my thoughts and experiences in Sicily. I wrote about my mom and dad, the discovery of my new family, and how something bad can turn into something good, if we're able to view it through a different lens. Piece by piece, I began to realize I might have a book to offer. I called my editor and approached her with the idea of changing the book to something else. She wasn't too keen on losing out on the book I'd originally promised, even if she had pushed out the date, but after I pitched the idea, she agreed to take a look at a partial before she decided.

My social media numbers plummeted as followers realized I wasn't the peppy, motivated leader I'd previously promised. I hesitated trying to rebrand myself until I decided how I wanted to show up. I thought about canceling my accounts and taking a detox, but my instincts kept leading me back to the platforms, whispering I could do me. Post what gave me joy. Share generously like I had in the past, without trying to force a certain outcome. I found that I was my most enthusiastic talking about my experiences in Sicily. So I leaned in.

I curated all the content I'd filmed over the past month and began matching the images with captions. Some were strictly for inspiration, and other times I wrote from that vulnerable place everyone was scared of. Each time I put something new out there, I started off anxious, then settled into my voice.

I was learning and growing. I was failing.

And then, slowly, I was succeeding.

On Thursdays, I jumped on a Zoom with my grandparents and tried to keep the time blocked out on my calendar. Seeing their faces on the screen gave me a boost, and we'd chat about everything, always ending on questions about Quint. Then Babba would do his humph thing and dark frown and tell me he missed me.

It always got me a tiny bit giddy, but I tried to act cool.

My cousins and I texted constantly through WhatsApp until they became so entwined in my daily life, I sometimes felt they were right up the road. Quint decided to come in October for two weeks, so I was bursting with excitement. I counted down the days as summer became fall. The leaves turned into an explosion of color and the sunlight glowed a rich sparkling gold. The air brimmed with scents of apples, pumpkins, and spices. I pulled boots from my closet, took out my flannel, and began recording my new podcast material.

I'd been home for a full two and a half months when one early evening, my doorbell rang.

When I peeked through the side window, I jerked back in shock. Jason stood on my doorstep, and he looked like he wasn't leaving until I opened the door. Biting my lip, I greeted him warily. "Hey. Everything okay?"

He gave me one of those megawatt smiles that dazzled. "Aurora! I know it's been a long time, but I really wanted to talk to you. Can I come in?"

I studied his muscled figure, clad in dark-wash jeans and a navy Henley that stretched ridiculously over his shoulders and chest. His thick blond hair blew in the wind. His crystal blue eyes were full of hope and a touch of contrition. He was amazingly handsome, and charming when he wanted to be. Once, I'd thought we might end up together. Marriage. Kids. Building a life.

But now?

There was . . . nothing. Just a flat pleasantness and polite hope he was well. But I couldn't send him away without hearing him out. He deserved to have full closure in person rather than over the phone. "Of course. You look great."

"So do you. You got a great tan. Lots of good food over there, huh?"

I smothered a smirk, knowing his assessing gaze had noticed the twelve pounds I'd put on. I was in no hurry to get it off and liked the way I felt. "Oh yeah. I had pasta and pizza daily. It was delicious."

His face blanched, but he tried to cover it, obviously off-kilter at my response. "Oh. Well, as long as you feel good."

"I do. Want a drink?"

"No, thanks. Aurora, I need to tell you something important." I waited, head cocked. "I think we made a big mistake."

I tamped down a sigh. It was going to be one of those conversations, huh? I couldn't help but tease him a little bit. "You think?"

He nodded and began to pace, obviously deep in thought and planning mode. "We both screwed up and committed errors in this relationship. I should have been more patient and I regret pushing you so hard. When you decided to stay in Sicily, I figured you were checked out from me. But I realized it wasn't me or us specifically. You needed to get your head on straight and be with your family for a while. I know I didn't understand the way you wanted me to—about losing your mom. I'm sorry for that."

My shoulders relaxed a bit. "Thank you, Jason," I said.

"Of course. I want to give us another try. I miss you. I wanted to call or text since you got back but figured you needed some boundaries. I saw you changed your podcast and dropped your clients. Are you happy with those moves?"

"Yeah, I really am."

"That's good, then. I like what you're doing with the audience dynamics. Who knows, I bet you could find a whole new batch of clients to help!"

I looked at him, thinking back on how delicately my mother tried to warn me. Jason wasn't a bad person. He was actually quite a good man, intent on success in his own way. He'd make another woman really happy.

Just not me.

"I'm sorry, Jason. I do appreciate you coming to see me, because we were serious about each other. But we're simply not a good fit. We won't make each other happy."

He blinked and scratched his head. "You made me happy. Didn't I make you happy?"

I smiled gently. "Not as much as I wanted."

"Oh. Well, that sucks." He waited to see if I had anything else to say, but when I didn't speak, he cleared his throat and moved toward the door. "Okay, I'll head out. I figured we owed it a try." He stepped outside and shot me a wry smile. "Bye, Aurora. Good luck with everything."

"You, too."

I watched him walk down my path, get in his car, and drive away.

And up above, I felt my mom smiling.

I PACED THE worn, thin carpet as crowds buzzed around me. My gaze kept bouncing back to the doorway as the clock ticked. Someone rammed into me with a bag but didn't apologize. The cries of cranky toddlers and hushed whispers of parents rose to my ears amid the scents of coffee, perfumes, and the sweaty tang of stress.

I froze as I recognized the broad shoulders and dark beard. The leisurely strides of a man who took life on his own terms. My heart leapt as he glanced around, then landed on me. For a few precious seconds, nothing existed but us and the connection that hadn't dimmed over space and time.

And then I ran hard and launched myself into his arms like in every rom-com I'd ever made fun of in my life. He caught me, murmuring my name while he swung me around, then dipped his mouth to take mine in a hungry kiss.

"*Amore*, you are here."

I clung to him and laughed. "Quint, I missed you so much. Welcome to New York."

His eyes shone bright with love. "I cannot wait to fall in love with your home like you have mine."

We linked arms as we headed to baggage claim, chattering nonstop about everything and nothing. It had been eleven weeks since we'd seen each other as I began to put the pieces back together from my career, and he made space to take two weeks away from the pub. I had an ambitious schedule for us both set up—including all the tourist sites, dinners out, and showing him everything about my work. It was important for Quint to see me outside of Sicily so he glimpsed all the parts I'd left behind.

The drive back from JFK was long, and we hit the usual traffic. When he commented on the busy roads, I cracked up. "The first time I took a cab from the airport to my Vrbo, I almost threw up. I remember thinking Italians must've been trained to drive in Manhattan."

He grinned, settling comfortably into the leather passenger seat. "Do you obey lights and signs?"

"Of course!"

He nodded. "Then you are better drivers."

We finally hit Cold Spring and walked into my house. Quint was voracious in his curiosity, touching every knickknack, studying photographs, and looking in my cupboards to see what type of food I carried. After I returned from Sicily, I'd begun to personalize my space a bit more, adding the gifts I'd brought back. Now, vibrant paintings decorated the neutral walls, and the kitchen had bright red, orange, and yellow towels, trivets, and mugs. He picked up the framed photo of me and my family by the pizzeria, and another one of Quint and me at the beach—the selfie we'd taken when I realized I'd fallen for him hard.

"Are you hungry?" I asked, kicking off my shoes and going to open a bottle of wine. "Or did you eat on the plane?"

He grunted. "That is not food. It is calories disguised as something edible."

My lip twitched. "I figured. That's why I cooked, so we don't have to go anywhere tonight. Let me heat everything up."

He wandered into the kitchen, kissing me and taking the bottle to uncork it. I rummaged through the refrigerator and took out two trays. I turned on the stove and he gave me the wineglass, lifting his own to tap mine.

"*Salute.*" His gaze delved into mine, but this time, his emotion burned bright and hot.

My voice came out husky. "*Salute.*"

We drank, staring deeply into each other's eyes, and I remembered that first night we made love and how it had all begun.

"What did you cook for me, *bella*?"

"Pasta with eggplant."

He placed his glass carefully on the counter. As he leaned in, his lips whispered over my hair, my cheek. His fingers stroked my back, his hips braced against mine. My body began to tremble, and then he took my glass and put it beside his. He ran his thumb over my lips, then cupped my cheeks. "And?"

My vision blurred and my focus narrowed to him. Finally, he was here, in my home. Finally, he belonged to me. "And antipasti. Artichokes. Cheese. Olives." His mouth drifted to my ear and I shivered. "Roasted peppers. That cured sausage you love."

His arms pulled me into his embrace. "And?"

I tipped my head up and fell into his eyes. "Bread."

His mouth quirked. Then he lifted me up and carried me to the bedroom, where I'd smartly left the door wide open.

"I cannot wait to feast later. Much later."

He kicked the door shut with his foot.

I realized he wasn't as hungry as I'd thought.

THE TWO WEEKS passed in a blur. He accompanied me to the podcast and watched as I interviewed guests, meeting my team and charming them with ease. He took pictures with me for my socials without hesitation, asking endless questions about how I decided what to post. He visited my parents' graves with me and held me while I cried.

We ate in restaurants across the Hudson Valley and Manhattan, trying a variety of both five-stars and well-known dives. We devoured hot dogs from food trucks, bacon burgers at Five

Guys, and slices of cheesecake at Junior's. I showed him the ugly beauty of being surrounded by endless towers of glass and metal, and lunching in the vivid green hills of Central Park. We drove to quirky small towns to pick apples and admire the changing leaves. We went horseback riding in the woods, had beers at McGillicuddy's Irish pub, and slow danced in the piano bar to old-school Billy Joel. Each place we explored seemed new, like I was seeing it for the first time through his eyes, and I cherished the gift of sharing my favorite places with the man I loved.

We sat together in my living room on the last night. Already, the ache of saying goodbye lodged in my chest. I laid my head on his shoulder as we settled in comfortable silence.

"What are we going to do?" I finally asked. "I don't want you to leave."

He played with my fingers, his grip a warm comfort. The gorgeous coral ring flashed in the light and gave me comfort, like my mother's medal. "I don't want to leave. Eventually, we will need to make a choice. For now, we can keep visiting each other. I cannot take you from a city you love. You're rebuilding a career that's important to you."

I'd been thinking the same thing. Since I returned from Sicily, I'd found a new balance for myself. I liked what I was putting together with the podcast, on my own terms. I'd lived in New York my whole life. This was where Mom and Dad had built a life, with me.

But . . .

As much as I had begun to lean in, there was still an emptiness following me. I was going through the steps of my life with satisfaction, but not with the joy I'd touched in Sicily. At first, I thought it was just my family and Quint I was missing. But in the past month, I'd begun to see it might be deeper.

Maybe I simply didn't belong here anymore.

I tilted my head up to look at him. "I appreciate your respecting my work and what I want to accomplish. And I changed a lot. I'm happier with my choices. Except—"

"Except?"

"I'm not truly happy here."

His gaze held mine. Hope reflected back, along with wariness. "Aurora, I don't want you to rush this decision. You need to think hard about how you see your life. Either way, I know we're meant to be together—I just want to move forward in your time. I'm not going anywhere."

His words calmed me. "Neither am I. But I can't see you settling here in New York, Quint. To leave your restaurant and Carmella? You belong there."

"I could make it work. Move in with you. Find a job at a restaurant to learn, eventually opening up my own. I could visit Sicily regularly and Carmella could stay here all summer."

"Or I could go to Sicily. Would I move in with you?"

"If you want, or we could get a new place. I'd like Carmella to stay with us until she's ready to move out on her own."

"Of course! It's possible I could run the podcast from overseas, along with social media. My job is probably more flexible than yours."

He stroked back my hair. "*Mia bella*, it's amazing what can be done when you meet the love of your life. I am open to trying what is best for us."

I jumped on his lap and began kissing him, and the conversation stalled out and morphed into other activities.

When Quint left, I returned to the house feeling lost. I looked around at the space I'd created, at the life I was building on my own. I'd kept my sessions with Dr. Sariah, recognizing that grief was an ongoing process and that Sicily hadn't cured it but offered a new pathway. There was still work to do and I was committed to showing up for myself.

Slowly, my eyes drifted shut.

I stood in my empty living room and quieted my mind. Listened to my breathing. And tuned in to the voice.

Where am I meant to be right now? I asked myself.

I waited, but silence was my only answer. Instead of giving up, I held on to my patience, not pressing, and asked again.

Sicily. Go to Sicily.

My lids flew open. My hand covered my mouth.

And then I began to laugh as the realization flowed through me with such natural ease, it was as if I'd been moving toward this decision since the first time Catena called me, since the first time my gaze met Quint's, since the first time I called my grandfather Babba.

"Thanks," I said aloud.

There was no answer, of course.

But I knew what I had to do.

TWENTY-FIVE

ONE YEAR LATER

"QUINT! OH MY God, come here!"

I stared at my laptop, blinking furiously. Had I read it right? Was it a dream, or had I actually manifested something this magical?

"What is it?" he asked, racing from the kitchen, where he'd been cooking dinner.

My finger shook as I pointed at the screen. "Can you read that? My editor sent it over and I think it's a mistake."

I held my breath and waited. A few moments passed. Quint turned to me and grinned, shaking his head. "You did it, *bella*. They love it."

I bit my lip. "It's the *New York Times*, right? The *Book Review*, right?"

"*Sì.* I am not surprised. It is a beautiful book, full of heart."

I read the words again, slowly.

A gorgeous, sprawling tale of a woman whose loss

becomes her greatest tool and triumph to create a new life . . .

Raw, honest, and vulnerable . . .

A talented new writer to watch . . .

Early reviews were streaming in and my publisher had already increased the print distribution after bookstore demand spiked. When I'd sent my editor a few chapters of the new manuscript, she'd agreed to change my contract and move up publication. This time, when she asked me to deliver on a tight deadline, I experienced no fear or dread. The words and ideas poured onto the page in a passionate rush. I ended up writing the first draft in three months, and my publisher decided to launch the book the following spring to get ahead of the summer reading club picks. The preorders already had the book ranking high on Amazon and Barnes & Noble. The buzz from early readers had been both gratifying and shocking.

I just hadn't expected much. I'd written the story for me, first, then my mom. It was a healing process and a gift. I'd thought it was a clever way to get out of my first disastrous contract, never believing the audience would be more than a blip.

But I was wrong.

Somehow, my social media posts of Sicily blew up, gaining me new followers. Once people heard about the book, it had exploded in preorders, taking all of us by surprise.

Dear God, they're calling me the next Elizabeth Gilbert.

Quint pulled me from the chair before I could read the review for the fourth time and spun me around. His hugs were still legendary, and I sank into his strength, the scent of citrus and spice and clean cotton filling my nostrils as I buried my head in his chest. "We have to call Catena and Theo and Carmella and Teresa."

"And Nonna and Babba. They're now local celebrities."

We laughed together. I'd gotten everyone's approval before sending the manuscript. Their reactions were pure excitement, so that made things easier. Sharing my family and private journey with the world was a big step.

After Quint came to visit me last fall and I made my decision, we spent the next few months preparing for my big move. I never looked back, nor regretted my choice.

Sciacca was home.

My family was ecstatic and helped in every way. Since I had all the documents from the church on my mother's birth, I was able to get the paperwork needed to move permanently. From the moment we made the decision, it seemed the universe opened up to allow us clear passage.

The podcast had a solid spring season and began to rebuild buzz. After ironing out a few kinks, I settled into a flow, working remotely with the team and my guests. I began writing the book, dragging my laptop to my favorite café, while I drank espresso and looked at the boats in the marina. I rented a small apartment near Quint.

And we got engaged.

The wedding was planned for the spring.

Still giddy from the review, I joined my fiancé at the table to eat, and then we made calls, arranging to see Nonna and Babba tomorrow. We cleaned up and headed out to Bar Sciacca to spread the good news to Catena and Theo. As we were walking in, Carmella called, saying her brother had texted the link to the review. We spoke for a while, and when I hung up,

Quint gave me a questioning look, hand paused on the door. "Coming in, *bella*?"

I smiled. "*Sì*. Be there in a minute. I just want to take a breath."

He nodded, understanding my need for space as he always did. He went inside and I heard an echo of greetings. I turned and walked around the building, to the bench where I'd first sat with Quint.

Gratitude overflowed in me, even as I noted not to get attached to the expectations for the book or what would happen next. I continued walking toward the square, hands in my pockets, my mind full of thoughts and memories.

The moon shimmered in an eerie crescent surrounded by stars. It was a weekday in deep fall. The streets were quiet and I closed my eyes. I breathed in the sharp air and thought about my mother as a young girl, running through the narrow side streets with her siblings, holding her father's hand as they walked into church every Sunday morning. I pictured her fighting at the dinner table where her cousins and aunts and uncles squeezed in, breaking bread and sharing pasta under the watchful eyes of Nonna and Babba. I imagined her meeting my father for the first time and the hard choices she made to be with him at any cost. I thought about how, years later, I'd find myself in the same place with a second chance for both of us. The way Babba laughed with me and the picture of Mom he carried in his pocket everywhere.

The images came to me like a slow-moving photo book.

Both had made mistakes. Perhaps my mother had believed Babba could never forgive her choice, so instead of facing rejection, she never reached out. Perhaps if she had, things would have been different. But life gave us free will, and choices could only be made to the best of our abilities, during a tiny snapshot of time. Mom didn't have the luxury of seeing the future.

Everyone had done their best.

But the circle of hurt and regret had now closed.

I thought of the dedication in my book, the words imprinted in my heart and soul.

For Mom.

Thank you for teaching me about love and for inspiring this story.

But most of all, thank you for being my mother.

Ti amo, Mamma.

I closed my eyes, tilted my head up, and felt a warmth cascade over me and through me, along with the faint scents of florals, of daffodils and sunshine. My skin prickled with awareness.

"I'm home, Mom," I whispered. "I'm home, just like you meant for me to be. And I miss you. We all miss you, but we're together now. And I'm happy."

I was met with silence, but I knew she was here. I knew every step in this journey, as painful as it was, had led me right here, back where I belonged. With a family and a man I'd fallen in love with.

I opened my eyes, wiping the tears from my cheeks, and turned to go into the pub, where everyone was waiting.

ACKNOWLEDGMENTS

EACH BOOK A writer finishes is both a gift and a lesson. Diving into the Sicilian culture so deeply and creating a strong, traditional Sicilian family who would jump off the page was a challenge. But along the way, I fell in love with these characters and all their joyful, broken pieces, reminding me again why family is so important. It was also a reminder that each family is different, full of good intentions and mistakes. Grace is sometimes needed. I'm so happy Aurora found hers . . . and her true love along the way.

Books are not written alone. It takes a hardworking tribe to get a creation past the finish line. I'd like to thank a variety of people who helped me deliver *To Sicily with Love* to readers' hands!

First up, thanks to the amazing team at Berkley. My editor, Kerry Donovan, for seeing and trusting my vision for this story. Thanks to Jessica Mangicaro and Tara O'Connor for their marketing and PR savvy, and their enthusiasm. Thanks to my copyeditor, Eileen Chetti, for catching all my silly mistakes, and to Kristi Yanta for giving me feedback on the first round before I panicked. To my agent, Kevan Lyon, for her support through all the stages of this book. Thanks to my assistant, Mandy Lawler, who keeps me organized so I can write.

Special thanks goes to Magan Vernon and Krista Bevsek for helping me with the detailed research in Sicily. They answered my questions, shared stories and pics, and helped me bring these small Sicilian towns to life on the page.

All mistakes are mine and mine alone.

A big thanks to my family. My husband, Ray, for all the amazing support. My boys, Jake and Josh, for being the best damn teenagers ever—you both are always cheering me on even when I complain nonstop about my deadlines! My mom, for feeding me amazing Italian food for all these years and loving everything I write. For my brother, Steve; my sisters-in-law, Dana and Carolyn; and my nieces and nephew: Taylor, Anna, Enzo, Kaitlyn, and Amanda. I love you all so much I can't put it into words.

Family is life.

Finally, thanks to my readers. We are sharing a journey together, and I'm honored you used your precious time to read this book. I am forever grateful for your support.

TO SICILY WITH LOVE

JENNIFER PROBST

READERS GUIDE

DISCUSSION QUESTIONS

1. When we first meet Aurora, she has her life completely under control, but the loss of her mother changes everything. Have you ever experienced an event that altered the course of your life? Did you feel any personal parallels to Aurora's emotional journey with grief? When did you feel most proud of her in this book?

2. Did you think Aurora was happy in her relationship with Jason? Do you believe she would have married him if she hadn't gone to Sicily?

3. What would you say are the main themes of the novel? Did you consider it optimistic that Aurora could find new happiness after losing someone so beloved in her life? What would you say was the most difficult moment of change for her?

4. Aurora's big, boisterous Italian family is steeped in tradition. Did you have any favorite scenes with them?

5. When Aurora goes to Sicily, she meets so many relatives who broaden her perspective on her life and her future. Which character do you feel had the biggest impact on Aurora during her time in Sicily?

6. The relationship between Aurora and her grandfather starts off rocky. Did you think Aurora was too hard on him, given that he'd lost so much time with his daughter? Or did you think he was too gruff and emotionally closed off as she tried to make a good impression?

7. Aurora and Quint start off as friends and their relationship evolves. Do you think an overseas romance can work? Do you believe they are meant to be together? Why or why not?

8. Would you ever use a DNA test to explore your heritage or family connections? Do you think this is a good idea? What unforeseen complications could you imagine arising?

9. Sicilian food is a big factor in the book. Are you an adventurous eater? Would you have eaten everything Aurora did, or called *basta* sooner?

10. What do you think Aurora is most thankful for after her life-changing summer in Italy?

Don’t miss Jennifer Probst’s

A WEDDING IN LAKE COMO

Available now!

ONE

AFTER

I STARED AT the embossed envelope, fingers gripping the sharp edges with such force, indentations cut into my tender flesh. The wedding invitation blurred before me, my name like a mockery in its perfect gold scrawled font.

Ava was getting married.

The breath left my lungs in a whoosh, so I allowed myself to drop into the kitchen chair. It was a long time before I decided to open the envelope. When I did, my French-manicured nail sliced through the wax seal, but I was beyond caring if the paint chipped. Like doing anything unpleasant in life, I learned to do it fast. Much better to take the hit of pain full force rather than in steady doses over time. I prefer a fast death.

In Ava's usual fashion, the invite was elegant, timeless, and spoke of her signature grace. The heavy stock paper was the color of rich butter, painted in thick gold-leaf brushstrokes that glittered. I skimmed the card.

You are cordially invited to the wedding of Ms. Ava Anastasia Aldaine to Mr. Theodore Roberto Barone . . .

The family invites you to a weekend of festivities at the Aldaine estate in Lake Como . . .

My gaze skipped over the words with greed. I didn't recognize the name of the man she'd finally decided to marry and wondered if it was a whirlwind affair, or if Ava had given in to her father's wishes and chosen a proper husband. Of course, it had been five years since we'd spoken, and I'd been ruthless in my denial of any information. Keeping her name off my social media search bar had been a coping mechanism, though there'd been many nights I wanted to drunken search for any nugget of information about her life. But I'd stayed disciplined. Too bad the success still rang hollow, but the years had taught me not to question the empty space. Better to keep it unfilled and have a life of truth than lies.

Even though lies felt so much sweeter.

I dropped the invitation on the table, but my gaze snagged on a small white card nestled within wispy golden tissue. Picking it up, I noticed it wasn't the usual RSVP card. Black marker bled into the fabric threads with a familiar, bold style I'd memorized long ago. This time, my heart paused in my chest.

Maddie—

Come to my wedding. I need to talk to you.

Please. It's important.

You made a promise.

Ava

I closed my eyes and fought back the whimper of pain that clutched my insides. Memories rushed through me like a stampede—of me and Ava and Chelsea drunken dancing under a full yellow moon with our arms linked; crowded in our dorm room with Harry Styles blasting on repeat, sharing secrets while painting our nails and recording silly TikTok videos, heads mashed together, smiles stretching our lips, the gleam and vigor of youth amid a bubble of love and trust that can only be found in the purest of friendships. Of Ava teaching me how to be brave when the doubts struck. Of Ava choosing me from the group that clamored to be in her magic circle, showering me with long hugs and whispers against my ear in the dark; of the familiar scent of rosemary and mint from her shampoo; of the clasp of her tapered fingers and joyous laughter and dazzling beauty that always made my heart stutter in appreciation and fierce pride that she belonged to me; to us. Ava was ours.

Until she wasn't.

I read the words again, hearing her lilting voice in my ear as if she were whispering to me. And for the first time in five years, the foundation of the wall I'd shored up and carefully built shook. The crack let in just enough of the past to make me question the decision to run and cut Ava out of my life forever.

A silly word, really. *Forever.* What really lasted forever? Certainly not love. Or youth. Not beauty or lust, dreams or certainty, not even friendship—the only thing I believed would never fail.

What about broken promises? Would this one steal a piece of my soul? Because there wasn't much left. I needed to salvage every bit that remained.

Dammit, why now? When I was so vulnerable?

I dropped the note on the table and got up, heading to the wine rack to grab a bottle even though it was only three in the afternoon. The expensive cabernet was bold and rich with burgundy and earth tones, so I sipped it slow and paced, pondering my options.

The quiet space around me that had once been my fortress felt like it was closing in on me. The expensive loft in Midtown Manhattan had been an indulgence, but I treasured privacy and, instead of hiring a decorator, decided to do most of the interior design myself.

Ebony black wood floors and vaulted ceilings gave the space breath, and the open-concept rooms allowed the furniture to delineate barriers. A spiral staircase led to my bedroom, and massive custom closets were transformed to house my social media shoots. I kept the eggshell-colored walls mostly bare, allowing a few retro art pieces from fashion history. Coco Chanel, Christian Dior, Cristóbal Balenciaga, and Donatella Versace all kept my secrets. The furniture was white and lush, accented with fluffy throw rugs, stuffed pillows, elegant candles, and hand-knit blankets. My kitchen was a trendy dream of clean white—cabinets, marbled granite, subway tile, and tiled floor in black and white invited cooking and lingering, one of my favorite activities since I'd become mostly a loner.

It was a feminine retreat now. I'd made sure after moving back to New York that I'd wiped away any last vestige of the life I'd had before.

I winced and took another sip.

Ava had always had an incredible sense of timing. Almost as if she sensed my weakening and decided to strike. I remembered how she always seemed to anticipate when I'd had enough of the madness—the sucking energy of her need for attention and love—and it was then she transformed into my favorite part of her: the joyful, free spirit filled with a warmth I'd never met in anyone else. She'd always been a mass of contradictions, ranging from drama to a heartfelt supportive mentor who knew exactly what was needed in the moment.

Another reason it was so easy to fall in love with her. But being friends with Ava had consequences. I just hadn't known how big a debt I'd need to pay until it was too late.

Scowling at my dark thoughts, I nursed my wine and eased out onto the balcony. New York City was already hot and muggy, the air unable to take flight and breathe, so it stuck on my skin and clothes and clogged my lungs, refusing to budge. I used to love everything about summer in the city. When everyone ran off to the Catskills or Hudson Valley, to beach trips and cool mountains, I'd hunker down and crawl deeper into the city I adored. Walk its streets for hours, explore hidden cafés and art shops, finding fashion treasures that rewarded only perseverance and patience. Getting lost amid strangers was oddly freeing, a balance of anonymity and crowds. It was here I'd first come alive and grown into my real self. Fresh from graduation, drunk on possibilities and dreaming of fame, I was at my most pure before reality hit and threw me onto a different path. One I wanted. One I paid for.

I lifted my head up and stared at the scatter of tall buildings that jammed the sky, housing both power and poverty, depending on who lived inside. How many times had I wondered if I never left for LA if everything would be different? It used to torture me, teasing my sanity, all those what-ifs. I tried to focus on all the wonderful things happening in my career, but I guess I was one of those crappy people who focused on what they didn't have rather than what they did.

One late night, I stumbled on a Tony Robbins seminar and was told life happens *for* me, not *to* me. I'd tried to change my viewpoint because it made things easier, but it was hard to keep the momentum up. Daily life and tasks eroded away the positivity, until I found myself waking up at 5 a.m. too many mornings in the same hopeless mood I'd started with.

My mind churned and I drank more wine and the memories pulled me back. I used to think my greatest loss would be my first love.

I should've realized Ava always had more power than him.

TWO

BEFORE

THE FIRST TIME my gaze landed on Ava Aldaine, I sensed my life would change.

She was sitting on the steps to the lecture hall, surrounded by a crew of laughing girls, all looking similar in subtle designer labels. Small leather crossbody bags, silky T-shirts with theme-driven mottos scrawled across the front, matched with low-heeled ankle boots with strappy gold buckles and heels. Even their carefully ripped jeans held an intention I'd never been able to inject into my own persona, one that screamed significance.

But Ava seemed more than a leader, more important than the typical high school prom queen. She practically glowed from within, pumping out energy to the surrounding crowd the way a guru offers energy shocks to a chanting audience. I paused before the steps, not knowing where to walk, and she looked up at me with extraordinary cobalt blue eyes, a deep dark blue that made you want to look closer. Rich, glossy waves of chestnut hair spilled down her back, and her heart-shaped face tilted upward, her lips stretching into a big smile, as if she'd met a good friend rather than a stranger staring stupidly at the blocked pathway. "Hey, you're in my English class. Madison, right?"

I nodded, still held mute by the strange feelings that rose up within me, a mix of longing and knowing, as if we had known each other before. Later on, I'd remember Ava said the same and called it kismet. Soul-sisters. I always loved the thought and would pull it tight to my chest when I found it hard to breathe. A reminder I was special.

"Love your outfit."

I tried not to gape. I had no money for top-rated brands, and I was obsessed with fashion. I'd mastered the art of finding cool vintage items or luxury fabrics and putting them together with flair. Unfortunately, my high school classmates mocked me for my crafty wardrobe. This was the first time I'd gotten a compliment. I wondered if she was joking, but her face was bright and open and . . . honest.

"Thanks."

Her crew had grown quiet, looking at me with the familiar judgment I was used to, but Ava only laughed and began to scoot her butt to the side. "Sorry, we're in your way. Procrastinating so we don't have to go in there yet, right, Chels?"

The girl sitting next to her nodded, curly blond hair bobbing at the motion. A slight gap between her front teeth stole my attention when she spoke. "How are we supposed to study poetry, for God's sake? Do I really care what the poet's intention was? All I care about is what we need to know to pass the test." Her big brown eyes rolled. "Why can't I just skip to my finance classes? No one gets a liberal arts education anymore. It's so old-school."

I couldn't help the words that sprang out. "I like liberal arts. It's like going to a buffet, a little bit of everything. Then I can figure out what I want more of."

Some of the girls snickered and I felt myself turning red. Ugh, why did I have to be so awkward? She wasn't looking for an actual answer!

Ava laughed, a bold, robust sound that commanded attention. "Love it. Havisham is really the Golden Corral of universities instead of the steak house it wants to be."

Chelsea laughed with her, and suddenly, everyone was laughing and I didn't feel like such an idiot.

I'd begun to relax, wondering if I could get myself to talk a bit more, when the sharp slap sounded against my eardrums. "I'm glad to see all of you have so much time to socialize and relax before my class. I'll be sure the questions for Friday's exam are hard enough to equal your confidence." Professor Lithman taught English and was known to be tough. She didn't pause, and the girls scrambled to give her a wide pathway, her smart black heels clicking on each of the steps like a countdown to doom. The overall groan made her chuckle just a bit as she entered the double doors.

"Better head in," Ava declared, standing up with an innate grace. Her bulky knit red sweater stopped just a few inches above the waist, flashing her flat belly. Dark-wash ripped jeans clung to her curves, then flared out at the ankle. Red flat-heeled boots added the perfect dash of style. I tried not to drool over her ensemble and her body as she shifted to grab her bag.

Her admirers pressed in around her like a protective layer, and I hurried past, head down. Sliding into my seat in the back row, I watched as students shuffled in, chatting and laughing with ease before Professor Lithman began class. I tried not to stare at Ava and her friends, wondering what it would be like to fit in and make friends easily.

Soon, I got caught up in the professor's lecture regarding Emily Dickinson, losing myself in the words that detailed the poet's struggle and deep emotion. I'd always loved dabbling in writing, finding it cathartic to spill all the crap from my mind onto paper.

"Ms. Davenport, I'd be interested to hear your thoughts on Dickinson's poem 'I'm Nobody! Who are you?'"

The attractive brunette who was one of Ava's sidekicks gave an audible sigh. I winced. There was one thing Professor Lithman hated, and it was attitude in her class. "It was a bit confusing to me," the girl offered. "I think she was angry that no one really recognized her since she stayed home all the time. So she was mad she was a nobody and mocked the ones who had fame and fortune since she was jealous."

"I see. Did you like the poem?" Professor Lithman asked.

Ava's friend tittered. "Not really. I find her works boring and stuffy. I wish she'd just say what she meant."

Professor Lithman nodded, though I could tell she wasn't too keen on the girl's answer. "Remember, Dickinson was commonly termed the poet of paradox. Any other ideas on Dickinson's intent or frame of reference for this popular poem?"

A few students offered shallow throwaway ideas. I knew this was an unpopular class, but I secretly liked it, along with Dickinson. Suddenly, Professor Lithman was gazing at me with intent. "Ms. Heart. I'd like your take on all of this. What did you get from the poem?"

Half of the class swung around to stare at me. I felt my cheeks flush and damned my fair, freckled skin for the betrayal. Oh, God, I always hated being put on the spot. Ava was looking at me curiously. I rarely spoke up.

"I liked the poem. It contained layers of wit many people don't see in her work."

The professor nodded. "Go on."

"I believe Dickinson actually enjoyed her solitude and had no wish to be out in society. She was happy to be a nobody, and the poem's tone seemed to be poking fun at others who want to chase attention or to look to be a someone in the world. I think she liked being whoever she wanted in the comfort of her room, even though we pity her."

"Interesting angle. What do you think she'd make of today's society?"

I couldn't help but laugh. "She'd despise social media. She'd probably think chasing likes is an asinine thing to be concerned about."

The class laughed, but I caught Ava's friends rolling their eyes at me. Ugh, why did she have to call me out? I wanted to be Dickinson right now and be left alone.

Professor Lithman nodded. "Excellent observation. Let's drill into the mechanics of the poem."

She went on, and I was blessedly ignored the rest of class.

After, I packed up and headed out. Ava fell into step with me. "I liked your answer in class," she said with a warm smile. "It's cool you like her poems."

I tried to ignore the glare from Ava's friends. "Oh, thanks."

"We're heading to the library to study for the exam." I was suddenly trapped by her piercing gaze. "Wanna study with us?"

A lump settled in my throat. I'd been having a hard time making friends my first semester. I hadn't attended any of the popular parties, and my roommate seemed to want nothing to do with me. All my visions of being different in college crumbled within the first two weeks. I nodded. "Sure. Thanks."

Most of the girls didn't seem thrilled. "We don't really have room for another person in our study group, Ava," Patricia Davenport said. "Sorry." Her tight smile was mocking and I wanted to slink away.

Ava's voice chilled. "Then maybe we should create another group."

Everyone froze. Chelsea broke the tension by bounding over and linking her arm with mine. "There's always room for one more. Please tell me you know more secrets you can help me with to understand that chick. I try, but I don't have a clue."

I grinned, my muscles relaxing into the casual embrace. "Actually, I do. You just need to look beyond the surface and think about what type of life she led. She struggled with depression for a reason."

"What do you think it was?" one of the girls challenged. "Being too weird for society?"

I acted on pure impulse. "A life with no orgasms," I said.

Ava and Chelsea broke into laughter.

Patricia looked pissed off.

Ava drifted to our side and linked her arm with Chelsea's. "You're funny," Ava declared. "Come on, let's go."

I couldn't help feeling pleased, glad I'd gone for the dramatic punch line. I loved to banter, but I was usually too shy to show my real personality. The rest of Ava's crowd hung back, and the three of us marched down the hallway to the library. For the first time, I felt I was part of something special. Giddiness fizzed in my veins like uncorked champagne.

Ava had chosen me.

Photo by Matt Simpkins Photography

Jennifer Probst is the *New York Times* bestselling author of the Billionaire Builders series, the Searching For . . . series, the Marriage to a Billionaire series, the Steele Brothers series, the Stay series, the Sunshine Sisters series, and the Meet Me in Italy series. Like some of her characters, Probst, along with her husband and two sons, calls New York's Hudson Valley home. When she isn't traveling to meet readers, she enjoys reading, watching "shameful reality television," and visiting a local Hudson Valley animal shelter.

VISIT JENNIFER PROBST ONLINE

JenniferProbst.com

X JenniferProbst

AuthorJenniferProbst

JenniferProbst.AuthorPage